One Year

Books by Mary McDonough

LESSONS FROM THE MOUNTAIN: *What I Learned From Erin Walton*

Published by Kensington Publishing Corporation

One Year

Mary McDonough

KENSINGTON BOOKS
http://www.kensingtonbooks.com

KENSINGTON BOOKS are published by

Kensington Publishing Corp.
119 West 40th Street
New York, NY 10018

All Kensington titles, imprints and distributed lines are available at special quantity discounts for bulk purchases for sales promotion, premiums, fund-raising, educational or institutional use.

Special book excerpts or customized printings can also be created to fit specific needs. For details, write or phone the office of the Kensington Special Sales Manager: Kensington Publishing Corp., 119 West 40th Street, New York, NY, 10018, Attn. Special Sales Department. Phone: 1-800-221-2647.

Kensington and the K logo Reg. U.S. Pat. & TM Off.

Library of Congress Card Catalogue Number: 2015931006

ISBN-13: 978-0-7582-9349-7
ISBN-10: 0-7582-9349-6
First Kensington Hardcover Edition: May 2015

eISBN-13: 978-0-7582-9350-3
eISBN-10: 0-7582-9350-X
First Kensington Electronic Edition: May 2015

10 9 8 7 6 5 4 3 2 1

Printed in the United States of America

For my parents.
Who taught me the importance of my roots and what it means to be
Irish, American, and Catholic.

Acknowledgments

This book came together through amazing people sharing their lives with me. So much of my foundation, my friends, family, and their beliefs are in this book. Over the years, I have adopted so many *parents*, *cousins*, and *sisters* into my life. I truly know family is what you make it and blood is not always thicker than water. My extended *family* is a testament to that belief.

None of this would have happened if not for John Scognamiglio, who always believed I could do things I only dreamed of. Thanks for your help, support, amazing vision, passion for books and the written word. I can't thank you enough for your patience, belief in me, and knowing I have more to share.

To all the women in my life who molded me into who I am. This book is about us and the love we share through the good and bad times. To me, we *are* family. So many thanks to: Kate for years of inspiration and book sharing, Maria for being the bomb whenever I call, Elise for all things Catholic, for listening and "getting" me so well, to Karen for leading me back to my purpose, to my Goddaughter Chelsea for the beautiful photos, Angalamabama for the walks, your ears, and the hair! A special thanks to Geri Jowell for sharing her experience of cerebral palsy with me. Hugs of gratitude to my *Godmother* Aunt Ellen, June, Sybil, Carol, Claire, Kari, Nancy, Cori, Mo, Ann, Nina, the +coffee gals, Bethie, Cheryl, and the Witches of Westminster.

To my incredible friends, I treasure you and am so grateful for your love and advice . . . always. Thanks for talking me off the ledge and reminding me who I am. Thanks to Tom for your wisdom, to Kevin for being the ultimate docent, Tim my executive assistant, Eric—the best mensch I know, Runtie for always being in my lap, to the Sacred Six and the Fabulous Five for showing me the importance of celebrating life.

To Sydnee, Robyn, and Kylie for reminding me how important it is to hold the women in our lives close . . . blood or not.

Eternal love to my brothers Michael and John, my touch stones to my past, present, and future. Thanks for remembering our childhood so I could write about it.

To the kind and durable Walton fans whose love of the show lifts me up. You are always there for us. To my incredible Facebook friends, you have supported this book from the moment I mentioned it to you. Your support in all I do in life and online is greatly appreciated. I hold you all as family.

To my Don, your love and support sustain me. I am so Blessed to call you husband.

THE FITZGIBBON FAMILY

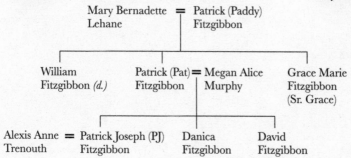

Mary Bernadette = Patrick (Paddy)
Lehane   Fitzgibbon

William   Patrick (Pat) = Megan Alice   Grace Marie
Fitzgibbon *(d.)*   Fitzgibbon   Murphy   Fitzgibbon
                                                        (Sr. Grace)

Alexis Anne = Patrick Joseph (PJ)   Danica   David
Trenouth   Fitzgibbon   Fitzgibbon   Fitzgibbon

CHAPTER 1

Mary Bernadette and Paddy Fitzgibbon had lived at 19 Honeysuckle Lane in the town of Oliver's Well, Virginia, for most of their married life. The town had been founded by a small band of English settlers in 1632, including one Noah Oliver, who had gone on to become its first elected official. The reason the town was called Oliver's Well and not Oliver's Landing or Oliver's Town, was lost to time. Presumably, Noah Oliver had had some doings with a well.

Over the almost four centuries of its existence, the town had grown to support a current population of almost three thousand people. There was a public grammar, middle, and high school, as well as a private academy. There was a community center, with a full kitchen for potluck suppers and an auditorium where the local amateur theatre group performed its plays. There was a library and an old-fashioned single-screen movie theatre. Small, locally owned businesses—hair salon, florist, dress shop, restaurants, jeweler—flourished alongside the branches of two area banks and an insurance company. The Oliver's Well Memorial Hospital was well regarded. The post office was a daily gathering place for the dissemination of gossip. There were no fast-food franchises or tattoo parlors.

In many ways, Oliver's Well was typical of any charming, historic American town, but many would argue that it had a unique appeal. Mrs. Fitzgibbon would be the most vocal and persuasive of those. At the age of twenty-one, Mary Bernadette, nee Lehane, had arrived in Oliver's Well from her native Ireland via New York City. Though the promised personal connection—the uncle of a friend of a friend—and the housekeeping job he was supposed to have provided her did not materialize, Mary Bernadette had decided to stay in Oliver's Well and make her way, liking what she saw of the quaint little town. There was little, if anything, that could deter her when she had decided on a goal. One of those goals was to marry the handsome and ambitious twenty-three-year-old factory worker named Paddy Fitzgibbon who she had met at the Church of the Immaculate Conception one bright Sunday morning.

Now, fifty-four years later, Mary Bernadette and her husband were getting ready to preside over New Year's Day festivities, surrounded by their family.

"Paddy," Mary Bernadette said from the door to the living room. "The garbage disposal is frozen again."

"I'll see to it," he replied, getting up from the armchair in which he was reading the day's edition of the *Oliver's Well Gazette*.

"And do it before your son arrives and tries to help you."

Paddy chuckled and followed his wife into the kitchen. "He means well, Mary. He just didn't inherit my handyman skills."

"Which is why I'll never understand why he always insists on 'giving things a go.'"

Paddy retrieved the tool he used when some bit of plastic wrap or chicken bone had managed to slip down the drain and cause the garbage disposal to grind to a halt.

"It was good to talk to Grace earlier, wasn't it, Mary?" he said, opening the cabinet below the sink for access to the works.

"It was," Mary Bernadette agreed. "We don't see enough of our daughter. And I wish she would call more often."

"Grace is a very busy woman. She does what she can."

Grace Marie Fitzgibbon—so called after her maternal grandmother, Mary Grace—was a nun in the small and highly unorthodox Order of Saint Prisca, Virgin Martyr. For those who wanted to know, Grace was happy to relate that Saint Prisca had met her grisly death in 270 CE. Paddy affectionately called Grace "our rebel," and indeed, her politics were as far removed from those of her parents as it was possible for them to be. Currently she was stationed in Los Angeles, though in past years she had been posted to Central and South America, or, as Mary Bernadette put it, the ends of the earth. "And what is your New Year's resolution?" Mary Bernadette had asked her daughter that morning, to which Grace had replied, "To speak the truth and shame the Devil. To rage against injustice." Well, that was Sister Grace for you.

It had been so many years now, Mary Bernadette thought, watching her husband tinkering away, since their children had lived under the roof of the house on Honeysuckle Lane. Built in the mid-nineteenth century, it was a handsome white clapboard structure with stark black shutters and a stately brick chimney. There were two floors, on the first of which could be found a living room, dining room, and kitchen, as well as a small room once used as a study and now as an extra bedroom, and finally a powder room that Paddy had added many years previously. On the second floor were a full bathroom and three bedrooms. In addition to a cottage behind the house, where Mary Bernadette and Paddy's grandson lived with his wife, there was a two-car garage and a garden shed on the property.

"Almost done," Paddy said, his voice muffled by the fact that the upper half of his body was inside the cabinet.

Mary Bernadette peered through the window over the sink, from where she could clearly see the cottage. "I wonder where PJ is," she said. "I thought he'd be here by now."

"I'm sure our grandson and his wife will be along at any moment."

Yes, Mary Bernadette thought. If Alexis wasn't dawdling. She was a good girl but had her faults like most, one of which, in Mary Bernadette's opinion, was a tendency to waste time. It was not a fault Mary Bernadette shared.

Now in her midseventies Mary Bernadette was still a striking woman. Her thick, snowy white hair had once been as dark as ink. Her eyes were still a clear blue, and she only wore glasses for close reading. For the New Year's Day celebration she had put on one of her favorite dresses, a dark blue wool A-line with a narrow, black patent leather belt at the waist. She was wearing the strand of pearls Paddy had given her on their fortieth anniversary, a pair of small pearl earrings left to her by her aunt Catherine, and her simple gold wedding band. The impression Mary Bernadette made upon virtually everyone she met—whether in her capacity as chairman of the Oliver's Well Historical Association or simply as a congregant at church—was one of power and elegance, competency and resolve. And when she smiled her famously dazzling smile, people were almost universally smitten. Mary Bernadette was aware of all this and took the attention she was paid as a matter of course.

"There, all fixed." Paddy emerged triumphant from under the sink. "I suppose one of these days I should replace the thing with a new one."

Mary Bernadette refrained from pointing out that he had been threatening a replacement for close to three years. She loved and respected her husband in spite of any shortcomings, which, to be honest, were too few to mention.

The patriarch of the Fitzgibbon clan was slim and wiry, though a hip replacement nine years earlier had left him with a slight hitch in his get along. His eyes were intensely blue. Mary Bernadette still considered him the most handsome man she had ever seen.

Paddy was retired now from Fitzgibbon Landscaping, the company he had founded as a young man, but with his grandson PJ in charge he was able to keep his hand in on a job he had loved. Every other Sunday he served as an usher at the Church of the Immaculate Conception, and he filled in when one of the readers had to be absent. In his leisure hours, he spent time with his friend Danny Kline (Danny's wife, Jeannette, was Mary Bernadette's dearest friend). Paddy, an only child who had been orphaned at sixteen, was genuinely well liked in Oliver's Well and greatly loved by his family. In that way, he had been heard to say, he was the richest man in town.

"Mmmm." Paddy smiled at his wife. "The dinner smells wonderful."

"Thank you," she said. Mary Bernadette was making roast beef (for which, in her opinion, she was justifiably famous), with mashed potatoes, green beans, and homemade rolls. For dessert, she had baked an apple pie (for which she also believed herself to be justifiably famous) and cookies studded with chocolate chips and bits of candy cane. The cookies would satisfy her grandchildren.

Mary Bernadette went back now to the living room. The Christmas decorations—including a real fir tree densely hung with ornaments and tinsel, a massive wreath made entirely of pinecones, and strings of blue and white lights in the windows—were still in place and would be until the Feast of the Epiphany, after which Mary Bernadette would carefully pack everything away until next holiday season. Her favorite decoration of all was the beautiful handcrafted crèche. It had pride of place on a side table in the living room, atop a blanket of Angel's Hair to represent snow. Mary Bernadette turned the statuette of St. Joseph a little to the right and straightened a camel that was threatening to topple over on his fluffy base. Then she checked to see that the bowls of nuts and ribbon candy and chocolates were still untouched. To assure this, she had covered each bowl with a piece of plastic wrap. It wasn't Banshee's behavior she was worried about. It was Mercy's.

Banshee—currently asleep on one of the armchairs—was Mary Bernadette's ten-year-old Siamese cat. She was long and lean, with lovely hyacinth blue eyes. Mary Bernadette had never told anyone but Paddy that she had purchased Banshee from a breeder in Arlington. She had a well-deserved reputation for frugality, and she did not relish the idea of people—her son, for instance—commenting on this one instance of extravagance. Anyway, intelligent and affectionate Banshee had proved well worth the expense.

Mercy, however . . . Mary Bernadette eyed her husband's shelter dog with a measure of suspicion. The creature, who for the past hours had been roaming the first floor of the house, sniffing at the oven, trying to snatch stray food from the kitchen table, and generally causing havoc, looked like two or more very different dogs randomly stuck together. There was a sort of ruff around her neck, though the rest of her fur was short. Her face was black, the ruff was a mottled white and gray, and her body was a patchwork of all three colors. Her eyes were ever so slightly crossed, giving her a quizzical expression, which suited her curious personality. Now, this curious personality was prompting her to sniff loudly at the straw in the Holy Family's crèche.

Paddy appeared in the doorway.

"That dog is a menace," Mary Bernadette said, turning to him. "Not even the baby Jesus is safe. Paddy, put her upstairs, won't you." Paddy was ostensibly in charge of the mutt, but while he doted on her and she adored him she never obeyed any of his commands. Mary Bernadette thought her husband's canine rather dim-witted.

"She'll just whine until I let her out, Mary, you know that. Besides, I think Jesus faced worse threats in his life than a dog's wet nose."

Mary Bernadette ignored the vaguely blasphemous comment and checked her watch. "Where is everybody?" she asked. "Dinner is almost ready, and there's nothing I hate worse than to serve a cold meal."

"They'll be here, Mary. They'll be here."

CHAPTER 2

"You know Mom's not going to let me watch the games today. We should have stayed in Annapolis. I swear, I don't know how Dad stands it."

Pat Fitzgibbon was driving Megan's Subaru Outback; Megan was beside him in the passenger seat, and the twins, David and Danica, were in the backseat, each plugged into an electronic device that allowed them to ignore their parents' boring conversations.

"I thought you were taping the games," Megan noted, with a glance at her husband's perfect profile.

"It's not the same," he grumbled.

Pat Fitzgibbon, Mary Bernadette and Paddy's older child, was tall like his mother and slim like his father. His eyes were a bright greenish blue. By the time he was thirty, his hair had turned an attractive steely gray. During the week he wore conservative dark suits with a white shirt and a red or blue tie, suitable attire for his job as a corporate attorney. On the weekends, he lived in jeans and T-shirts. On holidays, like this one, in deference to his mother, he wore a navy blazer, charcoal gray slacks, and a pale blue shirt. Mary Bernadette did not think jeans and T-shirts appropriate for grown men.

Megan wasn't entirely unsympathetic to her husband's complaints. They had gotten an invitation to a party at the home of friends, a couple with three children around the twins' age and a reputation for serving the finest wines. No doubt the Taylors would have had their big flat-screen TV tuned to the football games. The only reason the Fitzgibbons had turned down the enticing invitation was to make what Pat rightly called a command performance at his mother's house in Oliver's Well.

"I am sorry," Megan told her husband. "Let's make a pact that next New Year's Day we stay home."

"I'm holding you to that, Meg."

Megan, Pat's wife of over twenty-five years, was also a lawyer. Her light brown hair was cut into a sleek bob and she wore very little makeup. Her one personal indulgence was her collection of stylish eyeglasses. Today, she was wearing Prada frames. She would never tell her mother-in-law how much they had cost. Mary Bernadette did not entirely approve of personal spending. And she was the sort of woman who was always ready to tell you her opinion of your supposed faults or flaws. Formidable did not come near to describing the woman who was her mother-in-law. True, she had been duly forewarned that she would find Mary Bernadette—difficult. Megan remembered the first time Pat had brought her home to Oliver's Well to meet his parents. She had noted the horseshoe hung over the front door of number 19. Why a horseshoe, Megan had asked Pat. "It's for good luck," he had explained. "There was a horse in the stable the night Jesus was born."

"Was there? I thought it was a donkey Mary rode to Bethlehem. So why not a donkey's shoe?"

Pat had frowned. "Maybe that works just as well, but I don't want to be the one to suggest that my mother try something new or that she change her mind. And believe me, you don't want to be the one, either. She'll just take it as an insult."

No truer words had ever been spoken.

"Mom?" Danica had unplugged herself from her iPhone. "Are we almost there?"

Megan smiled over her shoulder at her daughter. "Every time we make this trip you ask me the same question at exactly this point. And the answer is always yes."

Danica nodded and went off into her electronic world again. She and David had turned twelve years old the previous October. Danica, older than her brother by five minutes (something she never let him forget), was also taller than David, who had been born with cerebral palsy, by a good two inches. The twins shared the same light brown hair and their father's bright greenish blue eyes, though David's were partly obscured by his glasses, which he had worn since he was small. He occasionally used crutches or a walker to aid his mobility, but more often than not Megan found them abandoned in unlikely places, like under the dining room table or behind the rosebushes.

"I hope my mother doesn't have my father running around all day fixing things," Pat blurted, his bad mood clearly unmoved. "The man is closing in on eighty, but she treats him like he's still a man of forty, ready to climb up a ladder or . . ." Pat clamped his mouth shut.

Megan spoke carefully. "You know you're exaggerating, Pat. Besides, your father is hardly an invalid. He enjoys being useful around the house." And, Megan thought, he enjoys dancing attendance on his wife, though most times Mary Bernadette didn't seem to notice his efforts. That, or after so many years of marriage she simply took her husband's attentions for granted.

"It will be good to see PJ and Alexis," Megan said. "I feel I'm not getting to know my daughter-in-law as well as I might. It's the distance between Annapolis and Oliver's Well, I suppose."

"She's a nice young woman," Pat said, "that's for sure. PJ is lucky."

Pat turned the car onto Honeysuckle Lane. Megan put her hand to her hair though she knew it was in place and straightened her skirt though it didn't need straightening. Mary Bernadette had that effect on people.

"If she tries to pull any of that sappy 'God bless us, every one' nonsense," Pat grumbled, "I'll . . ."

"You'll raise your glass like the rest of us and chime in."

"Hmm."

Pat pulled into the drive of number 19. He had barely shut off the engine before David and Danica were tumbling out of the backseat and making their way toward a house where they knew they would find two doting grandparents; plenty of candy; and, if they were really lucky, their grandmother's awesome cookies. Megan and her husband followed more slowly, arm in arm.

CHAPTER 3

"How do I look?" Alexis twirled before her husband so that her red circle skirt flared out like a bell.

PJ smiled and held out his hands. "Lovely as always."

Alexis went to him and allowed PJ to hold her close. She wished they didn't have to go to Mary Bernadette and Paddy's house, not just yet. As if he were reading her mind, PJ released her with a sigh.

"We'd better get a move on," he said. "My parents and the twins should be pulling up any minute. Grandmother will be eager to put dinner on the table."

"I just have to do my makeup," Alexis told him. "I won't be long."

"I'm going to check that I've set up everything correctly to record the games."

"Why is your grandmother so strict about not watching TV when the family is together?" Alexis asked.

PJ smiled over his shoulder as he left the bedroom. "You know what she's like," he said.

Alexis was certainly finding out what Mary Bernadette Fitzgibbon was like, and more so every day. She went into the bathroom, where the light was best, and carefully began to apply her makeup. And while she smoothed on moisturizer and then foundation, she remembered a recent conversation with PJ. They had been at his grandparents' house, of course.

"Look," she had whispered. "That's the third ornament Banshee's deliberately knocked off the Christmas tree!"

PJ had whispered in return. "And you'll notice she hasn't broken one of them."

"Why does your grandmother get upset when Mercy accidentally knocks an ornament off the tree with her tail but looks the other way when Banshee does it on purpose?"

"Because Banshee is hers, and Mercy is not."

"Oh. Has your grandmother always had a cat?"

"No. Not while my father and my aunt were growing up. Not while I was growing up, either. She has this superstition about cats sucking the breath out of small children while they sleep."

Alexis had laughed. "How medieval! But wasn't she concerned with Banshee being around David and Danica when they were little?"

"I can't explain my grandmother, Ali," PJ had said with a

shrug. "I mean, to other people her ideas might seem odd or inconsistent, but to her they make perfect sense."

Odd or inconsistent was right, but the last thing Alexis had a desire to do was to question or defy her husband's grandmother, the matriarch of the family. Still, there was the blanket of Angel Hair under that beautiful old crèche in Mary Bernadette's living room. . . .

"Isn't that incongruous?" Alexis had whispered to her husband, not long after the Banshee exchange. "I don't think the ancient Middle East got much snow."

PJ had grinned. "Grandmother likes to think otherwise."

"Well, it does look pretty. I suppose it can't hurt to suspend our disbelief."

"There's the spirit!"

Alexis Trenouth and PJ Fitzgibbon had married the previous March, after her graduation from college at the end of the fall term. Alexis was tall and willowy with large blue eyes and long blond hair. She had grown up in Philadelphia and loved the vibrancy of urban life, but she had fallen so very much in love with PJ that she had agreed to settle down with him in Oliver's Well. So far, living in the cottage on Mary Bernadette and Paddy's property, working as the office manager for Fitzgibbon Landscaping, and being PJ's wife was proving to be very satisfying indeed.

Alexis smiled as she heard PJ cry out, "Yes!" No doubt he was snatching a few minutes of a football game live while he could. PJ—Patrick Joseph—was a few inches over six feet, well built, with a classically handsome face. His eyes were even bluer than his wife's and were framed by long, dark lashes. His hair was almost black and naturally flopped over his left eye. He had a boyish, charismatic charm; a genuinely warm smile; and a sexiness that had nothing to do with pretense. He was, in the words of his beloved grandmother, "a real Irish charmer."

A moment later Alexis joined him in the living room. "I'm ready," she said.

PJ clicked off the TV and turned to her. "Thank you for being my wife," he said.

Alexis smiled. "What brought that on?"

"The fact that I love and adore you."

"Oh, is that all. . . ."

Hand in hand the pair made their way across the backyard to Mary Bernadette and Paddy's house.

"You're late," Mary Bernadette pronounced as they came through the back door and into the kitchen. "I was hoping to see you here before now."

"I'm sorry, Mary Bernadette," Alexis said automatically.

PJ hugged his grandmother and kissed her cheek. "Everything smells fantastic," he said. "I can't wait for dinner."

"Well," she said, disengaging herself, "you'll have to wait a bit longer. I slowed everything down when your father wasn't here by three as he promised."

PJ smiled at Alexis over his grandmother's head and then, taking his wife's hand, they went into the living room to greet the others. There was the usual chaos of hellos and how-are-yous, accented by Mercy's excited barking, and all followed by a warm hug for both PJ and Alexis from Megan. Alexis thought her in-laws were pretty wonderful people; they had made her feel welcome in the family right from the start, even before she and PJ had become engaged.

"Look at my cool new bracelet," Danica demanded, yanking on her sister-in-law's arm. "I made it myself from this kit I got for Christmas."

"It's awesome," Alexis said, which seemed exactly what Danica wanted to hear. The girl grinned and loped off toward a bowl of candy.

"Hey." David looked up at Alexis. "Do you want to hear this cool new song I downloaded?" He handed her his iPhone and earbuds, and Alexis pretended to like the cacophony screaming into her ears.

"That's . . . cool," she said, handing it all back to David. He, too, seemed to be satisfied, because he went off in the direction his sister had taken, toward the coffee table.

In spite of having known David for several years, Alexis still occasionally had to resist an impulse to "help" him. It was remarkable how well he managed for himself. She was impressed by his abilities as much as by his personality, but she had decided that it would probably sound condescending if she told him as much. No one else in the family made a big deal—or any deal at all—of David's having CP, so Alexis had learned to treat it matter-of-factly as well.

Mary Bernadette emerged from the kitchen and asked PJ to sharpen the carving knife. "And be sure to put the sharpening steel back in the drawer when you're done," she instructed, ushering him into the kitchen.

Paddy handed Megan and Alexis a glass of wine and gave his son a beer. "You both look lovely," Paddy said.

"What about me, Dad?"

Paddy pretended to grimace. "Now, Pat. Lovely isn't the word."

"David," Megan called to her son. "How many chocolates have you had?"

David chewed vigorously, swallowed, and assumed a look of complete innocence. "Two?" he called back.

Megan raised an eyebrow. "Just be sure you save room for dinner, please." And then she turned to Alexis. "What a ridiculous thing to say to a twelve-year-old. They always have room for more food."

Alexis laughed.

"It's time for dinner," Danica called from the door of the dining room. "Grandma says to come quickly so it won't get cold."

The Fitzgibbon family took their usual places at the table—Mary Bernadette at one end and her husband at the other—and Paddy led them in a traditional grace: "Bless us O Lord and these thy gifts, which we are about to receive from thy bounty, through Christ our Lord, Amen."

"So, what's your New Year's resolution, Grandpa?" PJ asked, taking a roll and passing the basket to his wife.

"I'm afraid I haven't decided on one yet," Paddy admitted.

"You need to make a resolution to make a resolution," David suggested. "Pass the gravy, please."

"I think that one should make a resolution every single day of the year, not just on the first of January. And keep it, of course," Mary Bernadette said.

"What sort of resolution, Grandma?" Danica asked, dropping a large pat of butter onto her mashed potatoes.

"To be productive," Mary Bernadette told her. "To avoid physical as well as spiritual laziness. Sloth is a sin."

Pat grinned. "I thought a sloth was a four-legged tree-dwelling animal from South America."

His mother gave him a look that Alexis thought could wither a freshly bloomed rose on its stalk. "Sin is nothing to joke about, Pat," Mary Bernadette said.

Pat looked like he was about to utter a retort, when David unwittingly—or not, Alexis wondered—intervened. "My New Year's resolution is to eat an entire gallon of ice cream at one time."

"Just don't come to me when you've got a stomachache afterward," Megan told her son.

When the pie, cookies, and coffee had been brought to the table with some fanfare, Mary Bernadette took her seat again. "I think," she said, "that it's time for a toast to the year ahead."

Everyone raised his or her glass.

"To the Fitzgibbons," Mary Bernadette said, with her famously dazzling smile. "May the new year bring us peace and prosperity."

"To the Fitzgibbons!"

Alexis saw Pat lean into his wife and whisper something.

"Do you have something you want to share with us all, Pat?" Mary Bernadette asked, eyebrows raised and glass still in the air.

Alexis bit her lip. Next to her PJ could barely hide a grin. Megan, too, looked ready to laugh.

"No, Mom," Pat replied. "Nothing at all."

CHAPTER 4

Jeannette and Danny Kline were at the Fitzgibbon house for their weekly dinner of pot roast, glazed carrots, and roasted potatoes, followed by a game of Monopoly. Banshee watched the proceedings from atop the fridge. Every so often Mercy would trot into the kitchen and with a swish of her tail knock any unattended game tokens or silverware off the table. Then Paddy would bring her into the living room with strict instructions for her to stay there. And before long she was back in the kitchen, tongue lolling. "That dog," Mary Bernadette would say. To which Paddy would murmur, "Now, Mary." The Fitzgibbons and the Klines had met at the Church of the Immaculate Conception more than fifty years before, when Father Murphy was in charge of the parish. The Klines had three daughters. The two older girls, Margaret and Kathleen, had long since moved out of state and married. Between them they had five children whom, unfortunately, Jeannette and Danny rarely got to see. Mary Bernadette might have felt pity for her friends if it were not for the fact that the Kline's youngest daughter, Maureen, still lived in Oliver's Well—she was a senior agent at Wharton Insurance on Main Street—and spent a good deal of time with her parents.

"It was a wonderful meal, Mary," Jeannette said, folding her napkin next to her empty plate. "Your pot roast is always a treat."

Jeanette was a pretty woman, with eyes that were remarkably green. She was almost as tall as Mary Bernadette, but a case of scoliosis that hadn't been diagnosed until she was fifty had left her slightly hunched and crooked. Though Jeannette never complained, Mary Bernadette knew her friend well enough to know that she was in constant pain. You could see the evidence in the lines of tension in her face, particularly when she had been sitting or standing for any length of time. Although in some ways the women were quite different, in this way they were alike. Each suffered quietly and with dignity.

"Excellent whiskey, Paddy," Danny said, after a first appreciative sip. "It almost makes a man feel young again." Years of physical labor in the contracting business in all sorts of weather conditions had finally caught up with Danny. He had lost weight over the past year, and his walk was missing some of its usual bounce. Mary Bernadette didn't like to notice signs of aging in her friends; they reminded her of her own process of decline, a process she was determined to ignore.

"I see, Mary, that there's a new Lenox curio box on the coffee table," Jeannette said, as she helped bring the dinner plates to the sink for rinsing.

"Yes, I found it at the thrift shop when I was dropping off a few of Paddy's old shirts. It's a fine piece, isn't it? I can't imagine why anyone would have let it go."

In spite of her frugality, Mary Bernadette was not a believer in the "less is more" aesthetic, and the thought of downsizing appalled her. She owned a complete set of Waterford crystal glasses in a pattern long since discontinued. There wasn't so much as a chip in one of them. Her Belleek tea set had pride of place on the credenza in the dining room. She had amassed no fewer than thirty-three Byers' collectibles figurines, which she kept entirely dust free, no easy task what with the intricate folds of cloth and the finely spun hair. Antique embroidered samplers, some stitched by her mother and her mother before her. Lacy doilies and fine linen table runners. Capodimonte porcelain flowers. There seemed no end to Mary Bernadette's "items of interest."

She was most proud, however, of the large collection of family photographs taken over the long years of her marriage. The entire Fitzgibbon family was represented, with the notable exception of William Patrick Fitzgibbon. Mary Bernadette and Paddy's first child had died at the tender age of eighteen months. Photographs of the little boy did exist, but Mary Bernadette kept them in a locked box to which she had the only key. Paddy had never protested this. He had never dared to interfere with his wife's mourning.

It would be difficult for a visitor to miss the fact that every photograph had been taken on an official occasion—at a wedding, a christening, on Christmas or Thanksgiving—so that every family member was in his or her Sunday best. This, too, was Mary Bernadette's doing. She was not the sort of woman to commemorate or celebrate sloppiness. She never left the house without applying powder and lipstick. She saw the habit of people wearing shorts or flip-flops to church as a sign of a larger breakdown of society. What had become of the virtues of modesty and propriety? If it wouldn't be calling too much attention to herself—and it would be—she would still wear white gloves and a veil to church, as she had been taught to do by her mother.

"Shall we begin?" Mary Bernadette said, taking her seat again at the table.

Paddy had set up the board, stacked the Chance and the Community Chest cards, and distributed the game tokens. Mary Bernadette was always the thimble. Jeannette was always the top hat. Danny was the old boot, and Paddy the Scottie. This evening, it was Danny's turn to be the bank. With a roll of the pair of dice, the game began.

"I ran into Leonard at the grocery store today," Jeannette said as she waited her turn. "He said he was passing the Kennington House early this morning and thought he saw a tramp asleep on the front steps."

"Nonsense," Mary Bernadette said, taking a small sip of her sherry. "We don't have tramps in Oliver's Well."

Jeannette laughed. "You're right, we don't. Leonard got out of his car to investigate and found that what he thought was a pile of clothing with a human being inside it was just a big, black garbage bag escaped from someone's lawn, no doubt in that windstorm we had the other night."

"Once an officer of the law, always an officer of the law. I've always said that attention to detail and an eye for trouble is what makes Leonard a fine CEO."

Leonard DeWitt was the Chief Operating Officer of the Oliver's Well Historical Association, of which both Mary Bernadette and Jeannette were long-standing members. Over the years Mary Bernadette had advanced to the position of chairman, an honorary post with the exception of the job of official spokesperson. And no one on the board would debate the fact that she was also the heart and soul of the organization. The latest successful project the OWHA had undertaken, under Mary Bernadette's guidance, was the salvation of the Joseph J. Stoker House. The house, barn, and what few outhouses remained intact had been privately held for generations until the OWHA had been able to buy the property three years earlier. The structures were in a sorry state and had required complete renovation including urgent structural repair. The most important parts of the work were done, though there were still a few interior finishes Mary Bernadette hoped to make in the years to come. Now the OWHA was ready to award the job for restoration of the twelve acres on which the structures stood, including a kitchen garden, flower garden, and small apple orchard. Five landscaping design firms, including Fitzgibbon Landscaping, had submitted bids and were scheduled to give presentations in the following weeks.

"Come to think of it," Jeannette said, "I haven't gotten an e-mail from Neal about the next meeting. He's never late sending it out."

Mary Bernadette frowned. "Machines. There's probably something wrong with his computer. In the old days we sent a notice through the mail."

"Which cost more of the board's money and took more of the secretary's time."

"Still," Mary Bernadette said. "Things got done."

"Speaking of things getting done, I do wish we had the money to buy the Branley Estate. I drove past earlier today and the main house has lost another window frame. The place will decay entirely if we don't get busy saving it."

"We'll find the money in time," Mary Bernadette said. "God willing."

Indeed, the Branley Estate represented the last major pie-in-the-sky piece of business for the OWHA to take on. The property had once belonged to a powerful robber baron of the late nineteenth century, a man named Septimus Hastings, who, unlike the majority of his class, had lived in relative simplicity in the original house that had been built in 1743 by one George Branley. Instead, he had used his vast wealth to purchase other buildings of the seventeenth and eighteenth centuries, move them fully intact from their original sites to his land, and fill them with furnishings and art from the period. In short, he had built a museum complex of no less than three houses, several barns (stocked with old farm implements and machines), a blacksmith's workshop, and a mill, complete with a water source and working waterwheel. After his death, several successive generations of the Hastings family proved to be without the financial acumen of their forebear and the estate had gradually fallen into ruin. Sometime in the 1940s it was sold to another family, whose finances had not fared much better than that of the Hastings. Sadly, at this point in time, the estate was almost entirely dilapidated. Much of the art had been sold off; some had been stolen. A fire in the 1950s had virtually destroyed one of the homes and most of the barns. Still, the Branley Estate represented a true prize of historical Oliver's Well just waiting to be brought back to life—whenever the OWHA could find the money to buy it.

"Have you seen today's *Lawrenceville Daily?*" Paddy asked, finishing his turn around the game board. "They interviewed Mary last week about her long tenure at the OWHA."

Jeannette nodded. "It was a wonderful article, very thoughtful and well written," she said. "And the photo is very flattering."

Mary Bernadette waved her hand in dismissal. "If I had known they would be sending a photographer, I would have worn my blue dress. But the possibility never even crossed my mind."

"It was what you said that was most impressive," Danny noted. "I'd babble away if a reporter ever wanted my opinion on anything other than, oh, I don't know, my favorite television show."

"I've always said that my Mary should have gone on the stage," Paddy said. "She's that good."

"Nonsense. I have no interest in acting and never have. I simply answer the questions the reporter puts to me as clearly as I am able. If I produce a quotable quote, then so be it."

"She's too modest," Paddy teased. "We all know her dazzling smile can light up a room."

This time, Mary Bernadette didn't protest the compliment.

The doorbell rang then, and Paddy went to answer it. When he retuned, Maureen Kline was with him.

"I'm sorry to interrupt," Maureen said. "I just came by to drop off those brochures you asked for. They should explain the changes to your homeowner's policy Paddy said you're considering."

"Thank you," Mary Bernadette said. "You'll stay for a cup of tea."

"No, I'm afraid I can't." Maureen handed Mary Bernadette a manila envelope. "I'm meeting a friend to see a movie."

"I haven't been to a movie in years," Mary Bernadette said. "Too much sex and violence."

Maureen grinned and was gone as quickly as she had come.

"I do wish she would meet a nice man and marry again." Jeannette sighed. "But I don't think that's what Maureen wants."

Mary Bernadette said only, "Hmm." There was no need to rehearse aloud the tragedy of Maureen's brief marriage, or Mary Bernadette's disappointment that her son Pat had not married the girl. Mary Bernadette had known Barry Long was a bum from the first moment she met him at Maureen's engagement party. But no one had listened to her warnings, and a few years later Maureen was divorced, without even a child to show for her efforts at civilizing the man. Well, Mary Bernadette thought now, there was no use in crying over spilled milk.

"Shall we continue the game?" she said. "Danny, I believe it's your turn."

As Danny moved the boot around the board, Mary Bernadette turned to Jeannette. "Did I tell you I finally managed to get Marilyn Windsor to donate her great-great-grandfather's diaries to the OWHA? It took almost three years, but I knew I'd succeed in the end."

Jeannette laughed. "You'd have made a great enforcer for some crime syndicate, Mary. Give me your embroidered cushions or I'll—"

"Now, that's enough of that. You know it's all in the interest of the OWHA."

"I do know, and I'm grateful. We all are. What made Marilyn change her mind?"

"I simply employed a good dose of flattery along with a sprinkling of guilt. I reminded her that the diaries are a vital and uniquely essential part of the history of Oliver's Well and that depriving the current and future generations of their study would be a travesty as well as an act of extreme selfishness on the part of the Windsor family."

Jeannette put her hand to her mouth, and Paddy flinched. Danny shook his head. "What are we going to do with you, Mary?" he said.

Mary Bernadette assumed a look of wide-eyed innocence. "Why, congratulate me, of course. My thimble has landed on a piece of property not owned by anyone at this table, and I intend to purchase it."

CHAPTER 5

Every other Friday, without fail, Mary Bernadette Fitzgibbon had afternoon tea with her friends Katie Keefe and Bonnie Eckman. The women lived three houses down from the Fitzgibbons on Honeysuckle Lane in a small and very charming house built in the late nineteenth century. If possible, Katie and Bonnie were even more meticulous housekeepers than Mary Bernadette; it was one of the things she liked most about them.

Katie and Bonnie had lived together for forty years, and though it was perfectly plain to those who wanted to see that they were more than "just friends," Mary Bernadette was not one of those people. Paddy, who fondly referred to Katie and Bonnie as "The Ladies," found this willful ignorance more amusing than frustrating, and had given up trying to bring his wife around to a more contemporary way of thinking.

Katie Keefe was seventy-one and recently retired from her job as accountant for several small businesses in Oliver's Well. She was a tiny woman, and standing or even sitting next to Mary Bernadette, who had often been described as statuesque, she appeared in danger of being physically overwhelmed. Her hair had been snowy white since she turned forty, and she wore it in a perfectly cut bob. Mary Bernadette happened to know that she paid the unheard-of sum of sixty dollars to a stylist in Lawrenceville for her haircuts.

Bonnie Eckman was seventy-three. She was not much taller than her partner (she would say, her better half) but three times again as round. If you were going to set yourself up as a cook, she was fond of saying, you had better know how to eat. For more than twenty years she had been a personal chef in D.C. and then, when the demands of that job had become too arduous and downright annoying ("Cooking isn't the problem, fussy clients are"), she and Katie had moved to Oliver's Well, where Bonnie had opened a small catering business. Though she had shut down the business several years earlier, she still occasionally provided the food for a friend's party. Mary Bernadette had a particular fondness for Bonnie's raspberry scones and was pleased to find a platter of them set out on the table, along with a large square of real butter. Mary Bernadette had no tolerance for phony butter—"congealed yellow oil," she called it—and neither did Bonnie. Mary Bernadette felt sure it was one of the many reasons that Bonnie's career had been such a success.

"Did you hear that Bill Harrison has filed for divorce from his

wife?" Mary Bernadette asked when the three women were settled at a small, round table in a cozily decorated alcove of the living room.

Katie put a hand to her heart. "No, I most certainly did not.
And three small children!"

"How did you hear about it, Mary Bernadette?" Bonnie asked.

"Tara herself told me," she admitted. "Seems he informed her
over dinner one night that he had fallen out of love with her."

"What an idiot!" Bonnie exclaimed.

"Bonnie," Katie scolded.

Mary Bernadette agreed with Bonnie's assessment of Bill
Harrison, but she declined to comment. She was often if not always the first to know the local gossip. For some reason people
seemed to want to confide in her, either about their own travails
or about the travails of others. Mary Bernadette was very careful
never to abuse this privilege—she *did* consider it a privilege—
and chose her own audience carefully. Unless, of course, someone had sworn her to secrecy. To hold and keep safe someone's
secret was even more of a privilege and a duty, and Mary Bernadette took her duties very seriously.

"It's fine weather we've been having, isn't it?" Katie noted
now, reaching for what Mary Bernadette noticed was her second
scone. Where she put all the food she ate was anybody's guess.
Mary Bernadette herself had always kept a strict watch over her
own diet. Gluttony was one of the Seven Deadly Sins.

"The best we can expect for winter in our little part of the
world, yes," Mary Bernadette noted. "My garden is flourishing."

"Speaking of gardens," Katie said, "and I don't mean to be
telling tales—I loathe gossip unless it serves some good purpose.
Of course, there's always the case when . . ."

Mary Bernadette tuned out Katie's ramblings and wondered
what good purpose her sharing the news of the Harrisons' divorce had served. Well, she decided, it would have been terribly
awkward had Katie and Bonnie *not* known and had run into Tara
Harrison in town and had asked an innocent question on the
order of, "And how is your lovely husband, Bill?" In fact, by

telling, Mary Bernadette had saved her friends a moment of potential social embarrassment.

"Just tell her what you heard, Katie," Bonnie instructed. "There's no need for a lengthy introduction."

"Well, all right. It's just that I was at the garden center in Waterville the other day, you know the one, and I ran into Eve Hennessy. Now, she knows you and I are friends, so I don't know what possessed her to say what she did—"

"Don't you?" Bonnie interrupted. "Human nature, Katie. Lousy human nature."

Katie frowned at her partner. "Anyway," she went on, "she mentioned how your garden and all of your landscaping is always so perfect and how it is unfair of you to enter the annual garden contest, what with your husband being a professional landscaper. She *implied* that he helped you win last year. I have to tell you, I was shocked, just shocked."

Mary Bernadette stiffened. "You know, of course, that Fitzgibbon Landscaping has consistently refused to be one of the sponsors of the contest because of my participation. It would be a conflict of interest, not to mention a breach of ethics. And I would never avail myself of Paddy's store of gardening supplies. I insist on purchasing my own supplies from my personal household budget."

"I know!" Katie shook her head. "You would *never* do anything unethical. Anybody who knows you knows that. That's what was so horrible about Eve's accusation!"

Bonnie grunted. "There will always be the sort of people who resent another's happiness and success. I think they're called 'haters' these days. Supposedly they're all over the Internet. Vile thing. My advice would be to ignore anything negative you hear, especially when it's about yourself."

"Oh," Mary Bernadette said, "I assure you I will ignore it! As my mother used to say, God rest her soul, an evil tongue is of the Devil; the merciful word is of God."

Bonnie nodded. "Amen. Now, let's change the subject."

"Will Pat and Megan be coming home for his birthday?" Katie asked. "It's the twenty-fifth, isn't it?"

"Yes, it is, and no," Mary Bernadette said. "They've decided to stay in Annapolis. I'm told the twins are baking a cake."

"I hate birthday parties, myself," Bonnie said. "Probably from having catered so many of them."

Mary Bernadette nodded. "Familiarity often breeds contempt."

"Now, that's a harsh sentiment," Katie said with a frown. "I'd prefer to think that familiarity breeds, well, fondness."

Bonnie grinned. "She's the Pollyanna of the family."

"I don't suppose," Mary Bernadette said, "that I might bring home a scone for Paddy? Only, of course, if it's not too much trouble."

Katie leaped from her chair. "Of course it's no trouble," she said, hurrying off to the kitchen for a piece of plastic wrap. "Anything for you, Mary Bernadette. Anything!"

CHAPTER 6

The board's vote had been unanimous, as Mary Bernadette had believed that it would be. Fitzgibbon Landscaping had been awarded the contract to restore the extensive grounds of the Joseph J. Stoker House. Five companies had competed for the job, one of them a very prestigious firm from D.C., and another a much talked about startup out of Lawrenceville, but in the end Oliver's Well's own Fitzgibbon Landscaping had proved once more to be the right company for the job.

Mary Bernadette took the kettle of steaming water to the kitchen table and poured the contents into her favorite teapot. If she weren't such a modest woman, she might be tempted to feel a bit smug about the success of her family's business. But everything they had achieved had been the result of hard work and the grace of God, and there was no good in being smug about either.

Just then, PJ burst into the kitchen through the back door. His hair looked windblown as if he had been caught in a sudden gust, and he was breathing heavily as if he had run to his grandparents' house all the way from the office.

"We got it!" he cried.

Though she was as excited as her grandson, Mary Bernadette smiled serenely. "Yes," she said. "I know. And fix your hair."

PJ pushed his hair back from his face. "Oh," he said. "Of course you know! Anyway, Leonard DeWitt called me at the office about an hour ago."

"The vote was unanimous."

"Really?" PJ laughed. "I have to admit that when it came down to just us and that Blue Sound Landscaping Design, I panicked. Talk about bells and whistles! Remember that video walk-through simulation and that whole presentation about some kind of computer project management software they use to make sure it's all on time and on budget? When Richard asked me how I keep a project on schedule and on budget, all I could say was that I commit to a schedule and a budget and I just make sure it happens! I was sure we were doomed."

"Well, I was never in doubt. There's no need for fuss when you've got quality, is what I've always said. I'm proud of you, PJ."

"Thanks, Grandmother. I'm going home. I can't wait to tell Alexis the good news."

"But the two of you will come back for dinner," Mary Bernadette said. "We'll celebrate."

"Sure. Around six?"

"Five-thirty would be better, but six if you must. And don't be late."

PJ grinned and hurried out through the back door. With pride, Mary Bernadette watched him go. There was no doubt in her mind that the Fitzgibbon family was blessed. The business her husband had worked so hard to establish was flourishing under the leadership of her grandson. Paddy and Mary Bernadette held positions of preeminence in Oliver's Well. The Oliver's Well Historical Association was continuing to excel under her own guidance. And of course, her son and his wife were successful in their own way. No matter that Pat had ungratefully turned his back on his father's legacy.

Mary Bernadette made the sign of the cross and offered up a prayer of thanksgiving. *Thank you, dear Lord, for the gifts you have bestowed upon us. May the Fitzgibbon family continue to be worthy of your favor. Amen.*

CHAPTER 7

Alexis was preparing a marinade for a Chinese beef dish. On the counter before her was a bottle of soy sauce, a small bowl of chopped garlic, a bottle of hoisin sauce, a jar of black bean paste, a bottle of sherry, a shaker of sugar, and a tin of five-spice powder. *If Mary Bernadette walked in right now and saw what I was making*, Alexis thought, *she would keel right over*. A "foodie" she was not.

Alexis and PJ had been living in the cottage behind Mary Bernadette's house for almost a year. It was a single-story structure with a crawl space in lieu of a proper attic, a kitchen that flowed into a living room, a small full bathroom, and a bedroom. There was a flower garden out front, and behind the cottage stretched two acres of land, at the edge of which stood three massive American beech trees. Alexis would have been glad to help with the maintenance of the property, but she wasn't much of a gardener. Well, she wasn't a gardener at *all*; she had even managed to kill innocent houseplants left in her care. For obvious reasons, she kept this bit of information from the clients of Fitzgibbon Landscaping.

There wasn't much she could productively do on the inside of the cottage, either, other than to keep it clean and bring her own small touches to a décor that Mary Bernadette had chosen long ago. But it wasn't as if they would be living in the cottage forever. Someday in the not too distant future she and PJ would buy a home of their own and then they could decorate as they pleased.

Alexis put the piece of flank steak into the marinade and the dish into the fridge. She got the rice cooker out from its cupboard. The kitchen was small but well stocked with appliances Alexis had received at her wedding shower and the flatware, dishes, and glassware Mary Bernadette had so generously provided. On the whole Alexis felt lucky to be living there. Really, the only thing that bothered her was the relative lack of privacy. She frequently came home from work to find things rearranged. It could only be Mary Bernadette, of course, and the image of her husband's imposing grandmother sneaking into the cottage to shuffle trinkets from one shelf to the next amused her. What could possibly be the point in such tiny, meaningless manipulations?

Only recently had Alexis begun to feel a hint of annoyance when she came home to find a vase moved from one end of a table to the other or the tablespoons stacked in the slot that had formerly held the teaspoons. Still, she had only become seriously upset when one afternoon the week before she walked in to the bedroom to find PJ's Christmas gift to her gone from the wall over her dresser. It had taken her almost ten minutes of frantic searching to find it tucked away in the bottom drawer of the small desk that sat in a corner of the living room.

The object that Mary Bernadette had found offensive was a black-and-white photo of a nude woman, the work of a critically acclaimed contemporary photographer named Adrienne Jonas. Alexis loved the photograph. She knew that the piece must have cost PJ an awful lot of money. It was a thoughtful gift, and it meant so much to her. The fact that Mary Bernadette had ventured into the bedroom of a husband and wife—a sacrosanct place, if you considered marriage holy, which as a Catholic Mary Bernadette was supposed to do!—and had in effect hidden a personal item of great sentimental value was just too much.

Still, after some reflection Alexis had decided not to mention the incident to PJ. If found out, Mary Bernadette might be embarrassed—though how she could think she *wouldn't* be found out was beyond Alexis's comprehension—and Alexis had no desire to cause trouble for any member of her new family. If she found the picture gone a second time, then she would tell PJ. Maybe.

Alexis looked at her watch. PJ would be home soon. She so looked forward to seeing him at the end of the workday, even though most days he was able to dash into the office for a quick hello. *I am lucky in more ways than one*, Alexis thought, smiling to herself. *I just hope I continue to deserve the happiness.*

CHAPTER 8

"Congratulate your husband!" PJ was standing in the doorway of the cottage, a grin on his face.

"Congratulations!" Alexis said. "Um, what for?"

"We got the contract. The one for the Joseph J. Stoker House!"

"Oh, PJ, that's fantastic!" Alexis threw her arms around her husband's neck and kissed him.

"I still can't believe we beat out Blue Sound Landscaping Design. It's like a miracle."

"Or maybe you're just supertalented," Alexis said. "Did you ever think of that?"

"If anyone is the talent, it's Grandpa. I'm just following in his footsteps."

He's too modest, Alexis thought. Then again, it was one of the things she loved about her husband, that and his devotion to the family's continuing legacy. She knew it hadn't been easy for PJ when he had decided to move to Oliver's Well to accept his grandfather's offer of an official role in the family business. For one, his father hadn't been pleased. Pat had told his son that he would be wasting his education, to which PJ, by his own account, had replied that no education was ever wasted, and that he *had* majored in American History. To PJ, the decision to build a life in a town founded in the seventeenth century made perfect sense. Who better to appreciate old architectural styles and indigenous landscaping? Who better to take over the family business than the grandson of Mary Bernadette Fitzgibbon, scion of the well-regarded Oliver's Well Historical Association?

"Why *didn't* your father join the family business?" Alexis asked now. "You never told me."

PJ shrugged. "It's no big secret. He just wasn't interested. I don't think he ever liked living in Oliver's Well. I've heard him say that before he was out of middle school he was dreaming of moving away."

"Interesting," Alexis said. "Growing up in Philadelphia I never dreamed about moving away from home. I thought that I'd stay in Philly forever."

"And now, here you are in little Oliver's Well."

"Yes. Here I am." *For better or worse*, Alexis added to herself. And that was yet to be seen, although so far, life in Oliver's Well was turning out to be pretty good, and that was all because of her wonderful husband.

"Oh," PJ said, "Grandmother wants us for dinner. I told her we'd be there no later than six."

Alexis frowned. "But I've already started prepping that Chinese beef dish you like. The meat is marinating in the fridge."

"I'm sure it can wait until tomorrow. After all, this is a celebration! You know, I couldn't have done it—gotten the job—without your support."

Alexis smiled. "Thank you. And you're right, it is a celebration. I'm so proud of you, PJ."

"Remember, it's really Grandpa we should be proud of. He's the one who built the business into what it is now. He's the one who made its good reputation. And I'm the one under the pressure not to let him down!"

"You can do it, PJ. I believe in you."

PJ put his arms around his wife's waist and pulled her close. "You know, we don't have to be at Grandmother's until six. . . ."

CHAPTER 9

Pat and Megan Fitzgibbon lived at 23 Garrison Terrace, Annapolis, in a modest two-story house built in the 1980s. There was a two-car garage and a backyard big enough for kicking around a soccer ball. There was also a paved area large enough for a picnic table and a charcoal grill and, when Pat was feeling particularly lazy on a hot summer Saturday, a chaise on which he liked to stretch out and read. Until he fell asleep, which usually happened about ten pages into the book.

They had bought the house shortly after PJ was born. When the twins came along twelve years later, the house had proved a bit snug for the five of them, but they had made do. Then PJ had gone off to college and the remaining Fitzgibbons had settled in more comfortably. They could afford a bigger house, one with a backyard large enough for a pool or a fanciful gazebo, but neither Pat nor Megan, who were both very busy people, really wanted the responsibilities that went with more real estate.

Megan was sitting in the living room in her favorite chair, a cup of her favorite tea by her side, and a novel by one of her favorite authors on her lap. All the elements were in place for a pleasant hour of reading, but her thoughts kept turning to her family. She had gotten a call from PJ earlier to say that Fitzgibbon Landscaping had been awarded the job of restoring the grounds of the Joseph J. Stoker House, one of the properties owned by the OWHA. Megan was proud of her son for having followed his heart. Pat, however, had been disappointed with PJ's decision to settle in Oliver's Well. If his oldest child didn't want to go to law school, at least, Pat thought, he could move to a big city where there were opportunities for good jobs with good futures. But PJ had very different ambitions. He had been working for Fitzgibbon Landscaping since the summer after freshman year of high school and already knew more about the business than his father had ever known or wanted to know. He had plans, he had told his parents, for future expansion and diversification. And of course, Paddy and Mary Bernadette were there to supervise and give counsel. One only had to hope that Mary Bernadette wouldn't smother her grandson in the process.

Megan took a sip of her tea. She knew all too well that in some ways PJ was closer to his grandparents than to his parents. She felt sad about that and still occasionally wondered what she and Pat might have done differently after the birth of the twins to keep their oldest child closer. But PJ didn't seem to feel any resentment toward his parents, and if he did, he wasn't showing it. At least, he wasn't showing it as far as *she* was concerned.

The truth of the matter was that PJ and his father always seemed to be annoyed with each other. In some respects they were very different people, and that alone might go far to explain why they simply didn't get along. Still, Megan suspected that the disconnect between her husband and his older son had something to do with Pat's unhappy childhood—and the obvious fact that Mary Bernadette preferred her grandson over her son.

Well, she thought now, finishing her tea, a past could never be erased, but it could be exorcised. Certainly Grace didn't seem to be suffering the ill effects of a troubled childhood, but then again she was in tight with God. And Megan was sure that when the formidable Grace Marie Fitzgibbon opened her mouth, God took heed.

"Am I interrupting?" It was her husband, leaning against the doorway.

"Hey," she said. "I was just thinking about you."

"You were? I hope you were thinking about the good stuff."

"Of course," Megan said with mock seriousness.

He came into the room, leaned down, and kissed her on the lips. "You're as beautiful as the day I met you."

Megan smiled. "Thanks. And you're as handsome. But frankly I'm surprised you remember anything about our first meeting."

"Here we go again . . ." Pat adopted a wide-eyed look of innocence. "Why, what do you mean, my dearest? How could I not remember the night I met the one and only love of my life?"

"Well, you *were* kind of drunk."

"I was not!" Pat protested. "Well, maybe just a little tipsy, but not too tipsy to ignore your shining beauty."

"You'd been out celebrating some baseball win with Charlie Howard. The guy who used to chew on a straw all the time."

"He was trying to quit smoking."

"I remember. And I never asked—did it work? The straw method?"

"No. Poor guy was back to the Camels about a week later. I wonder what ever happened to ol' Charlie. I haven't seen him since just after our wedding."

"You could Google him."

Pat grimaced. "I'm afraid of what I might find out."

"Do you remember what you were wearing?" Megan asked with a grin. "The night we met?"

"No," Pat said, again with the wide eyes of a person who enjoyed being a player in a well-practiced game. "At least, nothing's coming to mind."

Megan laughed. "You were wearing a bright red blazer with the sleeves pushed up to the elbow and shoulder pads that made you about seven feet wide."

"Darn the eighties! Anyway, I'm going to show you my gratitude for your being my wife yet again, so get ready to adore me. I've got a special treat for Valentine's Day."

"A special treat? Are you going to give me a clue?"

"Nope. But I promise you won't be disappointed."

Megan laughed. "I believe you. Oh, Pat, have you called PJ to congratulate him on getting that big job he was after?"

Her husband pulled his iPhone from his pocket. "I'll send him a text," he said, wandering out of the living room. *Well*, Megan thought, *a text is better than nothing*. With a sigh, she finally opened her book.

CHAPTER 10

Alexis had walked into the heart of town from Honeysuckle Lane, about a fifteen-minute amble along pleasant streets lined with willow oaks and an occasional American beech tree. The weather was fine. Traditionally, February was the driest month in this part of the state, with an afternoon high of forty degrees. But this year, temperatures had climbed into the upper forties on several occasions and there had been enough rain to nourish land that might otherwise have suffered, and *that* made PJ's job a little bit easier.

Alexis stopped at the post office to purchase stamps for the office, and then walked on to the bakery. She was craving one of Cookies 'n Crumpets' famous corn muffins. *My secret vice*, Alexis thought. *Corn muffins. Life in the fast lane!*

Well, she deserved a treat, didn't she? The night before, PJ had announced that they would be celebrating Valentine's Day with his grandparents. Alexis hadn't protested, but she had been disappointed. After all, this was their first Valentine's Day as a married couple, and though in the past Alexis would have laughed at such sentimentality, since meeting, falling in love with, and marrying PJ she put a lot of stock in romantic holidays, like the date they had first kissed. Sure, Valentine's Day was mostly just an excuse for candy and jewelry companies to go whole hog on marketing, but still, Alexis saw no harm in celebrating the holiday alone with her lovely husband.

Alexis pushed open the door to Cookies 'n Crumpets. There was a woman just inside by the display of wrapped sandwich breads, and Alexis knew immediately that she had met her before but the where, the when—and the name!—had entirely escaped her. Before a flush of embarrassment could invade her face, the woman put out her hand and said, "Maureen Kline."

"Oh," Alexis said, smiling now. "Of course. I'm sorry. I can be bad with faces. And with names, to be honest."

"No worries," Maureen said. "I don't think we've actually seen each other except in passing since your wedding."

"Right. Do you work in town?"

"Just down the block, at Wharton Insurance." Maureen laughed. "I've spent my entire life in Oliver's Well."

"So far, anyway."

"I'm not going anywhere. Someone's got to be around for the parents."

"Oh. But they're not ill, are they? Jeannette and Danny. I saw them just the other day . . ."

"No, they're not ill," Maureen said. "Just getting older, as are we all."

Alexis thought she detected a note of wistfulness in Maureen's voice, and she realized she didn't quite know what to say next.

"So, what do you and PJ have planned for your first Valentine's Day as husband and wife?" Maureen asked briskly.

Alexis was glad for the change of subject. "Actually," she said, "we'll be going out to dinner with PJ's grandparents."

Maureen smiled. "The Fitzgibbons live in each other's pockets. They're old-fashioned that way."

"I didn't mean to sound like I was complaining," Alexis added quickly.

"Of course not. And I didn't mean to sound critical. The Fitzgibbon family is like an extension of my own family, and sometimes when I'm talking about them I take liberties I suppose I shouldn't. So, where are you going for dinner?"

"The Angry Squire. Mary Bernadette knows the owner from the board of the OWHA."

"You're in for a treat," Maureen told her. "The food is very good and the atmosphere is charming. Richard Armstrong went to a lot of trouble to bring over most of the interior directly from England. And I'm sure you and PJ will find some time alone for a celebration. Young love always finds a way. At least, I vaguely remember that it does."

Again, Alexis detected that note of wistfulness.

Maureen suddenly looked at her watch and exclaimed, "Oops, I'm going to be late if I don't run. It was nice to see you, Alexis."

"You too," Alexis said, watching as Maureen dashed out the door and down the sidewalk. She was not a very attractive woman, Alexis thought, not physically anyway, and her skirt suit looked totally out of date. But she was friendly, and Alexis found that she liked Maureen, though she doubted they had much in common. Maureen was probably in her forties, more Megan's age than hers. More Alexis's own mother's age, at that. And imagine, she had lived her entire life in little Oliver's Well! Of course, that was PJ's intention, to live out the rest of his life in Oliver's Well. And as PJ's wife, Alexis would be spending the remainder of her days right here alongside him.

Wow, she thought, as she walked up to the counter to place her order for a corn muffin toasted with butter. That was a bit of a scary thought—the *remainder* of her days, as if her life was already mostly in the past. She would grow old and eventually die

in a charming but insular little Virginia town. Talk about mellow-
ing. If things continued in the way they were, her friends back
home in Philadelphia would hardly recognize her in a few years,
and not only because she would have gained twenty pounds from
eating too many corn muffins and too much of Mary Bernadette's
mashed potatoes!

Alexis paid for her muffin and took a seat at one of the little tables in the bakery. At that moment, she was not in the least concerned about becoming unrecognizable, not even to herself. She
was concerned with eating her muffin before it got cold.

CHAPTER 11

The moment she entered The Angry Squire, Alexis was charmed.
She had never been to England, but she had watched enough
period dramas and browsed enough art and history books to know that
Richard Armstrong had gotten the atmosphere just right. The lighting was low enough to be flattering but not interfere with the
reading of a menu. Everywhere one looked there was burnished
brass and dark, gleaming leather. The walls were decorated with
oil paintings of horses and men and women in powdered wigs.
Alexis wondered why she had never been to the restaurant before now and realized with a bit of a shock that she and PJ hadn't
gone out for as much as a drink or a movie in weeks. Or was it
months? Only a year into their marriage and already they were
acting like a couple that had been together for sixty, content to sit
side by side for an evening until one or both nodded off!

The menu was suitably conservative, and Alexis could see at a
glance why The Angry Squire was Mary Bernadette's favorite
restaurant. There was only one fish dish on the menu; the other

main course offerings were lamb, roast beef, and chicken. There was nothing even vaguely exotic on offer—no bok choy or cous-cous and certainly no escargot. The daily pasta special was spaghetti with meat sauce. The desserts were apple pie, choco-late cake, and chocolate and vanilla ice cream.

The waiter (a young man Mary Bernadette knew by name) had poured water and brought a basket of bread and butter to the table when PJ turned to Alexis and presented her with a small box wrapped in shiny red foil.

"Happy Valentine's Day," he said, leaning over and kissing her cheek.

Alexis blushed. She felt embarrassed opening the present in front of her husband's grandparents. But PJ urged her on. While her husband, Mary Bernadette, and Paddy watched, Alexis tore off the wrapping paper.

"Waste not, want not, as my mother used to say, God rest her soul." Mary Bernadette reached across the table for the discarded paper. "Some of this can be salvaged."

Alexis laughed. "Maybe a one-inch square!"

"Go ahead, Ali," PJ urged again. "Open it."

Alexis did, to find a small silver cross settled against a blue vel-vet background. It was not what she had hoped for.

"Oh," she said, looking up at the expectant faces around her. "It's very nice. Thank you. But I already have a cross."

"But not this one," Mary Bernadette explained. "This is Saint Brigid of Ireland's reed cross. You can look her up in my book of saints if you like. She's quite as famous as St. Patrick."

PJ laid a hand gently on Alexis's arm. "It was Grandmother's idea," he said.

Alexis felt chastened and determined to hide her disappoint-ment. "It's very pretty," she said, with a smile for her husband. "Thank you, PJ."

"It doesn't matter that it's pretty," Mary Bernadette pointed out. "What matters is that it symbolizes our faith."

PJ took his hand away from Alexis's arm. She smiled and closed the box. "Of course."

"Aren't you going to put it on?" PJ asked.

"Well, I would, but I'm already wearing a necklace." It was a small black pearl on a white gold chain, a gift from her parents.

A beat of silence followed this remark, and Alexis felt that she had committed a further crime of insensitivity. "But I'll take it off," she said, turning her back to PJ. "Can you help me with the clasp?"

"I'd highly recommend the steak," Mary Bernadette said now. "It's by far my favorite."

Alexis, now wearing the cross of St. Brigid, turned back to the others. "Actually," she said, "I was considering the lamb."

Her statement was met with a silence Alexis could only call expectant. "But I think I'll change my mind and go with the steak," she said.

The Fitzgibbon family smiled at her. "You won't regret it," Mary Bernadette said.

Chapter 12

Megan slit open the pale blue envelope. Inside she found a note of thanks from a woman who had attended a recent talk sponsored by the Cerebral Palsy Education Effort. Megan greatly appreciated such notes of thanks; they helped remind her that she was making a positive difference for the CP community.

Eight years earlier, Megan had met a man named Alec Clare at a legal conference, and during the course of a conversation she had learned that Alec had lost his brother, Ted, to suicide. The poor young man had been driven to take his own life as a result of all the teasing and bullying he had been subjected to by adults and kids alike who hadn't understood that his CP was not an illness or something shameful. Alec, who was only eleven when his brother died, was still haunted by the tragedy. Since graduating from law school he had been an advocate for tolerance and understanding of those with the condition.

Not long after meeting at the conference, it had occurred to Megan and Alec that they might establish an organization of their own to address a need for education and care among those families without the benefits of the financial security they themselves enjoyed. Thus the CPEE was born. In its current manifestation it had three functions. First, the education of the broader community about cerebral palsy, what it was, how it occurred, how it could be managed. This aspect included a schedule of lectures and presentations to schools and community organizations. David had given a talk only last year at the public middle school in a neighboring town. It had been fun, he said, and the prolonged applause at the end hadn't hurt his already substantial ego. Second, the CPEE offered support for the cerebral palsy community. This aspect included a website, a community blog and forum, and a call center where parents and caregivers could find information and resources. Finally, the CPEE had set up a separate foundation for research funding. Megan's work with the CPEE occupied enough of her time for her to realize that it would never have seen the light of day if she had kept a full-time position at Klausen, Robben, and Hill after the twins were born.

Megan filed the thank-you note with the others she had received that month. She was in the office she shared with Pat on the second floor of their home. Well, it was really Megan's office. Pat hated to bring his work from Cruz, Fitzgibbon, and Dengler home with him and would rather stay at the firm until nine at night to avoid "infecting" (that was his term) his private life with other people's woes.

It was interesting, Megan thought now. Though her husband was terribly protective of his wife and children, he had never seemed overly concerned with his parents' health and well-being; at times he had seemed almost indifferent to their progress toward old age. So it had come as some surprise when a few nights ago Pat suggested that he and Megan might make an effort to visit his parents more often.

"I know it's not exactly fun hanging out with Mary Bernadette and Paddy, but they *are* closing in on eighty," he had pointed out. "They could get into all sorts of trouble. What if my father fell off a ladder? He's always fixing something that doesn't need fixing or tinkering with the wiring on some old appliance."

"That's true," Megan had replied. "They *could* get into all sorts of trouble, and I'm glad to know that you're concerned, but there's a limit to what we can prevent. Even if we lived next door we couldn't stop one of them from falling down the stairs in the middle of the night or taking ill behind the wheel of a car."

"You're right, but that doesn't mean we can't check in more often."

"Maybe we should ask PJ to keep an eye on his grandparents."

Pat had frowned. "PJ and Alexis are just kids. They probably wouldn't even see a warning sign. Remember when my father had his hip replacement? PJ told me he hadn't noticed the man had developed a limp."

"True. The young never want to see indications of sickness or death. Well, not that any of us do, but the young seem particularly good at being blind to disaster."

"So, you agree?"

"Yes," Megan had said. "I agree that we should see your parents more often."

Megan still wondered what had prompted this sudden filial concern. And it wasn't lost on her that Pat's concerns lay mostly with his father. But that wasn't unusual. Sometimes she wondered if he cared for his mother at all.

Well, Pat's cool relationship with his mother hadn't inhibited his ability to express his love for his wife. For Valentine's Day he had given her a gorgeous ring, a round brilliant cut, bezel-set diamond in a yellow and white gold band. She had been secretly coveting it for months, and somehow Pat had divined her secret. He had presented the ring with a bouquet of her favorite flowers, pink peonies, and a box of very good chocolates. If she hadn't long ago forgiven him for wearing that disgusting red blazer (and for being polluted) the night they met, she would have forgiven him now.

Megan looked up at the copy of a popular English translation of The Prayer of St. Francis pinned to an old-fashioned corkboard over her desk.

> *Lord, make me an instrument of your peace.*
> *Where there is hatred, let me sow love;*
> *Where there is injury, pardon;*
> *Where there is doubt, faith;*
> *Where there is despair, hope;*
> *Where there is darkness, light;*
> *Where there is sadness, joy.*
> *Oh Divine Master, grant that*
> *I may not so much seek to be consoled, as to console;*
> *To be understood, as to understand;*
> *To be loved, as to love.*
> *For it is in giving that we receive.*
> *It is in pardoning that we are pardoned,*
> *And it is in dying that we are born*
> *To Eternal Life, Amen.*

The prayer summed up Megan's religious and moral philosophy. She wasn't at all certain about an Eternal Life, but she believed that the benefits of good behavior here on earth were enough to make the effort worthwhile. Not, of course, that her own behavior always met the high standards of St. Francis, but she did try to give rather than to receive. Take, for example, her wedding. Though she and Pat would have been perfectly content to get married at city hall, for the sake of family—or, as her mother would say, "for the look of it"—they had tied the knot at the Church of the Immaculate Conception in Oliver's Well. Even so, Mary Bernadette had made it known that she wasn't thrilled with her son and his new wife being only "cafeteria Catholics," picking and choosing what rules to follow and what rituals to perform. Even having their first child baptized in the church (with Jeannette and Danny Kline as godparents) and later, confirmed (PJ had taken his father's middle name, Christopher), had not entirely appeased Mary Bernadette.

But Megan had long ago realized that there never would be any appeasing her mother-in-law. At best one might succeed in placating her. In a perfect world, one might succeed in flying completely under her radar. But this was not a perfect world. For as long as Mary Bernadette lived and breathed she would probably never forgive her daughter-in-law for not joining the Oliver's Well Historical Association. Of course it had been entirely unrealistic of her to assume that Megan—who didn't even *live* in Oliver's Well—would have the time, let alone the inclination, to join. But Mary Bernadette wasn't a woman given to introspection. *That's not fair*, Megan thought now. Who knew what deep and searching thoughts plagued her mother-in-law in the middle of the night? All that anyone could tell for certain was that by day Mary Bernadette was a woman of action, a woman who at times might benefit from taking a moment to reflect before speaking her mind.

Megan sighed and tapped her pen smartly against her desk. The CPEE. The twins and their after-school activities. The law firm. The house. The grandparents. Lord knew she was busy enough, too busy by most people's standards. Still, lately she found herself wanting some new project she could sink her teeth into. Lately, she found herself ever so slightly *bored*. Maybe she was what Mary Bernadette called "a glutton for punishment." Except that Megan didn't find work a punishment at all. And she thought that if Mary Bernadette took the trouble to consider the idea, she might realize that she and her daughter-in-law were not so terribly different after all. They were both devoted to their family and to their causes. It was as simple as that.

"Mom?"

Megan turned away from her desk. Danica was leaning against the doorframe wearing what amounted to her uniform—a hoodie, a pair of skinny jeans, and UGG brand boots no matter how hot the day.

"What's up, honey?" she asked her daughter.

"Grandma called," Danica told her.

"Again? That's twice today."

"I know. I told her you were working."

Megan restrained a smile. "And what did she say to that?"

Danica shrugged. "What she always says. 'Oh, your mother spends too much time at work.' How come she never says that Dad spends too much time at work?"

"I guess your grandmother is just old-fashioned. She comes from a place where men work out in the big, wide world and women stay at home. Or, at least, a mental state if not an actual place."

"I don't get it. You work but you're *at* home! That should be okay, right?"

Megan laughed. "Well, I guess I can't really explain it after all."

Danica wrinkled her nose. "I like Grandma, I mean, I love her and all, but she has some weird ideas."

"Don't let her hear you say that."

"Oh, I won't," Danica promised. "That would be rude."

"Well, did she say what she wanted?"

Danica shrugged again. "Not really. I think she just wanted to talk."

"And did you? Talk, I mean?"

"She asked me about school. That's what she always asks me about, never my friends or soccer or debate team."

"Well, she knows the value of an education."

"I guess."

"Where's your brother?" Megan asked.

"He's in his room."

"I wonder if he's doing his homework or fooling around with a video game."

"It helps his dexterity, Mom."

"Which is all well and good, as long as he doesn't neglect his homework." Megan sighed. "I guess I should call Mary Bernadette back before it's time to start dinner."

Danica grinned. "I bet I know what she'll say."

Megan pitched her voice a bit lower than usual in an attempt to mimic her mother-in-law's commanding voice. " 'So, you're finally done with that work of yours for the day?' "

"Or: 'Oh, you didn't have to call me back. It was nothing.' And then she'll keep you on the phone for, like, an hour!"

Megan laughed. It was wrong to mock anyone—St. Francis would tell you that—let alone an older person, and behind her back to boot, but sometimes it just couldn't be helped.

CHAPTER 13

It was another unseasonably warm day, and Alexis was taking advantage of the weather to stretch out on a chaise lounge behind the cottage. She wasn't sure how the untiringly energetic Mary Bernadette would feel about her putting her feet up in the middle of the day—though it *was* a Saturday—but thought she was probably safe here, with only the beech trees as witnesses.

Mary Bernadette! It had been like being with a celebrity the other night at The Angry Squire. People kept stopping by the table to pay their respects to PJ's grandmother, and Richard Armstrong had delivered their desserts on the house. An elderly, very dapper man named Mr. Levitt had congratulated PJ on winning the Joseph J. Stoker House job and said he remembered the place from when he was very small. Would PJ like to borrow some photographs of the gardens before they had entirely gone to weed? PJ had thanked the man profusely, as had Mary Bernadette. "I've known him since I first came to Oliver's Well," she explained when Mr. Levitt had moved off. "And he was ancient even then."

And Mary Bernadette had been right about the steak. It was fantastic. Still, next time they went to The Angry Squire, Alexis was going to have the lamb come hell or high water, as she had heard Mary Bernadette say often enough. It was probably an expression she had come across in the bible, maybe something to do with Noah.

God, Alexis thought, *the woman's voice is everywhere!* No doubt about it, she had never met anyone even remotely like PJ's formidable grandmother. There certainly were no such people in her family. Alexis was an only child. Neither her father nor her mother had any siblings, and all of her grandparents had died before Alexis was born. But her parents had always been enough family for Alexis. They had encouraged her to feel good about herself, and she had grown up to expect a certain amount of attention and respect as her due.

Alexis glanced down at the new pair of jeans she was wearing. They had cost her $150. Well, they had cost her parents $150. Every month they sent her a substantial check. She had never mentioned this to PJ. The truth was that Trenouths weren't thrilled that Alexis was working as an office manager for a small family when she could have set her sights on a real career with a real income. If she had wanted to, of course, and that was the thing. Alexis hadn't wanted to and she still didn't want to. She was happy working for Fitzgibbon Landscaping. It kept her close to her husband and what he loved most—his family.

And that was something else Alexis's parents simply couldn't understand: her intense attraction to the Fitzgibbon clan. From the start of her relationship with PJ she had been drawn to the "otherness" of the Fitzgibbons. Their passionate membership in the Catholic Church excited her. She liked the fact that the Church provided landmarks by which a person could mark his progress through life. She liked the fact that those landmarks were marked by ceremony. When a child was born he was baptized; his godparents gave him a cross and there was a party in his honor.

Later came the occasion of his First Confession, and then his First Holy Communion, and then his confirmation, which involved the choosing of a sponsor and a "new" name to mark the passage into Christian adulthood and responsibility. All of this struck Alexis as fascinating, possibly because her own family had never identified with an ethnic or a religious group. What Alexis knew of organized religion she had gleaned from her studies of art and history and philosophy. But then she had met PJ and had chosen to join him in his faith.

Alexis touched the cross of St. Brigid resting against her chest. Though she had converted to Catholicism for her husband, she couldn't say that she really believed in all of the Church's teachings. She *did* enjoy the pomp and circumstance of the mass; the sheer theatricality of the ancient ceremonial and ritualistic practices appealed to her artistic nature. True, some bits were very puzzling, like the sacrament of the Eucharist. From what Alexis understood (and she knew that her understanding might be faulty), you were supposed to believe that you were incorporating the actual body and blood of Christ when you received the host and the Communion wine. She found the notion bizarre, though she would never insult PJ or his family by mentioning her discomfort. That was a topic for conversation with Father Robert. He had tried to explain to her the difference between belief and faith—supposedly, you could have faith without belief but not belief without faith—and he had counseled prayer and active good works as two ways in which she might experience God and Christ "in action." So far she was afraid she had failed to make much progress via either avenue.

But PJ was so grateful for what he called "the gift" of her conversion. Was conversion the right word in her case? After all, she hadn't belonged to another faith before belonging to the Catholic Church. She had sworn allegiance to nothing other than the American flag, and that without much thought.

Knowing PJ had changed all that. From the very first, Alexis had admired his passion for heritage and history. She had seen it as an indicator of a stable person, one who wouldn't succumb to the allure of someone or something new. PJ was someone who appreciated the value of tradition and inheritance.

Alexis looked fondly at her wedding ring. It had once belonged to Mary Bernadette's Aunt Catherine. "I think," Mary Bernadette had said, "that you should have this. It's been in my family now for almost ninety years." Alexis had thanked PJ's grandmother profusely, and it was only much later that night she remembered that she had had her heart set on a platinum wedding band, to match the platinum setting of her engagement ring. Oh well, she had reasoned. It was no longer a faux pas to mix metals. And if Kate Middleton could do it, well, then, it was all right for Alexis Trenouth, soon to be Alexis Fitzgibbon.

"Aren't you at least going to hyphenate your two names, like I did?" her mother had asked on the morning of the wedding. "Or are you going to subsume your entire identity in PJ's?" Oddly, Alexis couldn't remember her reply. Her parents also hadn't been happy about their daughter converting to Catholicism, but rather than argue with her they had simply said, "Do what you need to do. You can always get out of it later."

But Alexis didn't want to get out of any of it, not her marriage, not her membership in the Catholic Church, not her place in the Fitzgibbon clan. Though, if she were *completely* honest, lately a few things had given her pause. Take the matter of St. Brigid's cross. She had been hoping for an amethyst pendant and had even dropped a few hints to PJ. But he had taken his grandmother's advice and bought the cross instead. It was no big deal but . . .

And then there was the matter of the mail, delivered to a box next to his grandparents' mailbox. From the day they had moved in, Mary Bernadette had taken it upon herself to bring their mail to the cottage, making her privy to every card or bill or magazine they received. A few weeks ago, Alexis had worked up the nerve to suggest to Mary Bernadette that there was no need for her to act as courier, to which Mary Bernadette had replied, "It's no trouble at all." And that had been that.

Well, Alexis thought now, getting off the chaise lounge and

going back inside the cottage for a glass of water, her husband was worth putting up with a domineering grandmother living within spitting distance. He was kind and good, and every single day he told her how much he loved her. The fact that he was also physically perfect didn't hurt his case any. She was very much looking forward to having his children, though they were using birth control at the moment; they wanted to sock away a fair amount of money before starting a family. Very rarely was she careless, and she always felt badly when she realized she had forgotten to take her pill.

Alexis's musings came to an abrupt halt as she heard PJ pulling into the driveway. She rushed out of the cottage to greet him, a smile of welcome on her face.

CHAPTER 14

Alexis came into the kitchen of the big house to find her husband and his grandfather seated at the table. Paddy was in a jacket and tie, and PJ was wearing a jacket over an open-necked dress shirt. The sight of them all gussied up for church made Alexis smile.

"It's a puzzle," Paddy was saying. "And you did a soil test, you say?"

"Yup. No disease that I can see. I think I'm going to have to call in a plant pathologist."

Paddy whistled. "And that'll cost a pretty penny. Is there no other way?"

Each man now tapped his right cheek with his forefinger, a habit they shared. Alexis often wondered if PJ had consciously adopted his grandfather's habitual gesture, or if somehow it had seeped across to his unconscious. Or maybe the gesture had actually been inherited. Was such a thing possible?

Whatever the case with PJ and his grandfather, Alexis found it endearing. As far as she could tell, PJ and his *father* didn't share any physical habits. In fact, they didn't seem to share much of anything. Between PJ and Pat there was often a sense of competition or suspicion, as if neither one really knew what to expect from the other. She was sure she wasn't imagining it. She had seen Megan look with annoyance from her son to her husband when the two men were purposely misunderstanding each other.

"I can't understand why it's taking the lawyers so long to draw up the contract for the Stoker job," her husband said now. "They've written contracts for the OWHA before. It can't be so difficult."

"Maybe they're just really busy," Alexis suggested.

"I want everything to be squared away so that work can *begin*. Maybe I should call Leonard DeWitt and ask him to hurry the lawyers along."

"Be patient, PJ," Paddy said. "The course of business never runs smoothly. You don't want to give yourself a heart attack, worrying all the time."

PJ laughed. "You're right. I should learn how to be patient. I will. Someday."

"He's impossible, Paddy," Alexis said, putting her hands on her husband's shoulders. "You should see how agitated he gets when we're on a slow line at the grocery store."

"Just like his father," Paddy noted.

PJ frowned. "I'd like to think I'm a bit more patient than Dad!"

Mary Bernadette came into the kitchen then. She was wearing a skirt suit in a soft gray, with a pearl-colored silk blouse. Alexis suddenly felt underdressed in her white jeans and lightweight motorcycle style jacket.

"Is everyone ready?" Mary Bernadette asked. "We don't want to be late."

"Of course not," Paddy said, rising from his seat at the table.

"There's nothing more insulting to the priest and distracting to the congregation than people coming in late to mass."

"We've never been late to church, Mary, have we?"

Mary Bernadette frowned. "Only that once when Pat was about six and we couldn't find him when we were ready to leave the house. Do you remember, Paddy?"

Paddy nodded but said nothing.

"Where was he?" Alexis asked. "Was he okay?"

Before Mary Bernadette could reply, Paddy spoke. "That's an episode best left forgotten. Let's just say the poor lad was upset about something. He got over it soon enough."

Alexis shot a look to her husband, who shrugged and shook his head.

"PJ and I are taking our own car," Alexis said as the four Fitzgibbons made their way through the living room to the front door. "We want to see a movie in Westminster after church."

Mary Bernadette came to a sudden halt just inside the door. "Oh."

"Anything wrong, Grandmother?" PJ asked.

"It's just that I thought we might all have brunch together at The Angry Squire. But it's all right."

PJ looked at Alexis behind his grandmother's back and her heart sank just a little. "We can go to the movie some other time," she told her husband's grandmother.

Mary Bernadette bestowed one of her megawatt smiles upon Alexis, and as disappointed as Alexis was, she found herself smiling back. "Why, thank you, Alexis," Mary Bernadette said. "How nice of you."

The two older Fitzgibbons went out first, followed by PJ and Alexis. "Thank you," he whispered to his wife, and took her hand in his.

Alexis nodded. How little it took to make the people you loved happy, she thought. Just a little bit of sacrifice here and there.

CHAPTER 15

Mary Bernadette guided her car down Main Street. There, coming out of the bakery, was Marilyn Windsor, she of the old family diaries. Really, the woman had been unaccountably difficult about them, and for the life of her, Mary Bernadette couldn't see why she had put up such a fuss about letting the diaries go. It wasn't as if she really cared for them. How could she have when instead of being kept in a proper archival storage box they had been stuffed in a drawer of a table in her front hall where anyone could manhandle them? No matter now. The Oliver's Well Historical Association had gotten the diaries in the end.

Mary Bernadette peered ahead. Was that Alexis's car parked outside The Angry Squire? No, she realized as she drove past, it wasn't, but it was a similar make and color. She and Paddy had enjoyed a lovely Valentine's Day dinner with the young couple at Richard Armstrong's restaurant, though Alexis hadn't seemed very excited about the cross of St. Brigid that PJ had given her. Well, to be fair the religion was still new to her. Unlike the other Fitzgibbons, to whom their Catholicism was second nature, Alexis would have to grow into a sense of belonging and comfort. It would happen, given time.

Of course, there was always the possibility that she could turn out like Pat and Megan, who had moved beyond a sense of belonging and comfort into a state of alienation and, at times, active contempt. But that would *not* happen to her grandson's wife, not if Mary Bernadette had anything to say about it.

It had been at her suggestion that all four of them—Mary Bernadette and Paddy, PJ, and Alexis—had gone to church together for the Ash Wednesday service. "Remember man that thou art dust, and unto dust thou shall return." Though she had heard her son condemn the words as morbid, Mary Bernadette had always found them of great importance. It was important to keep one's pride in check and never to forget that life here on earth was not all pleasurable—nor was it meant be. Mary Bernadette had learned that lesson in a particularly brutal way when she lost her beloved William. Since his death there had been many times when she had wondered if perhaps she had found too much joy in her son; perhaps God had taken him away to remind her of the dangers of ignoring the trials and challenges He had sent his children. But the ways of God were inscrutable, and Mary Bernadette would never know why her baby had been taken from her. That there might have been no reason at all—that there might be no God or guiding principle behind the working of the world—was simply not something Mary Bernadette Fitzgibbon was capable of conceiving.

She came to a stop at the red light on the corner of Vine Street and nodded in greeting to Mrs. Kendrick, behind the wheel of the car to her left. Mrs. Kendrick was another member of the Church of the Immaculate Conception; Mary Bernadette had seen her there the day before, three small children in tow. Mary Bernadette very much doubted that Pat and Megan had taken the twins for ashes. For them, the season of Lent was devoid of spiritual meaning and Easter was merely a day on which it was acceptable to bite the ears off chocolate rabbits. For Mary Bernadette, and to a lesser extent her husband, Lent was a time of quiet introspection, self-denial, and repentance, and Easter a day of thankfulness.

The light turned green and Mary Bernadette continued on her way, eventually turning onto Haven Street and pulling into her usual spot outside the Wilson House, where the OWHA was headquartered. The building had once been owned by the descendants of one of the original settlers of Oliver's Well, a Richard Wilson, a woodworker, farmer, and mariner. It was one of the oldest surviving wood-framed houses in the region, built by Wilson himself. Originally, the house had sat on a twenty-five-acre plot; today, only five acres remained attached to the house. The structure resembled contemporary English precedents but was notably American in its extravagant use of wood. The original part of the house was a two-story structure, sided in rough clapboard, with a steeply sloped roof and a center brick chimney. Over the years, primarily in the eighteenth century, several additions had been made, and when the OWHA had acquired the house, there were some who wanted to remove them. In the end it was decided that the additions were part of the character of the building, so they remained.

The board regularly met in what had once been the dining room. The members of the board were responsible for hiring the CEO—currently, Leonard DeWitt—who served at their pleasure. He ran the operation—negotiating contracts, hiring and firing services—and made a report to the board at each meeting. The board itself was also in charge of setting broad policy, raising money, and approving major financial decisions and commitments. Mary Bernadette, seated at the chairman's customary place at one end of the long oval table, now surveyed her colleagues.

There was Jeannette, of course, seated just to her right. She had been a member of the board for almost as long as Mary Bernadette, currently the longest standing member. Though Jeannette was always ready and willing to volunteer her time and energy for tasks as small as stapling together sheets of paper to be distributed during tours, she had never aspired to hold a position of major responsibility, and generally kept a low profile among her colleagues.

To Jeannette's right sat Wallace Chadbourne, a small, spare man with a neat little mustache. He had been the principal of the local public high school for close to twenty years before retiring. He made it no secret that he would like to be the chairman in Mary Bernadette's place—"when she is ready to step down, of course, and not a moment sooner!"—but he didn't seem to realize that he didn't have the support of the other board members. Wallace was a smart-enough man, but he lacked the personality to inspire devotion in the way Mary Bernadette could. Even those members who occasionally chafed against her high-handed methods had no doubt of her abilities and kept their complaints to themselves. And of course there was Mary Bernadette's charm, which could, as her husband was fond of saying, "soothe the most savage beast you could drag in from the jungle."

Seated next to Wallace was Richard Armstrong, owner of The Angry Squire, congenial and very good at soothing irate tempers. He was taller than six feet and very thin. He had been happily married for almost thirty years before his wife had died of cancer. Since then, Richard had been on his own, though there were several single women in Oliver's Well who would very much like to walk down the aisle on his arm.

Next was Joyce Miller. She taught history at the private academy. Her husband was the pastor at the local Methodist church. Mary Bernadette had only met Martin Miller a few times, and she found him a genuinely unassuming, honestly kind, and somewhat baffled person. How he had come to marry Joyce was anyone's guess. (She was sure that Martin himself didn't know the answer to that.) Joyce and her husband had twin girls, aged five, who were often seen having a tantrum. Joyce was the youngest member of the board at thirty-eight. She was painfully thin, always on a strange diet, and almost always ready with a critical word about an absent colleague. To Mary Bernadette, Joyce seemed an unhappy woman, and a potentially dangerous one.

Anne Tribble, the next board member, was a gracious, good-natured woman who owned a very successful boutique called The Sophisticated Lady. Her husband, Joseph, a retired optometrist, had been confined to a wheelchair for some time after a car accident had left him partially paralyzed. That they were a devoted couple no one could doubt. Mary Bernadette had great respect for Anne, as a business owner, as a wife, and as a member of the board. The fact that no matter how trying things were at home, Anne always managed to be perfectly turned out only raised her in Mary Bernadette's esteem.

Leonard DeWitt, the aforementioned CEO of the organization, was a large man, tall and robust, with perpetually flushed cheeks and bright blue eyes. He was an honorably retired and highly decorated police chief from the D.C. area who had moved to Oliver's Well six years earlier. Within his first year of residence he had proved to be one of the most dedicated citizens Mary Bernadette had ever encountered. He lived in a small, very charming house that had been built in 1845, on what was one of the prettiest streets in Oliver's Well. All he would say of his personal past was that he had been married once but that his wife hadn't been happy married to a cop. He was an unabashed fan of Mary Bernadette and had been heard to say that she would have made an excellent law enforcement agent, given her unswerving ethical conduct and her ability to "grasp the right end of the stick."

Neal Hyatt, seated next to Leonard, was owner of the Hyatt Gallery, specializing in contemporary American art. He held a doctorate in twentieth-century American painting from the University of Chicago and was a guest lecturer at several area colleges. His dedication to the past of Oliver's Well was fierce—interesting, Mary Bernadette thought, given his professional specialty—and he was brilliantly suited to his job as the board's secretary. He was in his early forties, as was his life partner, Gregory Smith. As with her friends Katie and Bonnie, Mary Bernadette treated the men with great respect without formally acknowledging the complete nature of their relationship.

Finally, there was Norma Campbell, a very expensively preserved fifty-five-year-old woman. She lived on her own in an enormous house on an enormous estate, complete with a stable full of horses she didn't ride and a tennis court she never used. Rumor had it she was visited regularly each Saturday night by a gentleman in a large black sedan with Florida plates. Mary Bernadette had no time for such an obviously theatrical tale (concocted by Joyce Miller?), and as far as she was concerned, Norma's personal life was none of her business. Norma rarely showed much enthusiasm for the OWHA's projects and causes, and Mary Bernadette wasn't the only one to suspect that Norma was a dabbler, a lonely woman who saw holding a place on various boards and clubs around Oliver's Well as a way to pass the time of day. Still, she wasn't a troublemaker and she did contribute gener-

ously in a financial way to the upkeep of the historical Oliver's
Well, so Mary Bernadette saw no reason to object to her presence.

Now Mary Bernadette cleared her throat and called the meeting to order. Neal, in his capacity as secretary, read the minutes of
the last meeting. There followed a discussion of old business.
When that had been satisfactorily concluded, Leonard announced
that he was still investigating a new paint supplier and went on to
describe his findings. Mary Bernadette listened attentively.

CHAPTER 16

Alexis bounded into the Wilson House. The day was warm and
bright and she was feeling happy and energized. She wished
PJ weren't at work. If he were free she would steal him away for a
long drive with the windows down and music blaring.

The day before, Richard Armstrong, who usually conducted
the OWHA's Haunted Oliver's Well Tour, had asked Alexis if she
might fill in for him, as he was suffering a terrible cold. "Just follow the script," he said between sneezes. "And try not to be too
dramatic. No gore or guts. We don't want anyone having a fit
along the way."

"What should I do if someone *does* freak out?" she had asked.
To which Richard had replied, "Run."

So she had taken on the task and had enjoyed it immensely,
everything from the visit to Oliver's Well's oldest cemetery,
which dated from the seventeenth century, to the stately Kennington House, supposed residence of at least three ghosts, one
of whom was believed to be the spirit of a notorious rake named
Nehemiah Jones, who had met an ignominious if just end when

he had been run through by the irate husband of one of his conquests. Leading the tour had suited her love of theatre—she had been a member of the theatre club in high school and in college—a love that hadn't had much opportunity to make itself known since moving to Oliver's Well. There *was* an amateur theatre group in town, but Alexis hadn't ventured to join. She was reluctant to devote a chunk of time to other people that might better be spent with her new husband.

"There you are." It was Mary Bernadette, come in just ahead of Alexis and still wearing her classic, belted trench coat. "How did you succeed with the tour?" she asked.

"Great," Alexis said. "Everything went perfectly. Well, I did accidentally miscount the give-away pamphlets before I left. I was short three, but no one complained."

Mary Bernadette shook her head. "You must learn to check your supplies twice before beginning any tour."

"I did check twice. But . . ."

"Well, you'll know better next time."

Alexis felt chastened, as no doubt she was meant to be. Why did Mary Bernadette always have to find fault? Anyone could have miscounted a stack of pamphlets printed on slick paper, even the illustrious Mrs. Fitzgibbon. *And if Mary Bernadette had ever miscounted*, Alexis wondered, *would she have admitted her mistake?*

"That tour is ridiculous, anyway," Mary Bernadette was saying. "No one is rising from his grave until the Judgment Day. Of that, I am completely sure."

"Yes, but it brings in an awful lot of money. I mean, the tickets are thirty dollars each. We made, let me see . . ." Alexis did a quick mental calculation. "We made three hundred and sixty dollars today."

"Well, we all have to make sacrifices for the greater good. For the sake of the OWHA, I allow the tour to continue."

Alexis wondered if allowing the tour to continue really *was* Mary Bernadette's decision to make. True, she was the chairman, but wouldn't every member of the board have a right to vote on such a decision? "Anyway," she said, "the tour does no harm. I'm sure half the people who sign up for it don't really believe in ghosts."

"And the other half are desperately hoping to have their wits scared right out of their heads, if they had any wits to begin with. Bodies rising from the dead indeed."

"But what about Lazarus, in the New Testament?" Alexis asked. "He rose from the dead."

Mary Bernadette frowned. "That was a miracle, performed by Jesus for His own good reasons."

Strictly speaking, Alexis thought, couldn't you call Lazarus, and Jesus, for that matter, a zombie? And what about the Holy Spirit? He was a *spirit*, if not the sort that went around in torn sheets and rattling chains. But she held her tongue. She didn't want Mary Bernadette to accuse her of blaspheming. Still, to stir the pot was so tempting. . . .

"While I have you here," Mary Bernadette was saying now, "I want to talk to you about a project I think you'd be perfect for."

"What's that?" Alexis asked.

"It's called A Day in the Life. Most of the best historical societies have a version of it. You can research their attempts and make changes for the better. There's no reason the OWHA can't be number one in this enterprise."

"But what exactly is the enterprise?" Alexis asked.

"It's quite simple. You'll take a photograph every day at the same time and in the same place, say, at the corner of Main Street and Market Street, and post them on our website. The pictures will be a permanent record of life in Oliver's Well over time."

Alexis felt flattered. And for a moment she felt badly that she had been so harsh in her silent criticism of Mary Bernadette.

"I don't know what to say," she professed. "I'm not sure I'm qualified. I'm not a professional photographer."

"You'll do just fine," Mary Bernadette said firmly. "You'll be the official Contemporary Archivist of the OWHA."

"A picture every day? Even on holidays?"

"Even on holidays. Same time, same place."

Alexis thought about it. The project could be fun, and the title—Contemporary Archivist—was kind of cool. "Sure," she said. "When would I start?"

"How about first thing tomorrow? You can do some research tonight."

"Okay. Well, I guess I'd better get on home now so—"

Mary Bernadette sighed. "Just look at the condition of this room. Alexis, would you mind dusting the display cases before you go?"

Alexis did mind, but she found herself saying, "No, I don't mind at all."

Mary Bernadette bestowed one of her dazzling smiles. "The cleaning supplies are in the hall closet by the public restroom."

Mary Bernadette left, and Alexis went to the closet to retrieve a roll of paper towels and a bottle of glass cleaner. She wondered if other Contemporary Archivists were also unpaid housekeepers. And as she cleaned the tops of the display cases containing crumbling old letters and deeds, dented buttons, and tarnished flatware, Alexis hoped that the next time Mary Bernadette was in one of the supposedly haunted homes in Oliver's Well, she encountered something wrapped in a smelly shroud and covered in cobwebs and crawling with worms and spiders. The thought made her smile.

CHAPTER 17

Alexis and PJ were in the kitchen of the little cottage. It was almost six o'clock, and a pot of soup was simmering on the stove. Alexis was sorting through the mail, and PJ was texting a client.

"That smells great," PJ said, without looking up from his phone.

Alexis smiled. "Thanks. It's split pea with ham. Look," she said. "Another anniversary card. This one's from Craig and Anna."

"That was nice of them."

"Well, Craig *was* your best man," Alexis pointed out. "Anyway, I'm sure it was Anna who sent it. It's always the woman who sends the card."

PJ laughed. "That's a bit sexist, isn't it?"

Alexis shrugged and continued to go through the day's mail, which, per usual, Mary Bernadette had brought to the cottage. She smiled as she opened a card from her maid of honor, Diane DeLaurentis. "One year down," Diane had written. "A lifetime to go!" It had been Mary Bernadette's idea that PJ and Alexis marry on St. Patrick's Day, and though Alexis hadn't been keen on a March wedding (she had always envisioned an autumn wedding), she had agreed readily enough. The truth was, she had been so eager to marry PJ she would have married him in a garbage dump with a couple of howling cats for a band if his grandmother had wanted it.

PJ put down his phone and joined Alexis at the counter. "Ali," he said, taking her hand in his. "I need to talk to you about something."

Alexis stood Diane's card next to Craig and Anna's. "Sure. What's up?"

"I know we planned to go to Charleston for our anniversary, but I really think we should spend it in Oliver's Well."

Alexis was surprised. "But you were so excited by the idea of getting away. And we booked a room at that gorgeous old bed and breakfast."

"I *was* excited," PJ said. "I still am. I mean, excited to go someday. Look, Ali, we'll go to Charleston next year, I promise."

"But you promised we'd go *this* year. I don't understand. What's happened?"

PJ sighed. "Nothing happened. It's just that, well, Grandmother asked what we were planning, and when I told her we were going away for a few days she was disappointed. She'd been hoping we could all celebrate together."

"But it's *our* anniversary," Alexis said, "yours and mine, not hers. My parents always celebrate their anniversary alone, just the two of them."

"Grandmother is old, Ali. I know it will make her very happy to have us with her on our first anniversary. Who knows if she'll be around for next year's?"

Alexis laughed. "I think your grandmother is going to be around for the next twenty years!"

"Well, it's true she's never been sick a day in her life, but you never know. Please, Ali. This means a lot to her. It means a lot to me."

Alexis sighed. When PJ looked at her in that way, his bright blue eyes so wide and intent upon her, she could never say no. "Oh, of course it's okay," she said.

She had let him have is way. Rather, she had let Mary Bernadette have her way. And how, Alexis wondered, as her husband kissed her, had she allowed that to happen, again?

CHAPTER 18

"Ow." Megan had been trying to retrieve a dust ball from under the couch when her back began to protest. "All right," she muttered, slowly climbing to her feet. "The dust ball can stay."

There was no good reason for Megan to be chasing dust. The Fitzgibbons had a housekeeper, the daughter of one of the legal assistants in Pat's office. She came in once a week to give the house a thorough going-over, but Megan was not comfortable paying someone to clean up after her and had a tendency to do half of Sandra's job before the young woman arrived. Pat had argued that there was no reason for Megan to do any of the housework, what with her job, her role as family cook, and her chauffering the twins from pillar to post when Pat wasn't available. "Besides," he had pointed out, "we can afford the help. And Sandra appreciates the money. It's a win–win situation."

All reasonable arguments, but Megan knew—as did her husband—that she would continue to do most of the housekeeping. "You sound like my mother," Pat had said, "intent on being insanely self-sufficient. What are you trying to prove? And to whom?"

"Nothing," Megan had replied. "Nothing to no one. Just don't tell your mother, or mine for that matter, that we hire someone to clean our bathrooms."

Megan stowed the broom and dustpan in the kitchen closet and put the teakettle on to boil. Her dentist had advised her to cut down on the amount of tea she drank—it caused staining—but it was no use. She was addicted to the stuff, as was her formidable mother-in-law. Said mother-in-law had invited the Annapolis Fitzgibbons to Oliver's Well for St. Patrick's Day dinner. As much as Megan loved seeing her older son, especially on an important day like his wedding anniversary, the holiday fell midweek. And there was no suggesting to her mother-in-law that they postpone the celebration until the weekend. Megan had tried that once before. Mary Bernadette had reacted as if she had suggested they abandon Catholicism for the practices of the ancient Druids.

Well, the important thing, Megan thought now, was that PJ and Alexis had successfully negotiated the notoriously difficult first year of marriage. And that year had flown by. It was a cliché, but Megan doubted that anyone throughout the history of mankind had ever said, "Last year passed just at the right speed; it neither flew by nor did it drag." People were never going to be comfortable regarding the issue of time and never were they going to accept that it acted according to its own mysterious agenda. If, indeed, it had an agenda other than confusing and frustrating human beings, who might have created the crazy concept in the first place.

Anyway, it really did seem like only yesterday that PJ and Alexis had stood before the congregation and taken the vows of Holy Matrimony. It was a lovely wedding, and Megan would have considered it to be perfect if at any time during the weekend she and Pat had had the chance to speak privately to Olivia and Lester Trenouth. They had come to Oliver's Well the day before the wedding and put up at a B&B. They had chosen to host the rehearsal dinner at Le Petite Versailles, a chic and very expensive restaurant in Lawrenceville, a little over an hour's drive from Oliver's Well. Placecards indicated that Alexis was at one end of the table, her parents on either side of her. PJ was seated at the other end of the table, with his parents on either side of him. Mary Bernadette was seated next to Pat; Paddy next to Megan; David next to his grandmother; and Danica next to her grandfather. Megan had wondered if the seating plan had been designed to eliminate the necessity of the families getting to know each other. She had been disappointed. Mary Bernadette had been insulted.

And of course, no real conversation was possible on the day of a wedding but for the requisite comments at the reception (held in this case at the Wilson House, thanks to Mary Bernadette's exalted position on the board of the OWHA) on the bride's loveliness ("Isn't she the most beautiful bride you ever saw?"), the groom's manly demeanor ("He looks like a prince!"), and the quality of the food ("These are the best shrimp puffs I've ever had.").

Megan smiled as she remembered how Mary Bernadette had sailed around the reception like the *QE2* among a sea of lesser vessels, greeting guests and accepting congratulations as if she had orchestrated PJ and Alexis's relationship from the start. At the time Megan had felt a bit annoyed. In retrospect, she found her mother-in-law's behavior amusing. And she would never forget watching the bride and bridegroom as they danced to "The Twelfth of Never." They had made such a romantic pair, so beautiful and so madly in love it was almost disquieting to watch them, as if they were too perfect, too much the ideal to be anything but temporary and fragile.

Megan finished her tea, put the cup in the dishwasher, and headed upstairs to her office. It was time to abandon the reminiscing and get to the kind of work that paid the bills. Not the kind that made her back protest.

CHAPTER 19

Alexis had never paid much attention to the statue of St. Patrick that stood on a small table in a corner of Mary Bernadette's living room. In fact, she wasn't entirely sure she had even noticed it before now. It was a nice-enough statue, even though St. Patrick looked as if he had a bad headache. Then again, she had never seen an image of a saint smiling. She supposed saints didn't have much to smile about, what with all the self-sacrificing work they had to do, the miracles they had to perform, the sick they had to heal, and the gruesome, agonizing deaths they had to suffer.

"What are you doing over here in the corner?"

Alexis smiled at her husband. "Looking at St. Patrick. Why are there shamrocks on his robe? Decoration?"

The shamrock, PJ told her, was the tool with which St. Patrick taught the heathen the concept of the Holy Trinity. "Three leaves comprising one leaf. Three people or aspects comprising one God."

"Clever. And the staff?" Alexis asked.

"The staff was what he used to drive away the snakes plaguing the land," PJ explained. "Though some say it's actually a walking stick. It has something to do with his evangelical work, but I can't remember what."

Alexis turned away from the statue. "But is it all real?" she asked. "Did he really drive the snakes out of Ireland?"

PJ shrugged. "I don't think it matters if he did or he didn't. People like to believe that he did. The belief is what matters. The meanings behind the stories."

"But what was so bad about the snakes?"

"Maybe they were poisonous. And remember, snakes are a symbol for evil. Maybe there *were* no actual snakes. Maybe the snakes are meant to represent the old heathen beliefs."

"Right. The Garden of Eden and Satan in the form of the snake. Well, I guess it does make for a good story. Maybe not as good as *Snakes on a Plane . . .*"

PJ laughed. "Don't let Grandmother hear you! Good ol' St. Pat is one of her favorites."

Mary Bernadette announced that dinner was served. They gathered in the dining room and took their seats at the table, Mary Bernadette at one end and Paddy at the other; Jeannette to Paddy's right and Danny next to her; Alexis to Paddy's left and PJ next to her. Mary Bernadette had put out the good plates and the good silver and the good crystal. Underneath it all she had laid a beautiful cream lace cloth over a plain white cloth. Two tall, white candles framed a low centerpiece of mini green hydrangeas and pale orange roses. Mary Bernadette had explained that the candles were not to be lit for fear that wax might drip onto the fine cloths beneath.

Paddy said the grace and Mary Bernadette gave a toast to PJ and Alexis on their first anniversary as husband and wife. It was not as good as going to Charleston, but it was something. Besides, PJ's mother and father had sent a lovely card and a bouquet of white roses, and her own parents had sent a card with a generous check.

This evening Mary Bernadette had prepared a traditional meal of corned beef and cabbage. Alexis loathed corned beef and barely tolerated cabbage, but under Mary Bernadette's watchful eye she ate what she could. At least there was soda bread. Alexis was in love with Mary Bernadette's soda bread.

After the dinner plates had been cleared, and before dessert was brought in, Danny, who had a beautiful tenor voice, sang a few old Irish songs. Halfway through "Danny Boy," tears were pouring down Alexis's cheeks. She dabbed at her face with her napkin and pushed away untouched the small glass of Jameson that Paddy had poured.

"My wife's Irish is showing," PJ said to the others at the table. Alexis shot a look to PJ as she pointed to her full glass, only to be interrupted by Mary Bernadette.

"You know I don't care for stereotyping, PJ," Mary Bernadette scolded. "That the Irish are too fond of their liquor. That they're always ready to brawl. That they're maudlin fools."

"Oh, Grandmother, I was only joking." PJ got up and went to the head of the table, where he placated his grandmother with a hug and a kiss.

Mary Bernadette disengaged herself from her grandson and rose from her seat at the table. "Jeannette and I will get dessert now," she announced.

PJ sat next to Alexis again, and while Paddy and Danny talked quietly together, he said, somewhat sheepishly, "I'm sorry I said that, about your Irish showing. I didn't mean anything negative by it, really. And I'm sorry that I don't have an anniversary gift for you. The trip to Charleston was going to be my gift. But then Grandmother said she wanted us here and things are so busy at work, and I didn't get around to shopping."

Alexis tried to smile. She felt a headache coming on, either from the whiskey or the corned beef. What *was* corned beef, anyway? "It's okay," she said.

"We can go into Westminster this weekend if you want. There are lots of nice shops there, and you can pick out something special."

Alexis looked down at the two layers of tablecloths and thought of the care PJ had put into her birthday gift last November. He had given her a very high-quality edition of the collected works of Vermeer, one of her favorite painters. And then there had been the wonderful Christmas gift of the Adrienne Jonas photo. And then she thought about how his Valentine's gift had been chosen by Mary Bernadette. And now there was no anniversary gift at all, once again because his grandmother had intervened. And had Mary Bernadette even considered the deposit they had lost by canceling their reservation?

Alexis lifted her head and, perversely, she found herself telling her husband that it didn't matter that he had neglected to buy her a gift. "Besides," she said, "we should save our money so that we can buy a house of our own one day."

PJ smiled. "Or build onto the cottage. There's almost two acres out back, plenty of room to expand, especially when we start a family."

Alexis decided that this was not the moment to argue about moving out of the cottage. She thought of Maureen then, for no reason she could identify. "Too bad Maureen isn't here tonight," she said.

PJ looked surprised. "Why? I didn't think you really knew her."

"I don't. We met in town a few weeks back. She seems nice."

"She *is* nice. I guess. Honestly, I don't know much about her at all. Oh, except that she dated my father once."

"Really?" This surprised Alexis. "How do you know that?"

"Grandmother mentioned it, years ago. The relationship didn't last very long, though. My father broke it off."

"Huh. Does your mother know about it?" she asked.

"I assume so. There was nothing to hide. No secret love child, if that's what you're thinking."

"No, of course not. It's just interesting. Your mother seems so different from Maureen."

PJ laughed. "I think that's what attracted Dad to her. Besides, he told me he always thought of Maureen as more of a sister than a girlfriend, and you don't marry your sister."

"No, I guess not." Alexis lowered her voice to a whisper. "PJ, when can we go home?"

"Right after dessert."

"Promise?"

"Of course."

PJ joined the conversation between the other two men and

Alexis busied herself refolding her linen napkin. She had little faith that they *would* be going home right after dessert. Her husband had broken a promise or two before. But it was all right. She got up from the table to get an aspirin from her bag.

Chapter 20

Mary Bernadette had decided to present the coffee that evening in the silver service she had inherited from her father's sister, Catherine. Aunt Catherine had married well and, with no daughters of her own, had left her favorite niece a few good pieces of her accumulations, as well as her wedding band (now worn by Alexis). Mary Bernadette kept the coffeepot, creamer, and sugar bowl in sparkling shape, though she doubted that anyone else appreciated its beauty as she did.

For dessert, she had assembled a trifle in a large Waterford crystal bowl. The layers of ladyfingers, red gelatin, custard, and canned fruit cocktail, all soaked in sherry and topped with hand-whipped cream, made for a special dessert on a special occasion. It was only too bad that the entire family wasn't there to share it.

"Where is Maureen this evening?" Mary Bernadette asked. "I thought we might see her here. She knows that she's always welcome."

"At a party with some friends from her office," Jeannette said. "They get together every year. It's a nice group of people, Maureen says. And what about Pat and Megan?"

Mary Bernadette frowned. "At home. I don't understand why they didn't come down to Oliver's Well. It's not like they had other plans. Pat told me they're not even celebrating the holiday! Can you imagine?"

Jeannette shrugged. "Well, it is the middle of the week, and both Pat and Megan work and the twins have school tomorrow."

"That's not the point. How will David and Danica ever learn about their heritage if their parents don't keep up the traditions?"

"I'm sure the twins know about St. Patrick's Day. Doesn't everybody? It's not a holiday solely owned by the Irish, not anymore."

"If you mean, have the children seen those awful bits on TV with grown men in ridiculous leprechaun costumes eating cupcakes with green frosting and quaffing green beer, then, no, they *do not* know about St. Patrick's Day!"

"Well . . ."

"You might have talked some sense into Pat, Jeannette. You *are* his godmother."

"You mean I should have made him feel guilty that he wasn't coming to Oliver's Well?" Jeannette laughed. "Mary, the nonsense you talk!"

Mary Bernadette did not believe she had spoken nonsense, but she let the matter drop.

"Is everything all right with Alexis?" Jeannette asked now.

"Of course. Why would you ask?"

"Oh, it's just that she seems a bit—not her usual self today."

Mary Bernadette shook her head and busied herself with dessert plates and spoons. Really, Jeannette could be so melodramatic. If there was one thing Mary Bernadette was sure of, it was that her grandson and his wife were a happy young couple. Although she did have to wonder why Alexis wasn't pregnant yet. Maybe there was a medical problem. Maybe, God forbid, they were using birth control. Mary Bernadette was intelligent enough to know that there were situations in which birth control might have its very good uses—in spite of what her beloved Church had to say—but a young, married couple, employed and with the full support of their family, had, in Mary Bernadette's opinion, no business fiddling with it.

"The coffee's ready," Jeannette announced. "I'll carry it out."
Mary Bernadette picked up the bowl of trifle. "I'll be sure to
pour a nice, big cup for Alexis."

CHAPTER 21

Mary Bernadette opened the door of her bedroom closet and
removed a large black binder from the top shelf. It was the
third volume of her clippings file, something she had been keeping since giving her first interview on behalf of the Oliver's Well
Historical Association thirty years earlier. She had served on the
board for a few years at that point and was already considered a
valuable part of the organization. That was not pride speaking.
That was public fact. Since then, the Oliver's Well *Gazette* had described her career with the OWHA as "illustrious" and "inspiring."
Mary Bernadette perched on the edge of the neatly made bed
and opened the binder at random. Here was the article from a
Lawrenceville paper, chronicling the occasion on which she had
helped to facilitate the acquisition of the Spencer Homestead.
And here was an article that described how she had generously
acted as an unpaid advisor to the struggling historical society of a
small town in Massachusetts. For two months she had spent
countless hours on the phone with the members of the society,
sharing her experience and offering advice on everything from
preservation methods to garnering public support. Mary Bernadette
chose another page from the binder. Here was a piece from the
Gazette about the revival of the OWHA's educational programs for
children. It was by far the achievement of which she was the
most proud. Currently, the OWHA offered a variety of workshops

focused on the realities of childhood in the seventeenth, eighteenth, and nineteenth centuries. Participants learned in a hands-on way about the games children played, the lessons they were taught at school, the essential skills they learned at home, the songs they sang in church. Mary Bernadette also believed strongly in laying bare the harsher aspects of life long ago. Those who led the workshops, all volunteers from the community, were schooled in the sobering statistics of child mortality, the plaguelike diseases that could decimate a settlement almost overnight, the dangers of childbirth in a culture without advanced medical knowledge, and of course the terrible realities of war.

Grammar, middle, and high school classes from as far away as Lawrenceville and the even larger town of Nicholsborough came to Oliver's Well for these workshops, which included visits to the town's more important historical properties. In addition, for the past twelve summers, the OWHA had held a three-day camp during which children between the ages of twelve and fifteen had the opportunity to spend two nights in one of the homes on the historical register and live much as their ancestors had—eating the sort of meals they would have eaten, reading by candlelight, learning how to execute stitch work, tending to the family's farm or gardens. All in all, the educational program was enormously popular as well as being fairly, if not hugely, lucrative.

Mary Bernadette turned another page and ran a finger over a photographic image of the Wilson House, taken in the early twentieth century. She remembered as if it were yesterday the first time she had walked through the doors of the OWHA's headquarters with the intention of putting herself forward as a candidate for membership on the board. Pat was fifteen at the time, busy with after-school sports and his studies. Grace was only seven, but she had always been terribly independent and was perfectly capable of walking to a friend's house after classes to do her homework and wait for a parent to fetch her. Paddy, of course, had given his wife his full support.

Her motives for joining had been twofold. She had seen membership in the OWHA as a way to further the family's standing in Oliver's Well, and she had a genuine interest in the preservation of the town that had been her home since shortly after coming to the United States. She had been interviewed by the current chairman and then elected to the board unanimously.

Mary Bernadette flipped forward to a recent article and noted that she would soon need a fourth binder to allow the continued documentation of her career. Of course, the OWHA kept an official file at the Wilson House (currently, Anne was in charge of keeping it up to date), but Mary Bernadette's file was private. She made it a point never to take it out unless she was alone in the house. She didn't want her family to think that she was being vain, poring over articles in which her name appeared and her words were quoted. And then there were the photographs. She had always felt comfortable in front of a camera and was justifiably proud of several of the portraits that had appeared in newspapers and magazines over the years. Reviewing the file gave her a sense of accomplishment, and reminded her of why she bothered to work so devotedly for a cause that some unenlightened people might deem unimportant. And there was an added benefit to the documentation of her career. When she was dead and gone, the next generations of Fitzgibbons would have this treasury as something by which to remember her.

The phone rang and Mary Bernadette put the binder back on the shelf in the closet before answering the extension in the hall.

"Hi, Mom."

Mary Bernadette sat at the little table on which the phone and a notepad and pencil rested. "Grace," she said, "how good to hear from you."

She was immensely proud of having a daughter with a calling, especially in this day and age when it was regrettably rare. Still, it would have been nice if Grace could be stationed closer to home. It would have been nice if Grace had *wanted* to be stationed closer to home, but Grace seemed very happy to be working far away from the scene of her childhood. There were, she had said, so many people elsewhere that needed the help she could offer, whereas in prosperous Oliver's Well, the most good she might affect was to point out to a stupid teen that texting while driving was not a good idea.

"I'm sorry it's been so long."

"You're a busy woman. Still, it would be nice to hear from you more often."

Grace laughed. "Then you'll agree to getting an e-mail account?"

"I didn't say that."

"You know, Megan and I communicate all the time via e-mail or text when we can't carve out the time for the phone."

"Well, be that as it may . . ."

"And how are the Klines?" Grace asked. "How's Maureen?"

Mercifully her daughter had dropped the topic of twitting and tweets and God knew what else. "Maureen is fine," Mary Bernadette replied. "As far as I know. Certainly Jeannette hasn't said anything to the contrary."

It was no great secret that Mary Bernadette had always thought of Maureen Kline as a model of daughterly devotion. When her own daughter had chosen a life as a Bride of Christ, Mary Bernadette had hoped that Megan would prove to be her Maureen. But that hope had been dashed long ago, and now her expectations were directed toward her grandson's wife.

"That's good. And how's Dad?" Grace asked.

"Your father is fine."

"Good," Grace said. "Tell him I said hello."

"I don't suppose there's any way you might make it home for Easter?"

"Unlikely, Mom. Duty above all—you taught me that."

"Of course. Idleness is the fool's desire."

Grace laughed. "Well, I have to admit there are moments when I'd welcome a little idleness, but that's another conversation. So, how's everything with the OWHA?"

"Excellent. Alexis is finally showing some real interest. She led one of our most popular tours recently, and she's involved in an important photography project."

"That's nice to hear. Any pitter-patter of tiny feet in the offing?"

Mary Bernadette, who had been wondering about the same thing, pretended indifference. "I certainly have no idea when PJ and his wife are planning to start their family," she said. "And I certainly have no plan to ask them."

"Well, they're young. They have plenty of time. I hope they have some real fun before becoming parents. Live it up a bit. Maybe travel to some place exotic. Alexis has been abroad, hasn't she?"

"Yes. I believe so. But there's the business to run. PJ's now in charge, remember."

"I know. But it would do PJ good to expand his horizons. Especially before he's got the expense and responsibility of kids."

"He's quite happy right here at home," she said firmly. "Not that I would stand in his way if he wanted to travel a bit. But he doesn't."

"People say you can't miss what you've never known. And I suppose that's true for some. But for me?" Grace laughed. "I ached to see the big, wide world I knew absolutely nothing about. I wanted to experience what I didn't even know existed."

Mary Bernadette found that she was smiling. "I don't know who in the family you take after. Maybe some wayward seafarer, far back in the mists of time."

"Yes, well, right now I had better sail on over to the school. I'm supposed to be supervising the third grade's bake sale. You don't want to leave a bunch of eight- and nine-year-olds alone with trays of cupcakes and brownies."

"No," Mary Bernadette said, imagining the mess. "You most certainly do not."

CHAPTER 22

M ary Bernadette pulled into the space reserved for her outside the headquarters of Fitzgibbon Landscaping. Although
she no longer managed the company on a daily basis, she made it
a habit to visit the office regularly to review the accounts, to inspect the bathroom for cleanliness, to check the inventory of office staples, and to cast an eye over the condition of the reception
area (the candy bowl should always be filled and a box of tissues
always on hand). It wasn't that she didn't *trust* her grandson's
wife to keep things shipshape. It was that Mary Bernadette had
always believed that to get a job done properly one had to do it
oneself. And Alexis was young. Youth needed to be managed and
advised if it was to blossom into full maturity. Rules and regula-
tions and punishments for not following them were necessary for
true growth.

Today, Mary Bernadette had a particular mission in mind.
"Good morning, Alexis," she said, removing her trench and hanging it on the rack to the right of the door.

Alexis looked up briefly from her computer screen. "Good
morning," she said, her fingers tapping away on the keyboard at
great speed.

Mary Bernadette cast a critical eye over her grandson's wife.
While there was no denying that Alexis always made a clean and
neat appearance, there was something lacking when it came to
her ability to dress like a representative of an established and
reputable company. Take what she was wearing today—a blind-
ingly bright orange sweater and a pair of earrings that dangled to
her shoulders. Well, Mary Bernadette thought, she wouldn't be
surprised to learn that Mrs. Trenouth hadn't spent any time at all
teaching her daughter about seemly attire. The woman had come
to the wedding baring more cleavage than Oliver's Well had seen
on display in its three hundred or so years.

"Alexis," she said. "I'd like to talk to you for a moment."

"One sec, let me just . . . Done."

Alexis looked up again from the computer screen and smiled. "What is it, Mary Bernadette?"

"I was thinking," she said, "that you might want to dress a little more—appropriately—for the office."

Alexis's eyes widened. "But no one sees me," she said. "I mean, clients rarely come to the office. Most times PJ meets them at their homes."

"Still, you might want to wear more neutrals and less loud color." Mary Bernadette smiled. "In fact, I'll tell my friend Anne you'll be coming into her shop to try on a few things. The Sophisticated Lady is where I get all of my clothes."

"Oh." Alexis looked down at her orange sweater. "But I'm not sure—"

"Anne can always order your size if she doesn't have it in stock. She's very obliging that way, which is part of what makes her such a success in business. It's all about the customers, you see. When one of our clients comes into the office, he wants to be reassured his hard-earned money is being well spent. And a soberly dressed office staff adds to the atmosphere of responsibility and respectability. It reassures the client that Fitzgibbon Landscaping is not going to let him down. I'm sure you can see that."

Alexis nodded. "Yes. Sorry. I didn't mean to offend anyone."

Mary Bernadette turned her high-wattage smile on her grandson's wife. "Of course you didn't. Now, is there anything you need me for before I head off?"

Alexis smiled back, a bit anemically Mary Bernadette thought, and shook her head.

"Then I'll be off." And, retrieving her trench coat, she was.

CHAPTER 23

A lexis looked at the big clock over the stove. Where *was* he? She had been waiting impatiently for PJ to get home so that she could talk to him about what had happened earlier with his grandmother.

The fact was that Mary Bernadette had made her feel like a troublemaker. Alexis had *never* been a troublemaker—at least, no one had ever scolded her for being one—and it sat badly that now, as a married woman, she should be told that she was behaving—or, dressing—in a way that might upset people. And the worst part about the whole thing was the small, niggling doubt that Mary Bernadette was *right* in always correcting her and that she had been fooling herself, or that others had been fooling her, into thinking she was a sensible and sensitive person.

PJ had barely come through the door and tossed his jacket on the couch when Alexis blurted, "Your grandmother doesn't think I dress appropriately for the office."

"Hi to you, too."

"Sorry. Hi."

PJ came over and kissed his wife on the cheek. "Okay, so how do you know she doesn't think you dress appropriately? Did she say something?"

"Yes. Today. I mean, it's not like I'm showing up to work wearing a tank top and shorts! I'm always dressed nicely. Okay, sometimes I wear jeans, but it's not like they're ripped. And *everybody* wears jeans these days!"

"Well, you know how conservatively Grandmother dresses," PJ pointed out. "It's just her way. She's always been proper. Have you ever seen pictures of her from the sixties and seventies? It's as if the whole movement toward casual never happened in her world."

"But why does that have to be my way, too?"

PJ smiled. "I'm not saying you have to wear matching outfits. But I don't know, maybe you could make an effort to dress a bit more—what's the word? Formally? Just at the office. Just for Grandmother's sake."

"Well, sure, I guess. But it's . . ." Alexis hesitated.

"But it's what?" PJ asked.

"It's that your grandmother is always butting into our lives. We have virtually no privacy. She even coopted our anniversary!"

PJ frowned. "We talked about that. You said you understood."

"I did but . . . PJ, she tells me how to *file*. Everyone knows how to file! A goes before B goes before C!"

PJ laughed. "Okay, that's going a bit far, but I'm sure she's just trying to be helpful."

"And why does she insist on keeping paper files, anyway? Every time I suggest making everything electronic, she freaks out, like I'm suggesting setting fire to the place."

"She's wary of change. She always has been. It's one of the things that makes her such a force for the OWHA."

Alexis frowned. "You know, I could make us a lot more money working for someone else."

"But why would you want to work for a stranger?" PJ asked. "Besides, we make enough money. Well, we will, someday. There's plenty of time. And we have it really good here, don't we? The cottage is great."

Alexis half laughed. "Yeah. But she sneaks in when we're not home."

"What?"

Alexis bit her lip. She hadn't planned on telling PJ this, but the words had been spoken and she couldn't take them back.

"Your grandmother," she said. "She sneaks in. She rearranges things. Once she put the Adrienne Jonas portrait you gave me in the bottom drawer of the desk."

PJ burst out laughing. "That's hilarious!"

"It's not funny, PJ. And I know it's her. Who else would it be?"

"Well, the cottage *is* hers. She and my grandfather own it."

"But that doesn't give her the right to sneak in behind our backs!"

"She has a key, Ali. She's hardly sneaking in. Besides, maybe she just wants to make sure the place is okay."

"What do you mean by okay? Clean? Is she worried we're going to write on the walls or damage the woodwork?"

PJ sighed. "I'm sure she means well. She's just used to being in charge, that's all. It'll take some time before she realizes that she can trust us with the business. Once she's sure we're not going to bankrupt the family, she'll back off."

Why don't I believe that, Alexis thought. "Can't you ask her not to come in when we're not at home?"

PJ took her in his arms—she protested only a bit—and kissed her on the lips. "Oh, come on, Ali," he said. "Just think of her as, I don't know, as a good old-fashioned character out of a novel. She might be a little unusual, but she means absolutely no harm, believe me."

"Are you positive she doesn't read our mail? Envelopes can be steamed open and then resealed."

PJ sighed. "Ali."

Why, Alexis wondered, wouldn't her husband stand up for her? But then he kissed her again and she responded with more enthusiasm this time, and suddenly the craziness with Mary Bernadette really didn't seem all that important. At least, not as important as she had been making it out to be. At least, not at that moment.

PJ let her go. "I'm going to go see Grandpa for a bit," he said. "I need to buy a new mower and I want his opinion on the model."

"Don't be long," Alexis said. "I'm making one of your favorite dishes for dinner. Pasta with carbonara sauce."

PJ left the cottage and Alexis set to work preparing dinner. And while she worked she thought back to the early days of their relationship. PJ had told her all about his grandparents and their landscaping business, about his lawyer parents and his younger brother and sister, about his aunt who was a nun. He had told her that he loved them all and that especially after the birth of the twins his grandparents had become almost like parents to him. But Alexis had never really understood until now just *how* much they all meant to him. What she *had* understood was that PJ was a good-hearted and honest young man who loved his family. And there was nothing to complain about in that. His devotion had appealed to her. It had struck her as old-fashioned in a good, Hallmark Channel sort of way.

And now that she was a Fitzgibbon . . . well, she still did admire PJ's dedication to his family. Of course she did. It was just that it would be nice if he put her first, before the others. Wasn't that what a husband or a wife was supposed to do?

The bacon was cooked and sliced. An egg, still in its shell, sat in a bowl by the stove. The lettuce was washed and the vegetables were cut for a salad. The parmesan was grated. Alexis looked up at the big, round clock above the stove. It was now almost seven o'clock. PJ had been at his grandparents' house for a little over half an hour. She turned off the gas under the pan of boiling water.

A wave of annoyance swept through Alexis. She reached for her cell phone to call PJ, and then put it down. *Well,* she told herself firmly, *it could be worse. At least he's not out picking up women at bars.* And she poured a glass of wine. And she waited.

CHAPTER 24

Paddy and Mary Bernadette were having breakfast—including a pot of proper tea properly made—when the phone rang.

"I'll get it," Mary Bernadette told her husband. "Finish your eggs before they get cold."

A few moments later she hung the phone back on its base and returned to the table. "That was Richard Armstrong," she said. "He's just had some very interesting news."

Paddy put aside the morning paper. "Oh? And what is it?"

"It seems that we're to have a new member of the community," Mary Bernadette went on, her tone at odds with the excitement she felt. "Wynston Meadows has decided to take up residence in Oliver's Well. I'm sure you've heard of him. He made millions of dollars working for some sort of investment company. A hedge fund I think."

Paddy nodded. "I've seen the name in the papers."

"And word has it that he's heard of the OWHA's fine work and is interested in knowing more about us."

"Well," Paddy said, "I hope he won't be throwing wild parties and disturbing his neighbors."

"I don't think a man of importance like Wynston Meadows wastes his time on parties. He's probably at his desk until all hours, tending to business."

Paddy frowned. "Work hard and play hard, that's what those flashy types go for."

Mary Bernadette ignored her husband's last remark. "Given that he's already expressed an interest in the Oliver's Well Historical Association," she said, "he'll definitely want to make a contribution." *Maybe*, she thought, *a contribution big enough to allow us to finally achieve our greatest goal to date, the purchase of the Branley Estate.*

"We can't know that for sure," Paddy pointed out. "Don't leap to conclusions, Mary."

"Well, of course we can't know anything for sure. But it seems to me it would be in his best interest as a new and potentially important resident of Oliver's Well to show his support for our history and traditions."

Paddy murmured a reply and stuck his head back into the newspaper. Really, Mary Bernadette thought. He could be such a naysayer. Why did he bother to carry a four-leafed clover in his wallet if he didn't believe in the possibility of luck and good fortune?

The back door opened then, and PJ came into the kitchen. "Morning, everyone."

"Did you have your breakfast yet?" Mary Bernadette asked.

"No. Alexis left early for the office and there was only cold cereal in the house. I thought maybe you were whipping up some eggs."

Mary Bernadette got up from the table and went to the fridge. "Have you heard the news?" she asked. "Wynston Meadows has moved to town. Or is about to arrive, it's unclear as of yet."

"*The* Wynston Meadows?" PJ asked, taking the seat his grandmother had vacated. "The guy who's always in the paper? The one who owns, like, half of the East Coast? And he's only in his forties!"

Paddy rattled the paper and cleared his throat.

"One and the same," Mary Bernadette affirmed. "Richard Armstrong just called. There was a man at The Angry Squire last night. He'd just come down from D.C. and he told the bartender, that nice young man Jeff Brown, that the news all over D.C. is that Wynston Meadows has decided to make Oliver's Well his home. What's more, he's expressed a great interest in the OWHA."

Paddy coughed.

PJ accepted the plate of warm scrambled eggs his grandmother handed him. "This could be really good for Fitzgibbon Landscaping," he said. "He's bound to have bought some huge property. Maybe he'll want a water feature, or a walled herb garden. Boy, I'd love to design a good old-fashioned folly!"

Paddy looked out from behind his paper. "Now, don't go putting the cart before the horse."

His wife came back to the table with a plate of bacon and one of toast. "It's the bread you like, PJ. Not that cardboard stuff I found in your cupboard the other day."

"Alexis likes that. It's got a lot of fiber."

"Yes, well, what about taste?" Mary Bernadette turned to her husband. "Anyway, Paddy, PJ is not putting the cart before the horse. He's just thinking ahead, like a good businessman. He's spotted an opportunity and he won't let it pass."

Paddy retreated behind the Oliver's Well *Gazette* once more. Mary Bernadette watched with satisfaction as her grandson ate his breakfast.

CHAPTER 25

The phone continued to ring all that day at the Fitzgibbon house. First to call was Katie Keefe.

"Have you heard about the newest resident of Oliver's Well?" she asked without even a greeting.

Mary Bernadette felt a tiny stab of annoyance. She had been hoping to be the one to spread the news of Wynston Meadow's arrival. "Of course," she replied. "Richard Armstrong told me first thing this morning. How did you find out?"

"I was at the post office earlier, and it was all anyone was talking about."

Yes, Mary Bernadette thought. *The post office.* Richard made it a habit to stop in every morning at nine on the dot to collect mail for The Angry Squire. He would have told Kris Nelson, who was Oliver's Well's postmistress, and she would have told everyone who followed Richard.

"I suppose it is interesting news," Mary Bernadette said now.

"I read that his first wife was his high school sweetheart but that he left her for someone he met while he was at a conference in Berlin, once he'd made all his money. A German, I think. Or was she French? Anyway, she's gone now, too. I suppose he's in the market for wife number three, though I don't know how he'll find her in Oliver's Well!"

Maureen Kline was certainly out of the running, Mary Bernadette thought. She was too old and too plain for a man like Wynston Meadows, though once, back when she had been going out with Pat, she had been attractive enough. And what a travesty it would be if Norma Campbell set her sights on him, though she wouldn't put it past the woman. "His personal life," she said, "doesn't concern me. It's what he can do for Oliver's Well that's important."

"Of course. Do you think he'll want to join the OWHA?"

"As a matter of fact," Mary Bernadette replied, "I have it on good authority that he's already shown great interest in us. And if he's as smart as he's made out to be, I think we can expect him to approach us before long."

"Maybe . . . well, I shouldn't suggest it, but maybe *you* could approach *him*, Mary Bernadette. After all, you *are* the chairman of the OWHA."

Mary Bernadette smiled to herself. She would never admit to Katie that she had been thinking the exact same thing. It would seem self-important, as if she had too great an idea of herself. Modesty at all costs, her mother had often counseled.

"Well, Katie, that might be true," she replied, "but I think it best we wait for Mr. Meadows to settle in before any plans are laid."

"Oh, yes," Katie said. "Of course. You know best, Mary Bernadette. You always do."

A half hour later, it was Jeannette's turn to phone. She, too, had heard of Wynston Meadow's arrival—or imminent arrival; no one seemed to know for sure where he was at this exact moment, hovering over Oliver's Well in a private helicopter or having lunch at The Angry Squire.

"I read somewhere," Jeannette told her friend, "that he plans to run for political office. *What* office I don't exactly remember. But I'm sure it will be something important. A man like that wouldn't be content being just mayor of a tiny town!"

"As long as he focuses enough of his attention on Oliver's Well," Mary Bernadette replied, "he can run for president of the

United States for all it matters to me." *Imagine,* she thought, *being on a first-name basis with a future president of the greatest country on the face of the earth.*

"What do you think he'll be like?" Jeannette asked. "I've never met someone as rich and influential as Wynston Meadows."

Although her interest in the man was intensifying by the moment, Mary Bernadette still thought it best to feign nonchalance. "I have absolutely no idea," she said lightly.

"Can you imagine having all that money?"

"Character is more important than wealth, Jeannette."

"Oh, I know. Still, it's all very exciting."

Other members of the Oliver's Well Historical Association called after Jeannette. Wallace also wondered if they (not necessarily Mary Bernadette) should approach Mr. Meadows or wait until he approached them with an interest in becoming a benefactor. Leonard, former keeper of the peace that he was, wondered if Meadows's residence in Oliver's Well would mean more work for the tiny police department. "A man like that has enemies," he said. "And a lot of valuable items to steal." Mary Bernadette pointed out that a man like Mr. Meadows was sure to install a state-of-the-art alarm system and hire private guards. Leonard still wasn't convinced. Anne hoped that Wynston Meadows might prove a bright, new light in the community. Neal had done a Google search for him that morning and had learned he was the money behind the restoration of a WWII memorial column in Amherstville, Georgia, giving further credence to the rumor of his interest in the OWHA. Joyce had babbled on for a full six minutes about the possibility of the town's organizing a good old-fashioned welcoming committee to call on Wynston Meadows once he was settled. "A big basket of homemade jams and muffins," she said. "And a tea towel embroidered with 'Oliver's Well.'" Mary Bernadette thought it a ridiculous idea but held her tongue. The only member of the board who hadn't called was Norma. Well, Norma rarely had anything to contribute to a discussion. Why should things be any different now?

Mary Bernadette took no small satisfaction in the fact that *she* had been the one the other members of the OWHA had called to discuss the advent of Wynston Meadows, as if, chairman or not, she possessed some knowledge of their new neighbor or some sure sense of the role he was to play in the life of Oliver's Well.

Well, there was one thing about which Mary Bernadette Fitzgibbon *did* have a strong sense. In the months to come her career with the Oliver's Well Historical Association just might become even more illustrious and illuminating than it already had proved to be.

CHAPTER 26

"What the hell does Wynston Meadows want with little Oliver's Well?"

Pat and Megan Fitzgibbon were having a drink before dinner. Pat, fairly well connected in D.C. power circles, had heard from a colleague earlier that day that Wynston Meadows was about to descend upon the Fitzgibbons' hometown and that he had been going on about the "impressive little historical society" they had. This information did not sit well with Pat.

Megan shrugged. "Maybe he just wants some peace and quiet, a place where he can retreat when things get too crazy."

"Meg, a guy like Wynston Meadows doesn't know what the word *retreat* means, let alone *peace* or *quiet*. He thrives in the thick of the fray. Trust me, he's got some ulterior motive in moving to Oliver's Well. I just wish I knew what it was."

"Are you sure you're not being overly suspicious?"

"Very sure. That guy thinks the sun rises and sets on his whim.

I just hope Mom and her cronies aren't in for trouble if he decides to meddle with the OWHA. Maybe I should warn her, give her a heads-up or something."

"Is he really all that bad? I can't seem to recall reading much about him. What trouble could he possibly make for a small-town historical society?"

"He's that bad, Megan. And frankly, the thought of my mother charging into his line of sight makes me shudder. Those two would not be a good combination, trust me."

"Even so, the last thing you should do is try to warn her to watch out for him," Megan argued. "She'll be insulted. She'll think you're criticizing her abilities."

"Especially if the advice is coming from me."

"I didn't say that."

Pat smiled grimly. "You didn't need to. But you're right. She'll think I'm questioning her ability to make her own judgment of the man."

"Well, she is often right, Pat. You have to give her that."

"Yeah. My mother is not a stupid woman. Still, maybe *you* could mention something about this guy the next time you talk to her. She's never had any experience with someone so powerful. It's like a baby in diapers facing a rabid raccoon."

Megan laughed. "She won't take any more kindly to advice coming from me!"

"Maybe. Still . . ."

Megan kissed her husband on the cheek. "I'll see what I can do," she promised. "And if we're lucky, maybe the infamous Wynston Meadows really is moving to Oliver's Well for its beauty and charm, not to stage some evil coup d'état at the OWHA."

"From your mouth to God's ears."

"Pat. You're quoting your mother again."

"Darn. That woman is everywhere."

CHAPTER 27

Megan had been placing calls to and taking calls from her mother-in-law for decades and still she felt wary each time she picked up the phone. You never knew what to expect with Mary Bernadette Fitzgibbon. You never knew what bit of your life she would feel it necessary to critique or comment on.

The phone rang five times before Mary Bernadette picked up. Aside from the phone in the kitchen, there was only one extension in the house, and that was on the second-floor landing. Pat had talked to his mother about getting an additional extension somewhere between the two existing ones, but time and again his suggestion had been met with resistance ranging from polite refusal to angry dismissal.

"I hope nothing is wrong with the children," Mary Bernadette said as soon as Megan had identified herself.

"Everyone is in perfect health. I'm just calling to say hello, see how you and Paddy are doing."

"We're just fine, dear. Why wouldn't we be?"

Megan glanced at the Prayer of St. Francis posted above her desk. "No reason," she said. "And how is PJ? I haven't heard from him in over a week."

"Oh, he's got so much responsibility now and he's such a hard worker, I'm sure he just hasn't been able to find the time to call."

"Yes," Megan said. "That must be it. So, I heard a rumor that the big financial dealer Wynston Meadows is taking up residence in Oliver's Well."

"It's true," Mary Bernadette said. "I have it on good authority."

The Oliver's Well rumor mill. "Pat says that Wynston Meadows can be quite the shark in his business dealings."

"That's probably what makes him so successful."

"Yes. Still, Pat's a bit concerned that if Meadows decides to get involved with the OWHA he could be, well, disruptive."

Mary Bernadette laughed her distinctive, bell-like laugh. "First of all, Megan, the man has already expressed great interest in joining the OWHA, so yes, he will be involved. And second, I assure you I'm quite capable of handling myself in most any situation. I've dealt with a fair share of important people in my career as chairman and official spokesperson."

"Oh, I know that, of course," Megan said, "but some of the others on the board might be, well, overwhelmed."

"I've got the others well in hand," her mother-in-law replied tersely. "Megan, I'm sure it was Pat who put you up to this call of concern, but it's quite unnecessary, I promise you."

Megan knew when she had hit a wall with the inestimable Mary Bernadette Fitzgibbon. "Well," she said, "I'm glad to hear it. I'm sure Wynston Meadows will be wonderful to work with, assuming he *is* interested in the OWHA."

"As I said, I have it on good authority that he is *very* interested. Well, it's been nice chatting with you, Megan, but I'm due at the hairdresser in half an hour. And you know how I hate to be late."

"Lord," Megan murmured to her office when the call was over, "make me an instrument of your peace." She hoped that she hadn't done more harm than good by calling her mother-in-law. Mary Bernadette had pretty quickly adopted that imperious tone she reserved for when she suspected she was being second-guessed or insulted. The proud could be so sensitive to slights and so perverse, flying into the face of the very trouble they had been warned against, just to show that they could.

Megan next opened her e-mail to find an obviously bogus alert from her bank, a reminder from the library that a book was due back in three days, and a forwarded joke from Maureen Kline. Megan read the joke and shrugged; clearly she and Maureen didn't share a sense of humor. She wondered if Mary Bernadette would find the joke amusing. It was no secret that she had hoped Pat would marry the Klines' youngest daughter. But Pat had had other ideas. "I'm ashamed to admit this," he had told Megan years later, "but I think I asked Maureen out in the first place just to make my mother happy. And that's always a mistake."

"Trying to make someone else happy?" Megan had asked disingenuously.

"No," her husband had replied. "Trying to make Mary Bernadette Fitzgibbon happy."

CHAPTER 28

Mary Bernadette was sitting behind the desk in her small office at the Wilson House. She was dressed impeccably. Her hair was perfectly coiffed. Her back was straight.

The day before, Wynston Meadows had called and asked to meet with her. He was interested in learning more about the Oliver's Well Historical Association. Mary Bernadette had suggested he come to her office at ten that morning. It was five minutes to the hour. She had been at her desk since nine. She felt more excited than she ever had in her long career with the OWHA. She was sure that she and her beloved Oliver's Well were on the brink of greatness.

At exactly ten o'clock there was a knock on her door.

"Come in," she said.

A smiling Anne Tribble opened the door and showed in their visitor. Wynston Meadows stepped firmly into the office, hand outstretched. He walked directly to Mary Bernadette's desk. "Please, Mrs. Fitzgibbon," he said, "don't rise."

Mary Bernadette sat back and accepted his hand. "Mr. Meadows. Please, have a seat."

Mary Bernadette made a rapid assessment of the man's appearance. He was a little over six foot, with broad shoulders and slim hips—executives all went to the gym these days she had read. His hair was short but not too short, and still naturally brown; Mary Bernadette could always tell if a man dyed his hair. He was clean-shaven. He wore a gold watch that might have been a Rolex—she wasn't an expert on watches—and no other jewelry. Though it was still months until summer he sported a tan, leading Mary Bernadette to guess he had recently spent time vacationing at some exclusive resort, perhaps a place like Saint-Tropez. His navy suit fit him perfectly.

"Thank you so much for seeing me at such short notice," he said, opening one button of his jacket and sitting in the nineteenth-century guest chair facing the desk. "I must confess that I'm eager to establish myself in Oliver's Well." He smiled disarmingly. "I might never exactly blend into the woodwork, but I'd like to be regarded as a true member of the community."

"An admirable goal. Now, how exactly can I help you?" Mary Bernadette folded her hands on the desk and gave Wynston Meadows her dazzling smile.

"Tell me about the OWHA, its history, some of the highlights of its career. Tell me about its goals."

And so Mary Bernadette told him that the OWHA had been founded shortly after the end of the Second World War. Its first purchase was the Wilson House, which, after some initial restoration, became the association's headquarters as well as its central museum. More purchases of properties large and small followed. Awards had been won. Newspaper articles had been written. Programs had been instituted. And in 1979, Mary Bernadette had joined the board. When the chairman at the time, a very elderly man named Thomas Beckinridge, felt that he could no longer handle the duties of official spokesperson, he asked Mary Bernadette to take his place. She did, and to great acclaim. Eventually, she was chosen as chairman. "I've held the post for the past eleven years," she told Wynston Meadows. "We here at the OWHA go on much as we always have. There has been no need for any great change."

"All very impressive," Wynston Meadows said. "Do I dare hope there is a chance I might become a member of the OWHA's board?"

Mary Bernadette smiled. "I think there is a very good chance indeed, Mr. Meadows. In fact, I can't wait to present you to the board at our next meeting. Our secretary, Mr. Hyatt, will be in touch with the time and date."

Mary Bernadette came around her desk and accompanied Wynston Meadows to the front door, where they shook hands again. She watched as he got into his car—a new-model Mercedes—and drove off. Then she turned and walked purposefully back to her office. She would phone Neal immediately and tell him to send an e-mail calling a special meeting of the board a few days from now. On the list of new business he was to put the official introduction of Wynston Meadows. After all, Mr. Meadows had expressed his desire to become embedded in the life of Oliver's Well sooner rather than later. In an important matter such as this, delay would be wasteful.

CHAPTER 29

"This is so exciting," Jeannette whispered. She was wearing her best dress and had taken extra care with her hair. "He's just a person like every one of us," Mary Bernadette whispered back. She was wearing a small diamond stickpin in the lapel of her jacket. "He was perfectly charming at our meeting."

The two women had been the first to arrive at the Wilson House. Finally, every member of the board was in attendance, even Anne, who had had to close her shop in order to attend the quickly organized meeting, and Joyce, who must have called in sick. *Her students must be relieved*, Mary Bernadette thought, and she wasn't sorry for the sentiment.

"Ah," Mary Bernadette said, "here he is."

Wynston Meadows came into the room with a smile and a nod

of greeting. Mary Bernadette introduced him to each member of the board in turn. He had a kind or flattering word for each. When everyone had taken seats around the oval table, Mary Bernadette began the meeting.

"As you all know by now," she intoned, "Mr. Wynston Meadows, Oliver's Well's latest resident, has expressed an interest in becoming a member of the board of the Oliver's Well Historical Association. In your own words, Mr. Meadows, will you share the reasons behind your interest in becoming one of us?"

Wynston Meadows nodded. "I would be delighted," he said. "Most of you probably don't know that for many years my grandfather managed the county historical society museum in Smithstown. In fact, he lived on the second floor of the museum. When I was a boy I spent many an hour alone there when it was closed to the public, and I developed a love for the history of the region. Grandpa was a history buff, of course, and he'd often take me to visit old houses and historical sites—battlefields and whatnot. I've always looked back on those days as heaven. Now that I have the resources, and now that I'm a local, I feel a duty to help the Oliver's Well Historical Association with its important work."

Wallace began to clap, and the others joined in. "Commendable," Neal said. "What a wonderful story," Anne commented. Mary Bernadette nodded. Her expectations had been fulfilled. Here was a man who honored the important work of his grandfather, much as PJ was honoring the work of his own grandfather.

"Now, lest you think I'm getting in over my head"—and here, Wynston Meadows paused for the expected chuckles—"I'm a donor to several other historically minded missions, and I hold a spot on the D.C. Landmarks Commission. I think I can be of some service to you here in charming Oliver's Well."

Mary Bernadette looked to Leonard. He nodded. She looked to Neal and to Richard. They, too, were in agreement. A formal vote would not be necessary.

Mary Bernadette cleared her throat. "I speak for every member of the board then when I say welcome, Mr. Meadows, to the

Oliver's Well Historical Association. We look forward to many a year of benefiting from your knowledge and experience."

Wynston Meadows bowed his head in acknowledgment, and there was more applause. When it had died down, he rose from his seat. "I'm very pleased that you have accepted my plea. But now, I'm afraid I have to be off. Relocating is hell, as I'm sure everyone here knows. The moving company damaged my grand piano, and I've got an angry phone call to make."

"You'll receive an e-mail regarding the time and date of the next meeting," Neal told him.

"Until then." Wynston Meadows left the room, which immediately erupted in excited chatter. Wallace thought that the OWHA might now be able to enter one of the nationwide competitions for best restoration and beautification of a historical property. "Meadows's money," he said, "will finally help us go up against those other bigger and *hitherto* better funded historical societies."

Joyce had ideas of her own. "I've always thought the OWHA deserved national coverage," she said. "Why shouldn't one of us appear on a show like *Good Morning America*? Mr. Meadows's money could make that happen. He's bound to know people who could put us in touch with the networks. Maybe he even knows Oprah!"

"With money like his," Jeannette said, eyes shining, "the sky's the limit!"

"Virtue, not money, is everlasting wealth."

"What was that, Mary Bernadette?" Neal asked.

Mary Bernadette smiled and waved her hand dismissively.

Joyce turned to Anne. "Isn't he a handsome man?" she whispered. "In the old-fashioned way, not like one of these photoshopped boys you see on-screen today."

Anne nodded. "His eyes remind me of Richard Burton's. So clear and intense."

"Now, ladies," Leonard said. "It doesn't matter what the man looks like as long as he proves a devoted member of the OWHA. And he hasn't made any specific promises of financial support yet. Patience!"

Joyce rolled her eyes at Anne.

"I'll give a welcoming party at my house," Norma announced. "Say, a week from Saturday? I'll send invitations to all of the important business owners and other noteworthy people in Oliver's Well."

Mary Bernadette nodded. In truth, she would have liked to have hosted the welcoming party but had to admit that Norma's house was more suited to a large affair than her own. So she would let Norma have the honor of being hostess to Wynston Meadows because she was sure that she, Mary Bernadette Fitzgibbon, would be the one to appear on television once the OWHA became well known for its purchase and restoration of the Branley Estate. She *was* the senior member, the chairman, and the board's official spokesperson after all, and she could say without exaggeration that she made a fine appearance. Dignified without being stuffy, with the proper degree of wit and humor. And, she thought, in matters of preservation, age *always* trumped youth.

"Do you remember that about twenty years ago the OWHA produced a short film about the society's founding and early years?" Neal asked then.

Richard nodded. "And it would be wonderful to make another film documenting the time that's passed since the first one was made. Mr. Meadows might fund the cost of production, and we could host a grand premiere showing."

Mary Bernadette nodded in approval. "I'm sure my grandson's wife would love to direct a film about the OWHA," she said.

"But does she *know* anything about making a film?" Joyce asked.

Mary Bernadette dismissed the question as irrelevant. If Alexis didn't know, she would learn. "Of course she knows about making a film. Now," she said, "as long as we're here, do we have any business to discuss other than speculation about our future?"

There was a murmur of laughter and the members of the board got down to immediate, if less exciting, business.

CHAPTER 30

Mary Bernadette expertly steered her car past a group of workmen repairing a stretch of York Avenue. She enjoyed driving, and the fact that her car was always spotlessly clean and in perfect working order, and the fact that she had never once gotten a ticket, only added to the pleasure.

The meeting, she thought, had gone well. No, more than that, it had gone spectacularly well. She had firm expectations that she and Wynston Meadows would be staunch colleagues. She liked his handshake and the way he looked a person right in the eye as if to say, "I am listening to you, I am hearing what you have to say to me." His clothing, too, hit the perfect note. Today he had worn a two-button suit that, while clearly expensive—Mary Bernadette knew quality cut and fabric when she saw it—was not in the least showy or faddish. His shirt was brilliantly white and most likely hand-tailored. His tie had a modest stripe. On the whole, Mary Bernadette had approved, though if asked she might have suggested he use a bit less hair gel. But maybe that was the fashion among the power brokers in the big cities these days.

As she drove home through the town she loved so deeply, she imagined her new colleague coming to her for all manner of advice about the town's politics, its more important families, and the OWHA itself. She felt sure she could steer him in the right direction regarding the ways in which certain people attempted to get around the town's zoning laws and build monstrosities completely out of keeping with the atmosphere of Oliver's Well. And she could certainly drop a careful word in his ear regarding whom on the board he might trust as truly devoted to the cause and who was only out for his or her own social enhancement. It was no secret that Wallace was a bit of a glory hound. As for Joyce, well, she would throw her own mother under a truck if it served to elevate her status on the board. And who knew what silliness Norma was capable of perpetrating.

Yes, Mary Bernadette felt very sure of her rightful place of importance in the OWHA as well as in Oliver's Well. She had been the public face of organization for almost her entire tenure with the board and together with her husband had raised a family and grown a successful business within the town's bounds. People looked to the Fitzgibbons as a model of propriety and honest dealing. Their civic responsibility and devotion to the community were undeniable. With her support, Wynston Meadows would achieve his goal of becoming a true part of the community without any trouble at all.

For about a half a second Mary Bernadette wondered if her thoughts had strayed too far into the realm of pride. It could happen. Temptation was never far off. But then she reassured herself. She really was the least prideful person she knew. She made it a point never to brag or to enumerate her various successes on behalf of Oliver's Well. She was the last one to take credit for a triumph even when credit was due. The well-bred, she believed, were recognizable by their modesty and their humility.

Mary Bernadette pulled into the driveway of her home and noted with distaste that her neighbors across the street, the Burrows, still hadn't fixed that hanging window shutter.

The family was a nightmare from start to finish. Mike Burrows, the father, didn't even have a regular source of income. For about a month he had driven a delivery van for the specialty food shop on Main Street. An unfortunate crash (no one was hurt, but the van was demolished) had put an end to that. For a year or so he had worked at an old diner in town as a short-order cook. When the owner died, the diner was closed and Mike was out of another job. And for a while he had set himself up as "maker of furnishings." From what Paddy had gleaned from a few dissatisfied customers, Burrows was a builder of shoddy tables and chairs. Mary Bernadette dreaded the day when he would come to the Fitzgibbons asking for employment. She saw it as inevitable, as would be their response—a resounding no.

And the wife wasn't much better. When summer came, that dreadful Lucy Burrows would be out on the lawn in nothing but her bathing suit—a two-piece one, at that—sunning herself on a sagging plastic lounge for all the world to see. It wasn't right, a mother of two teenage children, exposing herself in so shameless and, yes, Mary Bernadette would say it, so low class a way.

Well, the character of the parents no doubt had informed the character of the teenage children. The boy, Buddy, didn't seem to be very bright, and he spent far too much time rolling up and down his family's driveway on a skateboard—when he wasn't falling off it. It created a dreadful racket, and no matter how many times Paddy asked him to take the skateboard somewhere else, Buddy, after apologizing and promising, simply showed up in the driveway the very next day.

His sister, Tiffany, whom they called Tiff, if one could believe it, was what PJ had told his grandmother was "a Goth," which seemed to mean that she found it necessary to wear black lipstick, innumerable piercings, and black rags in lieu of clothing. True, whenever she caught sight of Mary Bernadette she smiled and waved. But Mary Bernadette was not easily fooled by a friendly gesture. For all she knew the girl was practicing some evil form of magic in the family's basement. It didn't bear thinking about.

That their presence on Honeysuckle Lane brought down the property values of the other houses there could be no doubt. Thank God the Fitzgibbons had no plans to sell in the near future! PJ and Alexis would someday move into the big house and assume ownership, and their children after them would keep the family homestead. By then the Burrows would be long gone. One could only hope.

Mary Bernadette got out of her car and, with one last glance over her shoulder at the eyesore that was the Burrows' house, went into her own well-kept home.

CHAPTER 31

It was one o'clock on Saturday afternoon and Megan was at her desk. Pat was out buying something or other at the hardware store. David and Danica were in the backyard, kicking around a soccer ball.

Megan sighed and rubbed the back of her neck. She was ready for a nap. The CPEE had booked a well-respected child psychologist to give a talk in one of the meeting rooms at the library Monday afternoon, but he had canceled just that morning, having come down with a case of laryngitis. His wife had made the call to Megan, claiming he was completely without the power of speech and that she was enjoying the "blessed silence."

She had scrambled to find another qualified speaker available Monday afternoon, and after three hours of phone calls and e-mails and texts had finally gotten a commitment from another, slightly less well-respected child psychologist, whose fee was slightly higher than what the CPEE was generally comfortable paying. Still, crisis averted.

"You so cheated!" Megan flinched at the sound of her daughter's voice. "I saw you touch the ball with your hand!"

"I so did not!"

Megan rolled her eyes. That David and Danica loved each other there was no doubt, but for some reason they were always accusing one another of foul play. Even before they had the power of speech, one would point to the other in the middle of their play and make a sound that Megan could only call accusatory. A long-buried memory suddenly popped into her head. She and Pat had brought all three children to Oliver's Well for a visit with their grandparents. At one point, Megan and Mary Bernadette had been watching three-year-old David make his way across the living room to retrieve a toy car he had left on the coffee table.

"There but for the grace of God go I," Mary Bernadette had murmured.

The phrase had always infuriated Megan, and now the assumption that Mary Bernadette had been specially favored by God while her grandson had been ignored or passed over was really too much for her to bear without protest. It had been one of the only times she had ever argued with her mother-in-law, a futile gesture in the end as Mary Bernadette had blandly refused to see her point.

"All the expression implies," she had said, "is that I'm grateful for my blessings."

Megan had turned to her favorite prayer then, as she had so many times since. "Lord, make me an instrument of your peace. Where there is hatred, let me sow love. And please don't let me kill my mother-in-law."

Now that Mary Bernadette was on her mind. . . . Just that morning Megan had suddenly recalled having read something concerning Wynston Meadows's personal life. She could hardly believe it had slipped her mind. It seemed that a few years back, not long after his divorce, the much younger woman Meadows was dating had gone to the police with the claim that he routinely slapped her around. The charges, however, had been dropped— had the girlfriend been bought off or frightened into silence?— and the press had forgotten the story in a suspiciously short time.

Though the story was disturbing, Megan had decided there was no use in mentioning it to Mary Bernadette. First, no wrongdoing had been proved, and second, Mary Bernadette would reject outright another "word to the wise," especially one delivered by her daughter-in-law.

"Mom!" Danica roared. "David is cheating again! Tell him to stop!"

"I am not!" David roared back. "She's just jealous that I scored a goal because she stinks as a goalie!"

Megan sighed, walked over to the window, and leaned out. "Work it out yourselves," she called down. "Or I'm taking the ball away."

"That's so not fair!" Danica cried.

"Yeah, that's so not fair!" her brother echoed.

Megan shrugged and turned away from the window. Mom's the bad guy. Crisis averted.

CHAPTER 32

"Fancy running into you in Oliver's Well's only pharmacy!" Alexis laughed. "Hi, Maureen. It *is* a small town, isn't it?"

Maureen put her hand on Alexis's arm. "And it gets smaller the longer you've lived here."

"Is that a good thing?"

"Depends. I don't mean to sound enigmatic, but we all find out the answer to that question in time."

"Oh. Hey, I missed you at our St. Patrick's Day dinner. Well, at Mary Bernadette's dinner."

"I had a party to go to. It's the same group of us every year, mostly people from the office, and frankly, it's gotten pretty dismal." Maureen laughed. "But it's something to do."

Alexis smiled. "Well, maybe next year you could join us, instead. Not that it was all that exciting! Well, except for your father. He has a beautiful voice. And Mary Bernadette's soda bread *is* amazing."

"Yes, he does, and yes, it is."

"Did he ever sing professionally?"

Maureen looked startled by the question. "Oh, no. People like us don't reach for the stars. We're content with what's right here in front of us. At least, we're supposed to be. Wait. That sounded as if I was criticizing my parents, and I'm not. I'm actually criticizing myself."

Before Alexis could form a suitable reply to this oddly revealing statement, Maureen spoke again. "By the way, have you seen the famous Wynston Meadows around town? My mother can't stop talking about him. You'd think he was JFK resurrected."

"I might have," Alexis said, "but I have no idea what he looks like. I hate to admit this, but I don't really keep up with the local news the way I probably should."

"The town's agog with excitement. It's been ages since Oliver's Well had a genuine celebrity. Personally, his being here doesn't matter to me, unless of course he decides to make trouble in some way. But I can't see why he'd bother. What could Oliver's Well possibly mean to a man who could buy out Donald Trump?"

"I have no idea. Are you going to Norma Campbell's party, to welcome him to town?" Alexis asked.

"I haven't been invited," Maureen said. "Not important enough, but my boss is going. As are my parents, thanks to Mom's being on the board of the OWHA."

"Well, I have to go—PJ calls it a command performance—but I'm not really looking forward to it. It sounds pretty dull and stuffy to me."

Maureen laughed. "Take it from someone who's perfected the art of staying on the sidelines. No party is entirely dull or stuffy when you set yourself up as a people watcher. You avoid being drawn into boring chitchat and you get to observe all the odd behavior that comes out when an unlikely group of people are forced to socialize."

"I'm guessing that people are going to be stumbling over their own feet trying to get a word with Mr. Meadows."

"That could be worth a laugh! Well, I must run. Wharton Insurance waits for no man. Or in this case, woman."

Maureen headed back to her office and Alexis to her car. Maureen Kline, she thought, was a bit of a puzzle. What was that she had said about staying on the sidelines—did she really mean on the sidelines of life? And about people like her not reaching for the stars. And there was the fact that Maureen Kline was so plain, almost deliberately so. She dressed in such a dowdy way, she wore no makeup, and there were wide streaks of gray in her brown hair. Maybe she truly didn't care about her appearance. Maybe she was without vanity. Maybe that's what she meant by staying on the sidelines; she meant that she didn't like to call attention to herself. Alexis smiled as she got behind the wheel and started the engine. God knew *she* had her fair share of vanity! It had depressed her to go into The Sophisticated Lady and allow Anne Tribble—a very nice woman, in fact—to choose for her a few basic tops, blouses, pants, and skirts in tan and navy and taupe and white. "Perfect for the office," Anne had assured her. The clothing was well made, but every time Alexis wore the white blouse and navy pants or the tan silk top with the navy skirt to sit behind her desk at Fitzgibbon Landscaping, she felt like a bit of a fraud.

Vanity, thy name is woman. And this made Alexis think of nuns, who once had been compelled to live narrow, unadventurous lives stuck in some gloomy convent praying for sinners in the nasty outside world—and they certainly hadn't worn makeup or dyed their hair to cover the gray! But things had changed. A contemporary nun like PJ's Aunt Grace didn't spend her days contemplating the evils of everyday life. She was out making a difference for the better. The stories Alexis had heard from the family made Grace Fitzgibbon out to be a very dynamic woman, but Alexis couldn't quite tell if she was dynamic in the way that Mary Bernadette was dynamic, or dynamic in another, less— well, less annoying way.

Alexis pulled into her parking space and checked her cell phone. She had been gone from the office for almost forty minutes. If the dynamic Mary Bernadette had stopped by and found her gone, there would be hell to pay. Alexis got out of her car and hurried inside.

CHAPTER 33

PJ was behind the wheel of his grandparents' car. Mary Bernadette sat in front with him, and Alexis and Paddy sat in back. It was a beautiful night, not a cloud to dim a sky twinkling with stars. Ordinarily, Mary Bernadette didn't wax poetic about the weather, but this was a special evening after all, and she couldn't help but consider the clear skies and pleasantly balmy air a sign of good things to come to Oliver's Well.

"Every time I see Norma's place I'm impressed," PJ said as he pulled the car up behind a guest's minivan. "I'm dying to get the landscaping contract. The gardens are the only thing subpar about the estate."

"I don't know what a woman living alone needs with all this house," Mary Bernadette replied. "And I do agree that her gardens could use a more professional finish."

"Look," Alexis said. "Over there. A media van. Who asked for a TV crew?"

Mary Bernadette smoothed an invisible wrinkle on her dress and straightened her already straight shoulders. "I don't know," she admitted, "but I wouldn't be surprised if Mr. Meadows is responsible."

Norma Campbell had hired a staff of parking attendants, and PJ surrendered the keys to one of the white-shirted young men who were scurrying to and from the field behind the house that was serving as a parking lot. Mary Bernadette was of two minds about this. On one hand, she considered hired parking attendants an unnecessary expense. On the other, she admitted that it did probably cut down on confusion when people wanted to leave at the end of the night. And there *was* the matter of women's heels getting dirtied in that field, what with the horses and those large hairy dogs Norma was known to keep.

Mary Bernadette looked up at the façade of the house, complete with a rather grand staircase leading up to a rather grand porch with whitewashed columns. Right out of *Gone with the Wind*, Mary Bernadette thought. How theatrical, considering the house had been built only in the 1950s. Certainly not a candidate for the Historical Register.

The four Fitzgibbons made their way into the house. The ceiling of the front hall had to be almost twenty feet high. There was a suitably sweeping staircase. Massive urns held massive arrangements of flowers. The floor was marble. Mary Bernadette peered into a room off the hall. It was dense with detailed moldings and heavy draperies.

"It's a gorgeous house, isn't it?" Alexis said.

Mary Bernadette frowned. "I find it too grandiose, myself. And the décor is too ostentatious for my taste. Can you imagine the expense of keeping all those intricate carvings and silk draperies clean? But if it's what suits Norma . . ."

The four of them went through to the ballroom, Mary Bernadette leading the way with an air of deliberate nonchalance. It would never do to give Norma—or Wynston Meadows, for that matter— the erroneous idea that she was impressed by a display of mere *things*.

"I don't think I've ever been in a room this big," Paddy whispered. "Outside of a museum, that is."

"It's probably shut up for all but one day of the year," Mary Bernadette said dismissively. *Conspicuous consumption*, she thought. *Money is the root of all evil. And Greed is yet another of the Seven Deadly Sins.*

Three large, ornate chandeliers, sparkling with drops of faceted crystal, hung in a row down the center of the room. Tall, rectangular windows were evenly spaced along the right-hand wall. Along the left-hand wall was a series of enormous landscape paintings in a distinctly nineteenth-century style, each in an elaborate gilt frame. Mary Bernadette wondered if the paintings were copies or originals. Not that it mattered.

Waiters dressed in white shirts and black pants wove their way through the gathering guests with trays of appetizers and glasses of champagne. A very long table of more substantial fare sat beside an equally long table of desserts, featuring everything from cakes to tartlets, from fresh fruit to an ornate chocolate fountain. There was also a full bar. "Norma is running a risk serving so much alcohol," Mary Bernadette proclaimed.

Alexis laughed. "I don't think this is a crowd likely to get rowdy!"

"You never know," Mary Bernadette replied darkly. "I've known the drink to fell even the most upright man."

Alexis shrugged. Mary Bernadette resisted the urge to reprimand her. A shrug, in her opinion, was a gesture of disrespect. Her grandson's wife might as well have said, "Whatever," in that obnoxious tone people employed when using the word dismissively. But this was supposed to be a festive occasion, so Mary Bernadette let the slight go without comment.

A live band, its members wearing classic tuxedos, was playing selections from the American Songbook. "I must say the music is tasteful," Mary Bernadette noted.

Paddy nodded. "The woman doesn't stint, I'll say that for her. Look at the size of those shrimp!"

"I'll be back in a minute," PJ said, already moving off. "I want a word with Leonard."

"There's Mayor Rogers." Mary Bernadette frowned. "What in the world is his wife wearing? Sheila has more money than God and yet absolutely no taste in clothing."

"I didn't know there was so much wealth in Oliver's Well," Alexis said.

"It's here and there, some old some new," Paddy explained. "Norma's one of the more recent imports. When did she come here, Mary? Ten, twelve years ago?"

"Eleven years and three months ago, to be precise." She had a phenomenal memory for names and dates concerned in any way with Oliver's Well. Besides, Norma's arrival was not something she was likely to forget. It wasn't every day that a middle-aged woman with no discernable familial attachments and no employment set up house down the road.

"And there she is now," Alexis said. Norma, bedecked in a bronze lamé gown more suitable for a Met gala than a welcoming reception, got up on a platform at the far end of the room, and when the crowd went silent she introduced the guest of honor.

"Thank you," she said, "for coming here tonight on this very special occasion. I'm pleased to see the cream of the crop of Oliver's Well in my home."

"She speaks well enough," Paddy commented.

Mary Bernadette shook her head. "Her enunciation needs work."

"And now," Norma went on, "without further delay, I would like to introduce our guest of honor, a man many of you know about but, at the same time, a newcomer to our little town and to the Oliver's Well Historical Association, Wynston Meadows. Mr. Meadows grew up in nearby Smithstown, where he was steeped in the tradition of our rich regional architectural and cultural history. He serves on the boards of no fewer than three major companies and holds a position on the D.C. Landmarks Commission. We are excited and honored to welcome Wynston Meadows to our fold. Mr. Meadows?"

With reporters hovering and television crews filming, Wynston Meadows took the stage. He was dressed in a dark suit, white shirt, and red tie. He put his hand up to request the applause to stop, and when it did, he spoke. Mary Bernadette listened attentively.

"Thank you, Norma, for that lovely introduction, and thank you all for coming this evening to welcome me to Oliver's Well."

Sporadic applause broke out, and again Wynston Meadows raised his hand.

"I'm delighted to have been accepted to the board of the Oliver's Well Historical Association," he went on. "As Norma mentioned, I have a very personal and long-standing connection with the historic lands and buildings of this region. My grandfather, Dennis Meadows, was the curator of the Smithstown historical society's museum. I passed many a pleasant hour with him, both in the museum and on visits to historic sites in our region, and so

became passionate about the need to honor, protect, and pre-
serve our heritage in these assets. I've been fortunate in business"—he paused for the expected chuckles—"so with the
resources given to me I am happy to support the OWHA and
other organizations committed to similar goals."

Wynston Meadows paused again and looked thoughtfully at
the floor.

"Isn't he wonderful?" Mary Bernadette turned to find that
Jeannette and Danny had joined them.

"He is indeed," Mary Bernadette whispered back.

"Tonight," Meadows went on, "I would like to announce that
I will be working with the OWHA to explore the possibility of ac-
quiring and restoring the famous Branley Estate." This was met
with a general murmur of satisfaction. "To this end, I am pledg-
ing a total gift of twenty-five million dollars to the OWHA."

This time, the applause went on without Wynston Meadows
attempting to stop it. Mary Bernadette's palms stung with the
force of her own clapping. When it had finally died down of its
own accord, Wynston Meadows continued.

"This gift," he said, "will be made in five installments of five
million dollars over the next five years, with the first installment
available immediately toward the acquisition of the property that
the incomparable Mary Bernadette Fitzgibbon and her colleagues have worked so hard to position us to purchase."

Again, the room resounded with applause. Mary Bernadette
was brimming with pride. Jeannette squeezed her friend's arm in
her excitement, and Paddy, beaming, cleared his throat.

Wynston Meadows again held up a hand to quiet the crowd.
"Thank you," he said. "Thank you all. I'm happy to be able to
make this contribution to my new hometown, and I hope the addition of my energy and experience to the management of the
OWHA will help guide us along the new path ahead. Now, I'll let
everyone get back to enjoying Norma's wonderful hospitality."

Wynston Meadows left the platform to more thunderous applause.

"I think he did a very nice job," Mary Bernadette noted to her companions when the applause had finally come to an end and the crowd began to move off around the room. She was determined to act as if the gift of a vast sum of money to her beloved organization was not something out of the ordinary. Keep a calm head and a placid demeanor, her mother had often said. And no one will be the wiser.

Alexis smiled vaguely. Jeannette wiped a tear from the corner of her eye. Danny patted her shoulder.

"It was good of him to mention you specifically, Mary," Paddy said to his wife.

Mary Bernadette laughed. "Well, why wouldn't he have?"

"I just hope things at the OWHA don't change too drastically."

"What do you mean?" Jeannette asked.

"A new man will have new ideas. It's only natural."

"Nonsense," Mary Bernadette said. "A smart man knows to leave well enough alone."

"I hope so," her husband murmured. "But a new broom sweeps clean."

CHAPTER 34

Alexis watched as Mary Bernadette chatted with a woman in a truly awful green gown. PJ's grandmother really was the proverbial social butterfly, flitting from one person to the next, landing delicately, charming the person with her dazzling smile, and then fluttering off to the next. Well, maybe not a butterfly. More like a very impressive archangel descending with a flaming sword.

Mary Bernadette always made a striking appearance, but for this event she had outdone herself. Her dress was a shimmering shade of lilac, simple and elegant, accented by a thin silver belt at the waist. Around her shoulders she had draped a silvery shawl. She looked, Alexis thought, as if she had stepped out of a 1930s period drama, a woman of great wealth and dignity and graciousness. Next to her, even her handsome husband became a mere prop to her magnificence. PJ had paid his grandmother the grandest of compliments. They would have made any other woman blush with embarrassment, but Mary Bernadette had taken them in stride, as if they were only her due.

Alexis sighed and looked around at the mill of chattering people gathered to celebrate Wynston Meadows's arrival in Oliver's Well. She had almost been looking forward to the party after her chat with Maureen, but so far she had detected no interestingly odd behavior, and except for a few of the waiters there seemed to be no one even remotely her own age. And maybe the most disappointing of all, no one had complimented *her* on her appearance. She had spent some time assembling the outfit with the help of Mary Bernadette's friend Anne at The Sophisticated Lady. (Luckily, Anne's shop sold some clothing in colors other than neutrals!) Her dress was a very pale ice blue, form fitting without being clingy or revealing. Her heels and clutch were beaded silver, and in her ears she wore the diamond and platinum studs her parents had given her for college graduation. Alexis knew that she looked pretty spectacular, but not even her own supposedly besotted husband had paid her a compliment.

She spotted PJ across the room now, in conversation with a group of three middle-aged women. He seemed to be having a grand time. He was at his best in a crowd, able to chat with ease about anything from someone's ailing parent to the local softball team's latest win or loss. Alexis had always admired his remarkable social abilities (clearly, he had taken a lesson from his grandmother), but at that moment, as she stood alone watching him laughing with the ladies of Oliver's Well, she felt resentful and left out. She was only vaguely aware that she was reacting childishly.

"Oh, great," Alexis murmured. Mary Bernadette was heading

her way, and Alexis wondered wildly if there was some way she might escape before she descended. But there was none, short of melting into the ground like the Wicked Witch of the West. A convenient trick, that.

"Are you enjoying yourself, dear?" Mary Bernadette asked, with a darting glance at the half-empty glass of champagne Alexis held in her right hand.

"Yes," Alexis said. "It's a fantastic party."

Her husband's grandmother briefly laid a hand on her arm. "Because it doesn't look as if you are. You might try to smile a bit more. You *do* represent Fitzgibbon Landscaping. We all do." Mary Bernadette now looked at Alexis critically, as if seeing her for the first time that evening. "Well, I must say that your dress is very pretty."

At last, Alexis thought. *A compliment—and from Mary Bernadette!*

"Thank you," she said.

"Anne is a marvel, isn't she? She has impeccable taste."

"Yes, she's very stylish."

"She really knows what works for a woman." Mary Bernadette gave Alexis the once-over again. "She's very good at hiding a figure's flaws and emphasizing its good points."

Alexis, who hadn't been aware that her figure had any flaws, simply nodded.

"Ah, there's Father Robert and Reverend McMeans. I should say hello." Mary Bernadette sailed off, nodding to partygoers as if, Alexis thought, she were Catherine the Great at an affair of state.

Alexis drained the last of the champagne. Well, so much for compliments. And how, she wondered, had she become an ambassador for her husband's business? It wasn't a position she relished, unlike Mary Bernadette, who seemed to thrive on attention. Were all eyes in Oliver's Well really on her every movement? She didn't know how those society wives did it, or the wives of politicians, forcing seemly and proper behavior even when they wanted to scream and stomp and make a scene—or to be left alone.

"Well, hello, young Mrs. Fitzgibbon."

Alexis turned to see Leonard DeWitt at her side. She had met him a few times in the past year and thought him a genuinely nice person. "Hello, Mr. DeWitt," she said.

"Leonard, please. Otherwise I feel like an old man!"

Alexis laughed. "Leonard, then. Are you enjoying the party?"

"Magnificent party! Magnificent occasion! You know, I'm convinced it was Mary Bernadette's leadership of the OWHA that brought Mr. Meadows to our organization. Yes, she's the one who's really responsible for this great gift we've been given. She's a remarkable woman."

Leonard looked expectantly at Alexis, and dutifully she replied, "Yes, remarkable."

"Oh, there go the cheese puffs!" Leonard hurried off after the waiter, and Alexis contemplated going over to the bar.

"Alexis." The voice came from just behind her, close enough to make her jump.

She turned to find another member of the OWHA's board. "Hello, Mr. Chadbourne," she said, moving away an inch or two from the tiny man.

"Fine speech Meadows gave, wasn't it?" he asked.

Alexis nodded. In truth, she had hardly heard a word, except, of course, for the mention of twenty-five million dollars. *That* had gotten her attention.

"Meadows was absolutely right," Mr. Chadbourne was saying. "The board is now on a new path. And it *does* need a breath of fresh air. Things get stale, don't they, everything from bread to people. Yes, it's definitely time for a change."

Alexis wondered what she had missed by tuning out when the illustrious Wynston Meadows had taken the microphone. "Well, I—" she began.

"Yes, a change is long overdue, that's what I say."

Before Alexis could attempt another thwarted response, Wallace Chadbourne wandered off without a farewell.

Alexis spotted her husband again, this time talking to a man she recognized as the chief of police, and made her way over to him. By the time she reached him, the man had moved off.

"There you are," PJ said. He put his arm around her waist and planted a kiss on her cheek. "Did I tell you how beautiful you look tonight?"

"No," Alexis said. "You didn't."

"Well, you look beautiful. Are you having a good time?"

"Yes. It's—fun. But can we go home now?" she asked.

PJ took his arm from around her and looked at his watch. "I'll have to check with Grandmother," he said. "She might need to stick around for a bit longer. It's only nine o'clock."

Alexis sighed. "I told you we should have taken two cars so we could leave when we want to."

PJ frowned. "You know my grandparents don't like to drive after dark."

Alexis immediately felt chastened. "Right," she said. "Sorry. I forgot."

"Look, I'll go have a chat with Grandmother and see what she wants to do. Why don't you find my grandfather?"

Alexis nodded and watched as PJ, incredibly handsome in his navy suit, made his way through the throng of chattering guests.

CHAPTER 35

Alexis was sitting on the little step outside the cottage when she spotted David, a soccer ball under his arm, making his way toward her from the house.

"I saw your mom's car," Alexis called. "But I didn't know that you were with her."

Megan and her family had been visiting Oliver's Well more

frequently lately. Alexis certainly didn't mind. Nine times out of ten she would take PJ's mother over his grandmother. Well, to be honest, ten times out of ten. And the twins were always fun.

Danica, David explained to her now, was playing in a soccer tournament and her father was on transportation duty. David figured he would rather go on a road trip with his mom than stay at home alone.

"Is your sister a good player?" Alexis asked.

David shrugged. "She's won a few trophies. Hey, want to practice with me?"

Alexis eyed the soccer ball under David's arm with trepidation.

"I have to warn you," she said. "I stink at sports. I just can't do them. Something about my coordination, I guess."

"Don't use bad coordination as an excuse."

Alexis blushed. "Oh. I'm sorry."

"Don't be. Anyway, it's just for fun. I kind of stink too. My feet are, like, totally turned in. They weren't always that way."

"All right. But don't say I didn't warn you."

They kicked around the ball for about twenty minutes before Alexis called it quits. "I'm sorry, David," she said, dropping back onto the little step outside the cottage. "I didn't realize how out of shape I am."

With some difficulty, David joined her. Alexis resisted the impulse to help him without being asked to. She had learned so much about being with someone with a physical challenge since knowing David. For example, when she had first met him she had trouble understanding his speech. She had felt terribly embarrassed asking him to repeat himself, though David had been patient with her. And then one day it occurred to her that understanding David was simply a matter of learning to listen in a new way. It was a lot like becoming accustomed to a foreigner's accent. The foreigner's pronunciation wasn't the problem. The problem was that you were listening for your own pronunciation and rhythms instead of listening for his. Once Alexis had figured that out, understanding David's speech was simple.

"What brought you and your mom down to Oliver's Well today?" she asked.

"Mom's checking up on Grandma," David told her. "But we don't tell Grandma that's why we visit a lot lately."

"Oh. Is she sick?"

"No. But Mom and Dad think that since Grandma and Grandpa are, like, almost eighty, they should make sure they're okay, you know, not getting senile or anything."

Alexis wondered why Megan and Pat hadn't just asked her or PJ to keep an eye on the grandparents. Then again, the last thing she wanted was to become Mary Bernadette's secret caretaker! "Your grandmother is an interesting person," she said carefully.

"Yeah. I know."

"Sometimes I feel kind of, I don't know, insignificant when I'm around her."

David looked at Alexis and laughed. "Of course you do," he said. "That's what you're supposed to feel."

Alexis was taken aback. "What do you mean?" she asked.

"Grandma's the queen of the family. Everyone knows that. She likes it that way. Anyway, like my mom says, there's no point in pretending that she's not in charge or that she's going to change. It'll only make you unhappy."

"Oh."

David gave her a distinctly conspiratorial smile. "Don't tell anyone I told you this, okay?"

"Okay."

"My dad says Grandma is a pain in the butt."

Alexis put her hand to her mouth in a vain attempt to stifle a shout of laughter.

"I don't let her get to me like she gets to my parents," he said. "Grandma's just the way she is."

Well, Alexis thought, it was easy for David to be so nonchalant. He didn't live in Mary Bernadette's backyard! Still, he had a point.

"You're pretty smart, you know," she told him.

"Some people think I'm stupid because of the way I talk, but I know that I'm not."

"That's awful. Doesn't it make you angry when people make ridiculous assumptions based on appearances?"

"Mostly I ignore it, but it makes my sister furious. She's the one with the 'famous Irish temper.' That's what Grandma calls it."

"I don't think I've ever seen your sister angry," Alexis said.

"Just wait. She puffs up like a cat about to attack. Well, not really, but it feels that way. It's like, you feel the air around you crackling."

Alexis pretended to shudder. "Yikes. I'd better stay on her good side."

"Well, mostly she gets angry when someone does something bad to someone else. She doesn't blow up just for nothing. She's like an avenger or something."

"That's a relief, that she doesn't just go around kicking butt for no reason!"

"Does my brother have a temper?" David asked.

Alexis laughed. "PJ's one of the most laid-back, easygoing people I've ever met."

"Sometimes I can hardly remember what it was like when he lived with us."

"Right. You and your sister were, what, six or so when he went away to college?"

"Yeah. Here comes Mom."

Alexis noted, not for the first time, that her mother-in-law really was an attractive woman. It didn't hit you over the head like it did with some people. Still, she made an impression. Alexis hoped that when she was her mother-in-law's age she would have attained at least a bit of her easy poise.

"Has David been behaving?" Megan asked, with the ghost of a smile.

"No," Alexis replied promptly, causing David to guffaw. "He's been awful and rotten."

Megan laughed. "Come on, kiddo. Time to head back home."

Alexis stood with a little groan.

"Give me your hand?" David asked.

Alexis did, and David rose from the little step.

"Can't you stay for dinner?" Alexis's reason for asking was almost entirely selfish. It was so much easier to be with Mary Bernadette when Megan and her family were around.

But her mother-in-law shook her head. "Sorry, but no. We're going to an event at David and Danica's school this evening. In fact, if we don't leave now we're going to be late."

"Okay. Well, tell everyone I said hi."

"And give my love to PJ."

"Sure," Alexis promised. "And David? Thanks."

"For what?" he asked.

Alexis smiled at the boy. "Just, thanks."

She watched as David and his mother walked to her car, parked behind Mary Bernadette's in the driveway. David was right; his legs and feet were turned in so that the toes were almost facing each other. It had to be painful, let alone annoying for him. But there was no point in Alexis worrying about it, not with Megan and Pat in charge. They were fantastic parents.

Alexis watched Megan and David drive off and vowed to keep in mind David's advice about how to handle Mary Bernadette. *Out of the mouths of babes,* she thought, turning back to the cottage.

CHAPTER 36

"Good morning," Grace said. "Well, good afternoon to you."

"Greetings and salutations," Megan replied with a smile. She and her sister-in-law communicated with some frequency—thank God, Megan thought, for the convenience of texting—but not even Skype was as good as being in the same room with a person you cared for, face-to-face. Besides, when you used Skype or FaceTime there was the huge downside of having to see yourself on screen. Megan said as much to Grace.

"You know," Grace pointed out, "if you raise the computer to just the right height on the table—use a stack of books—you can avoid having to see the always unflattering view of your neck. Mostly."

Megan laughed. "I've yet to find that right height."

"And I know I'm not supposed to care about what my neck looks like," Grace said, "but I *am* my mother's daughter! Not that she would ever admit to being the least bit vain."

"God forbid! So, have you heard anything about the famous—or, infamous—Wynston Meadows moving to Oliver's Well?"

"Believe it or not, yes. I try to keep up on hometown news. Gives me something to chat about when I'm on the phone with Mom."

"Then you know he's joined the board of the OWHA. There was a big party in his honor, complete with reporters and a camera crew to advertise his pledge of twenty-five million dollars to the OWHA."

"Twenty-five million? Whoa."

"The *Gazette* ran a big piece about just how important that kind of financing is to the future of the town. And it paid its usual obeisance to the OWHA itself, of course. Needless to say the online news sources got hold of the story, too. I daresay Mr. Meadows has a hotline to the press."

"Let me guess," Grace said. "Mom has high hopes for taking him under her wing."

"She'd never admit as much, but I suspect that's her plan."

"And a man like this Meadows is rumored to be is not going to take kindly to the whims—that's what he'll call them—to the whims of a quirky old lady."

"I did try to warn her he might be too—big—to handle."

Grace laughed. "How'd that go?"

"Not well, I'm afraid. And I know she's encouraging PJ—not that he needs much encouraging—to make a bid for Meadows's business. He's bought a home in town, of course. Lots of acreage."

"Well, good luck to him. PJ has pluck. I just hope he also knows how to tread carefully."

"I hope so, too," Megan said. "He's determined to make a name for himself as his grandfather's heir. He wants to do everything in absolutely the right way, but he can be impatient. He gets that from his father."

"I remember the time Pat grabbed a baking sheet barehanded right out of the oven because he couldn't waste time in finding a dishtowel. There were cookies on the baking sheet, of course. I hope he's learned his lesson."

Megan laughed. "Not really! But forget about the Oliver's Well Fitzgibbons for a moment. I haven't asked about *your* life, Grace."

"No worries. I'm fit as a fiddle and busy as a bee."

"Which tells me next to nothing."

"Well, there isn't much to tell really, not about *me*, anyway. I could go on for days about the important stuff, like the interesting people I meet, but I won't."

"I've got time," Megan said. "And I'm genuinely interested."

"Thanks. I know you are. Unfortunately, I'm needed at the Angela House in fifteen minutes."

"What's the Angela House?"

"It's a sort of halfway home for women who've hit rock bottom for one reason or another." Grace raised an eyebrow. "I'm sorry to say there's often a man involved. Anyway, the women and their children can live there for a maximum of two years while they're taught basic life skills like balancing a budget and choosing healthy food at the supermarket. I'm one of a staff of volunteers who come in twice a month to give special workshops. Today it's Culinary Skills 101."

"I didn't know you liked to cook."

"I don't," Grace admitted. "Can't stand it. But I know the basics."

"I'm curious," Megan said. "Do the women know you're a nun?"

Grace laughed. "I don't mention it. It could turn some of the

women off, make them suspect I'm out to save their souls or
something equally as intrusive."

"I suppose it might," Megan agreed. "But other women might
be impressed to learn that being a nun in today's world has nothing to do with wearing hair shirts under long black habits and
beating schoolchildren with rulers."

"Oh, absolutely. And who knows, someone seeing me in action might even decide to take the veil! I suppose I'll have to
make a judgment call at some point. If I suspect one of the
women might benefit from knowing about my calling, then I'll
tell her. Then again, I couldn't ask her to keep a secret from her
fellow residents. That would be setting a bad example." Grace
laughed. "Maybe silence is the best policy after all!"

"Maybe," Megan agreed. "Cheerio until next time."

"Au revoir. Until we meet again over the airwaves or whatever
this stuff is." Grace laughed. "Sheesh! I sound like my mother!"

CHAPTER 37

The board of the OWHA was in session. Mary Bernadette had
opened the meeting, and Leonard had given his report.
Neal read the minutes of the last meeting. This was followed by
a discussion of old business, including the vexing issue of the
missing reams of printer paper from Leonard's office. A discussion of new business followed. Neal suggested that they reconsider their fire insurance. "There was a story out of Connecticut
yesterday," he said, "about a dreadful fire that broke out in the
headquarters of a town's historical society. The loss to the museum was enormous, and there just isn't enough money to go
about finding new items of interest. Not that anything can be re-

placed, of course." Leonard promised he would take another look at their policy. Thus far, Wynston Meadows had not contributed to the discussions, though he had been taking notes.

Mary Bernadette looked around the table. "Does anyone else have anything to add?"

"I do." Wynston Meadows smiled at his fellow board members. "I'd like to revisit the awarding of the contract for the Joseph J. Stoker House to Fitzgibbon Landscaping."

"Revisit?" Leonard said. "I don't understand."

"Well, let's put it this way. I was thoroughly surprised to learn that a small, family-run landscaping business beat out a large and very well-regarded outfit like Blue Sound. I know their work well. It's quite impressive. In fact, I've hired them myself in the past. And I'm on the board of trustees of East Coast Investments with the owner, Mark Summers. Nice guy. Very smart."

Mary Bernadette wasn't at all sure that she had heard correctly. She felt an unpleasant tingling in her stomach.

"And to be frank," Meadows continued, "I have to say that I'm slightly troubled by the whiff of favoritism surrounding the selection."

"But we've hired Fitzgibbon Landscaping many times," Richard said, with a quick glance at Mary Bernadette. "Their work is good enough for our needs."

Wynston Meadows raised his eyebrows. "Really?" he said. "Well, then, maybe the OWHA has been setting its standards too low. Anyway, what I propose is that we start over from the beginning. We'll send out another call for bids, choose the most promising candidates, and let them make their presentations. And this time, let's look with fresh eyes. Let's cast the net wider, try to draw in some new blood. If Fitzgibbon is indeed the best, no doubt it will be obvious."

A weighty silence descended on the room. Mary Bernadette felt it bearing down on her. She was deeply shocked by Wynston Meadows's suggestion and just as determined not to show it. It took her great effort to speak evenly.

"Mr. Meadows," she said, folding her hands on the table before her. "I assure you that Fitzgibbon Landscaping won the job fair and square."

Meadows smiled ever so slightly. "I wasn't implying otherwise, was I? Anyway, if Fitzgibbon Landscaping did win fair and square, as you insist that it did, its owners won't mind the board revisiting their decision, will they?"

The unpleasant tingling in Mary Bernadette's stomach rose rapidly to her head. Revisiting? Investigating, more like. As if she and her family were criminals! Before she could respond, Neal spoke up.

"Wynston—if I may call you that?—Wynston, as Richard pointed out, Fitzgibbon Landscaping has done many, many jobs for the OWHA over the years. Their reputation is impeccable, and the board had no doubt whatsoever—*has* no doubt whatsoever—that in this case as well, they are the right people to handle the landscape restoration of the Joseph J. Stoker House."

Leonard added, "Hear, hear," and Mary Bernadette gave both men a slight nod of thanks.

Joyce spoke now in her trademark thin and high-pitched voice. "I think what Mr. Meadows—Wynston—is suggesting can cause no harm."

Traitor, Mary Bernadette thought. Joyce was a jealous woman, prone to enjoying the discomfiture of anyone she suspected had life too easy. Mary Bernadette had seen it time and again, like when Lydia Daly, wife of Oliver's Well's most illustrious retired plastic surgeon, had been robbed of a good deal of jewelry while on a trip to D.C. How Joyce had gloated over the woman's misfortune! It was plain that Joyce's being married to a minister hadn't had much good effect on her character.

No one else voiced an opinion. Jeannette looked very pale. Anne was fiddling with her pen. Norma was gazing at the ceiling as if she were alone in the room. Wallace's eyes were darting around the table, as if, Mary Bernadette thought, he was looking for a clue as to what his opinion should be.

"Then it's settled," Wynston Meadows pronounced. "I'll send out a call for bids, and Mrs. Fitzgibbon, why don't you inform your grandson—it is your grandson who now runs things, isn't it?—that if he wants another chance at the job he'll have to prepare another bid. And maybe, if he makes it through the first stage of the competition, another presentation."

What was settled, Mary Bernadette wondered? Who had settled it? They hadn't voted to reopen the competition. Wynston Meadows had simply commandeered the decision. And Leonard, as CEO, was responsible for issuing a call for bids.

Meadows stood. "If there's nothing else to discuss," he said, "I say we adjourn this meeting."

"Mary Bernadette?" It was Leonard, his voice low.

"Oh," she said, shaking her head. "Yes. That will be fine."

"All right," Leonard said tightly. "Meeting adjourned."

Mary Bernadette retreated to her office and closed the door behind her. She couldn't bear to talk to anyone right then. Her self-control was enormous, but it, like everything else in the world, had its limits. God forbid a kind word from a fellow sympathetic board member—or a critical word from an unsympathetic one—might damage her defenses and force her to exhibit a regrettable show of emotion. Mary Bernadette break down in tears or lash out in anger? She would never be able to hold her head up in Oliver's Well again.

Something Mary Bernadette's mother used to say came to her mind then, as she straightened the blotter on her desk. "There's no heat like the heat of shame." Mary Grace Lehane had been right.

CHAPTER 38

Megan, Pat, and the twins had come down for the weekend, arriving in Oliver's Well at six-thirty that evening, setting back Mary Bernadette's preferred dinnertime by an hour. Megan had expected a reprimand or at least a critical comment, but her mother-in-law had said nothing at all about the matter.

The twins had gone off after dinner to the ice-cream shop in town with instructions not to get double scoops or extra sprinkles on their cones. Now, plates cleared, it was the six adult members of the family around the kitchen table. Megan would be the first to admit that her mother-in-law was an excellent cook, if her repertoire was a bit limited. But tonight the chicken had been dry and the mashed potatoes a bit sticky. She would never dream of pointing out these flaws, of course, and especially not this evening. Clearly, Wynston Meadows's proposed review of the awarding of the contract for the Joseph J. Stoker House had been a great shock to Mary Bernadette.

Her mother-in-law brought a pot of coffee to the table. She poured a cup for everyone, leaving herself until last. She took one sip and pushed her cup away.

"I simply can't believe that he's behaving in such an appalling manner." Mary Bernadette shook her head. "It's an outrage."

Megan hoped that her husband wouldn't say, "We told you so." When it came to his mother, he could be unnecessarily combative, even at times childish.

"Well," Pat said. "I'm not at all surprised."

"What do you mean?" Mary Bernadette demanded.

"I see the move for what it is—a political action on the part of a man who has to be in control of every little aspect of his life. You didn't really expect someone like Wynston Meadows to will-ingly take a backseat to a bunch of midlevel professionals, did you? Shopkeepers, housewives, and a retired police chief?"

"Pat," Megan said quietly but with an unmistakable note of warning.

"Did anyone even think to interview the man before accepting him to the board?" Pat asked. "Don't you have an interview procedure in place?"

Mary Bernadette smoothed a nonexistent wrinkle on her dress. "Wynston Meadows is not the sort of man you interview. He and I had a conversation."

Pat snorted. "Just as I thought."

Megan shot him a look of warning this time.

"Well," Paddy said, "what's done is done. But I do think what the man is implying is an affront to the family's honor."

"As do I," Mary Bernadette added. "He didn't come right out and accuse us of manipulating the board's vote, but he implied as much. God knows the man probably thinks we bribed our way to getting the job!"

Megan wasn't so sure that Wynston Meadows had implied any such thing. Mary Bernadette had been known to exaggerate and to jump to conclusions. "I'd suggest a wait-and-see attitude for the moment," she said. "And remember, what Meadows is asking for *is* within his rights as a board member, even if he went about it in a heavy-handed way."

Mary Bernadette shook her head. "Nonsense."

"Does he think I don't know how to run the business?" PJ looked to his grandfather. "Maybe I should confront Meadows man to man," he said. "See what this is really all about."

"Bad idea," Pat said.

"But—"

"Consider your grandmother," Paddy warned. "She has to work with the man. Just go along with the investigation, or the reconsideration, whatever he's calling it. After all, you won the job fair and square. You have nothing to hide."

Megan nodded in agreement, wondered why more people didn't listen to Paddy Fitzgibbon, and then answered her own question. Because all too often he couldn't get a word in edgewise, not when his wife was around.

"Of course we have nothing to hide," PJ said vehemently. "But even the suggestion of possible wrongdoing can infect people's good opinion of us. It's that old 'where there's smoke there's fire' idea. And let's face it, Grandpa, people *want* to believe the worst of others. It's human nature."

"Where did you get such a grim view of your fellow man?" Pat asked.

"PJ is right," Mary Bernadette said fiercely. "People love other people's misery. It's sad but true."

"No one will ever look at us in the same way again. It's like Meadows has infected us. He's planted a seed of suspicion."

Mary Bernadette nodded. "Misfortune follows fortune, inch by inch."

Pat sighed. "No one is going to listen to his nonsense. Everyone in Oliver's Well knows that the Fitzgibbon family is beyond reproach. Anyway, Mom, are you sure you're not imagining him accusing you of dastardly deeds? Maybe this reconsideration has nothing at all to do with you personally."

"I most certainly am not imagining it!" Mary Bernadette shook her head. "A man with loud talk makes truth itself seem folly."

Pat shared a look with Megan. "I think," he said, "that the doom and gloom attitude should stop right here."

"Hey," PJ said excitedly, as if an idea had just occurred to him. "Meadows can't start the search over again if I've already signed the contract. Right? I'll go to the lawyers first thing tomorrow morning and demand they get to work."

Megan looked down at her hands, folded on the table. Pat cleared his throat. "I'm afraid that's wishful thinking, son," he said. *Wishful and naïve*, Megan thought.

"Well, I guess there's no chance now of Fitzgibbon Landscaping getting Meadows's personal business," PJ said bitterly. "He'll probably hire that sophisticated Blue Sound Landscaping Design."

Alexis had been silent until then, alternately flipping through a home decorating magazine and a copy of the Oliver's Well *Gazette*. Now she looked up and said, "Did anyone see the review in today's paper about that new movie starring Jude Law? It sounds really great."

No one answered her question. Megan wasn't sure if anyone but she had even heard it asked. Within a moment the conversation about Meadows had resumed.

Alexis sighed, got up from the table, and left the kitchen. Again, no one but Megan seemed to notice her absence. It struck her as slightly peculiar that her daughter-in-law hadn't exhibited any interest in the conversation; in fact, she had seemed entirely unconcerned over what most of the other members of the Fitzgibbon family in the room were considering a crisis.

"So, what do we do now?" PJ asked.

"We forbear," Mary Bernadette intoned. "We endure the trials set before us."

Megan raised her eyebrows at her husband in warning.

"What you do now," Pat said, looking sternly from his mother to his son, "is go along with the reconsideration Meadows suggested like the professional people that you are."

CHAPTER 39

Mary Bernadette contemplated the arrangement of Sweet Williams on the credenza in the dining room. Her hands were folded before her, almost in an attitude of prayer. Her thoughts were fifty-three years in the past. It was on a bright April morning much like this one that she had discovered that she was pregnant with her first child.

She could still remember leaving the doctor's office, overcome with a happiness she had never known existed. She had been brimming with laughter (indeed, it had been difficult not to indulge in it) and goodwill and lightheartedness. "I am going to be a mother," she had whispered to the world, hardly able to believe her good fortune. And then in the front yard of the house adjacent to the doctor's she had spotted a bunch of Sweet Williams, and in that instant she knew beyond a shadow of a doubt that the child she was carrying was a boy. Her dreams had been answered. He would be named William after her father and brother. She had rushed home, eager to tell Paddy the good news, though she knew he wouldn't be home from the factory until evening. When he finally did arrive, she threw herself into his arms and with a flood of grateful tears told him that he would soon be a father. His joy had been almost as great as hers.

When Mary Bernadette was seven months pregnant they bought the house on Honeysuckle Lane, and she began her garden by planting Sweet Williams. She read in the seed catalogue that the delicate clusters of flowers in combinations of red and pink and white had long been a symbol of gallantry and fidelity, appropriate she thought to describe the Williams in her life. Later, after her son's early death, she had no doubt that he would have grown to display those virtues as well as many fine others. Consider the way in which he had so joyfully greeted her each morning when she came into his room, his smile wide and his eyes bright, his arms outstretched in welcome. Consider the way in which he had taken to kissing both of her cheeks each night before bed, first the right and then the left. Consider how very early on he had learned to share his toys with other children. Mary Bernadette put her hand to her heart. After all these years she could still feel the silkiness of his hair. She could still smell the sweetness of his skin after his bath. She could still feel the warm pressure of him asleep against her chest. She could still hear his voice saying "Mama."

Mary Bernadette moved the vase of flowers to the left a fraction of an inch so that it was in the exact center of the cloth beneath it. Carefully she wiped a drop of water from its side. In and of itself the vase was not worth more than the money she had paid for it. It was the fact that she took it out of her bedroom closet only for this one important occasion—to mark the anniversary of that glorious day when she learned she was with child—that gave it great value. In truth, it was the second vase to display her Sweet Williams. Pat had broken the first one when he was eleven. Mary Bernadette had been so very angry with him and had punished him accordingly. For three weeks he hadn't been allowed to see his friends after school, or to attend softball practice, or to watch television. She had taken him to see Father Murphy, who had given the boy a stern lecture on the Fifth Commandment. Pat was made to write, "Thou shalt honor thy father and mother" one thousand times and deliver it to Father Murphy the following Sunday.

Pat had been bewildered by his mother's severe response to the destruction of what he saw only as a "stupid old vase." But she had told him time and again not to throw his football around in the house. And time and again he had disobeyed her orders. The broken vase was the last straw. Paddy attempted to talk her into lessening the boy's punishment, but she had walked out of the room even as he was speaking.

To this day Mary Bernadette was ever so slightly embarrassed about the severity of her reaction to her son's misbehavior. Still, she had never apologized to the boy or, later, to the man. It would have required more courage (yes, she could admit that) than she had been—or was now—able to muster. It would have taken her too close to the subject of William, and she had made a solemn vow never to mention him to either of her surviving children.

With a final glance at the perfectly arranged flowers, Mary Bernadette went up to her bedroom. She opened the bottom drawer of her dresser and looked down at a small wooden box nestled among the neatly folded cotton cardigans.

It had all happened so quickly. One day William had come down with a cough. A week later, his breathing had become labored and a sudden high fever would not break. The family doctor urged Mary Bernadette and Paddy to take the child to the emergency room. They did. William was admitted immediately. And three days later he was dead.

She had been with her son when he died, and even if she lived to be one hundred years old she would never, ever forget the sheer horror that had overtaken her in that stale and murderous place. When the time had come for her to leave William, she had raged. It was the one and only time Mary Bernadette had cried in public or, as her mother would have said, made a scene. Even at the funeral she had been silent, her grief so heavy she could barely stand upright but refusing to lean on Paddy's arm or to remain seated when the rest of the congregation stood.

In the weeks after the funeral she had wanted to die. She had once prayed to God to release her from this life, even though she knew it was a sin to want your life at an end. Hardest to bear were the sincere condolences she met with the few times she managed to leave the house. It took every ounce of will power not to shout, "Leave me alone!" at the long and pitying faces that seemed to be everywhere, pursuing her.

Jeannette had counseled patience. "Time will ease your suffering, Mary." Paddy had sworn to do whatever she asked of him that would help console her in her pain. She didn't hear either of them. While Paddy broke down and wept in Jeannette's arms—"I am losing my wife. I don't know what to do."—Mary Bernadette sat by the bedroom window and stared for hours on end.

And then she had discovered that she was pregnant; it had happened before William passed away. The grief intensified. The pregnancy seemed a cruel thing for God to visit upon her at this dark time. She had gone to Father Murphy in her despair.

"I can't go through this again," she told him through the grate of the confessional, her voice as fierce and desperate as her words, her hands clenched. "I can't."

"You have no choice, Mary Bernadette," Father Murphy had told her. "It is God's will that you bear another child."

Father Murphy told her that she must find consolation in her faith. He was stern in his admonitions. "This is no time for coddling," he said. "You have a duty to the God who made you. Think of what Our Lady suffered. Surely your pain is nothing compared to hers."

Duty. Above all, one did one's duty.

She was never entirely sure if it was for Paddy's sake that she had forced herself to rally, or if it was for the sake of the innocent child she was carrying, a child she didn't want. Or was it her strength of will that ultimately saw her through? Certainly, Father Murphy's stern counsel had helped her to accept the burden she had been given to bear. Maybe also it was dread of the shame that resulted from failing to keep up appearances. Mary Bernadette wanted the people of Oliver's Well to respect her and her family, not to whisper behind their hands. "There goes that crazy Mrs. Fitzgibbon. She fell to pieces when her baby died. They had to take the second one away from her. Her husband divorced her and moved away. She's all alone now, the poor thing."

But burying her grief and assuming the appearance of normalcy cost Mary Bernadette. It was a slow and arduous process. She had to learn how to live with an ever present and unfathomable loneliness. She had to learn how to distance her innermost self from everyone, even her beloved husband. She had to learn how to be alone. And over the years, through sheer determination, she had succeeded in rising to the position she held now, that of family matriarch and highly regarded citizen of Oliver's Well. A person who had not been felled by loss. A person who had triumphed over death.

Mary Bernadette lifted the wooden box from the drawer, opened it with the key hidden in the pocket of a cardigan, and took out a small stack of photographs. So few pictures of William; he had died long before the days when parents documented their child's every move on video and cell phones, long before the days when parents shared their child's every landmark and accomplishment on the Internet. Here was a photo taken on the day of William's baptism; his godparents, cousins of Paddy's who had gone back to Ireland shortly after, stood next to Father Murphy. Here was the infant William on his first Christmas. Here was a photo of William's first birthday the following December, sitting in Jeannette's lap, laughing and clutching a ball. William cuddled in

Mary Bernadette's arms on Easter Sunday. William and his father after mass on St. Patrick's Day.

His smile had been infectious. His cheeks had been plump and rosy. His eyes had been large and blue. No one could ever take his place. Which was why on a day a few months into her second pregnancy, with a fierce determination and without even a moment of hesitation Mary Bernadette had ruthlessly purged the house of William's things. She could no longer bear the sight of the fuzzy blue blanket and the plastic fire truck and the canvas sneakers. She couldn't stand the thought of her second child wearing his brother's clothing or playing with his brother's toys. She removed his pictures from their frames and locked them away, hiding the key. Paddy had come home from work that evening to find the crib and stroller dismantled and a stack of boxes, sealed and labeled, waiting to be picked up by a representative of Catholic Charities. He had not protested his wife's actions. Only Jeannette had voiced a concern that Mary Bernadette's decision to remove all traces of William from sight was not the best way to mourn. "I'm afraid it will make things worse for you," she had said. "I wish you would reconsider." Mary Bernadette had given her friend a choice. Accede to her request not to mention her dead son's name to anyone ever again or consider the relationship over. Jeannette had reluctantly agreed.

The only personal effect of William's Mary Bernadette had kept was the cross his godparents had given him at his baptism. She took it out of the box now and kissed it. And then she put everything back into the box, locked it, and put it away.

Later that afternoon Jeannette came by with a banana bread still warm from the oven. "I made two loaves," she said. "Too much for just Danny and me."

"Thank you," Mary Bernadette said.

Jeannette gently touched the blooms in the vase. "So many years."

"And it still seems like yesterday."

"I'm sorry for that, Mary."

"We all have a burden to carry."

"Yes. And some burdens are heavier than others."

"My mother and father taught my brother and me that it was wrong to dwell on your troubles. They often told us that we should look to God when trials came upon us and get on with the life He gave us to endure."

Jeannette sighed. "That's all well and good as far as it goes, Mary. But I don't think that God would deny any of his children the comfort of tears."

Self-indulgence, Mary Bernadette thought. The time for tears had long since passed. She turned away now and cleared her throat. "I got a nice fresh chicken at the farmers' market this morning," she said. "I thought I'd roast it for dinner. It's one of Paddy's favorites, as you know. We can have the banana bread with it."

"Then I'll be on my way and let you get started. Good-bye, Mary."

"Good-bye, Jeannette."

CHAPTER 40

The light was perfect, and Alexis had already spent a very pleasant hour taking pictures of some of the more interesting old buildings along Main Street. At the moment she was standing in front of a lovely old building, on the ground floor of which a storefront bore a sign that read THE SHELBY GALLERY. (She had seen the sign before, of course, but had never ventured inside.) Alexis raised her camera to her eye and adjusted the focus. Suddenly the door opened and a man emerged from the gallery. Alexis lowered the camera.

"Hi," he said, coming forward and extending a hand. "I don't think we've met. I'm Morgan Shelby. This is my gallery. And my building, in fact."

"I'm Alexis," she replied, shaking his hand. "I'm sorry. Do you object to my taking a picture? It's just for me, not publication."

"Not at all. It's a beautiful bit of midnineteenth-century architecture, isn't it? I live on the top floor. I've got a great view of nothing. No ugly factories or high-rise apartment buildings. It's one good reason to live here and not in some suburban development."

Alexis took quick stock of Morgan Shelby. He was not terribly tall, certainly shorter than PJ, and slender, with longish dark blond hair tucked behind his ears. His eyes were brown. He was dressed in dark blue jeans and a white button-down shirt, open at the collar with the sleeves rolled halfway to his elbows. *He's very nice looking*, Alexis thought.

"So, did you grow up in Oliver's Well?" she asked.

"Oh, no," Morgan said. "I came here about five years ago from Baltimore, partly to get away from my Important Old Maryland Family. I love them, it's just that . . . well, let's leave it at that. Anyway, it was a risk, opening a gallery at the tender age of thirty, and on borrowed money. But I had—I still have—a real love of what I do, and to be honest, I've had a lot of luck."

Alexis smiled. "So you're here to stay."

"As long as people keep wanting to buy up the past. So, what brings you to town?"

"I'm married to PJ Fitzgibbon. You know, of Fitzgibbon Landscaping."

"Of course. They do fantastic work. A mom-and-pop organization, isn't it?"

"Yes. PJ's grandparents own it, though someday PJ will inherit the business. He's running it now."

Morgan smiled. "All in the family."

That was putting it mildly, Alexis thought. "Kind of, yes," she said. "You weren't at Norma Campbell's party for Wynston Meadows, were you?"

"No. I was invited—all the shop owners were—but I have an aversion to anything even remotely political. Inevitably, at a shindig like that, someone is going to ask your opinion on a town matter and you'll be in trouble no matter what you say, even 'I have no opinion at all.' Well, especially if you say that."

"No one asked me my opinion about anything to do with Oliver's Well," Alexis admitted. "No one asked me anything at all, come to think of it. Oh, except, how happy was I to be working for Fitzgibbon Landscaping."

"And what did you say to that?"

"Oh, I said that I was very happy. That was the expected answer."

"Was it the honest answer?" Morgan asked.

"Oh, yes, of course," she said quickly.

Morgan pointed to her camera. "Is that a Nikon D90?"

"Yes, it is. You know cameras?"

"A little. I'm always taking photos of interesting items I find in my travels—old furniture, artwork, that sort of thing. They give me a reference for research and that helps me decide whether I want to offer for the pieces."

"Do you travel a lot hunting out things for the gallery?" Alexis asked. She thought it sounded like fun, poking through people's attics for old lace dresses, or sifting through a collector's accumulation of antique salt and pepper shakers.

"A fair amount," Morgan said. "At the moment I'm pretty much fully stocked, so I really should sell some big items before I go out and spend more money."

"Oh," Alexis said. "Right."

"You know," Morgan said now, "there's a guy over in Westminster who restores and sells old cameras and equipment. His name is Bud Humphries, and his shop is called Shutterbug. Mention my name if you go in," Morgan said. "I can't promise he'll give you a discount, but he'll definitely give you his full attention."

"Thanks," Alexis said. "I appreciate the lead."

"No problem. Well, I should get back inside. There's always an armoire to polish."

Alexis laughed. "I guess I should get going, too. It was nice meeting you."

Morgan nodded. "I'm sure I'll see you around town."

He went back inside his shop and Alexis continued on along Main Street. *That was fun*, she thought. *What a nice guy.*

CHAPTER 41

Mary Bernadette was on her way to a meeting of the board of the OWHA. She had dressed with more than her usual care and attention to detail, even fastening an elaborate, rarely worn gold brooch to her dress. She would not allow anyone to see that she had been shaken by what had happened.

And what had happened was this. The Oliver's Well *Gazette* had run a story that morning about the OWHA's decision to revisit the selection of Fitzgibbon Landscaping for the Joseph J. Stoker House project. The writer of the article had speculated on the "interesting coincidence" of Mary Bernadette Fitzgibbon, the most senior member of the board, being in fact co-owner of the very landscaping firm that had been awarded this most recent and lucrative project. "While some are calling foul," she had written, "not everyone would agree that there is indeed a problem." The reporter had approached members of the board as well as other "respected citizens" for their opinions on the matter. Those interviewed had wished to remain anonymous.

"Everyone knows everything that goes on in this town," a man had told the reporter. "So I can guarantee that if there was a stink, we would have smelled it before now. The fact is that Mary Bernadette Fitzgibbon is the heart and soul of the OWHA. Nobody's done more to further that organization, and the Fitzgibbon outfit does outstanding work. Why shouldn't the OWHA hire them? What's the board supposed to do, hire someone from out of town who nobody knows?"

Indeed, Mary Bernadette had thought.

A woman went on record as saying, "When local people aren't allowed to work for our own historical society, then something's badly wrong. I say the Fitzgibbons have never been anything but good for this town."

Then why, Mary Bernadette had wondered, *had this woman not wanted her name mentioned?*

Another helpful resident of Oliver's Well had this to say: "Oh, the Fitzgibbon family has had things all tied up now for I don't know how long. It really is remarkable how they always get the most important contracts in Oliver's Well. Luck, I guess. Some people have all of it."

Luck, Mary Bernadette had thought, *has nothing to do with our success.*

Finally, yet another "worthy of the community" had commented: "They're a fine family and it's a fine landscaping business. Why would I lie?" Implying, Mary Bernadette had thought, that lying about the Fitzgibbons' collective character was indeed a possibility.

The reporter had concluded her piece with this line. "Further review of the OWHA contracts and board decisions is expected."

"They're making a mountain out of a molehill," Paddy had stated, tossing the paper onto the table and almost upsetting the sugar bowl. "It's wrong."

The mere hint of a scandal can blacken a good name. . . . Mary Bernadette pulled into her parking space at the Wilson House and gathered her dignity along with her handbag. But it was no use in pretending to herself that she was in full possession of her usual strong sense of purpose.

Mary Bernadette took her seat at the oval table. Wallace wouldn't meet her eye. Joyce displayed an almost manic friendliness, asking after Paddy and his "adorable puppy" as if she could possibly care. Leonard whispered in her ear, "I'd like to teach some people a lesson about loyalty and respect." Anne gently put her hand on Mary Bernadette's arm as she walked to her seat. Norma's expression was blank. Neal's expression was grim. Richard looked supremely uncomfortable, and Jeannette looked close to tears.

Finally, Wynston Meadows joined them. He took a seat and, without a greeting, he said, "I'm assuming we all read the article in this morning's paper."

There were murmurs of assent from around the table, but no one voiced a remark.

He turned to Mary Bernadette. "I know this might be unpleasant for you, Mrs. Fitzgibbon, but I assume that with all of your experience with the media as well as your many years on this board you're quite able to separate personal from professional concerns." Wynston Meadows looked carefully now at each member in turn. "As anyone on this board should be capable of doing."

Mary Bernadette gave a slight bow of her head. "Of course. And to that end—assuming this reconsideration of the Stoker project is going ahead—I hereby recuse myself from participation in the process and final vote."

"A wise move, Mrs. Fitzgibbon, as the reconsideration is most definitely going ahead. Leonard, Neal, whoever, can you get me a copy of the original request for bids? I'll need to study it and make corrections to the job description. If we're not clear upfront, the bids won't mean a thing."

The meeting continued with Mary Bernadette barely aware of the proceedings that Wynston Meadows was directing. Finally, after what seemed an interminable time, he called the meeting to an end. The other board members began to rise. Wallace stood up and knocked over his chair in the process. With much apologizing and flustering, he set it upright.

"No harm done," he said too loudly.

No one else seemed to pay attention to Wallace's mishap, but Mary Bernadette's heart constricted. It was an Irish superstition that a chair falling over when someone rose from it was an unlucky omen. Her own aunt Catherine had passed away only days after a neighbor had knocked over her chair after having come by for tea. Mary Bernadette hadn't thought of the incident in years, but now it sent a shiver through her.

"Mary Bernadette?"

She looked up to see Leonard standing by her side.

"Are you all right?" he asked. "You looked a million miles away."

Mary Bernadette rose carefully from her own chair. "Perfectly fine, Leonard," she said. "I'm perfectly fine."

CHAPTER 42

Mary Bernadette wondered what was taking the girl so long to answer the doorbell. She pressed it again. After what seemed like another inordinately long period of time, Alexis opened the door to the cottage.

"Oh," she said, rubbing her eyes with one hand. "Sorry. I was taking a nap."

In Mary Bernadette's opinion, naps were only for the very young and the very old. A healthy young woman should not be wasting precious hours lolling about in bed.

"Did you come by for a reason?" Alexis asked after she had closed the door. "I mean, can I help you with anything?"

Mary Bernadette smiled. "No, dear. I just stopped in to see how you were doing."

"Oh," Alexis said. "I'm fine."

Mary Bernadette glanced around the living room, and her eye fell on Alexis and PJ's formal wedding portrait, sitting on the mantel of the small fireplace. She was very glad she had been able to persuade Alexis to wear something modest. Alexis had first chosen a gown that was absolutely inappropriate for church. For that matter, Mary Bernadette couldn't imagine anyplace where it *would* be appropriate, although maybe there were night-clubs in Las Vegas where such a costume might be welcome. The neckline was so low as to be downright indecent, and the dress was cut so narrowly that it left very little to the imagination. Mary Bernadette shuddered at the memory of it.

"It looks very nice in here," she said now to her grandson's wife.

The girl is a good housekeeper, Mary Bernadette thought. *I'll give her that.* (As for being a good cook, well, Mary Bernadette wished Alexis would give up all those foreign spices she was so fond of using. They couldn't be good for anyone's stomach.) The bath-room was always spotless, and in general the cottage always had the look of having been "picked up" recently. Mary Bernadette's eye now roved toward the living room windows.

"What do you plan to use for spring and summer curtains?" she asked.

Alexis, who had been standing with her arms folded across her chest (rather defensively, Mary Bernadette thought), shrugged. "I hadn't thought about it," she said.

"Well, I think it's time that you do." Mary Bernadette walked over to one of the windows. "These are too heavy for the hot weather." She peered closely at the curtains, ones she herself had chosen. "Besides, they need a good washing. Just think about all the dirt you're breathing in. It's a miracle the two of you haven't been ill."

"Oh," Alexis said, still standing where she had been. "I'll take them to the dry cleaners as soon as I have the time."

"The dry cleaners! No, the dry cleaners are too expensive. You can wash these in my machine. See, the tag says machine wash-able."

"Fine."

"But then you'll need to put up a lightweight set. Maybe a pale green linen."

"I didn't change the curtains last year," Alexis argued. "Why do I have to change them now?"

Mary Bernadette sighed. Sometimes she thought she was the only one who cared about maintaining order in the Fitzgibbon family. "Well," she said, fingering the curtains, "if I had known . . . It looks as if I'll be the one providing the summer replacements since you don't seem to care. I'm sure I can find something decent in my linen closet. Or maybe at the fabric store in Smithstown."

"Mary Bernadette, please!"

"Yes, dear?"

"Look," Alexis said, finally unfolding her arms. "I don't want to use curtains at all. The blinds alone are fine."

"Blinds without curtains look cheap. Just look at the Burrows' house across the street if you don't believe me."

Alexis sighed. "Fine," she said. "Have it your way. You always do in the end." Then she retrieved her keys from a bowl on the kitchen counter and went to the door. "I'm going out for a while."

Mary Bernadette stood alone in the cottage, and for a strange, disconcerting moment she wondered what she had been doing there. She felt vaguely foolish. She had won her point with her grandson's wife, but the victory didn't feel at all like a victory should feel. She had won a ridiculous push-and-pull argument better suited for ten-year-olds than for adults.

She left the cottage, locking it with her own key, and returned to her own home.

CHAPTER 43

"I'm afraid we let a viper into our nest, Mary." Jeannette, sitting across the kitchen table from her friend, shook her head and sighed.

We have made a deal with the Devil, Mary Bernadette thought. She was deeply ashamed of her weakness. She had fallen prey to Wynston Meadows's charm. He had seduced her with flattery, and she had taken pride in his praise. He had tricked her into thinking that he considered her an equal when it was clear that he considered her of no importance whatsoever. She was beginning to suspect that he considered Oliver's Well equally insignificant.

"The man is running the meetings and making decisions as if he was the chairman or the CEO. Not that you or Leonard would ever act so high-handedly. It's deplorable, Mary, it really is."

"Yes," she said. "Deplorable." And she was the one who had brought this man into the fold.

"Nothing is going as we expected it to," Jeannette went on.

Her friend was right. Leonard had informed them that Meadows was being maddeningly vague about when he would be ready to make good on the first installment of his pledge. "In due time, he told me," Leonard complained. "What does that mean when we have business to conduct?" At the last meeting of the board Neal had pointed out that the Branley Estate was still on the market and the object of their fondest hopes. To which Meadows had replied, "I don't see any other buyer knocking on the door of the old place. Patience."

Jeannette poured more tea into their cups. "I guess it's no time to bring up funding for another film about the OWHA."

"I wouldn't think so," Mary Bernadette said. She raised her cup to her lips but put it down untouched.

"Did you see Joyce making eyes at the man? A more ridiculous sight I've never seen. And a married mother at that! Those girls of hers are already trouble. Imagine what they'll be like when they're teenagers, with Joyce for a role model."

"Yes," Mary Bernadette replied. "Imagine."

"And with the Stoker job stalled for who knows how long . . . well, I'm worried, Mary, and I don't mind telling you."

Mary Bernadette straightened her shoulders. "We'll see our way right, Jeannette," she said. "I have no doubt of that."

"Will we, Mary? Do you really think so?"

"Yes," Mary Bernadette lied. "I do think so. Would you like another scone?"

CHAPTER 44

The bell over the door tinkled loudly as Alexis entered the pricey little gift shop called the Billet Doux. Since she was small she had had a weakness for beautiful pens. No matter that she used a keyboard to write just about everything but a grocery list; there was something about a high-quality, well-designed pen that attracted her. By now she had amassed quite a collection—Cross and Montblanc and Waterman and Rosetta—but there was always one more to buy.

There was only one other customer in the shop, a woman Alexis recognized vaguely, and she was talking to the owner, who was stationed behind the counter. Neither woman acknowledged her entrance. *They must be sharing some pretty exciting gossip*, Alexis thought, *not to have been distracted by that bell*.

Alexis went directly to the shop's display of pens, vaguely aware of the low rise and fall of the women's voices.

". . . Mary Bernadette never did . . ."

Those words caught Alexis's full attention. She wasn't in the habit of eavesdropping but realized that she wouldn't mind over-hearing some juicy tidbit of gossip about PJ's formidable grand-mother.

". . . said it was all because of William."

In an attempt to hear more, Alexis took a few sideways steps closer to the women—and knocked into a stand of designer read-ing glasses. A few pairs of glasses fell to the floor, creating enough of a clatter for the women finally to realize they were not alone.

The customer—a woman Alexis now fully recognized from church, Susanna something or other—whirled around and the owner of the shop put her hand to her mouth.

"Sorry," Alexis said, her cheeks flaming.

"Oh, no worries." The owner hurried out from behind the counter and began to retrieve the fallen eyewear.

"I'd best be going now, Nance," Susanna said, walking rapidly toward the door.

William, Alexis thought, bending to help retrieve the spilled reading glasses. Could he have been Mary Bernadette's illicit lover? The idea made her cringe. If there was one person in the world she simply could *not* imagine having a lover, illicit or not, it was Mary Bernadette! How the woman had managed to conceive was a question for the ages.

"Do you need help finding anything?" the owner of the shop asked now, order restored.

"Oh," Alexis said. "No. I'll just take . . ." She looked down at the pen she held in her hand. It wasn't really the one she had wanted—she didn't like the particular shade of green on the shell—but she was embarrassed to have caused a fuss and wanted to be on her way. "I'll take this," she said.

Alexis made her purchase and left the Billet Doux behind. Standing outside the shop was a young couple about her age wearing ripped jeans, T-shirts, and rough boots. The guy sud-denly put his hand on the woman's waist, pulled her close, and kissed her. *They* probably weren't tied down to boring, dead-end jobs, Alexis thought. *They* probably didn't have to spend their entire social life with a suffocating family that obsessed about entirely trivial things like summer curtains and work-appropriate clothes and not being late to church.

Alexis walked on down Main Street. She hadn't mentioned to PJ the fight she had had with Mary Bernadette about the stupid curtains. Why should she have? All he seemed to care about these days was the evil Wynston Meadows. Really, she had never met a bunch of people who could blow a situation so wildly out of proportion! And their obsession with the trivial! She imagined that when Pat and Megan were home in Annapolis, they talked about all sorts of interesting things like the latest exhibit at the National Gallery or what was happening in a war-torn African country, but when they visited Oliver's Well, even her intelligent, well-educated in-laws seemed only able to endlessly hash and rehash the minutia of local gossip. It was enough to drive you mad, Alexis thought. Not that anyone really cared about what she thought. Okay, she knew she was being a bit self-pitying, but if you didn't pity yourself at times, who else would? Clutching the little shopping bag containing the pen she hadn't really wanted, Alexis continued on to her car.

CHAPTER 45

Alexis was making a savory version of a sweet breakfast dish called a "pannekoeken." No doubt Mary Bernadette would be appalled by the notion of what was essentially a pancake for dinner. Alexis had heard her say that the idea of cold pizza for breakfast was an abomination. Thankfully, PJ hadn't inherited his grandmother's ridiculously narrow culinary prejudices.

PJ was at the kitchen table reviewing plans for a garden he was helping to design with a guy from the landscaping department at the Home Depot over in Westminster.

"Who's William?" she asked, turning from the stove.

"What?" PJ's head shot up from his work.

"Who's William?"

PJ's expression became suspicious. "How do you know about him?" he asked.

Alexis laughed. "I don't! That's why I'm asking. I was in the Billet Doux today, and the woman behind the counter was chatting with a customer and I heard one of them say 'Mary Bernadette' and then something else I couldn't make out, and then something like, 'It was all because of William.' Then they saw me and stopped talking. I figured they had been talking about your grandmother because how many other women named Mary Bernadette do you know? And they clearly didn't want me to hear what they were saying."

PJ sighed and pushed aside the drawings. "I guess I'll have to tell you," he said. "Before my father was born my grandmother had a son. His name was William. He died when he was eighteen months old."

Alexis put her hand over her heart. "Oh, how sad!"

"It was pneumonia."

"The poor little thing!"

"Poor Grandmother."

"Of course. And poor Paddy, too." Alexis went to the table and sat next to her husband. "But why didn't you tell me before now?"

"It wasn't my secret to tell."

Alexis felt a bit stung. She didn't like being excluded from the knowledge of something that was obviously an important event in the family's history. "I don't understand," she said finally. "William isn't really a secret if those women in town know about him."

"They shouldn't have been talking about something that happened over fifty years ago."

Alexis didn't agree. She thought that the death of a child was significant enough to be talked about for one hundred years, but what she said was, "Who else knows?"

PJ shrugged. "Anyone who lived in Oliver's Well when William died, I guess. The Klines, for one. And my dad and my aunt found out from my grandfather at some point. Don't ask me how, because I don't know."

"So, is Mary Bernadette aware that Pat and Grace know about William?"

"I have no idea. Grandmother never talks about William, Alexis. Not even to my grandfather, at least according to my father. You have to promise never, ever to mention the baby to her. Or to anyone else, for that matter."

Alexis thought about this bit of information. It was as if Mary Bernadette was pretending to the world that the death—and the life?—had never happened. It didn't seem a very healthy thing to do. It seemed rather a very good way to keep alive and raw a grief that might by now have been alleviated. *If* that was what Mary Bernadette was doing, and of course Alexis couldn't be sure.

"Ali?"

"Sorry," she said. "I was just thinking. Of course I won't say anything. It must be so painful for her though, suffering alone all these years."

"My grandmother wants it that way. She knows what's best for her."

"So, how did *you* find out then?"

PJ frowned. "My father told me when I was in high school. I don't know why, really. I can't believe my grandmother would want me to know."

"So she's never mentioned William to *you*, either?"

"No. I told you, she doesn't talk about him to anyone."

"But why all the—mystery?"

"It's the way Grandmother wanted it. The way she still wants it."

"PJ?" Alexis put her hand over her husband's. "Why didn't you tell me? I mean, I'm your wife. Don't you trust me?"

"Of course I trust you, Ali. But like I said before, it's not my secret to tell."

"But you told me now."

"Only so that you wouldn't go around asking other people about William. If word got back to Grandmother that someone in her own family was talking about . . . well, she'd be devastated."

Alexis took her hand away from PJ's. "Do you really think I'm the sort of person to do something so—so callous?"

"No. Of course not. Sorry, this has taken me by surprise."

"Do your brother and sister know?"

PJ sighed. "Probably. Dad can't seem to keep his mouth shut about it."

"Maybe he wants his children to know so that they can—" Alexis cut herself off. She had been about to say "so that they can understand why she is the way she is."

PJ abruptly got up from the table. "Ali, can we drop this please? I don't feel right discussing Grandmother like this."

"Yes," she said. "All right."

"Thanks. I'll be right back. I want to check something in the garage."

When he had gone, Alexis went back to preparing dinner, but her mind was not on her task. Instead, she was now haunted by the idea of the poor dead child his own mother would not acknowledge to the world.

CHAPTER 46

Mary Bernadette glanced at her watch. It was ten minutes to three in the afternoon. Neal had called her earlier, asking if he could stop by that afternoon. He had sounded upset but

wouldn't give her a hint as to what was on his mind. Mary Bernadette, however, had a very good idea as to the nature of what was
bothering her friend and fellow board member.

He arrived promptly at three (Mary Bernadette had always admired his strict punctuality). He wore a pained expression. She
invited him in and offered him tea, but he declined any refresh-
ments.

"I'm sorry, Mary Bernadette," Neal said, when they were
seated in the living room. "I have something rather upsetting to
tell you. I debated telling you at all, but Gregory convinced me
that it was better you knew."

Mary Bernadette folded her hands in her lap. "Go ahead,
Neal."

Neal sighed. "All right. Wynston Meadows came to the gallery
yesterday, just as I was closing up. I assumed he was there to
browse, so I let him in. Imagine my surprise when he informed
me that his real reason for stopping by was to talk to me about
the OWHA—and the next thing I knew he was complaining
about the fact that you hadn't gone to college!"

Just as I suspected, Mary Bernadette said to her self. *Wynston
Meadows.* "I fail to see his point," she said calmly, though her
heart had begun to beat heavily.

"So did I! I *still* do. Anyway, he . . . God, this is awful, Mary
Bernadette. But he said he thought your lack of a formal education rendered you unable to fully grasp the nuances of the business aspects of the OWHA."

Mary Bernadette sat very still. It was a rare thing for her to be
at a loss for words, but at a loss she was.

"I defended you, Mary Bernadette," Neal told her. "I told him
that what he was saying was poppycock. I enumerated your many
victories on behalf of the OWHA. I told him that we had never
had a better guiding spirit. I told him that you were an excellent
public spokesperson, and we had the clippings file to prove it.
But he seemed entirely—well, entirely unconcerned. As if he'd
already convinced himself of a truth and that was that. No evidence to the contrary was going to sway him. When I had fin-

ished speaking he just—he just *grinned* and left. I have to say it was a very disconcerting experience."

"Yes," Mary Bernadette said now, rousing herself with some effort. "It must have been disquieting."

Neal leaned forward. "I'm going to quit the board, Mary Bernadette," he said. "In protest against his behavior toward you and also for my own sanity. I know he was responsible for the way that article in the Oliver's Well *Gazette* was written. It's hard not to think he paid someone on the editorial staff to give it such a nasty, insinuating slant. And I know he means to award the Stoker job to his friend. No, I don't like being in the same room with that man. And I'm not at all sure that *you* should stay where you are, for the sake of your own peace of mind."

Mary Bernadette swallowed against a lump that had come to her throat. She was touched that a fellow board member was willing to make a sacrifice for her sake. It was gratifying to know that she was appreciated. But at the same time, she felt badly about the fact that she was—however unintentionally—the cause of Neal's distress.

"I am going nowhere," she said finally, "and neither, I think, should you, Neal—certainly not on my behalf. The OWHA needs a man of your intelligence and integrity. I can't force you not to resign, but I can ask you quite seriously to reconsider."

Neal sighed and leaned back in his chair. "All right. If you're brave enough to stay, then I'll stay as well. I just wish that man would go back to where he came from. Though I can't imagine anyone wanting him *there*, either. Well, I've taken up enough of your time, Mary Bernadette."

Neal took his leave then, with a warm handshake and an encouraging smile. When he had gone, Mary Bernadette sat on the couch and allowed herself to lean against its back. She felt humiliated by this completely unnecessary delving into her personal past. She had never lied about not having gone to college, and of course she wasn't the least bit ashamed about it. Still, her lack of a degree was not something she had ever chosen to mention.

And why should she have? She felt certain that she was better read than most people in Oliver's Well. She believed that her opinions were generally well informed, and if at the same time as she viewed the world in a rational manner she also maintained a certain belief in the more mystical or fantastical aspects of her Catholicism, she did not find the two incompatible. Greater minds than hers had found truth in this paradox.

Besides, she wasn't the only other member of the board not to have graduated college. Jeannette had never attended; Richard Armstrong had quit halfway through ("too lazy," he had told Mary Bernadette with a shrug); and as for Norma, Mary was vague on all aspects of her past. For all anyone knew she could be a high school dropout.

But for a reason Mary Bernadette simply could not fathom, Wynston Meadows cared only about *her*, Mary Bernadette Fitzgibbon of Honeysuckle Lane. Only *her* qualifications, or lack thereof, seemed to matter to him. What *was* his game? Why had he gone to Neal with his complaint—if not because he knew that Neal, her friend, would come to her with the tale? Was the man really so eager to hurt and abuse her? But to what *end*? It was all intensely frustrating.

Mary Bernadette got up from the couch and went into the kitchen. She was not looking forward to telling Paddy about this further humiliation—Paddy hadn't gone to college, either, and it certainly hadn't held him back!—but she was not in the habit of keeping secrets from her husband.

In an attempt to tear her mind from thoughts of the inscrutable Wynston Meadows, Mary Bernadette sorted through the day's mail. There was a bill from the electric company; that would be paid immediately. There was an announcement of a public meeting to discuss the possibility of expanding the high school's gymnasium. Mary Bernadette didn't know enough about the proposed expansion or about the existing state of the gymnasium to have an opinion on the project. She made a mental note to attend the meeting. And there was an envelope from the committee behind Oliver's Well Annual Private Summer Garden

Contest. Mary Bernadette opened the envelope, knowing that inside she would find an entry form. She had participated in the contest for the past twenty years and had won first prize four times and had twice come in third. Now she stared down at the entry form and remembered Eve Hennessy's nasty suspicion that she had used her connection with her husband's landscaping business to cheat.

A wave of fear swept through Mary Bernadette. Bolstered by the smear campaign Wynston Meadows seemed to be mounting against the Fitzgibbon family, would Eve Hennessy find fresh reason to point a finger of accusation? Would she confront Mary Bernadette personally, or complain to the committee behind the contest that there was a cheater in their midst? *Am I to be the victim of yet another act of public and entirely undeserved humiliation?* Mary Bernadette asked herself.

Nonsense. Mary Bernadette straightened her shoulders and forcibly dismissed those worries from her mind. And then she tore the entry form in half. The contest really was an awful lot of trouble—never mind the twenty-five dollar entry fee—and for what? A piece of paper in a cheap wooden frame. She would skip the contest this year. She would not miss it at all.

CHAPTER 47

In the hearing of everyone seated at the bar at The Angry Squire, Wynston Meadows had told the bartender—"in all confidence"—that he had been shocked to learn that Mary Bernadette, the self-proclaimed face of the OWHA, had not gone to college. "As I was saying just the other day to Neal Hyatt," he had gone on, "I just don't see how a woman with virtually no formal education can properly understand the workings of a complicated organization like the OWHA. No wonder the board has a history of making bad decisions."

Within a matter of hours, word of the event had reached PJ Fitzgibbon, who had immediately gone to his grandmother. She told him that Neal had come to her after his encounter with Wynston Meadows; she told him that Neal had wanted to quit the board in support of his friend but that she had not allowed him to make the sacrifice. When Megan had called her son that morning, PJ had related all to her in turn.

And Megan had related all to her husband.

"Life in a small town." Pat snorted. "Sickening. Don't people have anything better to do than pass along the nonsense they hear over a beer?"

"Not only small towns," Megan said. "Any sort of community is prone to dissension. Infighting. Backstabbing. It's human nature, I'm afraid."

"Now you sound like my mother. Doom and gloom."

"Be that as it may," Megan said, "it really was a low blow. College wasn't an option for your mother at the time. Or for your father, for that matter. And if she chose not to get a degree later on, that's her business. Besides, there are plenty of morons walking around with college degrees."

"You don't need to defend my mother's intelligence to me, Meg. But you're right. Meadows's argument is ridiculous. Do you know how many billionaires never finished college? Too many to count."

"Do you think that Meadows is persecuting the Fitzgibbons just for the heck of it? Could he find it a sport of sorts? Do you think he's mentally unbalanced?"

"I think he's a jerk. And who knows his real motivations. Maybe he does get a perverse kick out of harassing old ladies. But my money's still on some dubious business deal he's got cooking. Did I tell you what I found out the other day?"

"I don't think so. About Meadows?"

"Yeah. A buddy of mine was telling me that a few years back Meadows was involved in a nasty stink relating to a public taking of land later sold to a developer. And no coincidence, it was a developer with whom Meadows had a long and lucrative relationship. There were claims of bad faith dealing and corruption, but they never stuck and nothing ever came of it. No official charges were filed and no one made a court appearance, though you can be sure the lawyers for both sides were busy enough."

"It's appalling, isn't it, how some people have so little sense of accountability."

"And so little decency. Mark my words, Meadows's motives in stirring up the board of the OWHA are nefarious."

"Nefarious?" Meg laughed. "You make him sound like a comic book villain."

"Villains don't always wear masks and leggings. Most times they wear business suits. I just wish I knew what his motives were specifically. What's he after?"

"Power?"

"He's got plenty of that already. But I don't know, power is addictive. Maybe he can't get enough of it."

"Money?"

"Same argument. Some people just can't stop, even when they have more than their share."

"Did I tell you there was a claim of domestic abuse against him a few years back? A girlfriend barely out of her teens. Nothing came of that, either."

Pat frowned. "Why am I not surprised? No, this guy means trouble, you can be sure of it. And I'm not happy about my family being in the thick of it."

CHAPTER 48

Alexis was cooking dinner, but for a moment she couldn't say what it was she was preparing. Her thoughts had wandered off so completely that she had to take a step away from the stove top and stare hard at the pot in which a chicken was poaching and at the saucepan in which some greens were beginning to burn before she remembered that she was making a chicken salad with a side of kale. The experience was disorienting.

Alexis turned off the heat under the saucepan and rubbed her eyes. Earlier that day she had spotted Morgan Shelby on Main Street and had waved but he hadn't seen her and had gone into his gallery. An insignificant incident, but one about which she felt oddly upset. A *non*-incident. Unless Morgan really *had* seen her but had chosen to ignore her. But why would he do that?

She turned from the stove now, wooden spoon in hand. "I guess it's futile to suggest that we have Easter dinner anywhere but your grandparents' house," she said. It was the last thing she had expected to come out of her mouth.

PJ, sitting at the kitchen table leafing through a gardening catalog, smiled. "What brought that up? And where else *would* we go?"

"My parents' house?"

"But they're not Catholic," PJ said. "And you told me they don't celebrate Easter. Besides, it's a Fitzgibbon tradition to spend Easter all together."

"It's just that I was talking to my mother the other day, and she said that she misses me. My father, too."

That was a lie. Her parents had said no such thing. But she felt frustrated. She felt thwarted and ignored. She felt that she wanted to start a fight.

"Well, why not go and visit them for a few days?" PJ suggested. "You've been working hard. You deserve a break. Besides, Grandmother could fill in for you at the office. She knows every inch of the business backward and forward."

In other words, Alexis thought, *I wouldn't be missed at all.*

"What if we asked my parents to come here for Easter weekend?" she said. "They could stay at a B&B in town." In fact, she doubted they would want to come to Oliver's Well, but for the sake of argument . . .

PJ looked dubious. "I don't know, Alexis. Easter is pretty important to my family."

"Are you saying that my family isn't welcome here?" she asked angrily.

"No, of course not. It's just that Easter is the most important holiday in the religious calendar. And your parents don't even go to church."

"*Your* parents only go to church on holidays, and not even on all holidays!"

"And believe me, Grandmother is not happy about it." PJ sighed. "Look, Ali, if you really want to ask them down—"

"No," she said. "That's okay."

"I mean, I guess they wouldn't have to go to church with us."

"PJ, I said it's okay."

"Are you angry?"

"No," Alexis lied. "I'm fine." She turned back to the stove.

"Okay. Hey, how would you feel about a couple of azalea bushes out front? My grandmother loves azaleas, especially the white ones, and she could really use some cheering up."

CHAPTER 49

Mary Bernadette was sweeping the front hall of the Wilson House. The OWHA had a woman who came in twice a week to vacuum the carpets, dust and polish the woodwork, and clean the bathrooms. Twice a year a professional crew came to clean every windowpane, inside and out. And several of the board members, Mary Bernadette being one of them, took it upon themselves to maintain general order and cleanliness. Which was why Mary Bernadette could be found that morning with broom in hand.

"Just the woman I wanted to talk to!"

Mary Bernadette's head jerked up, and she put a hand to her heart. Wynston Meadows stood only a few feet in front of her. She hadn't heard him come through the front door. Could he already have been in the building, keeping out of sight and waiting for a moment to come upon her so abruptly?

Nonsense. "Good morning, Mr. Meadows," she said.

"Doing a bit of domestic work, I see."

Mary Bernadette made no reply. She wondered if he had come to harass her about her nonexistent college career. She thought of how he had singled out Neal. Now, he was here alone with her. Was he separating each member from the group to better create chaos? But to what end?

"I've been thinking about our educational program," Wynston Meadows said suddenly, taking a step closer to her.

Our educational program? Mary Bernadette stiffened. What made him assume ownership when he had had nothing to do with the inception and growth of the program?

"Yes," she said carefully. "It's something of which we are very proud."

Wynston Meadows shook his head as if with genuine regret. "Well, I was looking at the numbers, and I'm afraid the program just doesn't make fiscal sense. The money we spend on those *craft* classes and whatnot could be put to better use. For example, it could be put toward the purchase and restoration of the Branley Estate. Assuming we decide that we really do want it."

Mary Bernadette could not quite believe what she was hearing. Had Wynston Meadows lied when he told everyone that since he was a small boy visiting his grandfather's museum he had had a love for the work of historical societies? And of course the OWHA wanted the Branley Estate! They had wanted it for years!

"With all due respect to the *numbers*," she replied, "it's the responsibility of the OWHA to educate the public. Eliminating or even cutting back on our educational program would greatly diminish the importance and the usefulness of the OWHA. You know, our educational program *has* won regional recognition for its excellence."

"Regional?" Wynston smiled. Rather, he showed his teeth. "How nice. But I can't agree with you that eliminating the program would cause any significant loss of support or interest in our enterprise. Take that three-day summer camp. I believe you spearheaded the development of that? A serious waste of time and resources."

Mary Bernadette frowned. "The good people of Oliver's Well volunteer to work with the children. Our expenses are quite—"

"I haven't gotten where I am today by throwing my money away," he said, speaking over her.

And it is *his money now, isn't it? Even though we haven't seen a penny of it yet.* Mary Bernadette schooled her tone to remain calm and even. "My grandchildren," she said, "attended the camp two years in a row. They had a wonderful time. They learned much more from the hands-on experience than they could learn from a book only."

Wynston Meadows cocked his head and grinned. "Now, Mary Bernadette, are we confusing family interests and the interests of business again?"

"Of course not. I was just—"

Suddenly, Mary Bernadette couldn't go on. She was frightened being alone with Wynston Meadows. He was young and strong. And he was rude and bullying. The way he said her name struck her as far too familiar. Since when had he stopped referring to her as Mrs. Fitzgibbon? He was standing too close.

As if sensing her unease and enjoying it, Wynston Meadows reached out and laid his hand heavily on her shoulder. "Well," he said, "I'll bring it up to the others. I have no doubt at least a few of them—the smarter ones—will see things my way."

He withdrew his hand and, without a farewell, he left the Wilson House.

Mary Bernadette stood as if frozen to the spot in the hallway. She felt as if she had been violated. She felt sick to her stomach. Wrenching herself into action, she threw the broom to the floor and rushed to the bathroom.

CHAPTER 50

"Those are nice curtains," PJ said. "Are they new?"

Alexis, sitting at the kitchen table with her laptop and browsing an online catalog of photography equipment, gave the curtains a withering look. In truth, the curtains themselves were nice enough. It was the fact of their being in her windows that annoyed her. "Yes," she said. "They're new."

PJ frowned. "I'm not sure we should be spending money on things like curtains, not when the Stoker job is still up in the air."

"We didn't pay for them," Alexis told him. "Your grandmother bought them. And she put them up."

"You didn't help her?"

"I couldn't. She did it when I was at the office."

"She shouldn't be up on a ladder at her age."

"She's probably in better shape than any of us," Alexis countered.

"Still," PJ said, "you should have told her not to hang them."

Alexis laughed in frustration. "I didn't even know she was coming over! I asked you to tell her not to barge in when we're not here, but you didn't, did you?"

In answer, PJ turned away and began to sort through the pile of mail on the counter—left there, of course, by his grandmother.

Alexis closed her laptop. "PJ," she said, "really, something's got to change. I wish—PJ, look at me, please."

He turned to her, his expression guarded. "What?"

"I don't know. Sometimes I wish that we lived somewhere else or that—that things were different."

PJ's guarded expression now erupted into one of annoyance. "God, Ali, your timing is great, you know that? My family is being harassed. I've probably lost the Stoker project for good. My grandmother's character is being maligned. The last thing I need is you going on about being bored or whatever it is you're complaining about this time."

Alexis felt the color flood to her face. In all the years she had known him, PJ had never raised his voice with her. She wasn't afraid; she *was* shocked. "I'm not complaining," she said, fighting to keep her voice steady. "I'm just trying to have a discussion about our lives. And by the way, it's *my* family, too. I'm a Fitzgibbon now."

"Then you shouldn't be whining. Don't you know anything about family loyalty? It's the most important thing there is."

"More important than personal happiness and fulfillment?" she shot back.

"Yes."

"More important than world peace?"

PJ tossed the pile of envelopes he was holding onto the counter. Several envelopes slid to the floor. "Alexis, don't be ridiculous."

"I don't mean to be ridiculous!" she cried. "It's just . . . Can't you see that your grandmother doesn't want you to live your own life?"

"That's nonsense. I'm totally living my own life."

"Well, I'm not living mine," Alexis said. "PJ, I know you love your grandmother, but you have to see that she wants to mold us into the new Mary Bernadette and Paddy."

"Ali, you're hallucinating. She doesn't want any such thing. Seriously, where do you come up with this stuff?"

"She even chose my wedding gown! She wouldn't let me wear a strapless dress in church. Because of *her* I wore long sleeves."

PJ shook his head. "But you looked beautiful. Besides, that was over a year ago. Why didn't you say something then if you were so unhappy?"

"Because I—" *Because I was in love. Because I wanted to please you and that meant pleasing her.* So then, what had changed? *She* had changed. Her eyes had been opened. What she had taken for charming had proved, upon closer inspection, to be—primitive. Backward.

PJ sighed. "Look," he said. "I'm going out for a while."

"But we haven't finished talking!"

PJ grabbed his car keys from the counter and a baseball cap from a peg on the wall. "You might not have finished," he said, "but I have."

He let the door slam behind him. Alexis flinched.

Alexis felt badly that she had never acknowledged her friend Diane's anniversary card. She felt badly that she hadn't sent her an e-mail since before Christmas. Diane's e-mails were always full of news about their friends from college—who was dating someone new; who had broken up; who had gotten a promotion; who had gotten tickets to hear a popular band in concert. Alexis's e-mails were full of news about PJ's family and not much else. *Maybe that's why I've been remiss with my correspondence,* she thought now. *I have virtually nothing to say.*

Before she could change her mind she punched in Diane's number.

"Diane? It's me, Alexis."

"Hey, my long lost friend. You never answered my last e-mail. Or text, for that matter. And why aren't you on Facebook?"

"Sorry," she said. "How are you?"

Diane laughed. "Oh, just peachy. The guy I was seeing for the past four months just dumped me by text. I mean, how clichéd!"

"Oh," Alexis said. "I'm sorry."

"Yeah. Well, he wasn't such a treat, anyway. So, what's up with you?"

Alexis hesitated. This probably wasn't a good time to complain about her woes to Diane but . . . "Well," she said, "things are, I don't know, not great. Lately, PJ and I always seem to be fighting. And his grandmother is impossible. She acts like she owns the two of us. She's even made me dress like her at the office!"

"What does she dress like?" Diane asked.

"That's not the point," Alexis said a bit testily. "The point is . . . The point is that nothing's really what I thought it would be."

"Ha! When is it ever? Look, Ali, you have things really easy compared to a lot of us. I mean, you live in that adorable little cottage virtually rent-free. You have a job you didn't even have to apply for, and there's no way your family is ever going to fire you. Talk about job security!"

"But I don't own the cottage," she pointed out. "And the job is boring."

"And you have no mortgage and your health insurance will never be yanked away. And then there's the fact that PJ is a great guy. I think if I had a guy as charming and handsome as PJ Fitzgibbon to come home to every night I'd willingly live in a dump and work in a coal mine."

Once, Alexis thought, *I would have, too.* "You're right," she told Diane. "Sorry. I guess I'm just in a bad mood."

"Eat a pint of ice cream."

"It'll make me feel better?"

"No. It'll give you serious gas and that'll take your mind off your troubles."

Alexis knew that her friend expected her to laugh, and so she did. "I'll think about it," she said. "Bye, Diane. And thanks."

"Sure. And send an e-mail once in a while, okay? Let me know the *good* stuff that's happening in your life."

"Okay," she said. "I will."

Alexis ended the call and plugged her cell phone into its charger. Well, she thought, *that* had been a mistake. The next time she felt she needed to talk to someone about her marriage she would . . . she would what?

She would keep her mouth shut.

CHAPTER 51

Megan was at her desk, reviewing the most recent correspondence from David's doctors. In the past two years the spasticity of David's muscles had been forcing his legs to turn inward. He was the furthest thing from a complainer, but the pain had become so great that he had broken down in tears one afternoon. And then there was his mounting frustration when the in-toeing slowed him down or, worse, made it difficult for him to do something as simple as pick up a pen he had dropped on the floor. And then there had been that horrible kid in school who only the week before had mimicked David's awkward progress down the hall. It was only one episode, but one was enough.

As a family—Danica had been included in the conversations—they and David's medical team had decided that David would undergo a surgery that would help return his legs to a normal position. The procedure was called derotation osteotomy. It wasn't a particularly risky operation, but recovery could take some time, which was why it had been scheduled for summer. David was at a good age for the surgery, too; he was almost fully grown, and as a result the condition probably wouldn't return once it had been reversed. Until July twenty-third he would continue his exercises to the best of his ability, eat right (easier said than done with a twelve-year-old boy), and take a small but consistent dose of ibuprofen.

In his characteristic, laid-back fashion David considered the surgery—his first, except for when his tonsils were removed—as just another blip on his radar. His exact words were, "It's no big deal." Sometimes, Megan just didn't know from where he had sprung. Neither she nor Pat would be so nonplussed if they were facing the surgical knife. And his sister had admitted her fears just the night before in a cascade of hot tears. As for PJ, he, too, was a worrier, a true Fitzgibbon in that respect as in so many others.

Megan and Pat had decided to keep David's surgery from Mary Bernadette and Paddy for the time being. The older Fitzgibbons were upset enough about what was happening with Wynston Meadows. Upset, but not willing to let his machinations interfere with their upcoming Easter celebrations.

"You do so much for the family," Megan had told her mother-in-law over the phone. "The least I can do is make Easter dinner for you." Characteristically, Mary Bernadette had refused. "The day I can no longer cook a meal for my family is the day they lay me in the ground," she had said stiffly. Megan had known better than to argue; it was common knowledge that it was near impossible to soothe the proud. Well, Megan would insist on cleaning up after the dinner; if she enlisted the help of Alexis and the twins, the work would be done before Mary Bernadette could finish her protest.

Megan filed the latest correspondence from David's doctor. She would never, ever forget how excited she and Pat had been when they learned she was pregnant after so many years of trying and failing. They had not told either set of parents—or PJ—

about the decision to pursue in vitro fertilization. The doctor had been honest with them. "It might not work the first time," she had said. "It might not work at all."

But they had been extremely lucky. Megan *had* conceived on the first attempt. The pregnancy had been fairly easy, and it was thought that the delivery would be without incident. Danica had arrived first, howling up a storm. David's entry into the world had not been so easy.

From the very first, Megan had the distinct feeling that Mary Bernadette blamed her daughter-in-law for her grandson's misfortune. Megan had felt bad enough, wondering if somehow she might have been responsible for her son's cerebral palsy—in spite of the doctors reassurance that she was not to blame for the challenges her infant son would face—without having to endure her mother-in-law's silent but felt condemnation. The fact that Danica had come into the world without trauma had only served to create another layer of guilt and discomfort.

Pat, too, had experienced his own emotional trials. Bonding with his second son hadn't come easily (not uncommon, a doctor had assured them), and that had made him feel guilty and angry and remorseful all at once.

Trouble had visited anew when Pat announced to his parents that he and Megan had decided not to have the twins baptized. Paddy was too well mannered to openly protest his son and daughter-in-law's decision. Mary Bernadette had no such compunctions. "You're making a terrible mistake," she had declared. "Mark my words, there will be consequences for this lapse. There's no excuse for alienating your children from God." Really, what could you say to that?

Megan sighed. In keeping with her promise to visit the elder Fitzgibbons more often, she was going down to Oliver's Well for Palm Sunday weekend. The twins would stay home with Pat, who more than likely would *not* take them to church. At some point during her visit, Megan was sure Mary Bernadette would say, "I'm assuming my son and grandchildren aren't attending church tomorrow?" And Megan would respond with a neutral comment, something on the order of, "I really don't know what their plans are." To which her mother-in-law would reply, "And why *don't* you know their plans?"

Suddenly Megan experienced a wonderfully absurd vision. She saw Mary Bernadette standing before the pearly gates of Heaven.

"So," Saint Peter asked her in his booming and imperious voice, "what makes you think you're worthy of eternal life with God?"

And Mary Bernadette replied, in just as booming and imperious a voice, "And what makes you think that *you* are?"

CHAPTER 52

Megan was in Mary Bernadette's kitchen, wrestling with a craving for a grilled cheese sandwich while worrying about her son's marriage. She would have to have been blind and deaf not to pick up on the tension between PJ and Alexis at dinner the night before. PJ had pointed out that Alexis had failed to pick up a container of milk as he had asked her to. Alexis had replied that she assumed he was perfectly capable of buying a container of milk all by himself. Then she had pointed out that except for their honeymoon, PJ had never traveled. PJ had replied, somewhat stiffly, that the state of Virginia offered all that he could ever imagine wanting and that if Alexis was restless there was nothing stopping her from taking a plane to parts unknown. Well, maybe there was nothing to worry about. Maybe PJ and Alexis were simply experiencing the ordinary, absurd grumpiness that was so much a part of any marriage.

Oh, to heck with it, Megan thought, going to the fridge for the sliced American cheese her mother-in-law always kept on hand. She took the package of cheese to the counter and retrieved the loaf of bread from the breadbox. She reached up to the magnetic rack along which Mary Bernadette's knives were stored in order of size, and as she did so she saw, through the window over the sink, the cottage door open. PJ stood just inside. Alexis rushed out past him. PJ seemed to be calling her back. Alexis whipped around to face him, arms raised over her head. It was clear that they were shouting at each other. In a moment, PJ slammed the door, and Alexis turned and ran toward the house.

Megan put a hand to her heart. The pantomime had suggested such anger.

A moment later the back door flung open and Alexis came stomping in. When she saw her mother-in-law she stopped cold. "Oh," she said. "I didn't know anyone was here."

Megan forced herself to smile. "Just me."

"I saw Mary Bernadette and Paddy drive off earlier. I thought . . ."

"They had an appointment with the eye doctor. Mary Bernadette thinks Paddy needs a new prescription. I know, I know they're *his* eyes, but . . ."

"I left a library book in the living room. I just came to get it."

"Yes, I saw it on the coffee table. A biography of Julia Margaret Cameron. A photographer, wasn't she? Did you enjoy it?"

"It was okay," Alexis said.

Megan indicated the loaf of bread and the stack of sliced cheese on the cutting board. "I'm making myself a grilled cheese sandwich," she said. "Would you like one?"

"No, thanks."

"I know I shouldn't be eating this when I'm going to be having one of Mary Bernadette's calorie-laden meals later, but I'm in the grips of a craving."

Alexis smiled a bit. "I've been craving Twinkies lately. It's weird because I don't even like Twinkies. I never did. But I ate them when I was a kid because my best friend did."

"Maybe what you're really craving is your old friend," Megan suggested carefully. "Or your childhood, a simpler time."

Alexis looked at a spot on the wall above Megan's head. "I never thought of that."

"PJ used to like Twinkies. Once his grandmother saw him eating one at our house, and let me tell you, she was not amused."

"Because they were artificial?"

Megan gave Alexis what she hoped was a conspiratorial look. "Because they weren't made from scratch by his loving mother."

"Oh."

Megan turned away and busied herself with making her lunch. "How are you and PJ doing these days?" she asked.

"Fine," Alexis replied quickly. "Great."

She's a terrible liar, Megan thought. "That's good. Because the first year of marriage can be pretty difficult, no matter how much you care about each other." Megan turned back to her daughter-in-law. "I remember Pat and I having some real blowups. They meant nothing much in the end, but I remember feeling so upset at the time, like things would never get better."

Alexis cleared her throat. "Well, we've been married for *over* a year now, so . . ."

"Yes." Megan went over to the stove and turned on the gas beneath a large cast-iron skillet. "Still, there's so much to learn about a person once you've moved in together."

"I guess. But PJ and I already knew each other pretty well before we got married. I guess we're just lucky."

"Well," Megan said, "I'm glad."

"I really should get going. To the office."

"Do you often go to the office on a Saturday?" Megan asked.

"You know what Mary Bernadette says. The Devil finds work for idle hands."

Megan smiled. "Yes, she *does* say that."

Alexis turned toward the living room, and then turned back. "Do you think she really believes in the Devil?" she asked.

"I think," Megan answered, "that she believes in Evil, with a capital 'e.'"

Alexis nodded. "Enjoy your sandwich," she said as she went through to the living room. A moment later, Megan heard the front door open and shut.

After lunch, Megan placed a call to her husband in Annapolis. Briefly, she outlined the scene she had witnessed between their son and his wife.

"So," she said, "I tried to get Alexis to open up, but it was a complete failure. She clearly didn't want to talk to me about her personal life."

"Well, that's not surprising, is it?" Pat replied. "She probably sees you—and me—as the enemy."

"I wish she wouldn't."

"You know, I've often wondered if a girl like Alexis would tire of a guy like PJ. Don't get me wrong," Pat said. "I love my son. But his sights don't seem to be set very high. And from what we know, Alexis has had a lot more experience of the wider world."

"And yet, she chose PJ," Megan pointed out.

"True."

"Besides, I'm not sure how worldly she really is. She might have traveled a bit, but there's something naïve about her."

"Really?" Pat said. "I don't think I've ever paid enough attention to her to know that. That's terrible of me, isn't it?"

"Normal enough. Besides, we haven't known her for all that long. It might be different if we all lived in the same town and spent more time with each other."

"Speaking of living in different places, when are you coming home? I miss you."

"You mean, the twins are driving you crazy."

"That too."

"After church tomorrow," Megan told him. "It's Palm Sunday, remember."

"Oh. Right. You're a good woman, Meg."

Megan shrugged. "I kind of like playing a member of the idiot mob when the Passion is read aloud. I mean, in real life, when do you get to call out, 'Crucify him!' without being thrown in jail?"

"Meg! You had better not let my mother hear you say that! She'd brand you a heretic and inaugurate a new Inquisition."

"Don't worry." Megan laughed. "It's my own dirty little secret."

CHAPTER 53

PJ pulled into the parking lot in front of Fitzgibbon Landscaping headquarters. His grandfather—accompanied by Mercy—was just getting out of his car. Paddy had driven to the office on his own because in a little while he was headed to Westminster to visit a recently widowed friend.

Mary Bernadette had made some noise about God resting on the seventh day and couldn't it all wait until the morning, but his grandfather, in a rare show of opposition, had replied that winter came fast upon the lazy and that it was never a good idea to put off until tomorrow what you could accomplish today. Not even Mary Bernadette could argue with that reasoning.

Fitzgibbon Landscaping was located on the outskirts of Oliver's Well on a road that was also home to what had once been Danny's construction company, a lumber yard, a small brewery, and a bike repair shop. The company's headquarters included the small building that housed the office, a tiny kitchenette, and a bathroom for employees; a parking yard for clients and workers; and a barn-sized building for the storage of landscaping equipment.

Paddy unlocked the door of the office and Mercy bounded in ahead of them. "Two o'clock," Paddy said, looking at the clock over the reception desk. "I should be out of here by two-thirty if I'm going to get to Charlie's and then back home for dinner." He went over to an old metal filing cabinet to search for information on a client who was giving PJ a hard time. "The man was always a bother," Paddy had told his grandson. "Born mean."

PJ went over to his wife's desk, once his grandmother's, and sank into the ergonomic chair Alexis had ordered, with some opposition from Mary Bernadette, who didn't see why a plain, old-fashioned office chair wasn't good enough. PJ rubbed his eyes. His wife's unhappiness was wearing him out. When the Passion had been reenacted at Palm Sunday services that morning, she had only mumbled the words. She had been silent when the other members of the congregation had recited the Apostle's Creed, and by the end of the sermon she had shredded her palm stalks into tiny curling strips. At one point PJ had been sorely tempted to ask why she had bothered to come to church at all if she was going to act so disrespectfully. As if she just didn't care. And Alexis had always been someone who cared. She had always been so earnest in her emotional commitments. It was one of the first things about her that had attracted him so strongly. And now . . . now it seemed that Alexis was a million miles away from him.

His mother had been with them at church. Before she got into her car to head back to Annapolis she had taken him aside and reminded him that he could call her at any time. Then she had told him that she loved him. For one crazy moment PJ had wanted her to hug and comfort him like she had when he was little, before the twins had come along. But it was only for one crazy moment.

PJ looked at the framed photograph next to Alexis's computer. It had been taken on their honeymoon in the California wine country. They had been so very happy then. He wished he knew how things had gone so wrong so quickly. He wished he knew if he was somehow to blame, but try as he might he just couldn't see what he might have done to make Alexis so miserable. He loved his wife. He treated her well. He wouldn't dream of doing otherwise. Tears welled in PJ's eyes, and he lowered his head so that his grandfather wouldn't see his distress. When he had composed himself, he saw that Paddy was holding a folder stuffed with papers. Mercy was sniffing at the jar of candy in the reception area.

"Grandpa," he said, "can I ask you something?"

"Of course, though I can't guarantee I'll know the answer."

PJ smiled, as he was expected to do. "When you and Grandmother were first married, did you fight a lot?"

Paddy cleared his throat. "Oh," he said, with a wave of his hand, "I hardly remember. That was a long time ago, PJ, over fifty years now."

"Yes," PJ pressed, "but I'm sure you have some memories of those days. Back before you had kids."

"Well, that was before the business, too," his grandfather said. "Money was tight. I was working shifts at the old furniture factory in Somerstown and your grandmother was keeping house. She was a whiz at managing the budget. You'd have thought we were millionaires, the way she kept everything looking new and neat as a pin. And the meals she would cook could have put a professional chef to shame."

"Yes," PJ said. "I wish Alexis would . . ." He wasn't quite sure how to go on.

"Now, Alexis is a young woman. And young women these days have other things on their minds besides cleaning and cooking, as well they might."

"Oh, I know. It's just that sometimes I think she's just lost interest in—" *In me*, PJ said silently. *And I need her.*

"You two need a break," Paddy said heartily. "Why don't you take your lovely wife away for a few days? A change of scene will do you good. A breath of fresh air helps clear the head. I can handle things back here."

PJ shook his head. "Now's not the time, Grandpa. Not with Meadows making trouble. How would it look if I left town just when my family is under attack?"

"Your wife is worth the risk," his grandfather insisted. "Your marriage is worth any sacrifice. Consider it, PJ. Now, I should be on my way. And don't be late for dinner. You know what your grandmother is like."

PJ managed a smile. "Punctuality is a virtue."

Carrying the file pertaining to the grumpy client, Paddy left the office with Mercy trotting along behind him. PJ sighed. He didn't feel particularly enlightened by the conversation, but he supposed that he hadn't really expected to. Verbal communication wasn't a big strength of the Fitzgibbon men—or, of his grandmother, for that matter. Still, he knew that his grandfather loved him as much as he loved his own son, and that was a great comfort.

PJ turned on the computer to check the account of a client who claimed to have been billed incorrectly. Alexis was in charge of billing, and so far she had never made a mistake. But there was always first time, as Mary Bernadette often said. Suddenly, he realized that he hadn't told Alexis they were expected at his grandparents' house for dinner. She should have assumed the invitation; all holy days and holidays were celebrated at Mary Bernadette and Paddy's. PJ sighed. Then why did he anticipate another fight when he got home to the cottage?

CHAPTER 54

Alexis turned the car onto Travis Lane. It was a gloomy day, drizzling since dawn and not predicted to get any brighter. The weather fit her melancholy mood. *Am I melancholy*, she wondered. *Or am I simply depressed?*

Well, there was plenty to be depressed about; Alexis strongly suspected that her mother-in-law had witnessed that stupid argument on Saturday. It had all been so silly. PJ had done a load of laundry into which he had accidentally tossed one of Alexis's delicate bras. It had come out of the dryer in tatters. Alexis had demanded an apology. PJ had refused to give one. "You shouldn't have left it in the bathroom," he had said. "I just scooped up everything that was hanging on the towel racks." The argument had escalated to a screaming match, stopping short only of foul language and name-calling.

And only moments later Megan had been asking all those questions about their relationship. Alexis felt embarrassed that she had been seen fighting with her husband. But she also felt annoyed. She and PJ were *never, ever* alone. There was always a Fitzgibbon lurking, ready with criticism and commentary.

Well, that wasn't entirely fair. Her mother-in-law never criticized, but as much as Alexis liked and admired her, she simply couldn't trust Megan to be sympathetic. Megan was PJ's mother. She would be *expected* to take her son's side, even if she thought he was in the wrong.

Alexis parked her car in a municipal lot, opened her umbrella, and walked in the direction of Main Street. She had decided that she would stroll by Morgan Shelby's gallery, and if it was open, she thought she might pop in to say hello.

The gallery was open. Alexis went inside to find Morgan with a customer, a tall, thin woman in a tightly belted trench, fedora set at a rakish angle, and very high-heeled shoes. The stylish woman fairly screamed money. There was no mistaking the diamonds on her hands and in her ears for anything but the real thing.

While she waited for Morgan to be free, Alexis took a look around the gallery. Though there were probably hundreds of items for sale, the gallery was very orderly. There was plenty of space around each large piece for a potential buyer to view all sides and angles. The lighting was perfect. The glass display cases were spotless. Alexis peered into one case and noted an engraved silver case for a lady's calling cards. *A more gracious time,* she thought. *Or, a more restricting time.*

Finally, the striking woman left and Morgan came over to Alexis.

"Sorry that took so long," he said.

"No problem."

"I think you brought me good luck. The woman who just left bought that dining table against the wall. And it's not an inexpensive piece."

Alexis smiled. "I doubt it was me who brought you luck," she said.

Morgan looked at his watch. It was clearly a vintage piece, and Alexis wondered if a woman had given it to him as a present. It hadn't occurred to her before that Morgan Shelby might be in a relationship. The notion slightly upset her, and she thought that maybe it had been a mistake to stop by the gallery. She was about to make an excuse to leave when Morgan preempted her.

"I was going to close up for lunch now," he said. "Why don't you stay? There's nothing too fascinating in my fridge at the moment, but I'm sure there's a yogurt or two."

Alexis hesitated, but only for a moment. "Sure," she said. "Why not?"

Morgan flipped the Open sign to Closed, locked the door to the gallery, and together they went up two steep and narrow flights of stairs to Morgan's top-floor apartment, where she found a veritable art studio rather than a normal apartment with couches and end tables and area rugs. In what might have been the living room there were three easels; a long worktable piled high with cans of paintbrushes, tubes of paint, and rags; several drop cloths covering the floor; and at least twenty-five canvases of various sizes, some blank, some showing evidence of charcoal sketching, others—mostly landscapes—seemingly finished.

"Just as I thought," Morgan called from the kitchen. "Two cartons of yogurt and some grapes and a bit of cheese. All right?"

Alexis joined him there. "Sure," she said. "So, let me guess. You paint."

Morgan laughed. "Yeah. I majored in painting as an undergraduate, not that it made me all that great of an artist, and then I went on to get a master's degree in American furniture from the Rhode Island School of Design."

"So . . . where *is* your furniture?"

Morgan laughed again. "Oh, it's normal enough in the bedroom and study. And as you can see, I do have a kitchen table."

"I majored in art history," Alexis told him, taking a seat at that
table on which Morgan had laid out their meager meal. "Nothing
very specialized because it was only undergraduate."

"So, if you went on to specialize, what area or period would
you choose?"

Alexis had to think about that question; the answer was not
readily to hand and that embarrassed her. "Maybe the Italian Re-
naissance," she finally said. "Or Cubism. I also like Vermeer a
lot." She laughed a bit nervously. "I guess I never really gave
much thought to specializing." *Or,* she realized, *to what really matters to me.*

"You're young," Morgan said. "You have time. Blueberry or
raspberry?"

"Raspberry, please. So why haven't you joined the Oliver's
Well Historical Association? I mean, obviously you have a great
interest in history."

"I told you I'm not into politics, remember?" Morgan laughed,
sitting down across from her. "I'm a lover, not a fighter."

"But the OWHA is hardly politics."

He raised a brow. "Isn't it?"

Alexis suddenly felt naïve. Of course it was politics. Just look
at what was going on with Wynston Meadows, and all because of
his promised millions. "My husband's grandmother is always trying to get me involved," she said. "In fact, I'm doing this Day in
the Life of Oliver's Well project for her."

"What's that about?"

Alexis explained.

Morgan frowned. "I have to say, it sounds a bit deadly."

"Why?"

"In a small town like this one," Morgan explained, "so well
regulated, change, if it happens at all, happens in increments. A
shop owner like me can't even put a potted plant on the sidewalk
unless he goes to the OWHA first for approval. You could take a

photo a day of Main Street for a full ten years and barely see the tiniest bit of change."

"Well," Alexis said, "I have to admit it's not the most exciting project I could imagine. But Mary Bernadette asked me to take it on, so . . ."

"Not the most challenging task for someone of your talent, either."

"But how do you know I have any talent? You've never seen my pictures."

Morgan grinned. "I know what kind of a camera you use. Someone who doesn't take her work seriously—someone without talent—isn't going to waste time and money on a piece of equipment that requires so much skill and attention."

Alexis felt herself blush. "Oh. Anyway, I think that Mary Bernadette would really like me to devote *all* of my spare time to the OWHA."

"And you don't want to."

"No." Alexis smiled. "I guess because of *family* politics. Mary Bernadette can be pretty overwhelming. She's the undisputed president of the Fitzgibbon family."

"More like the dictator. Sorry, but I've heard stories. Everyone in Oliver's Well has."

"Well, she's not as bad as all that. Most times. She's just used to getting her own way." *And maybe that's why she's so upset about Wynston Meadows*, Alexis thought. *He's not letting her get her own way.*

"Sounds like one of my aunts. People like that can be pretty exhausting."

"Yeah," Alexis admitted. "But I try not to let her boss me around too much."

"Well, good for you for standing up to her. For standing up for *yourself*."

Alexis wondered if she really was standing up for herself, for what mattered to her, or if she was only being the stubborn child, resisting Mary Bernadette just to prove that she could. At least being recalcitrant got her noticed in the family, but was it the kind of notoriety she really wanted? And what progress was she making in developing her own life, apart from the Fitzgibbons? These thoughts made her feel uncomfortably young.

"You probably should be getting back downstairs," she said now to Morgan.

Morgan glanced at the small scale grandfather clock on a shelf over the stove. "You're right. Time flies when you're having fun."

They went down to the first floor of the building and into the gallery.

"Oh," Morgan said. "I almost forgot. There's a show of twentieth-century Japanese woodblock prints at a gallery in Somerstown. Would you like to go to see it with me some afternoon?"

Alexis felt her heart speed up and hoped she wasn't blushing again. She hated that her emotions showed so plainly on her face.

"I always feel as if I've neglected my education in the Asian arts," Morgan went on. "I mean, I took an overview course in college, but one survey class is hardly enough to give you any real insight or expertise. And the field is so large."

"Can I let you know in a day or two?" Alexis asked. "I have to check with . . . I mean, I have to look at my work schedule for the next week."

"Of course. We don't need tickets, and I can be pretty flexible. Just let me know."

"I will," Alexis promised. "And thanks again for lunch."

Morgan smiled. "And thanks again for bringing me good luck."

Alexis put her key into the lock only to find that the door to Fitzgibbon Landscaping was already open. She pushed it in and saw Mary Bernadette seated at the desk that had once been hers.

"Oh," she said, as she stowed her wet umbrella in its stand. She hadn't seen Mary Bernadette's car in the lot out front. Where had she parked?

Mary Bernadette rose from her chair. "How long have you been away from the office?" she asked.

Alexis shrugged. "Only about an hour. Maybe a little more.

I—I had some errands to run." In truth, she had been gone close to two hours.

"Well, it was lucky that I happened to stop by to take the calls you missed."

"Was there anything important?" Alexis asked. *Please don't let her ask exactly where I've been,* she prayed silently. Alexis was not a good liar. She had always been proud of this, but now she wished that lies rolled smoothly off her tongue.

"All calls are important, Alexis. This is a business we run, not a hobby."

"I know, but I thought it would be all right if the voice mail picked up. I can always return calls."

"That might be, but people want to hear a live human voice, not the recording of one."

"Sorry." Alexis was glad that she was wearing one of her office-appropriate outfits. At least Mary Bernadette couldn't scold her about her clothing.

Mary Bernadette sighed. "Well, no great harm done. But next time you're going to be out and about during business hours, be sure to let me know so that I can cover for you."

"Yes. I will."

Alexis figuratively held her breath until Mary Bernadette had gathered her things—handbag, rain hat, trench coat, and umbrella—and left the office of Fitzgibbon Landscaping. Then she sank into the chair Mary Bernadette had so recently occupied. What had she been doing stopping by the office? Had she expected to find Alexis stealing from petty cash or filching paper clips? Like she had nothing better to do than undermine the family business through a series of petty crimes!

Alexis put her hands on her lap and took a deep breath. She felt dangerously close to an anxiety attack. She hadn't had one since high school, when for a very brief time she had been bullied by another girl. But she remembered the symptoms well enough.

What is happening to me? When she considered that for the rest of her long life *this* would be her reality—to be an insignificant part of the Fitzgibbon machine, forced to live by their rules and on their schedule—she was filled with dread. This *couldn't* be all that there was to her existence. Alexis had never really believed that a special calling would suddenly raise her above the average person plodding through the years, but surely her life had to contain some bigger *meaning*, some better *purpose* than sitting in this unattractive little office, paying bills and assuring impatient clients that Fitzgibbon Landscaping would indeed finish the job on time. There had to be more to her life than sitting in Mary Bernadette's kitchen two or three nights a week, eating variations of the same dinner, going over the same boring topics—what the weather was doing, who in town was getting a divorce, how pretty much everything and everybody was better in "the old days." And once she and PJ had children she would be ever more tightly bound to the Fitzgibbon way.

Unless she put a stop to the monotonous forward motion of her so-called life. But being married to PJ Fitzgibbon, how would she go about doing that? Alexis put her head in her hands and took several slow, deep breaths. There *was* no putting a stop to the inevitable. It was hopeless.

CHAPTER 55

Unlike the rest of the house, Mary Bernadette and Paddy's bedroom was furnished simply, almost sparsely. There was a queen-size bed and two oak dressers. There was one closet. A crucifix hung on the wall above the bed. A cross she had fashioned from the palm stalks received at church on Palm Sunday was propped against the small mirror over her dresser. Everything was spotless and in its proper place. A messy bedroom had always seemed to Mary Bernadette a sign of a suspect character.

On top of her dresser sat a framed black-and-white photograph of her parents standing outside the family's little house in Cork, Ireland. Next to it was a photograph of Mary Bernadette and her brother, William, taken when they were about ten and fourteen, respectively. She looked intently at the faces of her family. They were all gone now, dead and buried if not forgotten.

Her wedding portrait stood on Paddy's dresser in a silver gilt frame Grace had given her one Mother's Day. She and Paddy had been married after knowing each other for only a few months. For Mary Bernadette, the union had been less of a love match— though she certainly did love the man—than a practical choice of a helpmate. Mary Bernadette had known from the start (in the way that reasonable women knew these things) that she could count on Paddy Fitzgibbon to be sober and hardworking, a good provider for the family with which she hoped to be blessed. Mary Bernadette had never been a silly sentimental girl, not like so many (especially, she thought, these days) who went traipsing into marriage on the most ridiculous of whims only to wind up in divorce court a mere few years later or, maybe worse, stuck spending the rest of their lives with an entirely unsuitable man who drank or who couldn't keep a job.

Not having the money for a wedding gown, Mary Bernadette had borrowed a dress from a neighbor named Florence Bainbridge. It was pale blue, a bit out of date, but quite pretty. Most important, it fit. Her bouquet was a simple collection of white chrysanthemums. Paddy, who had served in the Korean War, looked incredibly handsome in his dress uniform. They had no money for a ring, so they had simply done without. A year later they had been able to afford a simple gold band; Mary Bernadette wore it to this day.

The reception had been held in the church's community room. The food—coffee and sandwiches—was provided by Mary Bernadette herself; Florence Bainbridge; and a Mrs. Tracey, who was the housekeeper for Father Murphy and the other priests in the rectory. Mrs. Tracey had made the cake, too, a three-layered affair covered in white buttercream with pink buttercream flowers. Next to the day of William's birth, her wedding day counted as the happiest day of Mary Bernadette's life.

Yes, she had been very lucky to find Paddy Fitzgibbon, and very wise, too, to recognize such quality. How far they had come together. How much they had endured.

Mary Bernadette straightened the crucifix above the bed; it had a habit of tilting to the right. It was Holy Thursday. She and Paddy had gone to the service at four that afternoon, in commemoration of the Last Supper, the Passover feast at which Jesus had washed the feet of his disciples. She had given PJ permission to skip the service so that he could spend the afternoon and evening with his old high school friend Peter Costello, come back to Oliver's Well to spend Easter with his family. Her grandson had been working endless hours since Wynston Meadows had first cast aspersions on the honesty of Fitzgibbon Landscaping, and Mary Bernadette believed that he deserved some time off.

Alexis had said that she would come to the service on her own, but Mary Bernadette had not seen her in the church, nor had she spotted Alexis's car in the parking lot afterward. She had never thought she would live to see the day when so many members of her own family would treat their faith so lightly.

Mary Bernadette left the bedroom and headed down to the kitchen to start the dinner. Well, she thought, nothing was ever the same from year to year, though you could try to fool yourself into believing that it was. Things changed, and often not for the better. Just look at what was happening to her beloved OWHA. But God had not put His children here on earth to complain. He had put them here to work hard and to do good deeds. And the reward for good behavior was the greatest reward of all.

Still, Mary Bernadette Fitzgibbon thought, opening the fridge to retrieve the package of pork chops she was planning to serve her husband, there *were* times when the changes and the sorrows and the trials were very, very hard to bear.

CHAPTER 56

Alexis tossed the empty bag of potato chips into the recycling bin under the sink. She had eaten the entire bag in a matter of moments. She did not feel guilty about this. She was sorry there wasn't another bag of chips in the house.

April seventeenth. Holy Thursday. Alexis had not gone to the service that afternoon, though she had told Mary Bernadette that she would. If it was okay for PJ to miss the service so that he could spend time with an old high school friend (imagine his grandmother actually giving PJ, a grown man, *permission* to skip church!), it had to be okay for her to miss it, too.

Tomorrow, though, was another thing. The Good Friday service, commemorating the moment of Jesus's death, was a command performance. Alexis sighed. She wished that PJ's mother would be with them; her presence on Palm Sunday had made participation in the mass bearable, especially when the congregation had been forced to enact the Passion. It had almost made Alexis laugh, the vehemence with which her mild-tempered mother-in-law had uttered the words 'Crucify him!' as if she were truly a member of that ancient angry mob.

But tomorrow . . . well, she would simply have to endure the somber service as best she could. In the meantime she was glad to be alone at the cottage for a few hours. She hoped Mary Bernadette wouldn't take it into her head to pay a call. She supposed she could simply not answer the door if she knocked. But Mary Bernadette might come in, anyway. She had a key and she did not like to be ignored.

Alexis reached for her cell phone. Her mother loved her, and the love wasn't dependent on her going to church every Sunday morning or using curtains along with blinds or dressing a certain way at the office. Her love was unconditional.

"Hi, Mom," she said, when her mother answered. "It's me, Alexis."

"Given the fact that you're my only child," Olivia Trenouth replied, "you really don't have to identify yourself."

"Right. It's just something you say, I guess."

"How's life in little Oliver's Well?"

"Fine," Alexis said automatically. And then, "Well, not really all that good."

Her mother laughed lightly. "Why am I not surprised? Okay, what's going on?"

"It's PJ's grandmother. Mary Bernadette."

"Ah, the matriarch."

"She thinks she owns me," Alexis said, the words tumbling out. "Most times I don't feel like a member of the family. I feel like unpaid labor. It's like she sees me as this, this robot, with no interests of my own, just available for whatever little chore needs doing. And then, when I do her bidding, she criticizes the way I've done it. I'm so tired of apologizing to her!"

"Let me guess. She's pressed you into joining that Hysterical Society of hers?"

"It's not only that." Alexis shot a look toward the front door and lowered her voice. "She has no sense of boundaries. She comes into the cottage whenever she likes. She expects PJ and me to do whatever she asks without question. And PJ doesn't seem to notice that anything is wrong with her behavior. He thinks I'm just being whiney when I try to talk to him about it."

"I didn't like her at all, you know," Olivia Trenouth said. "At your wedding she acted like *she* was the rightful center of attention. The way she worked the room like she was a visiting dignitary. And that horrid gown she wore! If it had been a nun's habit she would have shown more skin!"

Alexis didn't reply to that. Honestly, she had found Mary Bernadette's taupe-colored column gown very sophisticated. And in a funny way it had actually complemented her own gown, which Mary Bernadette had chosen.

"Darling," her mother went on, "you have to stand up to her. Your father and I didn't raise you to have some old woman with a deluded sense of her own importance push you around. And the longer you put off taking a stand, the harder it's going to be."

Alexis sighed. "I know, but PJ adores her. He really does. And she's not *all* bad. I mean, she does let us live in the cottage almost rent-free."

"Well," her mother said, "I've given you my advice. I'm afraid you're on your own, Alexis."

"I know. Oh, Happy Easter."

"Is Easter this weekend? Well, good luck with all that."

"Thanks, Mom. Say hello to Dad for me."

Alexis plugged her cell phone into its charger and then went over to the desk and took out the manila envelope in which she kept a few informal photos from her wedding. She sorted through and found the one of her parents posing in the lobby of the charming B&B where they had stayed. Olivia and Lester Trenouth were a handsome couple; they looked almost as if they were brother and sister, so well matched were they.

Alexis went into the bedroom and tucked the photograph into the frame of the mirror on her dresser. And suddenly, she was overwhelmed by a wave of nostalgia. She missed the myriad sounds and the bright lights of the big, bustling city where she had been born and raised. She missed the wonderful smells of Philly's famous Italian market, and she missed the long Saturday afternoons she had spent at the Museum of Art with her mother. She missed the marked change of seasons, a true fall and winter following a true spring and summer. She remembered the first time she had gone to see the Liberty Bell at the statehouse. She remembered the fun she had had hanging out with friends in Rittenhouse Square. She remembered a school trip to the Edgar Allan Poe House. Most of all, she missed waking up in her old bed and knowing without a shadow of a doubt that she was loved just for being Alexis. So many happy memories from a time long before her marriage, a time when life was so very easy and innocent.

Alexis rubbed her forehead. She felt unutterably weary. She decided not to wait up for PJ. They would probably only get in a fight if she did. Instead, she went straight to bed and was asleep almost at once.

CHAPTER 57

The twentieth of April. Easter Sunday. Another year gone, Megan thought. Another family gathering to mark the passing.

They had been home from church for some time. Megan was sitting in the living room with Alexis, each of them flipping idly through a copy of *Better Homes and Gardens*. Mary Bernadette had retreated to the kitchen, and Paddy, Pat, and PJ had gone off to examine something in the garage. Megan hoped they didn't start fooling around with oil cans or dirty rags while wearing their Sunday best. Pat ruined at least two good dress shirts a year by forgetting that he wasn't wearing a T-shirt.

Megan glanced at her daughter-in-law. She was wearing a very pretty dress that had the look of something from The Sophisticated Lady, and her hair was, as always, meticulously groomed, but there were dark circles under her eyes and lines around her mouth that made Megan hope Alexis hadn't been losing weight. The girl didn't have any to spare.

Suddenly, Danica and David burst into the living room. "Something's wrong, Mom," Danica said.

"What do you mean?" Megan asked her daughter.

Danica lowered her voice to a loud whisper. "Grandma didn't make us Easter baskets."

"We *are* kind of too old for Easter baskets," David said.

"Yeah, maybe. But I don't know, it feels weird not to have one."

"Are you sure?" Megan asked her children. "I mean, maybe she's just saving them to bring out later."

Danica shook her head. "No way. She always does things exactly the same, every year. There are no baskets on the sideboard in the dining room. That means there are no baskets anywhere."

Megan had to admit that her daughter was probably right. "Well, your grandmother has a lot on her mind right now," she said. "She probably just didn't have the time." But her words didn't ring true. Mary Bernadette was the sort of woman who *made* the time she needed.

"Or," Alexis said, "maybe she just forgot."

Danica laughed. "Grandma never forgets anything!"

"Don't mention the baskets to her, okay?" Megan said.

"Sure." David frowned. "But I was really looking forward to a Cadbury Creme Egg."

"Ugh," Danica said. "I don't know how you can eat those things. They gross me out."

"Like those Peeps you eat aren't disgusting?"

Megan left Alexis with her battling twins and went into the dining room to confirm what she already knew she would find. No Easter baskets. There were, however, the three white Easter lilies Megan had brought. She had put them in a vase—*not* the vase used for William's flowers, of course. Even if she were cruel enough to want to use that particular vase, she wouldn't know where to find it. Mary Bernadette kept it safely tucked away somewhere, as she kept all things associated with the baby she had lost. The baby no one dared mention in her presence.

Megan would never forget the night Pat had told her his family's deep, dark secret. They had been engaged for a few months, and Megan had already spent enough time with her future mother-in-law to realize that it was going to require a good deal of energy to bear up under Mary Bernadette's formidable personality, as well as to survive her frequent critical comments and sometimes downright insulting remarks. She didn't know what had made Pat tell her about William that particular night, other than perhaps the fact that he had talked to his mother on the phone earlier that day and, in his own words, the conversation had not gone well. Pat had apologized for not having shared the fact of William's life and death before then. "It's just that I'm so used to secrecy," he had explained. "And now I'm so, so tired of it." Megan had forgiven him immediately. And she had thanked him for telling her the crucial piece of information that from that time forward had helped her to withstand the gale force that was Mary Bernadette—a woman still grieving for her lost son. It had explained so much. It had allowed Megan to feel a degree of sympathy for her mother-in-law.

Megan wandered back into the living room. It was empty now. Alexis and the twins must have gone off to join the men. Megan took a seat in one of the rather uncomfortable armchairs that stood like sentinels on either side of the rather uncomfortable couch. There was to be no slouching in Mary Bernadette's house. She had seen to that.

All day Megan had been plagued by a sense that something bad was hovering in the air above the family, waiting to swoop down and destroy the already tentative peace of the household. What she felt was what her mother, quoting her mother before her, called a "fairy blast," a sense of general sadness and impending doom.

Forcefully—if not entirely successfully—Megan shook off the feelings of imminent misery, got up from the armchair once again, and went into the kitchen to ask Mary Bernadette if she could help with the meal. And of course, she thought, Mary Bernadette would say no.

CHAPTER 58

Alexis sat on the extremely uncomfortable couch in the living room. Paddy, in one of the equally uncomfortable armchairs, was reading the Sunday paper. Her in-laws and the twins were nowhere to be found—it was interesting, Alexis noted, how people seemed to disappear for significant amounts of time while visiting Mary Bernadette—and her husband was in the kitchen with his grandmother. *He* never seemed to need a respite from Mary Bernadette Fitzgibbon.

Alexis sighed. If Paddy heard, he didn't acknowledge that he had. She had been taught that Easter was a joyous occasion, but Mary Bernadette had made it feel like anything *but*. She had made Danica change her dress—a perfectly modest garment in Alexis's opinion—before leaving the house on the pretext that it was too provocative. Alexis wondered if Danica even knew what the word meant. She had chastised Paddy for having forgotten to trim the hedges out front. "But I trimmed them just the other day," he had protested. "Well, they've grown since then," Mary Bernadette had snapped. And on the way into church that morning, she had made a comment about the majority of the congregation not having been to mass since the previous Christmas. Pat had frowned and stormed ahead of the rest of the family. Obviously, he had assumed that his mother was criticizing his own rare appearances. Alexis couldn't blame him for being angry. In all the time she had known the Fitzgibbons, not once had she heard Mary Bernadette pay her son a compliment. Half of the time she wasn't even particularly *nice* to him. If William had lived, Alexis wondered, would Mary Bernadette have been any kinder or more pleasant to Pat?

It must be exhausting, Alexis thought, to be a person like Mary Bernadette, always seeing the negative in things. It was so much *easier* to be accepting and uncritical. But if PJ's grandmother was *always* so harsh and unrelenting, why did so many people like her? Why was she so ridiculously popular in Oliver's Well? Was it only with her family that she was—difficult?

Alexis heard the sound of PJ's laughter from the kitchen. Mary Bernadette was making a roast lamb with mint jelly, mashed potatoes, green beans, and rolls. For dessert, she had made a cake decorated with white icing and a sprinkling of pink sugar. It was the meal she made every Easter Sunday, without fail. Unless, Alexis thought, remembering the missing Easter baskets, the family was in for another unexpected turn.

PJ came into the living room then and perched next to her on the edge of the couch.

"It was a nice service," Alexis said to him. It was a silly thing to say, but suddenly she felt shy with her husband.

"Why aren't you wearing your claddagh necklace?" he asked quietly. "The one I gave you for our wedding. The one for special occasions."

Alexis automatically put her hand to her chest, where she felt the distinctive outline of the Cross of St. Brigid. "Because," she said, "I'm wearing this."

"Oh." PJ glanced over at his grandfather, still absorbed in the paper.

"But *you* gave me this, too." Alexis laughed, not because she found anything amusing but because she felt frustrated and confused. "It's not like I'm wearing a necklace from another man!" she whispered.

The moment the words were out of her mouth she regretted them. It had been a stupid and hurtful thing to say. PJ's expression became as rigid as the couch on which they sat.

"I would hope not," he said coldly. Then he got up and went back to the kitchen.

Alexis put her hand to her head. All these stupid traditions and superstitions! How were you supposed to keep track of them all? Even the claddagh ring came with instructions on how to wear it, depending on your relationship status. She couldn't believe she had once thought all of this—she looked around the room and spotted the statue of St. Patrick—all of this *nonsense* was attractive and interesting.

Escape. That was what she needed. She got up from the couch. She was about to head for the front door when the twins appeared and announced that dinner was being put onto the table.

Paddy emerged from his newspaper. "Well, then," he said, "let's not keep your grandmother waiting."

CHAPTER 59

Mary Bernadette was putting the final touches on the gravy. She was tired. It had been a trying day. She had felt on edge since the moment she had opened her eyes that morning. So when Paddy had finished breakfast and gone upstairs to dress for church, Mary Bernadette had turned to the family Bible for spiritual support. She opened it at random to Psalm 139 and read the words carefully, with the sure knowledge that they were meant specifically for her comfort at that particular moment.

"Deliver me, O Lord, from the evil man; rescue me from the unjust man . . . Keep me, O Lord, from the hand of the wicked . . . Who have proposed to supplant my steps . . . Hear, O Lord, the voice of my supplication."

After mass, while driving home with Paddy at the wheel and PJ and Alexis in the back seat, Mary Bernadette had spotted Wynston Meadows strolling along Main Street in jeans and a T-shirt. Clearly, he was not coming from church. Resolutely she had turned her face away from the window. If the others had also seen the Fitzgibbons' enemy, the unjust man pursuing them, the deceitful man with the lying tongue, they hadn't said.

Now Mary Bernadette, with PJ's help, brought the large serving platter and bowls to the dining room. She was glad when everyone was finally seated at the table; it was that much closer to when she could close the door on the members of her family. Paddy said grace and the plates were passed around. She felt irritable throughout the meal. She found her husband's attempts to draw her into conversation annoying and condescending. She noted that PJ and Alexis were barely speaking to each other and that Megan was more than usually cheerful in an oddly determined sort of way. Pat had been in a bad mood all day, almost surly, and now he was shoveling food into his mouth as if it were his last meal on earth. At least the twins were acting decently, though once or twice Mary Bernadette had caught Danica giving her an odd look, almost as if the girl had something she wanted to say but couldn't. Indigestion, that's what it was, Mary Bernadette decided. The girl had probably eaten too much too quickly, a bad habit she had picked up from her father.

As soon as it was not rude to do so, Mary Bernadette rose from her seat. "If everyone is finished," she said, "I'll clear the table." If anyone wanted another helping of lamb or potatoes, they weren't saying. Good. She would hurry along dessert. For once Mary Bernadette was glad that her son and his family were driving back to Annapolis that evening. And if Megan tried to insist that she and the twins clean up after the meal, Mary Bernadette would simply not allow it.

CHAPTER 60

Alexis had made her decision. She would go to the gallery in Somerstown with Morgan Shelby. She had been unsure of her answer to his invitation for days, but the disaster that was

Easter Sunday had made her decision. Not even the delightful presence of the twins had helped to cheer her after that stupid encounter with PJ.

The very next day she had taken off the Cross of St. Brigid and put it into her jewelry box next to the claddagh necklace and the cross Mary Bernadette and Paddy had given her. And then she had put on a beach glass pendant her friend Diane had given her for her twentieth birthday. If PJ chose to comment on it, she would . . . well, she wasn't sure what she would say, and she didn't care. Not really.

Alexis tried to take a sip of her morning coffee, but her stomach was whirring with nerves and she put the cup back on the counter. "I'm going to need to take a day off work to see an art show in Smithstown," she said. "It's only there for another week." She hadn't meant to lie about the location of the show. But she had.

PJ took a sip of his coffee before saying, "Did you ask Grandmother for permission?"

Alexis bristled. "She's not my boss."

PJ laughed and put his empty cup in the sink. "Actually, she kind of is, Alexis. She and Grandpa do own the company. They do sign our paychecks."

"Fine," Alexis said. "I'll ask her permission. But I'm going no matter what she says. The office can do without me for a day. Besides, she's always checking up on me there. I'm sure she'd love an entire day alone to poke around looking for my mistakes."

"Ali, come on!"

"I have a life, too, PJ! I can't spend every moment of my day concentrating on Fitzgibbon Landscaping and the OWHA."

"I didn't say that you had to! Ali, don't put words into my mouth, okay? I'm on your side."

It certainly didn't feel like her husband was on her side. But all she said was, "Sorry."

"I've got to go or I'll be late to the Petretti job. And I've got a new guy starting today." He kissed her on the cheek and left the cottage.

The moment PJ was gone, Alexis reached for her cell phone. She had seen Mary Bernadette drive off about twenty minutes before; she was an early riser and often out and about on her chores before PJ and Alexis left for work. Paddy, too, had gone off that morning; he and Danny had volunteered to help Father Robert tend to the church grounds. The Fitzgibbon house was empty.

"Mary Bernadette," Alexis said to the voice mail. "This is Alexis. I'm going to be taking next Thursday off to attend to some personal business. I wanted to give you plenty of notice. Thanks."

Alexis hated herself for being so cowardly, but the thought of lying to Mary Bernadette's face—or, rather, the thought of telling her another half truth—was just too intimidating. Anyway, there was nothing *wrong* in leaving someone a message.

Just as there was nothing *wrong* in spending a few hours in broad daylight with a man who wasn't your husband.

CHAPTER 61

Every Thursday morning of her married life without fail, Mary Bernadette changed the sheets on all the beds in the house. Every Friday morning she did the laundry and vacuuming. On Saturdays, she dusted and polished. Routine and order were the keys to keeping a clean and comfortable home.

So it was that on this Thursday morning, Mary Bernadette carried a set of fresh sheets and pillowcases into the bedroom she shared with her husband. Banshee watched intently from the top of the dresser as she pulled the dirty sheets off the mattress and piled them against the wall, to be taken down to the washing machine in the basement.

The fresh sheets were on the mattress and neatly tucked beneath it when Mary Bernadette became aware of a dull pain in her lower back. It happened often lately, especially when she bent to retrieve something that Paddy had dropped or to clean Banshee's litter box. She sat on the edge of the bed to rest.

Easter baskets. Suddenly, Mary Bernadette realized that she had forgotten to make Easter baskets for the twins. She put her hand to her face. She was appalled by her forgetfulness. She was embarrassed by her display of carelessness. How could she not have remembered something so obvious, something so ubiquitous as Easter baskets?

No one had mentioned the missing baskets, but they must all have noticed their absence. Her family's silence was worse, she thought, than if they had teased her about her forgetfulness. It was probably Megan who had made sure that no one spoke. She was always so sensitive to other people's feelings. It annoyed Mary Bernadette sometimes, that scrupulous concern. She believed that it was better to be made to face one's faults than to be shielded from them. It was better to be made to correct one's mistakes and to atone for one's sins than to be coddled and kept in a state of ignorance.

Sensing her agitation, Banshee jumped from the top of the dresser and onto the bed by her side. Mary Bernadette stroked her sleek back. The cat began to purr.

What is becoming of me, she asked herself. She had faced bigger threats than Wynston Meadows in the course of her long life. She had met and conquered tougher challenges. Was it that she was simply too old for this battle? Or could it be that God was punishing her for having committed the sin of overweening pride, assuming a degree of importance in Oliver's Well she had never actually achieved?

The world was fickle. Mary Bernadette realized that she might have been permanently plucked from her place in the sun, condemned now to live out her days in a place of shadow and shame. And if that were the case, well, then so be it.

"Banshee, my love," she said to her feline companion, "I must finish making this bed."

Banshee leaped to the floor. Mary Bernadette got up more slowly and, resolutely banishing her troubles from her mind, she got back to her Thursday morning chores.

CHAPTER 62

Alexis was dressed in her best pair of dark skinny jeans, a new white T-shirt, and a fitted black blazer, an appropriate outfit she thought for an afternoon visit to an art gallery—and not an outfit she had bought at Anne's shop. She had taken extra care with her hair and makeup, not for the intention of attracting male attention—no, not even Morgan Shelby's—but for her own pleasure. It had been ages since she had been anywhere outside of Oliver's Well other than to a garden supply center in Waterville with PJ and his grandfather. Try as she might, she just couldn't get excited about backhoes and garden gnomes.

At 9:15 she got behind the wheel of her car and set off on her adventure. She couldn't remember when she had last experienced that delicious mix of guilt and excitement that accompanied doing something you knew that you shouldn't be doing. But why *shouldn't* she be going on a little excursion with a friend? There was nothing whatsoever wrong in that.

At exactly ten o'clock Alexis arrived at the gallery in Somerstown. Morgan was waiting for her, wearing slim black pants and a taupe linen shirt. Alexis thought he looked great.

"Punctual," he said, opening the door of the gallery for her.

Alexis smiled. "It's one of my many talents."

There were two categories of prints on display at the Foss Gallery. In the first room were Binjin prints. Each depicted a beautiful woman dressed in a traditional Japanese kimono. She was always alone, sometimes contemplating her image in a mirror, sometimes applying her makeup or giving herself a pedicure. At other times she was in a landscape. One of these, a portrayal of a woman in a veritable storm of cherry blossoms, particularly charmed Alexis.

"The colors are really amazing, aren't they?" Morgan said. "So luminous."

"Mmm. And the mood is so serene. They're just lovely."

In the second room were landscapes. These images were just as beautiful; they depicted specific sites in Japan—rivers and towns and monuments—at sunsets and sunrises, in rainstorms and in snow showers. Morgan was greatly taken with a print of a spectacular waterfall. "I'm overwhelmed by the sheer beauty in this room," he told Alexis. Her own appreciation was keen, but Alexis suspected that Morgan, having gone to graduate school, was seeing things she wasn't trained to see. As for the names of the artists—Ito Shinsui, Kawase Hasui, Natori Shunsen—she had no idea how to pronounce them and hoped Morgan wouldn't ask her to try. She didn't want to appear foolish.

When they had finished viewing the exhibition—and Morgan had been in no rush to leave the gallery—he suggested they have lunch. "I know this little place a few blocks away," he said. "They have great soups. Do you like soup?"

"Who doesn't?"

"My college roommate. He couldn't abide soup of any kind. Bisques, broths, cream of whatever. Hated them all."

Alexis laughed. "Maybe he was traumatized by a soup at an early age."

"Or maybe," Morgan said, "he was just weird."

When they were seated at the restaurant and had each been served a bowl of corn chowder, Morgan said, "Guess who came into the gallery the other day? The illustrious Mr. Meadows."

"Really? Did he buy anything?" Alexis asked. *Imagine*, she

thought, *having all his millions! I wonder if shopping would ever get boring?*

"He looked. And he asked me to keep an eye out for an armoire by Stephen Trevelyan. He was a famous cabinetmaker in the late eighteenth century."

"Are his works hard to find?" Alexis asked.

"One in good condition can be, but I'll try my sources."

"So, what was he like, one on one?"

Morgan frowned. "Perfectly pleasant. But I got the distinct feeling that it was a very practiced act. He's a crafty man, no doubt. I wouldn't want to tangle with him."

"I think he's met his match with Mary Bernadette," Alexis said with a laugh. "She's the most bossy, most stubborn person I've ever met."

"But she's never made millions managing a hedge fund, has she?" Morgan asked. "And she doesn't handle the OWHA's finances and properties. Leonard DeWitt does that. And everyone knows that she doesn't like to travel. When was the last time she went even fifty miles from Oliver's Well? Did she ever hold a paying job other than office manager of her husband's company? I think you overestimate her, Alexis. I'm not saying she's not an intelligent woman, but I am saying that this time she's in way over her head. I've heard what's being said about how Meadows has been acting with the board members, treating them like his minions."

This was a perspective Alexis had never considered. Maybe Mary Bernadette Fitzgibbon *didn't* have what it took to withstand someone like Wynston Meadows. Maybe he really could destroy all that she had built, if only for sport. In fact, Mary Bernadette hadn't even gone to college. How had this rather unworldly woman managed to assume so much control and influence over so many people? Had it all been through the force of her personality and the strength of her will? But Morgan was probably right. Not even Mary Bernadette's formidable self could triumph over a man like Wynston Meadows, who traveled the world to dine with dignitaries, was an important presence on Wall Street, and was rumored to be considering a run for a major public office.

"Alexis?"

"Oh," she said. "Sorry. I was just thinking about what you said."

"Yes, well, let's not spend any more time talking—or thinking—about the Fitzgibbon matriarch. Tell me more about you. I mean, the you that has nothing to do with the Fitzgibbons."

Was there such a person? Alexis wondered. "Oh," she answered nervously. "There's really not much to tell."

"Let me give you a challenge."

"Okay."

"The next time I see you, you have to tell me three true facts about yourself. And not things like where you grew up—where did you grow up, anyway?—but things like your dream vacation, your favorite book as a child, what character trait you like best about yourself."

Alexis smiled. "Philadelphia," she said. "And I accept your challenge."

After lunch Morgan walked her to her car.

"This has been a great day, Alexis," he said. "I'm so glad you could join me."

Alexis willed herself not to blush. "Me too," she said. "I mean, thanks for suggesting this."

Without hesitation or forethought—at least, on Alexis's part—they shared a brief hug, after which Morgan jogged off to where he had parked his car.

With a slightly trembling hand, Alexis unlocked her door and slid behind the wheel. For much of the journey back to Oliver's Well she was in a bit of a haze. She had not touched another man so intimately since her first date with PJ. The result was that she felt exhilarated. She felt powerful. She felt as if she had proved something. She did not ask herself what she had proved or to whom.

It was only when she finally reached Oliver's Well and turned onto Main Street with the intention of making a quick stop at the pharmacy that full consciousness returned, for there was Mary Bernadette behind the wheel of her Volvo, less than three car lengths behind her.

Alexis's heart began to race. *Darn it*, she thought. Could Mary Bernadette have followed her that morning as she left Oliver's Well? Could she have seen the hug she and Morgan had shared? Could she have trailed Alexis back to Oliver's Well, eager to accuse her of a sinful assignation?

Alexis glanced again at the rearview mirror. Mary Bernadette's Volvo was gone. For a moment Alexis wondered if she had imagined it. She pulled into the nearest parking space, shut off the engine, and put her hand over her racing heart. *Oh God*, she thought, *why did I lie to PJ? Why couldn't I have been honest and told him that I was going on an outing with Morgan Shelby?*

But the answer was obvious. It was because she considered her relationship with Morgan to be wrong. You didn't keep a totally platonic friendship a secret, because you didn't *have* to keep it a secret.

"I am a deceitful person," she said to the interior of her car.

Alexis didn't have the presence of mind to go into the pharmacy and make small talk with the locals. Not now. She started the car again and headed back to Honeysuckle Lane. She was painfully aware of the fact that she should never have gone to the gallery with Morgan Shelby—and just as painfully aware of the fact that if he asked to spend time with her again, she would say yes.

CHAPTER 63

Megan had been surfing through Netflix when Pat came into the living room and with a dramatic sigh tossed himself onto the couch. The springs groaned.

Megan turned off the television. "What?" she asked.

"Nothing."

"Pat."

"Did your parents ever keep secrets from you and your brother?" he asked.

"I'm sure they did. All parents do."

Pat shifted, and the couch springs squeaked. "I mean, big secrets. Like a dead sibling."

"What makes you ask such a question now?" Megan asked. "Have you been talking to your mother?"

"No. Just thinking. Well, actually," he said, sitting up and sending a series of metal squeals into the room. "I was reading a short story in the *New Yorker* the other day about a guy whose parents never told him that his paternal grandfather had been incarcerated for murder, and a pretty grisly one at that."

"Can you blame them?" Megan asked. "I'd want to keep a disturbing secret like that from my child."

Pat shrugged. "It got me thinking about my own family. You know, almost from the beginning I knew there was some deep, dark family secret. I knew it in the way kids just *know* things. Eventually, Grace caught on, too. When I was about sixteen— that would make Grace about eight—I decided to ask Dad what he and Mom were hiding."

Megan had heard this story many times before, but if telling it again was helpful to her husband, she would listen patiently. "Did you actually come right out and ask your father what they were *hiding*?" she asked, as if the story were new to her.

"I've never been subtle, Meg."

"Obviously."

"So my father told me about William. It cost him; even a dumb teenager like me could see that. But I was grateful for his honesty."

"And he asked you never to mention William to your mother."

"Right. You know, and I'm sure I've told you this before, that when my father told me that my mother had had a baby before me, it really wasn't a surprise. It was as if I had always known someone else had come first. That someone had precedence over me."

"Still, better the mystery be a lost sibling than a heinous crime."

Pat frowned. "I haven't always been sure about that."

"Pat. You're being melodramatic."

"I was thinking about this, too," he went on. "There was something my mother used to say to Grace and me when we were growing up. We'd fall and cut our knees, or someone at school would be picking on one of us, or we'd be going through one of those trials that seem insurmountable to a child. Instead of being sympathetic or comforting, my mother would say, 'Offer it up to God.' Offer your pain or your sorrow as a sacrifice to God. I mean, that's the equivalent of saying, 'Tough luck, kid' or 'Shut up and deal with it.'"

"Yes," Megan said. "It *is* a pretty harsh concept for a child to grasp. Trauma as a sacrifice."

"I remember once, I guess I was about twelve or thirteen, I'd been in a fight after school and she told me to 'offer it up to God,' and I came back with something like, 'Why would God want my bloody nose?'"

Megan laughed. "Oh, Pat, you didn't!"

"I most certainly did."

"And were you punished?"

"With extreme prejudice. No playing with my friends for two weeks, and I had to go to confession, and let me tell you, Father Murphy was not a guy to let you off lightly. I was kneeling at the altar saying Our Father's and Hail Mary's for hours."

Megan grimaced on his behalf. She recalled another story her husband had told her. He had been about six years old and had learned that his mother had thrown out his favorite stuffed animal. Mary Bernadette had made no excuses for it. She hadn't pretended that the rabbit had gone to Heaven or that he had fallen in love with a lady rabbit and run off to be married. "It was filthy," she told him. "It was trash."

So the devastated child had run off and hidden, just before the family was to leave for church. When he was finally found, crying and crouched at the back of the linen closet, his mother had dragged him out and drawn back her hand to strike him. His father had managed to grab her arm before she made contact, but according to Pat, the result had been the same as if she had left a welt on his cheek. He remembered making a solemn vow—as intelligent, sensitive children often do—never to trust his mother again. It was a horrible story, and every time she thought of it Megan felt pity for the poor little boy her husband had been.

"She was never as harsh with Grace, my mother," Pat went on. "Unless Grace has been keeping secrets from me. It's odd, but I always thought that Mom was more lenient with Grace, or at least not as relentless with her criticism, because Grace didn't really care what Mary Bernadette thought of her. Let's put it this way. I was always trying to please my mother and failing. I don't think that Grace even bothered to try. Smart woman, my sister."

"Yes," Megan agreed. "She is. Look, why don't you try to get your mind off the family. Why don't you watch a movie with me."

"Sure," he said. "Okay." Pat flopped back down on the couch at full length. The springs screamed.

"Oh, and Pat?" Megan said, reaching for the remote.

"Yeah?"

"I think we need a new couch."

Chapter 64

Alexis and PJ were eating dinner. She was trying very earnestly to engage with her husband, to ask questions and to answer them in return, but all the while she was uncomfortably aware of a sort of emotional buzzing inside her, something that felt dangerous and destructive. She wanted PJ to finish his dinner and go away before she lost what little control she had of her emotions.

"That was a great meal, Alexis," he said, crumpling his napkin onto his plate.

"Thank you," she said. Her own meal was hardly touched. The buzzing inside her wouldn't allow her to eat.

"But I thought we were going to have chicken tonight. You said something about a recipe from that popular Israeli chef you're always going on about."

Alexis felt the hot color rush to her face. "I am not 'always going on about' anything or anyone," she retorted.

PJ leaned back on the hind legs of his chair. "Sorry. Anyway, I just thought you said we were going to have chicken."

"I changed my mind. Is that all right? Or should I have asked you for permission to have my very own thought? And don't sit like that. It drives me crazy."

PJ let the chair tip forward so that once again it rested on all four legs. "That's not what I meant at all," he protested.

"Then what did you mean?"

"Nothing. I was just making conversation. Really, Alexis, lately it seems that you've got a problem with everything I say and do!"

"That's not true!" she cried.

"Well, it sure feels like it. Am I really so objectionable? I'm not trying to be, really."

Alexis bit back a nasty reply. She did not want another screaming match. She did not. "Of course not," she said.

"You never used to criticize me the way you do now. Have I changed all that much since you met me?"

Alexis put her hands on her lap and clenched them into fists. "No."

"Then what's wrong?" PJ leaned forward and put out his hand as if to touch her shoulder. But he didn't touch her.

"Nothing," she said, looking down at her lap. "I'm sorry. I'm just tired."

PJ sighed and abruptly rose from the table. "I am, too. I spent half the day trying to teach myself a computerized project management program so I don't look like a complete fool compared to Blue Sound and whoever else Meadows is bringing in. Assuming I get that far in the bidding process, which doesn't seem likely. I'm going to bed. Good night."

Alexis sat alone at the table for some time, all energy dissipated. Her mind was blank, her body heavy. Eventually, she got up and loaded the dishwasher. She didn't have the energy to wash the pots and knives. They would keep until morning. Alexis sank wearily onto the couch. In the past weeks, PJ hadn't once asked about her work for the Day in the Life project. He hadn't once asked if she had seen more of Maureen Kline. He hadn't once suggested that they have dinner at The Angry Squire or that they take an evening walk, just the two of them. He was totally immersed in his own concerns. He probably hadn't even noticed the photo of her parents that was now on display in their bedroom. Why should he notice a photograph when he barely noticed his own wife right in front of him? God knows they hadn't had sex in an age.

Alexis rubbed her temples. She couldn't imagine a man like Morgan Shelby complaining that his wife hadn't served for dinner what she had promised to serve. She couldn't imagine a man like Morgan Shelby allowing his grandmother to break into his apartment and hide objects she found objectionable. She couldn't imagine a man like Morgan Shelby canceling an anniversary getaway just to please and placate that grandmother.

Alexis shook her head. What was she doing? It wasn't fair to compare PJ with Morgan. PJ was her husband, and she owed him a degree of respect. Besides, she really didn't *know* Morgan all that well. Comparisons were futile and childish. With a feeling akin to despair, Alexis turned off the lamp, wrapped a chenille throw around her shoulders, and lay down on the couch. It was the first time since they had been married that she and her husband slept apart.

CHAPTER 65

At seven o'clock the next morning, Alexis was at her usual station on the corner of Main Street and Market Street. Her daily shot was set up, and at exactly three minutes after seven she would press the shutter button and take the photograph.

And then, at two minutes past seven, she stepped back from the camera. *No,* she thought. *No more.* She detached the camera from the tripod and hung it around her neck. She folded the tripod. She had had enough of Mary Bernadette Fitzgibbon and of all she represented. She would no longer do the bidding of a domineering old woman who only had harsh words for her in return. Morgan, she thought, was right about the project, anyway. It was just busy work. Mary Bernadette had probably designed it specifically to keep Alexis out of trouble and within sight.

When her equipment was safely stowed in the trunk of her car, Alexis drove to the office where she set about making a pot of coffee as if the morning was just like any other, as if she hadn't just committed social suicide in terms of Oliver's Well, the OWHA, and most important the Fitzgibbon family. As she measured the ground coffee and filled the pot with water from the bathroom sink, as she took the carton of milk from the minifridge and took a plastic spoon from a drawer, she acknowledged that abandoning the project in the way that she had was an act of passive aggression. And she acknowledged that before long she would have to account for her action. But she would handle that inevitable confrontation when it came. After all, as Morgan had pointed out, Mary Bernadette wasn't as omnipotent as Alexis had made her out to be. She was just a bossy old woman.

When the coffee was brewed, Alexis, feeling oddly calm, poured a cup and sat at the computer. She logged on to the Internet and began a search for online jewelry stores. Maybe she would buy herself a new wedding ring, one that actually matched her engagement ring. One that had not been forced upon her by Mary Bernadette Fitzgibbon.

CHAPTER 66

"Bats in the belfry, eh?"

Leonard frowned. "Bats nesting under the eaves of an old building are no joking matter, I assure you."

Wynston Meadows waved his hand dismissively. "Then deal with it."

"It was my intention," Leonard replied, "to do just that."

Mary Bernadette shot a glance at Neal, who frowned in response. Not one person in the room, not even Wallace or Joyce, she was sure, would argue the fact that the mood of the board meetings these days was drastically different from the mood before Wynston Meadows had joined the ranks. There had always been a sense of community and friendship, a sense that a wise solution to any problem was sure to be found, because every person at the table was dedicated to the same end—the good of their hometown. Now the meetings were a trial, the mood anxious and tense, with little laughter and even less open conversation. And what was the shared goal now? The appeasement of Wynston Meadows in the hopes of getting his promised millions.

"Mary B., what do you say about bats in the belfry?"

Mary Bernadette startled. Meadows was showing his teeth in a facsimile of a smile. "My name," she said, "is Mary Bernadette. Mrs. Fitzgibbon will do just fine."

Meadows laughed. "That name of yours is quite a handful. Can't you cut us some slack?"

"No," she replied. "I cannot."

"Respectfully," Leonard said, "the lady has a right to her name."

With a little grin, Meadows bowed his head in assent.

"Has the call for bids on the Stoker job gone out?"

"Just about to. I'm a busy man, Leonard."

"Of course. I would be more than happy to—"

"No need."

"It is traditional for the CEO to handle—"

"What is this about new upholstery?" Meadows pointed to the day's agenda.

Anne cleared her throat. "The upholstery on several of the furnishings in the Kennington House is badly in need of repair or replacement."

"And?"

"And I've located a design firm in Richmond that specializes in reproductions of old fabrics. The firm we've used in the past went out of business so—"

Meadows laughed. "No surprise there."

"This new design firm," Neal said, taking over from Anne, "is a bit more expensive than the last, but their work has been recognized as outstanding by several major museums across the country. I think it's worth having them take a look at the pieces in question and submit a bid for the job."

"I don't agree. Why waste money on new cushion covers when no one is actually using the chairs and sofas?"

There was a stunned silence after Meadows's remark. Mary Bernadette doubted the evidence of her ears, but only for a moment. Wynston Meadows didn't care a fig for historical preservation. He had made that abundantly clear before.

Finally, Leonard said, "Wasting money? How is necessary maintenance wasting money? If our budget can sustain—"

But Meadows cut him off, again. "Let me assure you," he said, "that I know far more about budgets than anyone in this room."

"Of course you do," Wallace said hurriedly. "I certainly don't doubt that."

Mary Bernadette tightened her grip on her pen and looked to Richard, whose hands were pressed flat against the table as if to keep himself in check. Both Anne and Jeannette were pale. Neal's expression was grim. Norma was examining a large gold ring on her right hand. Joyce shifted in her chair and smiled at Wynston Meadows. "If Mr. Meadows thinks we shouldn't spend money on upholstery, then I say we should listen to him."

The woman literally simpers in his presence, Mary Bernadette thought with disgust. She wondered if Joyce's husband knew his wife was making eyes at another man. She had half a mind to speak to Martin. It would serve the woman right, and her husband a man of the cloth!

Abruptly, Meadows rose. "I've got an important meeting to attend," he said. "We'll deal with decorating issues some other time."

When he had gone, Richard slapped his hands against the table and turned to Joyce. "What would you suggest we do, Ms. Miller, invest in plastic slipcovers?"

Joyce's face turned a fierce shade of red, and Mary Bernadette repressed a smile.

CHAPTER 67

PJ was slumped on the couch, watching one of those awful reality shows about lumberjacks or alligator hunters. Alexis was convinced that he wasn't really paying attention to what was on the screen. She was sure that his thoughts were with his beloved grandmother and Fitzgibbon Landscaping, the only two things that mattered to him.

Alexis placed her hands on the edge of the kitchen sink. Her stomach was in a knot. No one from the OWHA seemed to have noticed that it had been days since she had posted a picture on the website. But someone would notice, and the thought frightened her, though not enough to make her pick up the project again and explain away her absence as forgetfulness. No. She most certainly would not go crawling back to Mary Bernadette and her pathetic Hysterical Society.

"Dude, those are some righteous mud flaps!" These words were followed by the roar of a truck's engine and raucous male laughter.

Alexis flinched. What was she *doing* here in Oliver's Well? Just that morning Diane had sent her an e-mail in which she shared the latest news about their old college crowd. Sue was still in med school, determinedly working toward her goal of becoming a pediatrician. Her fiancé, Marc, was doing well in law school. Stacy was moving to Paris for a year. Diane had gotten a raise and was planning a two-week vacation in Hawaii. Alexis's parents had sent an e-mail, too. They had spent the weekend in New York City, where they had attended the opening night of a new opera at the Met. They were planning a trip to Italy next spring.

And what, Alexis thought, *have I achieved lately?* Nothing. She had achieved nothing at all since marrying into the Fitzgibbon family. Alexis stared out through the kitchen window at Mary Bernadette and Paddy's house. It was entirely dark but for a dim light behind the curtains of their bedroom. Alexis had come to imagine the house as a sentinel, home to an all-seeing and all-knowing guard who took her duties very, very seriously. Mary Bernadette was like that mythical three-headed dog—Cerberus, was it?—whose job it was to guard the gates of Hell so that no one confined to its depths could escape. Well, maybe that was going a bit too far; Mary Bernadette wasn't *physically* terrifying. Still, Alexis believed that if she dared go out on her own one evening, Mary Bernadette, ever watching for misbehavior, would come stalking out of the house after her. And if she did manage to sneak out for a quick drink at The Angry Squire, the whole town would report the news to Mary Bernadette by morning. She still wasn't sure that PJ's grandmother hadn't followed her to Somerstown the other day.

She turned from the window. She wondered if she might talk to Maureen Kline about her discontent. She liked Maureen. But then she rejected the idea. Maureen herself had said that she considered the Fitzgibbon clan her family. She would choose Mary Bernadette and PJ over Alexis. She would have no choice. No, Alexis thought, she would have to be really desperate, even more than she felt now, to approach Maureen. There *was* Father Robert, of course. He would be bound to absolute confidentiality if she spoke to him in confession. But Father Robert was a friend of Mary Bernadette. Alexis doubted that even the threat of ex-communication was enough to keep him from running to PJ's grandmother with tales of her marital woes.

But what was the use in talking to *anyone*? Nothing would change unless her *husband* changed. She would always be a stranger in Oliver's Well unless PJ actively fought on her behalf for an important, independent place in the Fitzgibbons' world.

Alexis walked through the kitchen. "I'm going to bed," she said in the direction of the living room.

PJ didn't look away from the television screen. "Good night," he said.

Alexis sighed and closed the bedroom door behind her.

CHAPTER 68

Mary Bernadette was sitting at her kitchen table with a cup of strong tea. She was alone in the house. PJ had asked Paddy to go with him to meet a potential client. There was no doubt that Wynston Meadows's behavior had caused her grandson's self-confidence to plummet. It angered Mary Bernadette. And it frustrated her that she could do nothing about it, much as it frustrated her that she had been unable to do anything about the disastrous meeting of the OWHA board the night before.

Wynston Meadows had once again wrenched the meeting out of her control as soon as the first new item of business was introduced. And that item of business was the annual Oliver's Well Independence Day festivities. Each year since its inception, the OWHA had played an important role in the celebrations. Together with the fire department they sponsored a hot dog stand with all profits going directly to the maintenance of the historic firehouse, now a museum, on Parker Street. Together with the local florist they sponsored the sale of corsages of red, white, and blue carnations. All floral profits went to the upkeep of Oliver's Grove, the town's one recreational park.

Still, most people in Oliver's Well would agree that the OWHA's most important contribution to the Independence Day celebrations was the organization of the parade. At some point in the life of almost every resident of Oliver's Well, he or she had marched in the July Fourth parade—as a Girl or Boy Scout; as a member of the high school marching band; dressed as the town's seventeenth-century founders; as employees of small businesses, riding floats that illustrated their services; as members of the local VFW.

But the night before, Wynston Meadows had announced that he wanted to cancel the parade—"A rather pedestrian activity, pardon the pun"—in favor of a fancy dress costume ball, to which the majority of the town would not be invited. And those who would be invited would be asked to make a donation of what Mary Bernadette thought was a prohibitive sum to the OWHA. She might have her standards, but she did not favor exclusionary measures. She believed that the town's celebrations were for everyone to enjoy.

She hadn't been alone in her protest. "But the traditions are so important," Anne had pointed out. "Everyone looks forward to the parade, especially the children."

To which Wynston Meadows had replied, "Children don't make financial gifts."

"And what's more American than a parade?" Leonard had added. "Marching bands and floats and the veterans in their old uniforms."

"The veterans," Meadows had said, "would be smarter to stay in the comfort of their nursing homes. One of these days the paramedics will be peeling their dehydrated bodies off the pavement."

"It'll be a deeply unpopular decision, mark my words," Neal had pronounced. "I don't think losing the support of the majority of Oliver's Well is something the OWHA wants to risk."

To which Wynston Meadows had argued that the support of the majority of Oliver's Well was no longer necessary, now that he was on hand to back it up financially. No one had pointed out that the OWHA had yet to see a penny of his money. In the end, the matter had been tabled until the next meeting, to give those members of the board who hadn't voiced an opinion time to muster the courage to voice it.

Mary Bernadette had passed Wynston Meadows in the foyer on the way out of the Wilson House. He was on his cell phone and she had heard him say, "The most pathetic of the bunch is that Leonard DeWittless." She had left the building feeling slightly sick to her stomach.

She still felt unwell and uneasy. No one on the board was standing up to their "benefactor" for fear of losing his promised millions. Were they all so cowardly and disloyal? Except for Neal, who so gallantly had defended her intellectual abilities to Wynston Meadows and who had volunteered to resign from the board. But how could she blame her colleagues for what really came down to cautious, responsible behavior? Like every other person involved with the OWHA, Mary Bernadette was acutely aware of the importance of Meadows's promised money to the town. If he decided to withdraw his pledge, other donors both big and small, disappointed in the board's failure to keep the gift they had been given, might follow suit, leading to the disintegration of the OWHA. The unhappy fact of the matter was that the OWHA needed Wynston Meadows.

Mary Bernadette sighed. She truly had the town's best interest at heart, yet her pride would not allow her to resign as chairman, a position she was sure Wynston Meadows coveted. She had already recused herself from the upcoming vote regarding the contract for the restoration of the landscaping of the Stoker property. Wasn't that sacrifice enough?

If only the others would see what Mary Bernadette now saw so clearly, that Wynston Meadows was a genuine threat to the goals of the OWHA! Then they might act together to form the unanimous vote the bylaws required to remove him from the board. And lose the promised millions as a result. Of course, there was no guarantee that while Meadows remained on the board he would use those millions for the good of Oliver's Well, as he had promised. His word was not to be trusted.

Mary Bernadette took a sip of the now-cooled tea. Only that morning Paddy had attempted to talk to her about the disastrous situation, but she had silenced him immediately. Now she wasn't sure why she had, not when she felt so in need of support. *Poor man*, she thought now. *He is so good to me. And am I so good to him in return?*

She had never given even a passing thought to committing an infidelity. For more than fifty years she had made his every meal, washed and ironed and mended his clothes. She had managed the household budget and raised his children to be respectable, hardworking, moral people of whom he could be proud. She had nursed him through the flu and colds and a hip replacement.

But had she ever taken his hand, just to let him know that she loved him? Had she ever gently touched his cheek for no other reason than to see him smile? Maybe she had, a very long time ago, during the eighteen months of William's life when the days had been filled with joy and wonder and laughter. And then, it was all over. With William gone, gone too was the warm and happy woman she had been so briefly.

Banshee, in the way that cats have when their human companions were troubled, appeared at Mary Bernadette's side and wound her long, sleek body around her legs. Absentmindedly, Mary Bernadette reached down to stroke her.

It had been years and years since she had had to reflect on matters in the way she was being forced to now. For so long her life had been firmly under her control. Or so she had thought. Now Mary Bernadette suspected that she might have been assuming mastery over events that were essentially out of her realm. *Overweening pride.*

"Banshee," she said, looking down at her feline companion, for whom life was so blessedly simple. "Would you like a wee bit of milk?"

Banshee replied in the affirmative.

CHAPTER 69

PJ was alone in the cottage. He didn't know where Alexis had gone. She hadn't left a note, and he couldn't remember if she had mentioned that she had a doctor's appointment after work or if she had needed to run to the bank or even, he thought, if she had planned to see Maureen Kline. She had mentioned once that she liked Maureen. Maybe they had become friends. PJ just didn't know.

He sat at the kitchen table, nervously drumming his fingers against it. Something was badly wrong. He could feel it. At the gas station earlier that day he had waved to Jim Toth, someone he had known since childhood. Jim, filling up his car two pumps down the line, had not waved back. On the way back to the office he got a text from a new client, canceling the job. And later, when PJ stopped in Cookies 'n Crumpets for a cup of coffee, he could have sworn that the other customers in the bakery had looked at him with suspicion and hostility.

It was only on the way home that the awful thought occurred to him. Wynston Meadows might be a creep, but he was a smart man. Could he be right, after all, in implying that Mary Bernadette had behaved unethically during her tenure at the OWHA, resulting in Fitzgibbon Landscaping being awarded so many lucrative contracts?

And there was something else. If Mary Bernadette were indeed guilty of professional misconduct, Paddy would have to know about it. How could a husband and wife keep such a thing a secret from one another, especially a pair like his grandparents, their lives so harmoniously intertwined for so many years?

PJ jumped from his seat and stalked over to the window from where he had a clear view of his grandparents' house. No. It was a ridiculous thought. But Paddy *was* the owner of Fitzgibbon Landscaping, and he *had* been its leader for forty years. How could he *not* know if something underhanded had been going on? And if he truly hadn't known, why hadn't he? What did that say about his abilities as a leader?

Or, PJ thought, *maybe I've fallen victim to the power of rumor.* He remembered what he had predicted back when Wynston Meadows had demanded a reconsideration of Fitzgibbon Landscaping having been awarded the Stoker job. Even the hint of a scandal, however false, might ruin a good reputation. If he could doubt the honesty of his own beloved grandparents, then no wonder a stranger might, too.

PJ rubbed his eyes. He wished there were someone with whom he could share his doubts. He certainly couldn't talk to Alexis. These days he felt as if he barely knew the woman he had married. *He* hadn't changed—he had given it a lot of thought and he was sure of that—but she certainly had. He just didn't feel— he didn't feel *safe* with her like he once had. Protected. Back when they had first started dating and all throughout their courtship and the first months of their marriage, Alexis had been the most patient listener, the most supportive person he had ever known, other than his grandmother and his mother. He had been so certain that Alexis would prove to be the perfect wife for him, that she would so easily become one of the family. He had been so certain that she would *understand*. But now, she had grown troublingly disloyal to the Fitzgibbon cause. To him. Who was to say that just for the spite of it she wouldn't tell someone of his suspicions—Leonard DeWitt or even Wynston Meadows?

And he certainly couldn't turn to his father for advice or consolation. They had never been close, and the passing years seemed to be pulling them even further apart. For some reason, just plain stubbornness or something more twisted, Pat Fitzgibbon couldn't appreciate—let alone accept—his son's decision to work for the family business. Sometimes PJ wondered if the reason his father wouldn't support him was because of the glaringly obvious animosity between Pat and his own mother. At times PJ had thought that his father actually hated her.

PJ sighed. He had never felt so alone in his entire life. Not even in the weeks just after the twins were born when everyone seemed to forget his existence. Not even when his high school girlfriend had dumped him on the eve of the junior prom for someone he had thought to be his friend. Not even when Alexis had spent that one summer during college traveling abroad on her own, leaving him behind in Oliver's Well living with and working for his grandparents. To this day he still didn't understand why she had felt the need to be apart from him for two entire months.

Yes, PJ thought now, turning angrily away from the window. That was it. His own scandalously disloyal thoughts *had* to be the result of his wife's influence. She had never really fit into the world of the Fitzgibbons, and she had never really tried to. Her dislike of his family was infecting him with the disease of false and unsupported suspicion. And to think that his wife wore his great aunt Catherine's wedding ring as her own. It was a travesty.

Suddenly, PJ couldn't stand being in the cottage for one moment longer. He grabbed his keys, went out to the truck, and pointed it in the direction of The Angry Squire.

He did not leave a note for his wife.

CHAPTER 70

Mary Bernadette did not believe in caller ID. She found it only slightly less rude than call waiting. Still, at this moment, she wished she had known who was on the other end of the line before she picked up the receiver.

"Hello, Mary Bernadette." It was Joyce Miller, with that tinny, almost desperate note in her voice Mary Bernadette found so annoying.

"Oh, hello, Joyce," Mary Bernadette said, with just enough enthusiasm to be polite.

"I have some rather disturbing news, I'm afraid."

Mary Bernadette allowed her usually dignified demeanor (which she made it a point to maintain even when alone) to slip just long enough to roll her eyes at the kitchen wall. What was it now? Joyce could make a mountain out of a molehill. She might have found a nail missing from a baseboard at the Wilson House and convinced herself the entire edifice was about to collapse.

"Yes?" she said.

"Well, I'm afraid that Alexis has abandoned the Day in the Life project."

Mary Bernadette felt a sharp twinge of pain behind her left eye. "What do you mean she's abandoned the project?" she asked, careful to keep her tone even.

"Just what I said. She hasn't logged a photo in days and days. I suppose I could have gone straight to Alexis for an explanation, but I thought that I had better come to you first. After all, you *were* the one who gave her the job."

"There must be some mistake," Mary Bernadette replied promptly. Silently, she damned herself for not having looked at the OWHA website in days. She might have spotted the absence and dealt with it without anyone else being the wiser.

"No, I don't think so," Joyce said, with her thin laugh. "But then again, Alexis being your family, I'm sure you'll get to the bottom of this little mystery before anyone else on the board notices that something is wrong. Unless they already have."

"Yes," Mary Bernadette said. "I'm sure there's a perfectly good explanation. Good-bye, Joyce."

Mary Bernadette sank into a seat at the kitchen table. She was angry. She was hurt. She was embarrassed. She simply could not understand how her beloved grandson's wife could care so little for her and by extension for the good name of the Fitzgibbon family. Why hadn't the girl come to her if she wanted to leave the project? There was no excuse for such behavior. It was downright underhanded. Well, Mary Bernadette thought, no good deed goes unpunished, and that was for certain. And the thought of Wynston Meadows learning of Alexis's act of treason (that wasn't too strong a word for it) horrified her. Alexis's bad behavior would only give the man more ammunition in his already powerful and inexplicable campaign against the Fitzgibbons.

Mary Bernadette abruptly rose from the table. She would accomplish nothing by sitting there and stewing. She would deal with the situation immediately.

CHAPTER 71

Alexis opened the door only after Mary Bernadette had knocked several times. "Oh," she said. "It's you."

Mary Bernadette resisted a very strong desire to slap Alexis's face. "May I come in?" she asked.

Alexis opened the door wider and stepped back to allow Mary Bernadette to pass.

"PJ's not here," she said.

"It's you I've come to speak with. Let me get straight to the point. I've been told that you haven't been keeping up with the Day in the Life of Oliver's Well project. Is that true?"

Color flooded the girl's cheeks, and she turned away. "Yes."

"Why is that?"

Alexis turned back to her and shrugged. "It was boring. I was tired of it."

"A Fitzgibbon," Mary Bernadette said, keeping a tight rein on her temper, "does not just walk away from responsibility. You've sullied our good name and you've let down the Oliver's Well Historical Association."

Alexis laughed a bit wildly. "Don't be so dramatic. No one cares about that project, anyway. It was a bad idea in the first place."

"I'll be the judge of that. And there is no excuse for not coming to me and asking to be let go of the task. The least you could have done was to stay on until I found someone to replace you."

"Come to you?" The girl's voice was a shriek. "Are you kidding? Like you would actually *listen* to me? God, Mary Bernadette, I am so tired of doing your bidding. Nothing I do is ever good enough for you. I just want to be left alone!"

Mary Bernadette steadied her breathing before she spoke. "Well," she said, "perhaps you should have thought of that before marrying my grandson. You're part of this family now, for better or worse. You don't have the right to be 'left alone.' You owe the family your active presence. We all do."

"Presence! Well, on that note, I want you to keep your *presence* out of my home. I want you to stop coming in to the cottage when I'm out and rearranging my things. I want you to stop snooping through my mail. I'll have the lock changed, if you don't!"

Mary Bernadette felt as if she had sustained a physical blow. No one had ever had the audacity to speak to her so rudely. "I might remind you," she said, "that I own this cottage."

Alexis laughed. "Oh, you never let me forget that! But you don't own *me*, even if my last name is Fitzgibbon!"

There followed a heavy, vibrating silence; Mary Bernadette could feel the weight of it pressing on her shoulders. "There are times," she said, "when I regret that it is."

CHAPTER 72

Alexis felt sick to her stomach as she waited for PJ to come home from work that evening. She knew without a doubt that Mary Bernadette would have waylaid him and told him her version of what had happened that afternoon. And she strongly suspected that she would have to fight for her side of the encounter to be heard.

Finally, she saw him coming from his grandparents' house, and when he was within a few feet of the door she threw it open. PJ's face was dark with an emotion Alexis couldn't identify. It frightened her.

"I've just talked to Grandmother," he said stiffly, walking into the cottage.

Alexis closed the door. "I bet she told you *her* version of what happened this afternoon."

"The way I see it, there's only one version of the story. You walked away from a job Grandmother was nice enough to give you without telling her—without telling anyone—that you wanted to quit."

"But there was a reason, PJ! Let me—"

"And then when Grandmother confronted you about what you had done, you didn't even have the decency to apologize. Instead, you threatened to change the locks against her."

"But she—"

"You should *never* have shown such disrespect."

"Me?" Alexis cried. "What about her?"

PJ laughed unpleasantly. "What sort of disrespect has she shown you? She gave you a job at Fitzgibbon Landscaping. She gave you a home. She gave you a special role in the OWHA. And look how you betrayed her."

"But I didn't *ask* for any of those things. I didn't—"

"I'm disappointed in you, Alexis. I never expected this sort of thing from you, of all people. You used to be so . . . so good. So trustworthy."

Alexis balled her hands into fists at her side. "God," she cried, "you sound like you're my father, not my husband! What has that woman done to you?"

"*That woman* helped raise me. *That woman* has been nothing but good and generous to me. And to think that I doubted her for even one minute . . ."

"What?"

"Nothing."

"Did she tell you she wishes my last name wasn't Fitzgibbon?" Alexis demanded. "She hates me, PJ."

"Can you blame her, when you do something so underhanded?"

Alexis felt her stomach heave. She was badly shocked. She wanted to tell her husband to leave the cottage. *She* wanted to leave the cottage. But the fear of no one coming to her rescue rendered her speechless.

PJ shook his head and made a dismissive gesture with his hand. "I'll take care of my own dinner," he said. He stalked out of the cottage, leaving the door to slam behind him. A moment later, Alexis heard his truck drive off.

He had been gone for almost four hours.

Alexis opened the front door of the cottage and peered out to Honeysuckle Lane. She listened for the sound of her husband's truck. She saw and heard nothing. She went back inside and closed the door behind her.

PJ had never gone off like this, not ever in all the years they had been together. Alexis was worried. She was still a bit angry, but she was scared, too. And she was weak with remorse. She should have behaved with more dignity when Mary Bernadette had confronted her that afternoon. Had she really threatened to change the locks on the cottage? Had she really meant what she had said about wanting to be left alone? Well, she had been left alone now, and it didn't feel very good at all.

With a shuddering sigh Alexis sank onto the couch and put her head in her hands. She hadn't been able to eat anything after PJ had stormed out and now vaguely wondered if she should make a cup of tea. But the effort seemed too great.

Her husband had not listened to her side of the story. He had called her conduct underhanded. He had said that he was disappointed in her. He had told her she had acted disrespectfully. He had accused her of betraying the family. His family. And in a way, she had betrayed them. Alexis had known that from the moment she had stowed her camera in the trunk of her car and driven away from the sight of the Day in the Life project. She had known there would be consequences. And she hadn't much cared. But now . . .

Alexis lifted her head. Was that the sound of a truck's engine slowing? She rushed over to the door and flung it open. The only sound she heard now was a call of a night bird. *Please God*, she prayed silently, *let him be all right*. Even though the thought of what PJ might say to her when he got home frightened her— what if he said he no longer loved her?—she wanted him home safely. With her. Where he belonged.

She closed the door again and waited, painfully aware that only a few yards away PJ's grandmother waited, too.

CHAPTER 73

"**M**om? We have to talk."

Megan was glad that her older son had called. After mass on Palm Sunday she had reminded him that she was always available should he be in need of advice, but she hadn't entertained a great conviction that he would indeed turn to her for help.

Megan listened now as PJ recounted an extraordinary story about Alexis quitting her photography work for the OWHA without telling anyone, and then about the terrible fight that had ensued between Alexis and Mary Bernadette when the truth had come out. Everything about PJ's tale bothered Megan, particularly her son's obvious preference for his grandmother's point of view.

"I just can't believe she was so rude to Grandmother," he said now. "What was she thinking?"

"I don't know," Megan said honestly. "Have you asked her?"

PJ didn't reply to that question. Instead, he said, "It's like suddenly she doesn't want anything to do with my family. What have we ever done to her that's so bad?"

"Maybe," Megan said carefully, "Alexis wants to make a new family, just with you. The Fitzgibbon dynamic can be overwhelming, even to those of us who've been on the inside for some time. Are you sure you've really considered her position in all this?"

PJ laughed. "Her position? Her position is that she's my wife. She should be my ally, my partner."

"And you're her husband. You should be *her* ally and partner, not your grandmother's."

"But—"

Megan pushed on. "Maybe I have no right to be quoting at you," she said, "given the fact that I go to church only about three times a year, but you would do well to remember the words of the Bible. 'A man shall leave his father and mother and cleave to his wife; and the two shall be as one.' Or something like that."

PJ sighed. "Why are you taking Alexis's side in this?" he asked in a distinctly plaintive tone.

"I'm not taking anyone's side, PJ," Megan replied patiently. "All I'm suggesting is that you take another look at the situation that's built up between your wife and your grandmother and consider whether you can do something to soothe wounded feelings."

PJ didn't reply.

"Look, I know things are tough right now, with Wynston Meadows being a pain—"

"A pain? He's being a lot more than that, Mom! He's trying to make us out to be criminals! And I don't have the time to handle two major crises at once!"

Megan put a hand to her head. Her son was sorely trying her usually equitable nature. "Well, PJ," she said. "You'd better make the time, because a marriage is not a joke. And crises don't happen all in a row, nice and neat. If there's one thing life has taught me it's that when trouble hits, it hits hard and all at once."

"But Mom—"

"Look, PJ, I've got to go."

"All right."

"One final word of advice, though you probably don't want to hear it."

"You're right," he said. "I don't."

"Keep your grandmother out of this situation between you and Alexis."

Megan didn't wait for her son to respond. Instead, she pressed the End button. She hated to feel disappointed in one of her children, even for a moment, but she *was* disappointed in PJ. His behavior was immature and selfish. Megan's eyes found the Prayer of St. Francis on the wall above her desk. PJ, she thought, would be well advised to learn how to work for pardon and for love, rather than for injury and hate.

CHAPTER 74

"I agree that what she did was wrong, but it wasn't a crime, Mary."

Mary Bernadette and her husband were sitting across from each other at the kitchen table. Two barely touched cups of tea sat in front of them.

"Her irresponsible actions," Mary Bernadette replied, "have further painted this family in a bad light."

Paddy sighed and took a sip of his lukewarm tea. "She was no more than immature."

Mary Bernadette pushed her own cup away from her. "Fine," she said, "take her side, but I have no further use for that girl. I wish I had never given her my aunt Catherine's wedding ring. She has no right to be wearing it."

"Now, Mary," Paddy said. "You don't mean that."

"Don't I? In fact, I hope the marriage ends before too much more time passes."

Paddy's face grew red. "Divorce is a terrible thing to wish upon anyone," he said angrily. "You should be ashamed of yourself."

Mary Bernadette was speechless for a moment. Her husband had never contradicted her so strongly. But in another moment, she had found her voice. "I'm not in the least ashamed of myself," she said. "I have my family's best interests at heart. I have my grandson's happiness to consider. Someone has to take charge when things go awry."

"Mary, PJ's marriage is between PJ and his wife."

"Be that as it may, I can't in all good conscience sit idly by while my grandson's wife wreaks havoc with our good name. Reputation is more enduring than life. My poor mother, God rest her soul, used to say that, and she was right."

"A family's reputation means nothing next to—"

Mary Bernadette rose from the table. "That's final, Paddy. Now, I'm going to bed."

Leaving her husband to put the teacups in the dishwasher, Mary Bernadette climbed the stairs to their bedroom and closed the door behind her. She looked at her reflection in the mirror over her dresser. Her eyes, usually so keen and bright, looked dull. She felt unhappy and afraid. She was not in the habit of losing her temper, and yet she had been losing it often lately, too often. Her admirable self-control was slipping away. And to what living creature could she turn for help? She was trapped within the bonds of privacy she herself had put in place long ago. Her isolation was her own doing.

Mary Bernadette opened the bottom drawer of her dresser and reached for the locked box containing the photographs of William. And then she withdrew her hand. Suddenly, without warning, there had come that needle-sharp worry, that dreadful suspicion that somehow she had been responsible for her son's untimely death. More than fifty years had passed, but still in her darker moments Mary Bernadette was assaulted by feelings of guilt that her child's passing had been a divine punishment for her overweening pride in him, for the intense joy she had found in his presence.

"A man may be his own ruin," her father used to say. "It's a wedge from itself that splits the oak tree." All the years after his death Mary Bernadette could still hear his voice, rich and mellow, as if he were right there in the room with her. Her beloved father. He had been right about most things but . . .

Mary Bernadette shook her head. No. The fault for William's death did *not* lie within her. It *could* not. And neither was she the author of her current woes. The cause there was to be found in the person of Wynston Meadows. And a family might be its own ruin, too, Mary Bernadette reflected, with one troublesome member acting as the wedge that drove the unit apart. And that wedge was her grandson's wife.

Mary Bernadette reached into the drawer now for her old missal. Its black leather covers were soft with age, the thin paper almost fuzzy. She turned to the last page and read aloud a prayer written there in her mother's hand. It had often brought her comfort.

"Oh, Mary, who had the victory over all women, give me victory now over my enemies, that they may fall to the ground, as wheat when it is mown."

Mary Bernadette gently closed the old book. "Amen," she said.

CHAPTER 75

The only other time Alexis had been in Oliver's Well Memorial Cemetery was when she had substituted for Richard Armstrong in leading the Haunted Oliver's Well tour. That was long before she had known anything about William Fitzgibbon. The cemetery wasn't Catholic, but Alexis thought that Mary Bernadette's devotion to Oliver's Well might have convinced her to lay her child to rest in the company of the town's earliest settlers. If William's grave was not to be found here, Alexis would look elsewhere for it. She had a very strong need to visit the little boy's place of rest.

The cemetery was a jumble of half-crumbling headstones dating back to the early seventeenth century and newer, shiny marble memorials erected as late as the 1980s. There were a few mausoleums, largely covered in lichen and moss. Some areas were overgrown with weeds, though other areas were well cared for. Alexis wondered if the cemetery was owned by the OWHA. She had never bothered to ask.

Alexis had no clear idea of where to begin her search. She didn't want to ask the custodian for help in locating the site. She didn't want it advertised around town that she was aware that William Fitzgibbon had lived and died. But luck was with Alexis, and she found the gravesite before long. It was, as she knew it would be, well tended, probably by Mary Bernadette herself.

William Patrick Fitzgibbon
Beloved Son
His Soul Now Resides with God

Alexis felt immeasurable sadness descend upon her. *So few words to commemorate a life,* she thought. *The poor little thing.* She hoped that he hadn't suffered, but a child that young wouldn't understand that he was dying; he wouldn't understand why he was in pain. All he might have known was that his mother wasn't making him better. All he might have known was confusion. And it was awful to imagine what it must have taken Mary Bernadette to survive the death of her firstborn and to find the courage to give birth to more children. Every time Mary Bernadette kissed her second son and her daughter good night, had she wondered if they, too, would be taken from her before their time?

Alexis gently touched the stone. She didn't know if PJ had ever visited William's grave. She wouldn't ask him, not now. She wouldn't tell him that she had been here, either. He might think she had no right to pay her respects. He might think she was being careless with the heavy veil of silence his grandmother had chosen to lay over the past.

But maybe she was being unfair to PJ. She had to learn how to school her thoughts toward reconciliation and kindness. She *had* to. So much was at stake. Alexis sat carefully on a crumbling stone bench not far from the headstone. She had been thinking about how it might have been for Megan when she first came to the Fitzgibbon family. There was no doubt in her mind that her mother-in-law had met with much of the same domineering behavior from Mary Bernadette as Alexis was experiencing now. She saw the way Mary Bernadette still criticized her. But Megan was such a strong person, so much more mature than Alexis felt she would ever be. And she had a husband who stood up for her no matter what.

How sad, Alexis thought now. Once she had believed that she would find all the meaning and purpose she needed in being PJ's wife. But now, being his wife didn't seem enough at all. Maybe it had been foolish to think that she could find perfect fulfillment only in relation to another person. She was embarrassed that she had fallen victim to such an archaic way of thinking. How—and why—had she so absorbed the notion of . . . of subservience? Was she so fundamentally lazy that the notion of forging her own life was unappealing? Or was she at heart a coward, afraid that if she tried her hand at an important task—like living an examined life of her own—she would fail and not find the energy to try again?

Alexis sighed. She wanted to pray for peace of mind, but she didn't quite know how. As best as she could, she put aside all distracting thoughts and began to recite the Lord's Prayer.

> *Our Father, who art in heaven*
> *hallowed be thy Name.*
> *Thy kingdom come,*
> *thy will be done,*
> *on earth as it is in heaven.*
> *Give us this day our daily bread*
> *And forgive us our trespasses,*
> *as we forgive those who trespass against us.*
> *And lead us not into temptation*
> *but deliver us from evil. Amen.*

Forgive us our trespasses/as we forgive those who trespass against us. Alexis knew that she should forgive Mary Bernadette for her interference and her insults, but she wasn't sure that she could. And she believed that Mary Bernadette should forgive *her* for having abandoned the project for the OWHA, but she wasn't sure that Mary Bernadette would. And PJ ... Did he need forgiveness? Was it wrong of him to love his grandmother to the point of ignoring his own wife? Yes, of course it was. But was love to be regulated and restricted? That couldn't be right, either.

What was true forgiveness, anyway, Alexis wondered, looking at little William's grave. Could anyone, even the wisest person, understand the nature of something so intangible? Was forgiveness real, or was it just an end product of the human desire for peace? Did it matter?

And lead us not into temptation ... Oh, those words came too close for comfort! Morgan Shelby certainly presented a temptation for her to break her marriage vows, and for the sake of what? Momentary physical excitement? Alexis sighed. It was no good. She felt more troubled and tormented for her efforts at prayer.

Prayer was supposed to comfort those in need, but too often Alexis found that it only made her more acutely aware of her misery.

"God," she said now, "if you are there and if you hear me, please help me. Please help me see my way through this troubled time."

And oddly enough, after a few moments Alexis did feel a small sense of peace steal over her. She wondered if it was a gift from William.

CHAPTER 76

That evening, Alexis made one of PJ's favorite meals—oven-fried chicken with crispy kale and home fries. After dinner, during which neither had spoken much, she reached across the table and laid her hand on his. He flinched, but he did not pull away.

"PJ," Alexis said. "I want to apologize. For . . . well, for everything. I . . . I don't know what came over me for a while. . . . But I'm very sorry. I hope you can forgive me."

PJ seemed to sag in relief. He laid his other hand over hers. "It's all right," he said. "Of course I forgive you. And I'm sorry, too. Really, I am. Will you forgive me?"

Alexis nodded. PJ's apology had sounded entirely sincere. But she suspected he had no real idea what he was apologizing for. She suspected that he just wanted things back the way they had been, before her discontent had taken shape. Maybe that was all she could expect of him. Maybe that was enough.

"I can't stand being mad at each other," he said. "It hurts too much."

"I know," she said softly. "I feel the same way."

"I hate when we fight. It's all so . . . so pointless."

"Yes," she said, though she believed that there were points to be made.

"We never used to fight like this. But ever since that Wynston Meadows came to town . . ." PJ frowned and shook his head.

Alexis refrained from pointing out that her discontent had begun before Wynston Meadows landed in Oliver's Well. *Maybe, she thought, I should speak. Maybe this is part of the problem.* But she held her tongue. This truce was too new, too fragile.

"Have you apologized yet to Grandmother?" PJ asked.

"Not yet," she said, forcing a smile. "But I will."

"Good. Then everything can get back to normal."

"Yes," she said. "Back to normal."

PJ stood, and still holding her hand he led her to the bedroom. They made love for the first time in a long while. After, in an attempt to maintain the delicate atmosphere of reconciliation, Alexis suggested they watch a movie together, something they hadn't done in months.

"Great idea," PJ said. "I'll make some popcorn. And let's watch something funny. We've had enough doom and gloom around here lately."

Alexis waited on the couch for her husband. She felt vaguely depressed and at the same time vaguely comforted. She knew that nothing had been solved, but at least a bit of the tension between them had lifted, if only for the moment. And for that she was grateful.

PJ came into the living room carrying an enormous bowl of popcorn. He was smiling. Alexis couldn't remember when she had last seen him smile, and it made her smile in return. He put the bowl on the coffee table and sat down next to her. Alexis took his hand.

"How about *Caddyshack*?" PJ suggested.

Alexis nodded. "Sure," she said. It was one of PJ's favorite movies. She had watched it with him five or six times. And she found it more boring with each viewing. But she had never told him that, and she wouldn't tell him that now. Since the beginning of their relationship she had hated to disappoint or to disagree with him. PJ was a sensitive person. She had always been so careful of his feelings. She would try to be careful of them still. After all, she loved him. She loved him.

CHAPTER 77

Mary Bernadette locked the front door and turned toward the driveway. "Oh Lord," she muttered. There was her neighbor, Lucy Burrows, hurrying up the drive, a big smile on her overly made-up face.

"Mrs. F!" she called. "I'm glad I caught you."

"Mrs. Burrows." Mary Bernadette hated being called Mrs. F (let alone Mary B.)—it was so common—but she had long ago stopped correcting Lucy Burrows, as her admonitions fell on deaf ears.

Lucy came to a panting halt. Mary Bernadette noted with distaste that her bra straps—bright pink—were showing. "You look lovely as always," Lucy said.

"Thank you." *It's because my underwear is safely secured*, she added silently.

"Mike and I are having a small party Saturday night, just a few people from the neighborhood and one or two from Mike's job. Did you know he's got a new job? It's at the dry cleaners. Anyway, very casual, pigs in a blanket and chips and dip, though if you wanted to bring something fancier, you're welcome to! Oh, what I mean is, we'd love it if you and Paddy could come, too. Starts at seven and goes on till who knows when!"

Mary Bernadette was briefly stunned. There was very little in the entire known world that she would like to do less than to spend an evening hobnobbing with the Burrows and their mates. Really, she thought, what had possessed the woman to invite people so clearly not of their social circle?

"Thank you," she said, regaining her voice, "but I'm afraid we have a prior commitment that evening."

"Oh, that's too bad," Lucy said. "Well, maybe some other time then."

Mary Bernadette smiled slightly.

It was then that Lucy reached out and put her hand on Mary Bernadette's arm. "You take care, Mrs. F.," she said, lowering her voice to a whisper. "Don't let them rich types get you down. Pardon my French." Lucy removed her hand and hurried back across the street to her house with the perpetually broken shutter.

Mary Bernadette got into her car and sat for a moment before starting the engine. The encounter had left a bad taste in her mouth. The last thing she wanted was pity from the likes of Lucy Burrows. And that's what the invitation to that dreadful party had been, an act of pity. The last thing Mary Bernadette wanted from *anyone* was pity.

CHAPTER 78

"Where's your brother?" Alexis asked.

"At home with Dad," Danica told her. "They're going to someplace where they've got pool tables and video games and pizza and beer. Well, the beer is for Dad."

Alexis and Danica were sitting at the picnic table behind the cottage, a picnic table she and PJ never used these days. They were eating tuna salad sandwiches.

"This is a really good sandwich," Danica said around a mouth full of food. "Grandma's tuna is so bland."

"She doesn't add fresh dill. Or onions, for that matter."

Danica took a long drink of water and smacked her lips when done. "Don't tell anyone, but I hate when I have to eat lunch at her house," she admitted. "She never lets me have dessert. I have to wait until after dinner."

Alexis smiled. "Don't worry. I know where PJ keeps his secret stash of M&M's."

"Awesome!" Danica took another huge bite of her sandwich, chewed, and swallowed. "And another thing," she said. "Grandma tried to give me this old blouse of hers. I mean, I guess it's nice of her to give me stuff but . . ." Danica lowered her voice to her loud whisper. "It has a *bow* at the neck. What's that about?"

Alexis bit back another smile. "What did you say?"

"I didn't know *what* to say! Luckily, Mom was there too, and she said something like, oh, thanks, Mary Bernadette, but Danica has too many clothes already—which I do *not*!—and why don't you give it to the charity shop."

Brave woman, Alexis thought. To say no to Mary Bernadette Fitzgibbon! "Was your grandmother upset?" she asked.

Danica shrugged. "I don't know. I just ran out here!"

Now Alexis did laugh. "Well, I'm glad you did."

Danica finished the sandwich Alexis had made for her and wiped her mouth with her sleeve, ignoring the paper napkin by her plate.

"You know," she said. "I usually think of PJ as my uncle, not my brother. It doesn't really make a difference, right?"

"I guess not."

"And I think of you as my aunt. Is that okay?"

"Sure," Alexis said. "I mean, it's nice that you consider me family."

"Of course you're family! You're married to my brother. You have our name."

Yes, she did now have the privilege—or the burden—of the Fitzgibbon name, that much was true. But it didn't really make her Fitzgibbon material, did it? Maybe she simply wasn't meant to be a part of this family. After all, she had come to suspect that in some way she had married PJ under false pretenses—her own, not his. In spite of her genuine love for him, she had married PJ while under the delusion that he and he alone would provide a fulfilling life for her.

"You don't have a boyfriend, do you?" she asked Danica.

Danica grimaced. "No way! And I'm not ever getting married, either. I'm going to live all by myself in a huge mansion with lots of dogs. We can't have a dog now because David's allergic—not superallergic but sort of—but when I grow up I'm going to have at least ten. Maybe a few more. And definitely a pug and a husky."

"It sounds like heaven," Alexis noted. "Animals are a lot less trouble than people."

Danica nodded. "Oh," she said, her tone quite serious, "they are *way* less trouble. Um, can we get the M&M's now?"

CHAPTER 79

Mary Bernadette had just finished stocking the drawer under the toaster oven with clean dishtowels and was now busy straightening the knives on their magnetic rack. Ordinarily she took some pleasure and satisfaction from such simple domestic chores, but today her spirits simply refused to rise above a level very close to depression.

In fact, all week her spirits had been low. Megan and Danica had visited the day before, and while Mary Bernadette usually welcomed a visit from her daughter-in-law and granddaughter, on this occasion she had found herself eager for them to leave.

And it had occurred to her that her granddaughter might not like her very much. Danica had darted out of the house just before lunch without an explanation of where she was going. Alexis had called a moment later to say that Danica would be having lunch with her. And Megan hadn't seemed at all concerned that her daughter had so unceremoniously fled. Well, other people's parenting choices had always been a mystery to Mary Bernadette.

A knock at the front door dragged Mary Bernadette from her thoughts. She opened it to find Katie Keefe on the doorstep.

"I hope I'm not disturbing you," Katie said. "I know you're always so busy."

"Not at all," she said. "Come in."

Mary Bernadette led Katie to the kitchen and offered her a cup of tea.

"Oh, no, thank you, Mary Bernadette. I've only got a moment but I just had to tell you the most appalling thing, and it isn't fit for the phone."

Mary Bernadette frowned. Was there no end to bad news these days? "Has anyone been hurt?" she asked. "Is Bonnie all right?"

"Oh, Bonnie is fine, but she's part of my story! Bonnie ran into Eve Hennessy yesterday afternoon at the library. And Eve had the nerve to march up to her and say right out of the blue that your not entering the garden contest this year was a sure sign of guilt, a downright admission of past wrongdoing. That was the exact phrase she used, 'past wrongdoing.' Can you imagine!"

Yes, thought Mary Bernadette with a sudden sense of great weariness. *I can imagine all sorts of things.*

Katie went on with her tale. "Bonnie told her what's what, you can be sure of that. She said the librarian, you know, Lillian Ross, threatened to ask her to leave if she didn't lower her voice!"

"Yes," Mary Bernadette said, trying and failing to find a polite way to ask her neighbor to leave. "Bonnie can be excitable."

Katie sighed. "There's some in this town who just love to make mischief, and Eve Hennessy is one of them. Do you know what I heard about her?"

"How could I?" Mary Bernadette replied. Really, Katie could be such a trial.

"I heard, and it was from a good authority, that she ran off with a much older man when she was in high school and had to be dragged back by the police. After that, her father put her in a private boarding school so there was always someone to keep an eye on her."

"Who was the good authority?" Mary Bernadette asked, though she had no interest in the answer. She had come to know all too well how damaging gossip could be.

"Well, I shouldn't say, but it was Kris Nelson from the post office. *She* had the story from Sara Gates, Marilyn Windsor's housekeeper. It only goes to show that some people are bad news from the start."

"Yes," Mary Bernadette said. "Some people are troublesome."

Katie put her hand on Mary Bernadette's arm. "You know," she said, "Bonnie and I will stick by you till the end, no matter what."

Mary Bernadette managed a smile. "Thank you," she said. "I appreciate your loyalty."

When Katie had finally gone off, Mary Bernadette sank into a chair at the kitchen table. She wondered if Lillian Ross had overheard the details of Eve's conversation with Bonnie. And who else had Eve approached with her poisonous accusations and lies? Had Wynston Meadows himself heard this latest calumny?

Katie had sworn her allegiance "till the end." Now Mary Bernadette found herself wondering what that end would look like. She wondered if that end was near. She wondered if Wynston Meadows would indeed be the death of her.

CHAPTER 80

"Magnolia, gingko, dogwood, and lacebark pine," Alexis said, pointing to each tree in turn. "Paddy Fitzgibbon taught me their names."

"Impressive! I can hardly tell a rose from a daffodil."

Morgan had invited Alexis to a picnic lunch in Oliver's Grove. Alexis had brought sandwiches from the Pink Rose Café, and Morgan had contributed bottled water and a monstrous blondie from Cookies 'n Crumpets for them to share.

The meeting was perfectly innocent. Still, Alexis knew it would be a disaster if any member of the Fitzgibbon family should happen to spot them. But she hadn't been afraid enough not to come.

"Do you remember the challenge I gave you when we were in Somerstown?" Morgan asked, unwrapping his sandwich.

"To tell you three things about myself. True things." *Things that have nothing to do with the Fitzgibbons.*

"And?"

Alexis laughed uncomfortably. "I'm still thinking about it."

"It shouldn't be difficult to know yourself, should it?"

"No," she admitted. "It shouldn't be. Still, I need a little more time."

"I had an idea the other day," Morgan said a few minutes later. "Why don't you come to work for me at the gallery."

Alexis almost choked on her sandwich. It was the last thing she had expected to hear from him. "Are you kidding?" she said when she had swallowed.

Morgan shrugged. "Why would I be kidding?"

"But what would I *do*?"

"Well, you'd start out as an assistant, help me with the business end of things. Over time, you'd learn about the objects themselves—how to recognize real from fake, how to identify makers' marks, how to date unmarked pieces. It would be a great education."

"Well, it certainly would be different from writing checks and taking complaints, which is pretty much all I do at Fitzgibbon Landscaping," Alexis admitted. "And learning about antiques sounds really *interesting*."

"I think it is, but then again, I'm an antiques nerd."

"I wouldn't say you're a nerd. You're an expert."

Morgan laughed. "Or so I make people believe. Seriously, Alexis, you're wasting your artistic talents being an office manager."

"Well, I can't argue with that."

"I could teach you the business from the ground up. Someday, if you wanted, you could open your own gallery. As long as you don't compete directly with me!"

Alexis took a deep breath. The idea was immensely appealing. But it was impossible. "She'd never let me leave," Alexis said, putting her sandwich on the bench by her side, all appetite gone. "Mary Bernadette, I mean. It's not that she likes me. I'm sure she'd love me to just disappear from her life. But as long as I'm here she wants to control me. No, it's more than that. She wants to *break* me."

"That bad?" Gently and briefly Morgan touched her hand.

"You have no idea," Alexis said, her voice ever so slightly cracking.

"Your husband's grandmother doesn't own you," Morgan said. "You're an adult. You're your own person."

"Of course. But you don't understand. It wouldn't be possible to leave Fitzgibbon Landscaping. My husband . . ." *My husband,* she thought, *has already scolded me for defying Saint Mary Bernadette.*

"What?" Morgan pressed. "What about him?"

Alexis shook her head. She couldn't talk about PJ with Morgan. She wouldn't. "The family would think I was being terribly disloyal," she said carefully. "They've never had a stranger working in the office."

And PJ would leave me, she thought. *He would take his grand-mother's side, again. He apologized the other night—and so did I—and we meant it, but nothing has really changed. And do I care?* At that moment, Alexis truly didn't know the answer to that question.

Morgan sighed. "I hate to see you so unhappy, Alexis."

She turned away and stared blindly at a sweetbay magnolia tree. Its blooms, Paddy had told her, smelled like lemons. *Oh God,* she thought. *What am I going to do?*

"Well," Morgan said after a moment, "just think about my offer, okay?"

She turned back to him. "Thank you, Morgan," she said. "Really."

Morgan bundled his trash into his paper bag and got up. "I'd better run. Someone's coming to the gallery at two to look at a set of flatware. Take care of yourself, Alexis."

Alexis sat alone for some time, staring ahead and seeing nothing. She could no longer deny that her feelings for Morgan had deepened into something that felt a lot like love. She wanted very badly to kiss him and to be kissed by him. Beyond that she didn't dare allow herself to imagine.

She wondered if Morgan had offered her a job as an excuse to be close to her and realized that she didn't care if he had. She would like to be close to him, too. Working side by side with someone she cared for. . . . Once she had thought she would find that sort of perfect companionship with PJ. Once she had harbored the fantasy of being part of an old-fashioned family business, part of an old-fashioned *family.* But what a fool she had been, thinking that PJ could give her a ready-made life. No one could do that. Not even Morgan Shelby.

Alexis sighed, gathered the remains of her lunch, and walked slowly back to her car. Fitzgibbon Landscaping was waiting.

Chapter 81

Alexis checked her watch. It would be at least forty minutes before PJ got home from work. There was plenty of time to make a call to her mother, but she did not want to make the call from the cottage. Mary Bernadette might have planted a listening device in the bookcase. PJ might be lurking under a window, just out of sight. Yes, Alexis knew she was being ridiculously paranoid, but she couldn't shake the feeling that her every move was being scrutinized. She scribbled a note for her husband. She told him she had gone out for a walk. Well, that was true as far as it went.

She left the cottage and walked down Honeysuckle Lane. At the end of the street she turned on to Austin Road, where she made the call on her cell phone. She continued to walk away from the cottage as she talked to her mother.

"I don't know how it happened, Mom," Alexis said after they had exchanged greetings. "For a while everything was fine. And now, I just feel so—so trapped."

"I told you marrying that boy was a bad idea," Olivia Trenouth replied.

Alexis laughed in surprise. "You never said anything of the kind!"

"Well, I certainly thought it. I still do. And your father agrees with me. We both feel that he's immature. We both feel that he relies on you to agree with his every whim without protest. Not that we think he's a bad person. Just a little too self-centered."

"I can't believe I'm hearing this," Alexis said. "Why *didn't* you say anything to me? Why didn't you *warn* me?"

Olivia Trenouth sighed. "Because you wouldn't have listened to me. You know I'm right about that, Alexis. Young love is blind and stubborn."

Yes, she admitted. It was. "But what am I supposed to do now?" she asked.

"I don't know, Alexis. Get away from that little town for a while. Come back to Philadelphia. Do you know who was asking for you? Damian Branson, that wonderful young doctor who treated your father a few years back. He couldn't believe it when he heard you'd married and moved to the country."

"It's not entirely rural," Alexis replied lamely. A vague image of Dr. Branson passed before her eyes. He was tall, she remembered. And he had kind eyes. Was her mother attempting to play matchmaker?

"But it's not the metropolis! What sort of career opportunities can there possibly be for you in Oliver's Well?" Olivia Trenouth asked.

A career as a gallery owner? But was that what *she* really wanted, or was it only what Morgan wanted for her? "I don't know," she said honestly. "Look, I should go now. Thanks, Mom."

Her mother laughed. "I don't know that I've done anything for which I deserve thanks. Be well, Alexis."

Alexis tucked her cell phone into her pocket. Well, at least she knew that her parents were willing to take her in if she separated from her husband. That was something for which to be grateful. They might feel that she had made a mistake by marrying PJ Fitzgibbon, but they had no interest in punishing her for it. Alexis sighed and turned back toward her narrow little life on Honeysuckle Lane.

CHAPTER 82

"What's wrong, Mary? Your face is a thundercloud."
Mary Bernadette pulled a chair out from the kitchen table, where her husband sat with a cup of tea, and dropped into it with less than her usual grace.

"I'll tell you what's wrong," she said. "Wynston Meadows is what's wrong."

"Now, calm down," Paddy said in his much practiced soothing voice. "What did he do this time?"

"I received a call earlier from Marilyn Windsor. She was having dinner at The Angry Squire last night and she overheard Wynston Meadows talking to Jack Burton from the bank. She swears his exact words were 'Mary Bernadette Fitzgibbon wasn't even born in this town, let alone this country, yet she acts as if she's the sole and proper heiress to its history.'"

Paddy shook his head. "Gossip," he said. "There should be a law against it."

"What gives him the right to defame me like this?"

"Nothing gives him the right, Mary," Paddy assured her.

"Doesn't a flag fly proudly outside my home? Don't I march in the Independence Day Parade every year, no matter the weather? Don't I vote in every single election? I'm as much a citizen of the United States as Wynston Meadows!"

"No one doubts that, Mary."

"Don't they? Mr. Meadows certainly does!"

"Gossip, again. Marilyn Windsor shouldn't have passed on Mr. Meadows's words. There was no need for you to hear them. They've only caused you more worry."

Mary Bernadette shook her head. "Marilyn only meant to warn me. Forewarned is forearmed."

"I'm not so sure she meant well," Paddy argued. "Maybe she

regrets having given you those family diaries. Maybe this was a way to get back at you for . . ."

"For what, Paddy?" Mary Bernadette demanded. "For persuading her to donate a valuable item to the OWHA for the benefit of the entire town?"

Paddy said no more on the subject of Marilyn Windsor.

Mary Bernadette suddenly got up from the table, her chair screeching against the tiled floor. "I defy that man to name every president of these great United States and in order."

"Mary. Please, let it go."

She did not respond to her husband. Paddy sighed, got up from the table, and brought his teacup to the sink. "I'm going to take Mercy for a walk," he said.

When he was gone, Mary Bernadette continued to fume. As much as she knew that a good Catholic was called upon to forgive her enemies, in this case she simply could not do so. And she would never admit—especially not to her husband—that at times she felt a murderous rage against the man, when she wasn't feeling out of her wits with fear.

Mary Bernadette made the sign of the cross, bowed her head, and prayed. When the prayer had been uttered, she made the sign of the cross again. "No," she said with conviction, to the air around her, to whoever would listen. "Wynston Meadows does not deserve my forgiveness."

CHAPTER 83

"The procedure is called derotation osteotomy. It involves cutting the femur and repositioning the ball of the femur in the hip socket," Pat told his mother over the phone the next morning.

"And why is this necessary?" Mary Bernadette asked, her hand over her heart.

"Because his hips are coming out of the sockets. The spastic muscles are causing abnormal forces on the bone. The result is what they call in-toeing, which is just what it sounds like. You've seen how David's gait has deteriorated in the past two years."

"Yes. Of course. Both legs will be . . . will be broken?"

"Cut, yes. They'll insert a metal plate in each femur so the legs will stay in their new position, pointing straight ahead. He probably won't need a cast, just some bandages over the incisions. Recovery could take some time, which is why we're doing this in the summer. Maybe four weeks or so depending on how comfortable he feels getting back to everyday activities."

"And how long will he be in the hospital?"

"Four or five days. And he'll probably need a walker for a bit, and some meds and a muscle relaxant for the pain. And, of course, he'll work with a physical therapist. But David's a pro at actively managing his CP. I know he'll be a fantastic patient. He's one hundred percent in favor of the surgery."

"Of course he'll be a good patient."

"Hopefully," Pat went on, "when all this is over he won't be in constant pain. Not that he complains, but it's a lousy way to live, always compensating for pain. It holds him back, and David hates being held back, in anything."

"Yes," Mary Bernadette said, very carefully. "Well, thank you for informing me. We'll certainly all be praying for him."

"I'm sure you will be, Mom. Say hi to Dad for me. And don't

worry, all right? If you or Dad have any questions about David's surgery, call Meg or me. Okay?"

Mary Bernadette promised her son and hung up the receiver. She took a seat at the kitchen table. Her worst fears were being realized. People went into the hospital and never came out. Children. Children like her son William and now perhaps her grandson David. To purposely cut into a child's legs ... It was an abomination.

They should have listened to me, she thought, her hands squeezing into fists. She had warned her son that something terrible would happen if David and his sister weren't baptized. Hadn't her mother and her aunt Catherine told her that children who weren't baptized were prey to the fairies, evil and mischievous creatures who would snatch the children right out of their cribs and make off with them, leaving behind a weak and mewling thing for the grieving mother to support.

And so Mary Bernadette had wondered about her grandson, no matter that David's affliction had occurred at birth, before he could possibly have been baptized. Paddy had laughed at her fears. "Now, Mary," he had said, "fairies stealing babies indeed! It's just a silly old superstition and you know it. Besides, Danica is just fine and she's not baptized, either."

"God works in mysterious ways," she had replied. "No doubt he has some trial planned for her, too."

Her husband had admonished her. "Are you saying that your grandson is a changeling child? Mary, get ahold of yourself. Next you'll be seeing leprechauns behind the hedges!"

Paddy was right, of course. They were awful old superstitions, full of trickery and malice around every bend. They had no place in the modern world. Yet they had pursued her all her life and now they would not let her rest for two moments at a time.

Mary Bernadette unclenched her hands and folded them on the table before her. She knew that despair was a sin. She knew that it was wrong to question God's wisdom. She knew also that she wanted very badly to release her fears and her anguish in a

great and awful howl. Maybe then God would finally hear and
come to her rescue.

But she would never do it.

CHAPTER 84

Megan was in the kitchen preparing dinner when she heard
her husband pull up the driveway. A few minutes later he
appeared, yanking off his tie and opening the top buttons of his
shirt.

"Hi," he said. "Smells good."

"Hi. It should. I'm sautéing onions in butter."

"Heaven. Where are the twins?" Pat asked, retrieving a bottle
of red wine from the cupboard and loudly scrambling through
the drawer that housed the corkscrew.

"In their rooms," Megan said, "doing homework. Or so they say."

Pat opened the bottle and poured them each a glass. "Sante,"
he said.

"Your good health." Megan took an appreciative sip of the
cabernet.

"I did something very stupid today," Pat announced.

"Oh?" Megan said, turning back to the stove. "What was it?"

"I called PJ."

Megan looked over her shoulder at her husband. "You never
call PJ."

"Seems there's a good reason for that."

"Okay, what happened?" Megan asked. She turned off the
heat under the saucepan and turned back to her husband.

"In a fit of self-righteousness and know-it-all-icity, I suggested again that he might convince Dad to sell the company. I

suggested that he finally go to law school and escape all that small-town nonsense and in-fighting. Not to mention his grandmother's overwhelming influence. Well, I kept that bit to myself."

Megan winced. "And what did he say to all that?"

"He wasn't receptive. Wait, that's an understatement. He told me to back off. He said that he'd made his decision and was sticking to it. He said that he was happy."

"Well, he is an adult, Pat. He has a right to make up his own mind. Which is not to say that on some level I wish he had settled somewhere other than Oliver's Well. But it's his life to lead, not ours."

"I know. I just wanted to help, but I guess I screwed things up even more."

"I wouldn't say that. Exactly."

Pat finished his glass of wine. "Anyway," he said, "I couldn't keep my mind on work after that, so I spent most of the afternoon thinking about how I've—let's say, how I've related to my oldest son. And you know what I realized?"

"What?" Megan asked.

"I realized that I've been behaving too much like how my parents behaved when I made the decision to reject the family business. In other words, I've failed to accept PJ for who he is. Not me. His own man."

And haven't I been hinting as much for years, Megan thought. What she said was, "I think all parents have to struggle at some point with the idea of a child being an entirely separate person."

"Don't try to make things easy for me, Meg. I know when I've been wrong. I know when I've been pigheaded."

"Well . . ."

"But I'm still worried about my mother and PJ. She's got undue influence over him. She could ruin PJ's marriage if she had a mind to."

Megan nodded. "I agree. But if PJ *is* weak enough to allow his grandmother's interference to destroy his marriage, then the fault lies with PJ as much as it does with Mary Bernadette."

"You'd think that with all her professions of faith she'd take the sacrament of marriage a bit more seriously."

"Your mother," Megan noted, "like most people, exercises selective morality. She believes that not all of the rules apply to her all of the time."

Pat was quiet and Megan let him be.

"I think we should go down to Oliver's Well again this weekend," he said after a time. "I want to apologize to PJ face-to-face."

"All right. I'll see if I can get the kids situated at a friend's house for Saturday night. Danica's been going on about a sleepover with Rachel. And David loves any excuse to hang out with Clay. His parents got a pool table, and it seems David's determined to become a shark."

"He didn't tell me that. Sheesh, another son I'm alienating."

"Pat. Stop it. He didn't even tell me. Danica told me in passing."

"So they're already at the age when they're hiding stuff from their parents. Where does the time go, Meg?"

Megan laughed. "If I had a good answer to that," she said, "we'd be rich."

CHAPTER 85

It was a Saturday in late April, about three in the afternoon. Megan and Pat had just arrived at the house on Honeysuckle Lane.

"Why aren't the twins with you?" Mary Bernadette asked her son as she poured him a cup of tea.

Pat sighed. "Mom, I already told you over the phone. They each have a sleepover."

Mary Bernadette frowned. "I don't understand the need for parents to let their children sleep in other people's homes. I certainly didn't let you or your sister spend the night in some strange house where who knows what might have gone on."

"I'm aware," Pat said. "Not that it bothered *me* all that much, but I remember Grace being pretty pissed about it."

"She most certainly was not—annoyed. Grace was always a sensible girl."

"A sensible girl who really wanted to sleep over at her friend's house and eat junk food and stay up all night watching movies and talking about boys."

"That's all in the past," Megan said. "There's no point in digging it up."

"Let sleeping dogs lie," Paddy murmured.

Mary Bernadette would happily have continued to press her point about the dangers and silliness of sleepovers. Still, there were other matters that needed to be addressed.

"Is it really necessary that the poor boy go under the knife?" she asked her son.

Pat rolled his eyes. It was a rude habit Mary Bernadette had failed to break him of long ago. True, she occasionally indulged, but only when she was alone. "Yes, Mom," he said, "it is. Do you really think we would put our child through surgery if it *wasn't* necessary?"

"Doctors can be persuasive, and all for their own benefit. It's why I never go to them. They can talk all manner of foolishness." *And they failed to save the life of my son,* she added silently. *They might as well have killed him outright.*

"David's doctors are wonderful," Megan said. "We have complete faith in them."

The woman is so naïve, Mary Bernadette thought. *What kind of lawyer must she be if she can be so easily deceived?*

"He should be in a special school," she said now, "one where the teachers and nurses know how to properly take care of a child with David's affliction."

"Mom, that word—"

Mary Bernadette ignored her son's interruption. "All that running around and trying to keep up with the normal children is probably why his legs are in the state they're in."

"Actually, Mary Bernadette—"

Mary Bernadette ignored her daughter-in-law's interruption as well. Would no one listen to her any longer? Would no one give her thoughts and opinions the consideration and respect they deserved?

"You should have had those children baptized," she said firmly.

Pat sighed. "Mom, we've been over this before. Baptized or not, David would still have CP."

"I've tried to tell her," Paddy said quietly. "Time and again."

And then Mary Bernadette had had enough, enough of being ignored, and doubted, and treated with disrespect. "Poor David!" she cried. "We should have taken that child away from the two of you when he was born. We might have done something positive for him! Instead, look at what's become of the boy, and not even going to Heaven when he dies!"

With a strange sense of detachment, Mary Bernadette watched her family react to her words. For a very brief moment she wondered if she had indeed said what she thought that she had. *We should have taken that child away from the two of you.*

"Mary—" Paddy put out his hand, as if to reach for her, but then stepped back. Vaguely, Mary Bernadette wondered if her husband was afraid that she might slap him away. Vaguely, she thought that she might.

Megan got up from the table and quietly left the kitchen. No stomping of feet or slamming of doors. No muttering under her breath and no angry looks. Not a tear in her eye. *Unnatural,* Mary Bernadette thought. *Does nothing move that woman?*

Pat now took a step toward his mother, his fists clenched at his side. "That was reprehensible," he said angrily. "That was completely disrespectful of the mother of my children. And of me, your own son."

Mary Bernadette turned from Pat and Paddy. She wished they would both go away. Shame warred with anger in her breast. Embarrassment wrestled with pride. "When wrathful words arise, a closed mouth is soothing." She heard her father's voice whispering in her ear. She shivered.

Pat's laugh was angry and dark. "I don't know why I bother to come here anymore," he said, and walked resolutely out of the room.

Paddy cleared his throat. "Mary," he said, quietly but forcefully, "you were cruel. Apologize now, before it's too late. If it's not too late already."

Mary Bernadette kept her back to her husband. "I have nothing for which to apologize," she said, her voice a bit shrill. "I simply spoke my mind." *I spoke*, she added silently, *the violence in my heart*.

"If not for Pat's sake, then for Megan's," Paddy went on. "Megan has always been so good to you, to all of us. She doesn't deserve to be treated so shabbily."

"I've said what I've said." Mary Bernadette turned again to face her husband. She realized that her hands were shaking, and she put them firmly on the back of a chair.

"Mary, you're flushed. Sit down and let me make you another cup of tea."

"I don't need a cup of tea, thank you. I'm perfectly fine." She walked over to the oven. With a hand still trembling she turned it on to preheat. "I must start dinner now. Would you like peas or string beans this evening, Paddy?"

"Mary—"

"I think it will be peas."

She heard her husband leave the kitchen. When he was gone, Mary Bernadette put a hand to her aching head.

CHAPTER 86

Pat opened the door to the bedroom that had been his as a child. It was where he and Megan regularly stayed when they visited his parents. There was that awful crucifix on the wall over the old wooden dresser. Pat envisioned tearing it down and chucking it out the window. There was a rocking chair big enough only for a toddler or a teddy bear. And there was the old narrow bed that his mother had never replaced with one more suitable for two people. Pat had always thought it was because Mary Bernadette refused to encourage even a married couple lying together under her roof.

Megan was sitting on the edge of that narrow bed, her hands folded in her lap. Pat had another vision of rushing back downstairs and shoving his mother against a wall. With effort he composed himself and sat down next to his wife.

"Are you all right?" he asked.

"I'm fine."

"Well, I'm not. I'm furious."

Megan sighed. "Look, she's under terrible stress, what with Wynston Meadows and the obvious trouble between Alexis and PJ. You know how she dotes on PJ."

"Don't make excuses for her. The woman implied we're unfit parents. I can take her garbage, after fifty years of it. But to say something so despicable to you is unforgivable."

"I'm not making excuses," Megan protested, "not exactly. I'm just trying to explain her to you—and to myself. There are reasons behind her behavior, motives. There *have* to be, and if I can understand them I can better handle her."

Pat laughed. "Did it ever occur to you that she's just a nasty person? That she acts in the wretched way she does and says the hurtful things she says just for the heck of it?"

"No. I don't believe that. I'm tempted to at times, but no."

"Then you're a better person than I am, Meg. Maybe it's due to that Prayer of St. Francis you're so fond of."

"No," Megan said. "It's just that we have different perspectives. You're her son, her child. You inherited all that sadness about William. You had to deal with all the pressure she put on you to be like him, all the unfair comparisons to what a dead boy might have been."

Pat sighed. "When you put it like that it sounds so macabre and Victorian. It *is* pretty insane, isn't it, to be jealous of the dead. You know, sometimes, even now, I wonder what my life would have been like if William had lived. What my mother would have been like. I wonder if we'd all have been happier. Well, of course we would have."

"It's said there's no pain as horrible as the death of a child," Megan reminded him. "Losing William truly might have warped your mother's capacity for happiness. I can't imagine what losing PJ or David or Danica would do to me."

Pat put his arm around his wife. "You wouldn't take out your grief on the surviving children. You wouldn't exclude your husband from your mourning. You wouldn't become like my mother, so cold and deliberate. So hard."

"So unhappy."

"Do you want to go home right now?" Pat asked.

"No. That would just make things worse. We'll stay, have dinner, then we can leave tomorrow after you talk with PJ."

"I almost forgot that's why we came here in the first place. He won't be at dinner tonight?"

Megan shook her head. "He said something about having other plans."

"Yeah. Avoiding me. But Megan, what if my mother erupts again?"

"She won't. I suspect she feels badly about what happened. I suspect she'll do her best to act as if it never *did* happen."

"Well, dinner should be a real treat."

"You'll behave, won't you, Pat?"

"For you, Meg, I'd do anything." He pulled his wife to his breast and held her tightly.

"And if I suddenly decide to throw a punch," his wife whispered in his ear, "be sure to stop me."

CHAPTER 87

Alexis took a deep breath and pushed opened the door to the Shelby Gallery. She hadn't seen Morgan since their picnic lunch the week before. She had planned her visits to downtown Oliver's Well to be as brief and as infrequent as she could manage, and she had studiously avoided even glancing in the direction of the gallery. But she couldn't avoid Morgan forever. She owed him an answer to his incredibly kind and generous offer of a job. Maybe it was also a self-serving offer. But what was wrong with someone *wanting* to be with her?

After many a sleepless night and many a tortured waking moment, Alexis had decided that there was no way in good conscience she could work with Morgan Shelby and not put her marriage at a grave risk of complete failure. And a failure of her short-lived marriage would be mortifying. She did not think she could stand the shame.

Alexis's decision did not bring her contentment. She wanted to be happy. She believed that she *deserved* to be happy and she wasn't, not now, and she simply couldn't see how she could ever be, not with things the way they were in the world of the Fitzgibbons. At best it could be said that she and PJ were carefully co-existing. It was no way to live. But she had taken a solemn vow before God and her family and her friends to love and to cherish PJ Fitzgibbon for the rest of her life, and she was determined to do everything in her power to keep that vow. She was determined.

Morgan was standing behind the counter when she came through the door. "Hi," he said with a smile. "It's been a while."

Alexis thought there was a slight nervousness in his manner, though she suspected that what she perceived was merely a projection of her own distress.

"I've been busy," she said.

"That's good. Better than being bored, anyway."

Alexis attempted a smile and failed. "I've been doing a lot of thinking," she said.

Morgan came around the counter. "Why don't we talk in back?"

Alexis was torn. She didn't want to be entirely alone with Morgan. But she didn't want what she had to say to be interrupted by the arrival of a customer. "All right," she said. She followed him back to the small hall at the foot of the stairs that led to his apartment.

"Now," Morgan said. "What have you been thinking about?"

"I can't accept your offer of a job," Alexis told him. "I wish I could, but I can't."

Morgan's expression darkened. "Is it because of—"

"No. Yes."

"Alexis, I—"

"Please, Morgan. I can't—"

Morgan put his hands on her arms and looked at her searchingly. Alexis felt her body lean forward, toward him. And then their faces were very close. Alexis closed her eyes. Her resolve melted away. What there had been of her resistance dissipated. *Let it happen then. I want it to happen.* She felt his warm breath on her cheeks. *This is the turning point. There will be no going back. After this moment I will have committed adultery.* And then with a cry, she opened her eyes and tore out of Morgan's embrace.

"I'm sorry," she said, her hand on her heart. "I shouldn't have . . . I'm so sorry."

Morgan shook his head. "It's all right. It was my fault."

"No, it was mine," Alexis insisted. "The fault is entirely mine."

"Alexis, please—" Morgan reached out a hand but did not come toward her.

"I have to go now," Alexis said, tears beginning to dribble down her face. "I—I can't see you again." Then she turned and ran.

"Alexis, wait!"

The door slammed behind her, its bell furiously clapping. Alexis ran until she was out of sight of the gallery. Then she turned off Main Street onto a block of private homes and, panting, came to a stop. She wiped ineffectually at the tears coursing down her cheeks. She was horrified by her behavior. It *was* all her fault. Morgan Shelby was a good man. She had led him on. She had acted inappropriately. She shouldn't have gone to the gallery today. She should simply have called Morgan and told him that she couldn't accept his offer of a job and then she should have vowed never to seek him out again.

Alexis took a deep, shuddering breath. All along she had been telling herself that there was nothing inappropriate in her relationship with Morgan, and yet all along she had been acting as if their relationship *was* inappropriate. She had never mentioned him to PJ. She had lied about where she had been while spending time with Morgan. She had sat at the dinner table beside her husband, fantasizing about another man.

Yes, Alexis thought, standing alone outside a trim little brick house with a pretty little garden, *I am as guilty of betrayal as if I'd been sharing Morgan Shelby's bed.*

CHAPTER 88

"Alexis!"

Alexis whirled around. It was Maureen Kline. It seemed like ages since they had last met.

"I saw you from the corner," Maureen said. "Forgive me for saying so, but you don't look so good. Oh no, you've been crying. Are you sick?"

"Yes." Alexis put her hand to her forehead. "No. Oh, I don't know . . ."

"Look, come to my house. You're in a good old-fashioned state of distress and we don't want the populace of Oliver's Well making assumptions."

Alexis let herself be led back to Main Street and then to Maureen's car, which was parked outside her office. Ten minutes later the two women were sitting in Maureen's kitchen, a pitcher of water, a bottle of whiskey, and two glasses on the table before them.

"Medicinal purposes, you understand," Maureen said with a smile.

Alexis managed an answering smile and took a bracing sip of the whiskey Maureen poured for her.

"Now," Maureen said, "tell me what's happened."

Alexis did. She told her about how stifled she had come to feel, living in the cottage in full view of PJ's grandparents. She told her about how Mary Bernadette was always criticizing her and about how PJ never stood up for her. She told her about how she felt at a dead end. And she told her about how she had met Morgan Shelby. He had been nice to her. They had talked about interesting things, things not related to Fitzgibbon Landscaping and the OWHA. He had shown interest in her photography. He had said that he believed in her talent. She did not mention his offer of a job. She did not mention that they had almost kissed.

Alexis sighed. "And that's the whole awful story in a nutshell. I never meant to—to become so attracted to Morgan. And I love my husband. I do. It's just that things between us are so awful right now. It's just that I'm so confused."

Maureen finished her whiskey and put the glass down with a thump. "Look," she said, "the first thing we need to do is avoid social disaster. Given the reputation of the Fitzgibbon family and Wynston Meadows's determination to tarnish it, you're a natural target for the gossips."

Alexis put her hands to her head. "Oh God, what have I done!"

"Nothing yet, if you're telling me the truth."

"I am," Alexis said, amazed that her cheeks weren't flaming with the lie. "I swear."

"All right. The thing is Alexis, you need to be very, very careful when you live in a town like Oliver's Well. I said once that the Fitzgibbons live in each other's back pockets. Well, the same might be said of everyone here. When my former husband was cheating on me, most of the town knew before I did. Unfortunately, I learned about his bad behavior from an old busybody who took some pleasure in letting me know."

Alexis leaned across the table and put her hand on Maureen's arm. "I'm so sorry."

Maureen looked down at her empty glass. "People can turn vicious in the presence of another person's grief, even those who are usually quite kind."

"It's awful here," Alexis said vehemently, sitting back in her seat. "I hate it."

"Oliver's Well isn't worse than any other small town. And there's the flip side of the coin. When someone is in real trouble, the neighbors come out in force to help."

"Is that really true, Maureen? Or is it just a tale people in small towns tell themselves to make the stifling life they live bearable?"

Maureen did not answer the question; Alexis thought her silence spoke volumes.

"You need," Maureen said then, "to keep far away from Morgan Shelby. That's the first step toward making things right. Hopefully anyone who might have seen you together will soon forget what they saw if there's nothing new to remind them. And then you have to talk honestly to PJ."

"But I can't let him know about my feelings for Morgan!" Alexis protested. "He'd be devastated!"

Maureen hesitated a moment before replying. "Yes, well, generally speaking I'm not a fan of secrecy between husband and wife, but in this case I think you're right. From what I know of PJ he's not—forgive me—not mature enough to handle that sort of revelation. He's a lovely young man, but he's got a fair amount of growing up to do. Still, you do have to tell him, calmly and clearly, that you need a—let's say, a path of your own, something that belongs only to you and not the rest of the family." Maureen paused. "Come to think of it, I'm not sure he'd take kindly to that, either, not with his—attachment—to his grandmother and the Family Ideal. Alexis, I'm sorry. I'm afraid I'm not very good at giving advice."

Alexis smiled. "But you're kind. You listened to me. I finally feel there's someone in Oliver's Well I can trust. You *won't* say anything to anyone, will you?"

"The cone of silence is firmly in place. Now, would you like me to drive you home?"

Alexis shook her head. "Thanks, but I left my car in the municipal lot."

And, Alexis thought as she got up from the table, *to think I once was tempted to dismiss Maureen as someone merely resigned to a life of boredom. There's so much more to her. PJ isn't the only one who needs to grow up.*

CHAPTER 89

"Hi," Megan said when her sister-in-law's smiling face appeared on her computer screen. "You're looking cheery."

"I just heard some good news," Grace explained. "One of the women who's been living at the Angela House got accepted to our community college. And she's been awarded enough of a scholarship so that she can actually *go*. It's a huge step in the right direction for her."

"How wonderful."

"It'll be tough going, no doubt. But she's got a support system in place for pretty much the first time in her life so . . ."

Megan smiled. "Do you ever stop to realize just how lucky you are and how supremely good you have it in this cruel world?"

"Every minute. So, what's up with you?"

"Well," Megan said, "there's this." And she related what had happened in Mary Bernadette's kitchen the last time she and Pat had visited. She had debated the benefit of telling her sister-in-law, and in the end she had decided that the very ferocity of the attack merited some attention and perhaps another point of view.

"I'd never felt such vitriol coming from another human being," she told Grace. "And having it directed at me, well, it's not something I'll soon forget. Nor will Pat."

Grace raised her eyebrows and whistled. "Oh boy. Meg, I'm so sorry. There's no excuse for my mother's bad behavior. She's in her right mind, isn't she?"

"Actually, I'm not so sure," Megan admitted. "I can't help but wonder if she isn't having a mental breakdown. She's always been a firecracker, but lately she goes off at the slightest provocation."

"It *could* all come down to the stress she's under because of Meadows's antics. Still, to turn on her family is not the answer."

"No, it isn't. And to make matters worse, Pat wants nothing to do with her. He thinks we should just cut ties, but I can't walk away that easily. I mean, the last thing I want is a rift between factions of Fitzgibbons. PJ dotes on his grandmother, for better or worse, and Paddy—well, I imagine it's been hard on him at times, being Mr. Mary Bernadette, but he's devoted to her. I have to respect that."

Grace laughed. "And *I'm* the Bride of Christ! Meg, you put me to shame. Anyway, I wish Dad had some degree of control over her. Even a bit of influence would do."

"Well, if he ever did, he doesn't have it now. Not that I can see."

"Poor Dad."

"And then there's PJ and Alexis."

"What's going on there?" Grace asked.

"I don't really know," Megan admitted. "They seem to have lost their way. Alexis won't talk to me at all, and I've had one fairly disastrous conversation with PJ, who was being a bit of an obtuse jerk. Not knowing all the details or what's at the root of the problem makes it very difficult to help in any real way."

"It's up to PJ and Alexis to ask for help," Grace pointed out. "No one accepts help until they're ready for it."

"Of course you're right. It's just so sad. They had so much potential as a couple. They were so *glad* to be with each other."

"How much do you think Mom's got to do with their marital woes?" Grace asked.

"I'm pretty sure she's part and parcel, which is another reason I want to avoid a big, definitive split in the family. It will only make PJ cling even more tightly to his grandmother, and there's no way that would be good for his marriage."

"Good point. Look, Meg, have you been praying lately?"

"Does repeating the Prayer of St. Francis a few times a day count?"

Grace laughed. "Well, you know there are ways of praying without just parroting old words. They might be helpful just now."

"I guess you're right. But good old Saint Francis works for me."

"Then stick to him. You know, a colleague of mine is fond of saying that an everyday saint is someone who willingly spends time with the sad and the ill. Someone who looks for the kernel of good in the disagreeable."

Megan laughed. "Well, that leaves me out!"

"No. I think it describes you quite accurately. *You* should be the one in the habit."

"I think Pat would have something to say about that!"

"Yes," Grace said. "I think he might."

CHAPTER 90

Alexis fiddled with her bracelet. She was nervous. PJ would *have* to listen to her. She would have to *make* him listen, because the last time she had been alone with Morgan Shelby she had teetered dangerously on the brink of undeniable betrayal. That sort of thing must never happen again. She knew that. She loved her husband. But she was deeply unhappy. She knew that, too.

PJ was leaning against the kitchen counter, staring down at the screen of his iPhone.

"PJ?" she said.

"Hmm," he replied, without looking up.

"Can we talk? It's important."

"Sure."

He looked at her now, his expression wary. For all they had apologized to each other, she no longer felt comfortable with PJ. Why should he feel comfortable with her?

"I'd like us to see a therapist," she said.

"A therapist?" PJ laughed. "You've got to be kidding!"

Alexis sighed. She had been afraid of this reaction. What had her mother and Maureen said about PJ? That he was immature.

"Why would I be kidding?" she asked. "I've given it a lot of thought and I really don't think we're equipped to handle this—problem—on our own. We don't have the skills."

"Jargon," PJ muttered.

With some effort, Alexis kept her temper. "There are a few couples therapists in Westminster and in Smithstown. I've checked them out online and—"

"No. Alexis. That's not going to happen."

"Why not?"

"We don't need 'skills' to take care of our problems. And we don't need outsiders butting into our personal business."

"Who do you mean by 'we'?" Alexis asked. "You and me or the Fitzgibbons?"

PJ didn't answer.

"My God, you're such a throwback!" Alexis cried, all effort to curb her emotions fled. "Going to therapy doesn't come with a social stigma anymore, you know."

"I'm sorry, Alexis, but no therapy. It's a waste of time and money."

"Money's more important than our marriage?"

PJ rolled his eyes. "I didn't say that."

Alexis turned abruptly away from her husband. She spotted her crystal rosary beads heaped on a shelf of the bookcase. ALEXIS FITZGIBBON was engraved upon the back of the cross. Mary Bernadette and Paddy had given it to her on her wedding day. Alexis remembered showing it to her mother. "What an artifact," she had commented. "I can't see you actually *using* it. And I still don't know why you gave up your own name." Then her mother had smiled. "I hope I recognize you at this time next year. But I fear you're becoming a stranger."

A stranger to my own self, she thought now. Was she no longer her own person? *Had* becoming a Fitzgibbon erased all that was unique and special about her, all that could be cherished and admired as purely her own? All the resolutions and promises she had made, all the prayers she had offered, now seemed pointless in the face of this fresh wave of despair.

Alexis continued to stare at the string of rosary beads. Once it had seemed a symbol of the loving bond between her and the other Fitzgibbons. Now it seemed a heavy, painful, punishing chain, binding her in servitude to people who felt no genuine love for her as a unique and individual person. It had to go. Alexis stalked over to the bookcase and snatched up the string of rosary beads. And in one smooth move she turned and threw it at her husband.

"Alexis!" The rosary hit him in the stomach and fell to the floor in a glittering pile.

"Why don't we just get a divorce and end this nightmare!" she shouted.

Even as the words were coming out of her mouth Alexis knew that a divorce wasn't what she wanted, but her desperation was so great, the feeling of being trapped and unknown was so strong, she just didn't know what salvation she might hope for.

PJ picked up the rosary beads and held them in his fist. His face was a mask of horror and disbelief. Alexis thought that it probably mirrored her own.

"No one in my family gets divorced," he said coldly. "It's simply not done."

"Even if they're miserable?"

PJ didn't respond.

Alexis laughed even as she felt tears stream from her eyes. "Well, maybe you'll be the first, the trailblazer, the innovator!"

"No! We absolutely cannot get a divorce. My grandmother would be devastated!"

"I don't care about your grandmother! How would *you* feel if I left you?"

"I'd feel . . ." PJ's voice suddenly became almost pleading in tone. "Alexis, the thought of divorce never crossed my mind. Things are tough right now, but they'll get better. I promise."

"Will they?" Alexis shook her head. "PJ, sometimes I feel like a stranger to myself. I feel like I'm turning into, I don't know, some alien being. I can't even remember what I was like before we got married, before I met you and your family."

"That's ridiculous, Ali. Listen to what you're saying!"

Alexis took a deep, shuddering breath and wiped the tears from her cheeks. "I never wanted things to be this way."

PJ took a step closer to her. "You knew what my family was like when you married me," he said. "I *told* you how close we were."

"Yes. You did. But I had no idea they could be so . . . so overbearing. So suffocating. Not all of them. Not your grandfather. Not your parents."

"So you're blaming my grandmother again!"

"No. Not entirely." *I'm blaming you,* she thought. *And I'm blaming myself, too. But I don't want to say that out loud. I can't, not yet.*

"You can't ask me to abandon my family, Alexis. I simply won't do it."

Alexis looked at the man she had promised to love and cherish until death parted them. "Not even for me?" she asked.

PJ had no reply.

"Then maybe we *should* get a divorce," she said sadly. "Maybe I'm not the right wife for you. Next time, you should let your grandmother choose the woman you marry."

PJ looked down at the string of rosary beads still clenched in his hand as if it were a foreign, somehow poisonous object. And then he tossed it onto the couch and stalked to the front door.

"PJ, wait!" Alexis cried.

A moment later she heard his truck tear out of the driveway. What had happened to the mild-mannered man she had fallen in love with and married? She prayed that he wouldn't do something stupid. If he got hurt it would be her fault, and in spite of her anger she didn't know how she would live with the crushing guilt.

Alexis dropped to her knees. She felt utterly hopeless. She was afraid of what she might do. She was afraid of what she might fail to do. "Oh, God," she whispered to the empty room. "Help me. Please, help me."

CHAPTER 91

Mary Bernadette was alone in the kitchen when it happened. Her vision blurred. And then, her vision went away. And then, her vision came back again.

The event had taken place in less than a second. Well, perhaps it had been more like thirty seconds, but it had passed and her vision was once again perfect. No harm had been done. Nothing at all was the matter. Mary Bernadette closed her eyes and opened them again. *You see? There is nothing wrong.*

Still. What if it happened again while she was behind the wheel of her car or crossing Main Street during a busy time of the afternoon? What if it happened while she was receiving Communion at mass, with the entire congregation a witness to her debility?

Don't be silly, Mary Bernadette scolded, slapping her palm against the counter for emphasis. *No one would have to know that you had gone blind for a moment. Not even Father Robert. Didn't Paddy always say you could have gone onto the stage?*

But could she really act her way out of sudden blindness? *All right,* she thought. *I am frightened. What of it?* Nothing would ever induce her to worry anyone in her family by telling them what had happened—or to go to a doctor. It had been a momentary aberration, a glitch in her otherwise hardy system. Maybe she was dehydrated. Jeannette had often suggested that she drink more water. *Fine, then,* Mary Bernadette thought, going over to the sink. *I'll have a glass of water.*

She brought the glass to the table and took a seat. Banshee, with her usual emotional acumen, appeared from nowhere and jumped in Mary Bernadette's lap. "Your mother is getting silly in her old age," she told the purring cat. "Thinking that she had gone blind."

There came a knock on the front door. It was Jeannette's signature knock, three short raps followed by two. With some reluctance Mary Bernadette asked Banshee to get down. She was not in the mood for company, especially that of her oldest friend. Old friends were the ones who recognized you through even your best, most distorting of disguises.

"Are you all right, Mary?" Jeannette asked at once when Mary Bernadette had opened the door. "You look troubled."

"I'm perfectly fine."

"Well, I don't believe you."

"Believe what you like."

Mary Bernadette led her into the kitchen. "Would you like a cup of tea?"

"Don't go to the trouble, Mary."

"It's no trouble whatever." Mary Bernadette set about preparing the tea, putting the kettle on to boil, fetching the milk from the fridge and the sugar bowl from its place on a shelf. She put out a plate of cookies and measured loose tea into the pot. Then she brought the teapot to the table and sat across from her friend.

Jeannette gave her a searching glance. "Mary," she said, "I've been thinking. Maybe it would be best if PJ dropped out of the running for the Stoker project. After all, the bids just came in, thanks to Mr. Meadows's delaying, and they haven't even been considered yet, and you know as well as I do that Mr. Meadows is not going to cast his vote for Fitzgibbon Landscaping. And he'll strong-arm others to vote against PJ, too."

"No." Mary Bernadette shook her head and wished that she hadn't as it resulted in a sharp pain at the very top of her head. "That's a terrible idea," she went on. "For PJ to give up now would be to admit wrongdoing, and he's done nothing wrong. And neither has any member of the Fitzgibbon family."

"I know you're entirely innocent, Mary, you and Paddy and PJ. But sometimes it's best to turn the other cheek."

"No," Mary Bernadette said. "Not in this instance."

"Well, I hope you know best. I don't like what this is doing to you, Mary, not one bit. And I don't mind telling you."

Mary Bernadette didn't reply.

Jeannette sighed. "I'll let myself out," she said. "Thank you for the tea."

When Jeannette had gone, Mary Bernadette sat very still. She wondered how many other members of the OWHA thought she should instruct PJ to relinquish the disputed contract. The thought of facing a delegation of her peers requesting PJ's withdrawal from the competition filled her with dread. How would she ever show her face in Oliver's Well after such a humiliation? All that she had worked for, all the sacrifices she had made . . . would it all be for naught because some wicked man from D.C. had taken a violent dislike to her?

Banshee appeared again, gave an uncharacteristically soft mew, and jumped into her mistress's lap. Mary Bernadette laid her hand on the cat's back and realized that her hand was trembling.

CHAPTER 92

"And Danny and Maureen are doing well?" Megan asked. She was sitting at her desk in her home office, eyeing an untidy stack of paperwork relating to a legal case on which she was currently working.

"Yes, just fine," Jeannette replied. "It's Mary Bernadette I am calling about."

I might have known, Megan thought. "What is it?"

"I suggested to her that PJ might withdraw his bid from the competition for the Joseph J. Stoker House job. Just to calm things down a bit in the family."

"Let me guess. Your suggestion didn't go over well."

Jeannette sighed. "I'm afraid she's pretty angry with me right now. It's not the first time, though, and it certainly won't be the last."

"I'm sorry, Jeannette."

"I am, too. I've never seen Mary be so unreasonable."

"Yes. She's more prickly than ever, that's for sure."

"Could it be something as simple as high blood pressure?" Jeannette wondered.

"We'll never know. Not without Mary Bernadette agreeing to see a doctor. You know what she says. God will decide when it's her time to go, not the medical establishment."

"Yes, but do you think she would be willing to take her pressure with one of those machines you can buy at the pharmacy?" Jeannette asked. "She'd be in the privacy of her own home."

"Doubtful. But Paddy might have more luck persuading her than either of us."

"Do you think so? I know it's probably terrible of me to say this, but sometimes I wonder if she's heard a word he's said in the past fifty years."

"I wonder that, too. But who else stands a chance of getting through to her?"

"PJ?" Jeannette suggested.

"The problem with PJ is that he's in complete denial about his grandmother being a fallible human being. It's not very healthy, I know. When something does happen to prove her human, PJ is going to be hit very hard by the reality."

"And I daresay what with the, well, what with the tension between PJ and Alexis these days—it's obvious to everyone, Megan, no need to deny it—he might be even less likely to consider that his grandmother needs help."

"You're probably right," Megan said. "I really worry about those two, PJ and Alexis. They're so on edge with each other."

Jeannette sighed. "Do you remember how the year started on such a happy note? And now, so much seems to be at risk."

"How are you holding up under the pressure at the OWHA?" Megan asked.

"Not all that well, I'm afraid," Jeannette admitted. "I fear that

I'm betraying Mary Bernadette by not speaking out against Mr. Meadows or by quitting the board in protest. But I'm not sure that either of those actions would really make a difference. Honestly, I'm not even sure the man knows my name. What would it matter to him if I walked out? He'd see it as one less minor annoyance for him to put up with. One less silly old lady."

"It's a terribly frustrating situation."

"I wish I could say that trust in God will see everyone through, but I'm afraid my faith isn't what it used to be."

Whose is, Megan thought. "Thanks for keeping me up to date, Jeannette."

"She would hate it if she knew we were talking about her this way, you know. Worried. Concerned."

"I know," Megan replied. "Which is why she'll never find out. Bye, Jeannette."

Megan frowned at the corkboard over her desk. Why, she wondered, was the board of the OWHA putting up with Wynston Meadows if he was causing them such distress? From all she had heard his behavior was far from professional, and the members had to suspect by now that he didn't care at all about historical Oliver's Well. Were they so overwhelmed by the Great Man that their courage and good sense had completely abandoned them? Didn't it occur to them that other people besides Wynston Meadows had money and that if they really wanted to purchase the Branley Estate they could go about it in some other way, step up their fund-raising efforts for one? No doubt Wynston Meadows had created a bit of a mess, but there were always methods by which a mess could be cleaned up. You just had to employ some creative thinking.

It's official, Megan thought. *I'm angry at Wynston Meadows for his bad behavior and I'm annoyed with the board members who are acting like frightened children. Maybe I should stick my nose in where it might not be wanted and call Leonard DeWitt. He's got—*

The buzzing of her cell phone interrupted this consideration. It was Alec Clare.

"Got a few minutes to talk about next year's CPEE budget?" he asked.

"Sure," Megan said. All thoughts of the OWHA went out of her mind.

CHAPTER 93

Alexis felt that she had lived the last two days at breakneck speed. She had certainly lived them in the deepest secrecy.

The last time she and PJ had had sex was the night they had reconciled, and so much for reconciliation. Since then they had had that terrible fight when she had thrown her rosary at him. She was still appalled at her behavior and still angry with PJ for so thoroughly rejecting her suggestion that they see a therapist.

And now, this.

She had always been regular, so when her period failed to appear on its appointed date she had rushed to a pharmacy in Lawrenceville, a town where, she hoped, nobody would recognize her. The last thing she wanted was the rumor mill to get grinding. The test told her that she was pregnant. She had immediately called her doctor and made an appointment for that very afternoon. It had been hard to bring a smile to her face when the pregnancy was confirmed, hard to accept the congratulations of the nurse practitioner when she had given her a stack of informational brochures about prenatal health and nutrition.

Alexis, sitting at her kitchen table, pushed the pile of brochures away from her. She felt horribly torn between sorrow and joy. On her wedding day she had taken a vow to "accept children willingly from God." At the time she had considered it worthy of a giggle, given that everyone over the age of eleven knew that

God wasn't the one who made babies. Now, unexpectedly pregnant . . . well, there was absolutely nothing to giggle about.

One thing was for sure. She was in no rush to tell her mother. "What were you thinking," she would say, "getting pregnant by a man with whom you're miserable."

What *had* she been thinking? Why had she been careless enough to get pregnant now? Had she, unconsciously, been hoping to bind PJ closer to her? Had it been a desperate tactic to turn him away from his grandmother and toward her, the mother of his child? And what did the fact of the pregnancy say about any feelings she had had for Morgan Shelby? Could she really have been falling in love with him if at the same time she had allowed herself to get pregnant with her husband's child?

Alexis rubbed her temples. No. She had not been in love with Morgan. She had harbored feelings. She had thought that she needed him. But she had not loved him, and she knew this now without a doubt because in spite of her distress she was happy to be pregnant with PJ's child. Not Morgan's child. Her husband's.

But what if her marriage couldn't be saved? Alexis looked at her wedding ring—Aunt Catherine's wedding ring—and remembered the morning she had walked away from the Day in the Life project. She had gone to the office where she had browsed websites in search of a new wedding ring, but in the end she hadn't had the nerve to buy one. She might have been bold enough to turn her back unceremoniously on the OWHA, but she had not been bold enough to replace her wedding ring in such an underhanded manner.

Alexis reached for one of the brochures. *The Importance of Vaccinations.* Childhood disease wasn't the greatest thing she feared. The greatest thing she feared was bringing a child into a home rife with unhappiness, a home on the brink of destruction.

Slowly, she got up from the table and went into the bedroom. She took from the closet the box in which she kept the notes and small tokens of affection PJ had given her since the earliest days of their relationship. The earliest days. Alexis had been a college freshman and PJ a junior. A mutual acquaintance introduced them in the lobby of the movie theatre on campus. Alexis had fallen instantly in love. PJ Fitzgibbon was the most beautiful man she had ever seen. From that first moment there had never been any doubt in her mind that he was the one with whom she would spend the rest of her life.

But PJ hadn't felt the same way, at least not at first. He hardly seemed to notice her in the following weeks. More than once he had passed her on the quad without a greeting. He was rumored to be dating a girl at another college. But Alexis was steadfast. She vowed to wait for him to realize that she was his bride. She knew that someday he would. So she watched and worshipped from afar until one magical day he *did* notice her. And since that precious moment they had been inseparable. Until now.

Among the cards and dried flowers and ticket stubs and funny drawings, Alexis found a piece of paper on which, in PJ's familiar hand, were written the words with which he had proposed. "O woman, loved by me, mayest thou give me thy heart, thy soul and thy body." He had taken the words from a book of native Irish wisdom and lore collected by Lady Wilde, mother of Oscar. To Alexis, his proposal had demonstrated the measure of the man that he was. Romantic. Thoughtful. Devoted. Yes, that PJ Fitzgibbon was the man Alexis had loved. He was the man she *still* loved. He was the man with whom she had pledged to spend the rest of her life.

Now the question was, did that man still exist?

CHAPTER 94

Two days later Alexis stood at the kitchen window, watching for her husband's truck. She had decided that she could no longer carry the burden of her secret alone. And PJ had every right to know that he was going to be a father.

At a quarter after five he came through the front door of the cottage. He looked tired, almost haggard. For a moment Alexis hesitated. She didn't want to add to his troubles. But then she had to speak. For better or worse. In sickness and in health.

"I have something to tell you, PJ," she said. "It's very important."

PJ looked at her warily as he hung his jacket on the back of a chair. "What is it?"

"I'm pregnant."

For a long moment PJ did not reply. Finally, just when Alexis was about to repeat her announcement, he said, "Are you sure?"

"Yes. I've been to see the doctor. It's very early days, but I'm definitely pregnant."

PJ ran his hand through his hair. "Wow."

"I know we wanted to wait a bit," Alexis said. "But . . . well, I guess God had other plans."

PJ smiled and shook his head. "A baby."

"You're not angry?" she asked hopefully.

"No," he said. "Of course not."

"It was what we wanted. A family."

"Yes. A family. But maybe . . ." PJ looked down at the floor. "Maybe we shouldn't say anything right away. To—to the others."

"Right. It's a first pregnancy, and there's always a chance I could lose the baby. . . ." Alexis felt tears choking her. This was supposed to be a joyous, shout it from the mountaintop moment. And it wasn't.

PJ looked back to her. "We'll wait until we're more sure. Until everything is—settled."

Until we're settled. Until our marriage is more sure. Or until our marriage is over.

PJ reached for her and she went to him. A hug had never made her feel so sad, and she began to sob. When the sobs quieted, they sat together on the couch.

"How do you feel?" PJ asked. "I mean, physically."

"Fine."

"Good. Is there anything I can get for you? Would you like a cup of tea?"

"No," she said, wiping her face with the back of her hand. "But thanks."

"We should be toasting the occasion with champagne."

"Not me. Sparkling water."

PJ reached for her hand and squeezed it gently. "Right. Do you remember how we used to talk for hours about baby names? Sean or James. Fiona or Allison."

Alexis rested her head on PJ's shoulder. "That was fun, wasn't it?"

"Yeah. It was. And we used to argue about how many kids we would have."

"You said you wanted six."

"And you said you wanted five."

"How silly we were," Alexis whispered.

"No," PJ said. "Not silly. Hopeful. Happy."

"And now?"

PJ kissed the top of Alexis's head. "Hopeful," he said. "And yes, happy."

Alexis felt her eyes flood with tears again, but this time they weren't tears of sadness.

"Thank you for being my husband," she said.

PJ turned to embrace her. "Thank you for being my wife."

CHAPTER 95

Was it a universal truth that every family, no matter how loving, had its drama and its tensions? Was there really no such thing as a truly harmonious family?

Of course there's no such thing, Megan reminded herself. *Be real.*

Megan was in her home office where she was supposed to be working on a matter for the CPEE. Instead, her mind was lost in thoughts of the family Fitzgibbon. Take Pat's admission that his apology to PJ had not gone over very well. "I don't think he believed I was genuinely sorry," he had told her only the night before. "Well, I can't say that I blame him. I've been harping on PJ about his choice of career for years. I'll just have to prove to him that I've finally accepted his decisions. And that I respect them."

Megan shook her head. What a weekend *that* had been! At dinner Saturday evening Mary Bernadette had acted as if nothing brutal had come out of her mouth only hours earlier, even complimenting Megan on her blouse, while poor Paddy had blushed and stammered his way through the meal. Pat, for his part, had glowered and grimaced.

Mary Bernadette and Megan had not talked since the morning after "The Incident" (it was what Megan had taken to calling it rather than using Pat's term, which involved a very graphic vulgarity). She did not feel badly about this, as time apart was often necessary in order for healing to begin. Besides, if they were to talk, what could they possibly say to each other? What topics would be safe enough not to elicit a fresh character assassination? Well, there was always the weather, but with Mary Bernadette behaving more cantankerous than ever, maybe even the weather wasn't a neutral enough topic.

Megan glanced at the photograph of her parents that sat to the left of her laptop. In almost every way you could imagine, Mary Bernadette and Kathleen Murphy were in stark contrast. Kathleen was one of the nicest people there was, easy to get along with and never critical or unkind. Left alone for more than fifteen minutes with Mary Bernadette, Kathleen would emerge shaking and chattering like a hiker who had just come face-to-face with a hungry puma on a deserted mountain trail. Megan grinned at her choice of dramatic imagery. Well, maybe that was a *bit* unfair. After all, the few times the two women had been in each other's company—for instance, at Megan's and then at PJ's wedding—there had been no spilling of blood.

Next to the photograph of Megan's parents sat a photograph of her brother Edward and his family. They lived only minutes from the elder Murphys. Edward's wife, Judy, got along splendidly with her in-laws. Kara and Jason, now teenagers, visited their grandparents without parental prompting. *Maybe my brother has succeeded in creating a truly harmonious family,* Megan thought now. *If so, he's a better person than I am.*

The truth was that Megan felt guilty that she wasn't available to her parents in the way her brother was. For better or worse she had chosen to devote her energies to Paddy and Mary Bernadette, though lately she wondered if she was doing a very good job of ensuring their well-being. Anyway, she knew this sort of thing often happened. Familial duties were divided, sometimes with intention and careful planning and at other times—well, at other times things just turned out the way they did.

On impulse, Megan reached for her cell phone and dialed her parents' number. (Like Mary Bernadette and Paddy, they had only a landline.) "Mom?"

"Meggie! It's so good to hear from you! I just got the latest pictures you sent through the e-mail. Gosh, the twins are getting so big!"

Megan laughed, happy to hear her mother's voice. "You should see our food bill!"

"And how's everything with PJ? I haven't heard from him in an age. He must be so busy running that company."

Megan grimaced. She hated to lie, but she didn't want her

mother to worry about her oldest grandchild. "He's fine," she said. "Everything's going well."

"Good. I sent PJ and Alexis a card for their anniversary. What a lovely wedding that was!"

"It was lovely, yes."

"And how are Pat's parents?" Kathleen Murphy asked.

Megan was beginning to regret this call. "Fine," she said. "Mary Bernadette's very busy with the historical society. And Paddy's enjoying retirement."

"Do tell them I was asking for them, won't you?"

Megan promised and listened as her mother began a very complicated story of what had happened at the last meeting of the parish council, of which she was a long-standing member. And as she listened she suddenly remembered thinking that she should call Leonard DeWitt about the current state of the OWHA. Or had she finally decided against getting involved in matters probably beyond her control?

"So," her mother said, "what do you think of that!"

Megan scrambled for a suitable reply. "I think," she said, "that it's quite—unbelievable."

Her mother laughed. "That's exactly what I thought!"

CHAPTER 96

Since the doctor had confirmed that Alexis was pregnant, life, every little bit of it, from the glass of juice she poured PJ in the morning, to the Japanese snowbell tree blooming in the yard, to the ringing of the bell atop the Episcopal church, felt that much more precious. Everything had taken on a glow of importance. And it was all due to the tiny, nascent bit of life inside her, a life to which she already felt a very strong connection. That tiny bit of life had also opened her to a further compassion for what Mary Bernadette Fitzgibbon must have endured when she lost her baby William.

It was clear what she had to do. She had to apologize to PJ's grandmother. She knew that she should have done so long before now—she had promised PJ that she would—and she hoped that her apology would still be worth something.

Alexis found Mary Bernadette in her kitchen, sitting at the table with an untouched cup of tea in front of her. She was impeccably groomed as usual, though Alexis thought she looked tired.

"Mary Bernadette, may I talk to you?" she asked.

It took a long moment before PJ's grandmother looked up at her. "What?" she said. "Oh. Yes. Would you like a cup of tea?"

She made as if to rise. *Always the good hostess,* Alexis thought, *even to those she dislikes.*

"No, thank you," she said. "I just want to say that I'm sorry for quitting the Day in the Life project like I did. I shouldn't have just walked away. You were right. I should have come to you first."

"Yes. All right."

"I'm sure there's someone else who wouldn't mind taking it over."

"Yes, of course."

"Maybe a photography student at one of the local colleges," Alexis suggested. "I could make some calls to the art departments if you'd like."

"No," Mary Bernadette said. "That's all right."

"Well, let me know if I can help find a replacement."

Mary Bernadette picked up her spoon and began to stir the tea. When after a moment she didn't reply, Alexis left the house.

That was a strange encounter, she thought as she walked to her car. She had never seen Mary Bernadette so distracted. She was usually the most focused person in the room. Her ability to pay close attention to every conversation going on around her—and to interject her own opinion in any one of them—was astounding to witness. Maybe, Alexis thought, as she got behind the wheel, Mary Bernadette wasn't feeling well. She knew she couldn't mention this idea to PJ. Relations between them were so delicate she was afraid that *anything* she said about Mary Bernadette would seem to PJ like an insult. She could, she supposed, call her mother-in-law, but what would she say? She had no proof of Mary Bernadette's being sick. Anyway, Mary Bernadette was probably just worried about the current state of the situation at the OWHA.

But what *was* the current state of the OWHA situation? Alexis realized that she had paid virtually no attention to its doings in the past weeks. She wasn't even sure that PJ was still in the running for that Stoker project. And that was because she hadn't bothered to ask her husband.

It was a painful realization, that her self-absorption had isolated her from the people who were now her family, and for that Alexis felt genuine regret. And she wondered, as she pulled out of the driveway and onto Honeysuckle Lane, just how much of her disaffection had been due to sheer laziness. Loving a person was arduous, day-to-day toil, but it was worth it in the end. Sometimes. Hopefully, most times.

Alexis sighed. There was much for which she had to make amends.

CHAPTER 97

Mary Bernadette had been cleaning the good china for the past half an hour, something she did once every month though the set was used only on Thanksgiving and Christmas. Things could get dusty even stored in a cabinet, and wasn't it more efficient to keep things clean and in order on a regular basis?

Carefully, she wiped each piece with a damp towel and then with a dry one. Dinner plates. Salad plates. Dessert plates. Dessert bowels. Serving bowls and cups and saucers. A gravy boat with a ladle, and a covered butter dish. There were ten settings, well over a hundred pieces of china in all. She finished drying a cup and set it down on the table with the others. But somehow it did not meet the table. Somehow it fell to the floor and shattered into tiny pieces.

"Foolish woman," Mary Bernadette muttered. "You should be more careful."

She went to the closet for the broom and dustpan and began to gather up the ruins of the cup. This was the second time in the past two weeks she had been uncharacteristically clumsy. The first was when she had been sweeping the kitchen after breakfast one morning and the broom had simply fallen from her hand. The sudden noise as it hit the floor had caused Banshee to leap to the top of the fridge and Mary Bernadette to flinch.

She tightened her grip on the broom now, finished sweeping up the remains of the cup, and dumped the shards and slivers into the trash receptacle under the sink. Then she sat at the table where a large portion of the china was still waiting to be cleaned. And now that she was off her feet, she realized that she was tired. She stifled a yawn, as if to give in to it would indicate a loss of moral fiber. Naps were for the very young and the very old. She had always held by that.

Mary Bernadette comforted herself now with the thought that there had been no witness to her clumsy behavior. She was especially glad that her daughter-in-law hadn't been visiting. She hadn't spoken to or seen Megan since the morning after she had "attacked" her. That word was not the one she would have chosen, but her son seemed to think it appropriate. In the past few days she had become aware of a small sense of remorse. Perhaps she shouldn't have been so—adamant—in expressing her opinions about David's care and religious upbringing. But what was done was done, and there was little if any purpose in bringing up past incidents and reopening old wounds, even for the sake of an apology. Take, for example, the time when Pat was little and had hid in the linen closet just as the family was about to leave for Sunday mass. She had never apologized to him for her angry reaction to his misbehavior, and she highly doubted he had any recollection of the incident at this late date. So many things were better left unsaid and undisturbed.

Of course, there were times when a belated apology was welcome. It had been decent of Alexis to apologize for her conduct regarding the OWHA, but it was probably PJ who had encouraged her to do so. Mary Bernadette doubted Alexis cared for anything but her own interests, whatever they were. If only PJ had come to her for advice before proposing to Alexis, she might have convinced him of his folly in choosing someone from such a different background. Again, what was done was done.

Like Pat's decision to reject a role in the family business. Like Grace's decision to work far from Oliver's Well. Like William's having died so terribly young. There was nothing she could do about any of it.

Mary Bernadette thought of the shards of china now in the trash can among the remains of meals and plastic bags of dirty cat litter and empty rolls of toilet paper. It was just a broken cup, and yet she experienced now a terrible pang of loss, as if the cup had value far beyond its practical purpose as a drinking vessel. She put her elbow on the table and her head in her hand. If her son were to walk into the kitchen right then, he would scold her for breaking her own rule. How many times had she punished her children for the offense of an elbow on the table and so many more like it? Too many to count, she thought. And what did any of it matter now? What had any of it ever mattered?

CHAPTER 98

The first time Alexis had been at Maureen Kline's house she had been too distressed to notice much of the décor. Now she took the time to survey the living room. On a long credenza, framed photographs stood in a perfectly straight line. Alexis recognized Jeannette and Danny, and she assumed that the other people in the pictures were Maureen's sisters, brothers-in-law, and their children. There was a couch with a taupe-colored slipcover slightly too small for it. The coffee table was a glass top on a chrome base, a very 1970s-looking piece. There was a standing lamp similar to one Alexis remembered seeing in the house of a friend's great-grandmother. The two armchairs had the distinct look of having been bought at a resale shop.

On the whole, there was very little sense of coherent style. Maybe "things"—beautiful furniture and thick carpets and good art hanging on the wall—just didn't rate high on Maureen's list of what was important in life. Or maybe, Alexis thought, she just didn't have the money to spend on high-quality furnishings.

Maureen had set out two cups of steaming tea and a plate of store-bought cookies on the coffee table.

"Thanks for having me over," Alexis said.

"I like having company," Maureen explained. "Not that I have anyone over all that often. And I like you, Alexis. I know I'm old enough to be your mother, but I'd like to think of us as friends."

Alexis smiled. "I'm not sure what I have to offer. It seems I'm always coming to you with a crisis."

"I don't mind. Anyway, by this time in my life I should have accumulated a store of practical knowledge worth sharing. Note I didn't say that I actually *have* accumulated such a store. So, tell me what's going on. Why did you want to see me?"

Alexis took a deep breath. "I'm pregnant," she said. "And yes, the baby is PJ's. There's no doubt of that."

"Thank God. Still, I know this must be so difficult."

Alexis laughed unhappily. "That's putting it mildly."

"Are you going to go through with the pregnancy?" Maureen asked gently.

"Yes, no matter what. My parents would help me if PJ and I— if we break up."

"Let's not even consider that possibility right now."

"But why not?" Alexis challenged. "Sometimes I feel so—defeated. The future looks so bleak. I'm trying to imagine *something* changing for the better, but I can't. And I've always considered myself a creative person. So much for that."

"Well, there *are* options other than divorce."

Alexis forced a smile.

"Look," Maureen said, "my divorce pretty much had to happen unless I wanted to live the rest of my life as the pitied, neglected wife of a rampant cheater. And I didn't. Still, divorce is not something I would wish on my most hated enemy, supposing I had one. And even when divorce does seem necessary, I'd still advise anyone who asked to try every other solution before it."

"Like therapy?" Alexis said. "No good. PJ refuses to go."

"Stubborn Irishman, that's what he is."

"He's afraid his grandmother will find out."

Maureen rolled her eyes. "That one!"

"Anyway, we're keeping the pregnancy a secret for now, but I just had to tell someone or go mad. Because in spite of what I just said about feeling defeated, I'm happy to be pregnant. I really am."

"I'm glad for you, Alexis. I . . . I never had children, as I'm sure you know by now. But I'm always happy for those who do."

"Did you want children?" Alexis asked.

"Yes." Maureen's reply was prompt. "But it didn't happen in my marriage, and after that . . . Let's just say I'm not cut out to be a single mom. Well, I'll revise that. It's not in me to *seek* to become a single parent."

"I'm sorry, Maureen. Why is nothing ever simple? Why does it always seem there's trouble around every bend?"

Maureen laughed. "I'm not equipped to have a coherent conversation about existentialism, if that's the name for the sort of questions you're posing. Have another cookie."

Alexis did. "I know this doesn't have anything to do with my being pregnant," she ventured after a moment, "and maybe I have no right to bring it up, but . . . but I heard that you and PJ's father used to date."

Maureen took a sip of her tea before answering. "Are people still talking about that ancient history?"

"No. It was just PJ who mentioned it to me once."

"Yes, well, our relationship came before Pat met Megan. And it didn't last very long. Pat never considered us serious. But I did. At least, I hoped that things would get serious. I was disappointed when the relationship fizzled out. I think I almost would have preferred a bang to the whimper that marked the end."

Was Pat Fitzgibbon the love of Maureen's life, Alexis wondered. If so, how terribly sad. "I'm sorry," she said. "I shouldn't have mentioned it."

Maureen shrugged. "And then I met the charming Barry and married him. Not the greatest decision I ever made."

"Do you hate him?" she asked. "I mean, Pat."

"God, no! Pat's a great guy. We just weren't meant to be. I think he saw me more as one of the family than as someone he might marry. There was no mystery about me for him, you see. I was just little Maureen Kline, the girl next door." Maureen frowned down at her teacup. "In fact," she went on, "sometimes it feels like that's the way the entire town sees me. The girl next door, nothing remarkable. Then again, that's what I get for sticking around Oliver's Well my whole life."

"Couldn't you leave? Couldn't you start over somewhere else?"

Maureen shook her head. "Too late. I missed whatever chance I might have had after the divorce, when I was feeling so awfully humiliated. But I was too—too shattered to make a move then.

Now the duty to my family takes precedence over my own wants. I don't know why I'm telling you these depressing things. Sorry."

Alexis recalled the wistfulness she had detected in Maureen's voice the first time they had run into each other at the bakery. What might have been for her, she wondered, if things had been different. If she had been lucky in love. "I wish you *were* part of the family," Alexis said, with a strong rush of emotion.

"Then we might hate each other," Maureen said briskly. "I'll make us some more tea."

CHAPTER 99

It was Saturday, the tenth of May, the day before Mother's Day. Mary Bernadette was home alone. It wasn't her habit to watch television in the middle of the day, but on a whim she had decided to catch the afternoon edition of the local news. There seemed to be nothing of great interest going on in Smithstown or Waterville. Westminster reported a rise in unemployment among its recent high school graduates. One of Lawrenceville's finest citizens had been caught on camera sneaking out of a "house of ill repute." And there was a fire in downtown Somerstown that had already claimed one life. Mary Bernadette made the sign of the cross and said a prayer for the soul of the victim.

"And in Oliver's Well news . . ."

There on the screen was a reporter she hadn't seen before, a rather oily-looking man, Mary Bernadette thought, wearing an old trench coat and sporting the type of mustache she hadn't known men to wear for more than forty years. Something about the bushes behind the man looked familiar. . . .

"That's my lawn he's standing on," Mary Bernadette said to the living room. "That's my property!"

". . . so given the recent allegations of wrongdoing on the part of Fitzgibbon Landscaping, this reporter decided to snare the lioness in her own den Friday afternoon."

Mary Bernadette stood abruptly. The remote slid from her lap to the floor.

"Even after repeated knocking," the reporter continued, "Mary Bernadette Fitzgibbon refused to answer the door to us. One can't help but ask, what is the woman hiding?"

"That's a lie!" Mary Bernadette protested. "I was at the hairdresser yesterday afternoon! He's lying!"

Mary Bernadette put a hand to her head. She wished she knew why she was being persecuted by Wynston Meadows. What had she ever done to justify this one man's hatred? She wasn't perfect. She knew that. But hadn't she always tried to act according to the word of God? Hadn't she always followed the Golden Rule and treated others as she would have them treat her? Then why, why was this happening?

And then her moment of fury was followed by abject fear. What else could this evil man do to her? Would he succeed in destroying her family, too? Would the good name of the Fitzgibbon family, already tarnished, be entirely and forever blackened?

The news show droned on. Or had it now gone to commercial? Mary Bernadette peered at the television screen. It was blurry. Something must be wrong with the cable. The sound was odd, too, a sort of buzz. She felt—funny. She was vaguely aware that Banshee was crying and that Mercy was making a pitiful noise.

I must call someone.

The idea seemed to have come from someone else, but it struck Mary Bernadette as a sound one. There was only one problem. The phone was in the kitchen and she was in the living room. Well, then, she would go to the kitchen. She took a step and fell to the floor. And then she felt a wonderful sense of peace envelope her.

Could it be? Am I about to join my sweet baby William?

It was her last conscious thought.

CHAPTER 100

Megan shut off the engine of her car and got out from behind the wheel. *Here I am,* she thought, *back again.* The car could probably drive itself to and from Oliver's Well by this point.

As Megan got closer to the front door, she heard Banshee howling. But there was something different in it, something frantic, as if the animal was terrified. It was a sound Mary Bernadette would never ignore. And she had to be home, because her car was in the driveway. . . .

"Darn it," Megan muttered, fumbling with her keys in her sudden haste. "Come on, come on!"

And then the key was turning in the lock and Megan threw open the door to find Mary Bernadette in a heap on the living room floor. The television was on. Banshee was circling Mary Bernadette madly. Mercy was crouched in the doorway of the dining room, whimpering. The rest of the house appeared to be empty; at least, Paddy's car was not parked outside.

"Oh, God, let her be all right," Megan murmured as she grabbed her cell phone from her bag and called for an ambulance.

She knelt down by her mother-in-law's prone body. "Mary Bernadette, can you hear me?" she asked. "Mary Bernadette?"

She was afraid to touch her. She had no medical training; she didn't even know CPR and cursed herself for it. Thankfully, it was only a moment or two later that Megan heard the siren and the Oliver's Well Emergency Corps pulled up outside the house. The door was still open as she had left it, and two paramedics came hurrying inside. Banshee dashed up the stairs, and Mercy retreated in the direction of the kitchen.

"I found her like this less than five minutes ago," Megan said to the man and woman who now bent over Mary Bernadette. "She was alone when . . ."

"Megan?"

It was Lucy Burrows and her daughter standing in the doorway.

"Poor Mrs. F!" Lucy cried. "What happened?"

Megan shook her head. "I don't know."

"Well, what can we do to help?"

"What?" Megan's mind went blank.

Lucy nodded. "I'll go find Paddy and take him to the hospital."

"Oh," Megan said, her intelligence returning. "Yes. Call the office first," she suggested. "If he's not there, Alexis might know where he's gone. If not, call Danny Kline, or check the bar at The Angry Squire. Sometimes he goes there for lunch."

"Right." Lucy Burrows dashed off.

"I'll look after Mrs. F's kitty," Tiff said. "Everyone knows how much she loves that kitty."

"Thank you. And would it be too much to ask that you walk Mercy, too? If none of us is back home by evening? There's a spare set of keys under the back door mat."

"Sure. She's a great old mutt!"

"Thank you, Tiff," Megan said. "I'll lock up and follow the ambulance in my car."

Less than five minutes later the paramedics had loaded Mary Bernadette onto a stretcher and into the ambulance. Megan pulled out directly behind to make the fifteen-minute drive to the hospital. "The old pain in the butt," she muttered, wiping away a tear. "I'll kill her if she dies."

CHAPTER 101

That evening, Jeannette and Paddy and Megan and Danny sat around the Fitzgibbon kitchen table, attempting to eat a dinner for which no one had much appetite. Megan had suggested that PJ and Alexis join them, but her son was too distraught to be with other people. At least, Megan thought, Alexis was staying at his side. Things between the young couple might not be hopeless.

"A stroke. I still can't believe it." Jeannette sighed and put down her fork, her hamburger and string beans neglected. "She's always been the picture of health. Well, thank God it was as minor as it was. It was a good thing you came along so quickly, Megan."

Megan reached across the table and laid her hand on her father-in-law's arm. "Yes," she said. "A good thing."

Paddy shook his head. His eyes were red rimmed from crying, and his voice was ragged. "All these years I bowed to her will," he said, "rather than acting on her behalf. Even when I knew she wasn't feeling well, I never forced her to see a doctor."

"We all bowed to her will." Megan took her hand from Paddy's arm. "It wasn't just you."

"Did we have much choice?" Jeannette said. "Mary Bernadette established herself as almost entirely independent and self-sufficient long ago. There's no use pretending things were otherwise."

"Jeannette is right," Megan said. "I'm not saying that Mary Bernadette brought this on herself—never blame the victim. But she did make it very hard for anyone who loved her—who *loves* her—to help."

"She was always so strong. . . ."

"She still *is* strong, Paddy," Jeannette said firmly. "Don't forget that. It will take more than a stroke to fell the oak that is Mary Bernadette Fitzgibbon."

Danny nodded. "Amen to that."

"I know no one is very hungry," Megan said now, "but we should all try to eat. Especially you, Paddy. You need to keep up your strength for your wife's sake."

"But does she really need me?" Paddy asked. "Did she ever?"

There was an awkward silence following those plaintive words. Danny cleared his throat and poked his fork into his cold hamburger. Jeannette caught Megan's eye and frowned. Megan thought that her father-in-law looked resigned to some great and permanent disappointment or sorrow.

Slowly, as if in pain, Paddy rose from the table. "I'm going to bed," he said. "Call me if there's any word from the hospital."

CHAPTER 102

*W*ell, Mary Bernadette thought, *this is quite a way to celebrate Mother's Day, hooked up to a bunch of tubes and wires, flat on my back in a hospital bed.* The celebratory meal she had planned to serve that afternoon would have to be postponed until the following Sunday; she was certain she would be home by then. She didn't know why such a fuss was being made about her. Her husband, sitting in a chair by the side of her bed, looked as if he were the one who had had a stroke. His face was ashen, and there were dark circles under his eyes. She was sure he hadn't slept at all the night before. Silly man, when there was really nothing to worry about.

The doctor who had visited her earlier that morning, a man

who looked no older than her grandson PJ, had told her that she was no longer in immediate danger but that she would not be released until the doctors had conducted a series of exams. "What sort of exams?" she had asked warily. One never knew with doctors. They were always poking and prodding in places God never meant one to be poked and prodded. And they let perfectly innocent people die.

The doctor had explained that they would be looking for a clot that might have been the source of the stroke; finding it might help prevent another stroke from occurring. Or something to that effect; Mary Bernadette couldn't quite remember. She did recall, however, that the doctor had said that she was lucky. The stroke might have been much worse than it had been. Her speech had not been affected, and in all likelihood she would need only minor physical therapy to rehabilitate her right side. Mary Bernadette thought that getting back to her housework would do just as well.

When the doctor had gone off, Mary Bernadette had duly said a prayer of thanks to God for having spared her. And then she had asked for the strength to endure the time she would be forced to spend in the same place where her beloved son had breathed his last. The place that terrified her.

Now, Mary Bernadette thought, looking again at her husband, she should say another prayer asking God to spare Paddy Fitzgibbon from his worry.

"You gave me quite a shock, Mary," Paddy said with a small, pathetic smile.

"Yes, well, I gave myself quite a shock, too. A stroke? Are the doctors sure?"

"Yes. Very sure."

Mary Bernadette sighed and plucked at the thin blanket under which she lay. "It's all very annoying. I'm afraid my memory of what exactly happened is a bit vague. It seemed as if one minute I was just fine, watching that awful news program, and then . . ." The memories of those few moments, no matter how vague, frightened her. "Well," she said briskly, "here I am now, in this dreadful place."

Paddy managed the ghost of a smile. "Now, don't let the nurses hear you say that, Mary."

"No, no, of course I won't. Paddy? How did you know I'd been taken ill?"

"Lucy Burrows hunted me down at the office. She drove me to the hospital."

Mary Bernadette, weakened as she was, couldn't hide her horror. "In that old jalopy of hers? It's a wonder you both didn't die in a fiery wreck!"

"Well, we didn't."

"Who is looking after Banshee while I'm in this aw—this place?"

"Tiffany Burrows. And she'll walk Mercy when I'm not there."

"Lord save us."

"Now, Mary," Paddy admonished. "The Burrows are good neighbors. And don't worry, I'll make sure Banshee gets as much attention as Mercy until . . . until you come home."

He wiped a tear from his cheek, and for a heroic moment Mary Bernadette struggled to keep her own eyes dry. She succeeded. Paddy got up from the chair then and perched on the edge of his wife's bed. He took her hand in both of his. And Mary Bernadette felt just a little bit ashamed. She had never been very nice to the Burrows. What possible motive could the family have for being so neighborly? Could it be that they were just—kind? Good Samaritans. It was a startling thought.

"Where are the others?" she asked now. "Where's Pat?"

"He's on his way from Annapolis."

"Who . . . Oh, this is so frustrating, but I can't remember exactly how I got here. And don't say in an ambulance."

Paddy smiled. "Megan found you. She heard Banshee through the door and knew something was wrong."

Mary Bernadette closed her eyes. How embarrassing that her daughter-in-law had seen her in such a vulnerable and undignified condition. But there was nothing to do about it now. And might such embarrassment really only be vanity?

"Grace will be here tomorrow."

Mary Bernadette opened her eyes. "When was the last time we saw her, Paddy?"

"Almost two years ago now."

"Too long."

"Yes. But she has such important work to do."

"Yes. Are you eating, Paddy?"

"I haven't had an appetite."

"Now, don't be silly. You need your strength. You tell Megan to make you a proper dinner tonight. I assume she's staying at the house?"

"Yes. She drove me here, in fact. Would you like to see her? She's in the waiting room."

Mary Bernadette flinched. She couldn't bear to face her daughter-in-law yet. "Not right now," she said. "I'm suddenly very tired."

"Of course. She'll understand."

Paddy continued to sit by her side, holding her hand in both of his, while Mary Bernadette felt herself drifting off to sleep.

CHAPTER 103

Grace arrived in Oliver's Well the following afternoon. She was wearing an ancient pair of jeans and a navy sweatshirt. Her hair was pulled back into a miniscule ponytail, from which several strands had escaped. She knew that unless her mother was entirely unconscious, she would make note of her daughter's casual attire and find it unfitting for a Bride of Christ. Oh, she might not actually say anything, but Grace knew her mother extremely well. She would see the criticism in Mary Bernadette's eyes.

She went directly to the hospital from the airport. She had known what she was going to find there—she had visited countless numbers of people in the hospital suffering from all sorts of nasty ailments—but the fact was that this was *her mother*. Nothing could ever prepare a child for the loss of a parent.

Grace, she scolded silently, as she looked down at her mother stretched out on the bed, *don't be an idiot. The woman is alive.* And she would not let her mother see her distress. She had inherited Mary Bernadette's poker face and now put it firmly in place.

"You look well, Mom. Considering you've had a stroke." Grace bent down and kissed her mother's pale cheek.

"Very amusing, my dear. How was your flight? I can't imagine ever getting on a plane again, not with the way the world is these days. Terrorists around every corner."

"The flight was fine, Mom. Uneventful. Not even a colicky baby."

Mary Bernadette glanced at her daughter from head to toe. *And there it is*, Grace thought. *The criticism.* "Have you been to the house yet?"

"No," Grace replied. "I wanted to come straight here."

Mary Bernadette sighed. "I wish I knew what was going on in my own home. It's very tiresome not knowing things. Is Banshee being properly fed? What about my plants? Has anyone been watering them? Make sure the mail is brought in. Don't let it accumulate in the box. Thieves notice such things."

Grace smiled. "Now, Mom," she said, "don't worry. Megan's got everything under control. Katie and Bonnie will help with Dad's meals. And Buddy Burrows will see to the lawn."

"That's your father's job. He's very particular about it."

"Yes," Grace said, "but Dad agreed. He wants to spend every spare moment with his wife, not pushing a lawn mower and pulling up weeds. And Mike Burrows will take the garbage to the dump."

Mary Bernadette made a sort of *humph* sound, and Grace bit back a smile.

"This is very important, Grace," Mary Bernadette said now, her voice determined. "I don't want anyone but the family coming here to see me. And Father Robert, of course."

"Not even Jeannette?" Grace asked.

"All right. Jeannette. But no one else. Promise me. Especially not anyone on the board of the OWHA. I don't want anyone to see me . . . to see me like this."

Grace promised.

"Did your brother arrive yet?" Mary Bernadette asked.

"Yes. Pat's been in Oliver's Well since last evening. Hasn't he come to see you yet?"

"No."

"I'll drag him in. You know how squeamish he gets around sick people." That was a lie, but Grace didn't have the heart to voice what both women knew. Pat hadn't been to see his mother because he didn't want to see her. Could it really be, Grace thought, that her brother didn't care at all for his mother? Megan had told her that Pat wanted to cut all ties with Mary Bernadette. *Well,* Grace decided, *not if I have anything to say about it.*

"Yes," Mary Bernadette said. "I'm sure that's it. A weak stomach."

"Right. He's very concerned that you get well."

"No one has to worry about that."

Grace smiled. "I daresay we don't. Now, Mom, why don't you get some rest while I go and introduce myself to the nurses."

Mary Bernadette sighed. "I must admit I do feel a bit weary."

Grace kissed her mother on the forehead and straightened her blankets before going out into the hall. Only then did she allow herself the luxury of a tear.

CHAPTER 104

Megan was dusting the living room of Mary Bernadette's house. Grace and Paddy were at the hospital. Pat was home in Annapolis; he said he'd been called back on an emergency. Megan knew he was lying. He just hadn't been able to work up the nerve or the courage or whatever it was he needed to visit his mother. "She's stable and you're all here," he had said, avoiding his wife's eyes. "She doesn't need me." Megan had let him go without protest.

A photo of Mary Bernadette and Paddy in the early days of their marriage, dressed smartly for church, arm in arm and smiling directly into the camera. Mary Bernadette with the two-year-old twins on her lap, the kitten Banshee perched on a branch of the brightly decorated Christmas tree. Mary Bernadette and Megan on Megan's wedding day. *If only I had known what I was getting into,* Megan thought, gently wiping the glass with the dust cloth.

Like her husband, Megan hadn't seen her mother-in-law since she had been admitted to the hospital, but not for lack of trying. She supposed that the indomitable Mary Bernadette was likely embarrassed by the fact that the woman she had so horribly maligned only weeks earlier had been the one to see her safely to the hospital. *Well,* Megan thought, *I'm not going away. She'll have to see me at some point, so it might as well be on her own terms.*

Megan went to the kitchen, put the dust cloth in the broom closet, and put water on to boil. After a cup of tea she would call home. The twins would soon be out of school and eager for an update. Danica had burst into tears on hearing of Mary Bernadette's stroke and had gone on about not having been nice to her about the blouse with the bow. David had offered to take a leave of absence from school in order to move in with his grandfather and "help out." He had argued, very reasonably, that he could make up the missed course work during the summer while he recuperated from his surgery. Megan's heart had swelled with pride, though she had had to tell David that Grace and the neighbors had everything under control.

And me? Megan wondered. *What am I doing to help?* She turned off the gas under the teakettle and, taking a tea bag from the pocket of her jacket, dropped it into a cup. Mary Bernadette would be horrified if she knew someone was using a tea bag in her home, but Megan was just too lazy to make a real pot of tea the way her mother-in-law insisted on. Quality over convenience was Mary Bernadette's motto.

And was there anything wrong with that? No, Megan decided, there wasn't. Her mother-in-law believed in setting high standards. She never shied away from hard work or what might seem like an impossible task. And here was the germ of an idea. . . . There might just be a way in which she could help Mary Bernadette, and the rest of the family, and even Oliver's Well if . . . if she could somehow rid the OWHA of the pest that was Wynston Meadows. *I'll be the Exterminator,* she thought, and laughed out loud. Her weapons would be her intelligence, her doggedness, and her devotion to her family. Really, she should have taken action back when the thought had first occurred to her after that call of concern from Jeannette.

It was going to difficult, of that she was certain. It might prove to be impossible. But she *had* been feeling a bit bored in the past months, hadn't she? Going up against Wynston Meadows was sure to be anything but boring, especially since she had no clear idea of how she was going to do it. An immediate goal might be to get herself a place on the board. Then, armed with more information about how the board functioned and a better sense of Meadows's intentions regarding it, she might try to hunt out concrete reasons to doubt his integrity and his dedication to Oliver's Well. Ultimately, she would have to convince the others to oust Meadows—and lose all the money he had promised as a result. *This is ridiculous,* she thought. *No one is going to listen to me. Why even bother?* "Because it's the right thing to do," she told the room. Tilting at windmills, maybe; after all, the man had neatly avoided criminal charges in the past. Who was she to think she could succeed where others had failed? But still, it was the right thing to do.

Megan finished her tea and stuffed the tea bag down into the garbage can where Mary Bernadette, should she be home in the next day or two, wouldn't see it. The woman missed nothing, so Megan knew that her campaign to oust Meadows would have to be carried out with stealth. Further agitation was to be avoided at all costs if Mary Bernadette were to fully recover from the stroke—and she had to, if only for Paddy's sake.

The hard part would be getting the other members of the OWHA board to agree to keep quiet about her involvement. She would have to be very firm about it, "respectfully requesting their silence for the sake of their dear friend and colleague." She might exaggerate her mother-in-law's condition just a wee bit, make her out to be in a more fragile state than she was, in the hopes that not even the miserable Joyce Miller or the Great Man himself would be cruel enough to risk Mary Bernadette's health by bothering her with OWHA business. And she would have to enlist the help of her family in keeping the newspapers out of reach. And she would have to ask the hospital staff not to engage in any conversation with the patient about a topic more serious than what was for lunch.

This is sounding like a mission mounted by the CIA! Megan thought. It would be a long shot, keeping the keenly curious Mary Bernadette in ignorance for as long as she was recovering, and the attempt might fail, but when and if it did Megan hoped that she would already have made some headway toward her goal. Her impossible dream?

Megan returned to the living room. Pat in a sailor suit. She picked up the photograph and smiled. The poor kid looked miserable. What would he say when she told him of her plan that was barely a plan? Megan suspected that his reaction might be worth capturing on video. It might become a YouTube sensation, a husband in the act of declaring his wife completely and totally insane.

CHAPTER 105

"**A**re you hungry, Grandmother? Can I get you anything from the cafeteria?"

It was the second time her husband had asked that question in the past fifteen minutes. Alexis felt her heart break. He looked so very young at that moment. So very young and so very vulnerable.

"No, thank you, my dear," Mary Bernadette replied, which was exactly what she had told her grandson the first time he had asked.

PJ was sitting in the chair next to the bed, from which he could easily hold his grandmother's hand. Alexis stood at the foot of bed. She wasn't sure she had the right to be any closer. Looking down at Mary Bernadette, Alexis remembered what Morgan had said at lunch the afternoon they had gone to the gallery in Somerstown. He had suggested that Mary Bernadette might not be as omnipotent as she appeared. Well, she had indeed been laid low. *How the mighty have fallen,* Alexis thought. She took no joy or satisfaction in this. It made her uneasy to see PJ's grandmother in a situation of almost total dependence. Someone like Mary Bernadette Fitzgibbon wasn't supposed to be susceptible to human frailty. People relied on her to be above and beyond the reach of common mortality.

How ridiculous, Alexis thought. *And yet, that's how I've felt about her. Maybe we all have.* It was true that she couldn't pretend to like

PJ's grandmother very much—and sometimes she didn't like her at all—but to see her lying in this narrow hospital bed dressed only in a flimsy johnny, her finger bare of her wedding ring, and without the powder and muted pink lipstick she always wore, was deeply disturbing.

We are all going to die, Alexis thought, unconsciously putting her hand against her stomach. *Life is so very precious, and so very fleeting.*

"Are you comfortable, Grandmother? Do you want me to adjust the pillows?"

Mary Bernadette smiled. "You're a good boy," she said. "The pillows are fine."

Poor PJ. He had cried for hours the night Mary Bernadette had been taken ill, and Alexis had been powerless to console him. She had suspected his tears were for more than just his grandmother. She had suspected they were also for their marriage, for their unborn child, for all of the lost chances of kindness and understanding between them.

"You'll be good as new, Grandmother, I promise."

"Of course I will. There was never any doubt about it."

"Is there anything you need from home?" Alexis asked. "Any personal items?"

"No, thank you, dear," Mary Bernadette replied. "If I do need anything, Grace will bring it to me."

"Okay. I'll let you two have some time alone, then."

Alexis left and took a seat in the waiting room down the hall. The atmosphere was hushed. There was a poor selection of old magazines, many with pages sloppily torn out and coffee rings obscuring print. The light was dim. A woman around her mother-in-law's age was the only other occupant of the room. She was looking off into space while twisting a tissue in her hands. Her eyes were red and swollen. Alexis said a silent prayer for the woman.

After some time PJ joined her. He sat in the chair next to hers and took her hand. Neither spoke. Alexis found the silence a comfort and hoped that her husband did, too. This moment, she thought, was a sign of the healing between them. At least PJ wasn't retreating into himself and shutting her out. At least he wasn't turning to another woman for comfort, as she had almost turned to another man.

"Are you ready to go home?" she asked PJ gently.

PJ nodded.

They rose, and still holding hands, they left the hospital.

CHAPTER 106

Megan Fitzgibbon pulled into one of the parking spaces reserved for visitors to the Wilson House. She was wearing one of her best and most conservative suits. She was armed with knowledge of Meadows's dubious prior real estate dealings and his shameful romantic past. She was filled with a sense of righteousness. And she was going to crash a meeting of the board of the OWHA. Asking for an interview would have allowed time for prevarication or downright refusal. It was much more difficult to turn away someone right in front of you than it was to fire off a dismissive e-mail. As predicted, Pat thought she was crazy but he knew better than to try to stop her.

Here goes, Megan thought, stepping into the front hall of the old building. The others had already gathered in the former dining room, and Megan joined them. And there, leaning casually against the mantel of the fireplace, was the Great Man himself. Megan could feel his energy across the room; there was something brutal in it. She experienced a moment of panic. *No wonder everyone is so intimidated by the man,* she thought. But the panic was followed by the return of her resolve. She walked resolutely toward him and put out her hand.

"Mr. Meadows," she said. "How do you do? My name is Megan Fitzgibbon. I'm married to Mary Bernadette's son. I've heard so much about you and your—work—in Oliver's Well."

Meadows shook her hand briefly. "Another Mrs. Fitzgibbon," he said, with barely concealed—was it amusement? "I'm afraid I didn't even know that you existed."

Megan laughed. *Fine*, she thought. *If that's the way you want to play it.* "Well," she said, "I can't claim to be as popular as you are, but in my own little sphere I'm not without influence."

"As you say, in your own little sphere. Well, it looks as if the meeting is about to start. You'll be on your way then."

"Oh, no," Megan replied. "I have a matter I would like to present to the board. Leonard assured me I was welcome to attend the meeting."

Leonard had done no such thing, but Meadows didn't need to know that.

Meadows raised an eyebrow. "Indeed? Well, then, I suggest you take a seat at the table. We do have a temporary vacancy, as you know."

Thanks to you, Megan thought, as she joined the others. In answer to their surprised expressions she simply smiled.

Neal had been selected as temporary chairman in Mary Bernadette's place. Why, Megan wondered, hadn't Meadows commandeered that honor? No doubt he had his reasons. Neal opened the meeting and read the minutes from the last meeting, as was his duty as secretary. When old business had been discussed—rather summarily, Megan thought, disturbed by the general timidity and silence of the board; it did not bode well for her mission—Wynston Meadows took over.

"As you can see, we have a Mrs. Fitzgibbon in our midst today. To what do we owe this—this honor?"

"I'd like," Megan said, folding her hands on the table before her, "to put myself up as temporary replacement for Mary Bernadette. Not, of course, as chairman." Megan smiled at Neal, who nodded his acknowledgment. "But as a representative of a family whose lives have been deeply involved with the life of Oliver's

Well for over fifty years. As a representative of a woman whose passion for historical accuracy and integrity is undeniable."

Meadows sat back in his chair and crossed his legs. "And what qualifies you for membership on the board?" he asked, showing his teeth.

Megan looked from one board member to the next. Joyce frowned. Wallace looked away. Norma's face was expressionless. Jeannette smiled feebly. "As many of you know," she went on, "even though I make my home in Annapolis, I've been what I like to think of as an honorary member of the Oliver's Well community for over twenty-five years. And during that time I've made it my business to keep up with everything that's happening locally, from the debate about the new high school gymnasium to the mayor's proposed ban on plastic grocery bags. My mother-in-law is an excellent source of information."

This last remark was met with appreciative laughter from Richard and Leonard. Neal and Anne and Jeannette smiled.

"And as cofounder and copresident of the Cerebral Palsy Education Effort I'm well acquainted with the workings of boards and committees. I'm also a practicing lawyer with a professional knowledge of contracts and negotiation. Finally, I have a vested interest in keeping the Fitzgibbon family in the service of Oliver's Well. The town has been good to us, and we feel it our duty to be good to it in return. My son and his wife plan to raise a family here in Oliver's Well, and my husband and I want our grandchildren to have the same wonderful experience of the town as my mother- and father-in-law and my husband and his sister have had."

Megan's final remarks were followed by a silence that was distinctly anxious. Covertly or quite openly, everyone at the table looked to Wynston Meadows. Megan found his expression inscrutable. Clearly, the next move would be his and his alone. *Jesus,* she thought. *What was I thinking?*

"Well," he said heartily after a long moment of letting them hang, "let's put it to a vote, shall we?"

Megan was surprised that he hadn't shut her down with one

swipe. She sat patiently while paper ballots were passed around and then collected by Neal Hyatt. He unfolded and read each ballot, and separated them into two unequal piles. When he was done he looked first at Wynston Meadows and then to her. "Welcome to the board, Mrs. Fitzgibbon," he said, with an unmistakable note of relief in his voice.

"Megan, please. And thank you, Neal."

Megan looked at Wynston Meadows and once again couldn't quite read the expression on his face. She thought it might be surprise, heavily masked by annoyance.

"Just until the good lady returns," he said to Megan. "If, indeed, she does return."

What a creep, Megan thought. But what did it matter? She was on the board. Step one was accomplished.

After the meeting—conducted by Meadows and at which nothing of significance was decided or rejected—Richard Armstrong walked to the parking lot with Megan. "I'm so glad you're doing this," he told her. "I've been so worried about Mary Bernadette for the past months. Most of us have. She was trying to be so strong."

"Yes."

"And we were all letting her down. Not one of us ever stood up to Wynston Meadows. We valued money over the well-being of our friend and colleague."

"It's a complicated situation, Richard," Megan said soothingly.

Richard glanced around, as if to be sure there was no one to overhear, but by now the parking lot was empty. "I was one of the people they quoted in that article," he said softly. "I was the one who said, 'Why would I lie' about the Fitzgibbons. It came across all wrong. I was appalled when the article was published, but I've been too embarrassed to say anything. Please, Mary Bernadette must know that I'm her staunch friend."

Megan put her hand on Richard's arm. "I'm sure she does. And the others? Do you know who else gave a quote to the *Gazette*?"

"Not for sure, but I can make a pretty good guess."

"Joyce or Wallace?"

Richard nodded. "Yes."

"You know I can't promise any miracles. I'm not even sure of my game plan yet. But you can help me impress upon every member of the board the need for complete secrecy as far as my membership goes. I mean, it must be kept from Mary Bernadette for as long as possible. Honestly, I'm not sure how she'd feel about my butting in. I don't want to cause her more anxiety."

"Leave it to me. I'll have a talk with each one privately. I can be persuasive when I need to be."

Megan smiled. "What about Wynston Meadows?"

"I suspect that if he's asked not to do a particular thing he goes right out and does it. I think we're just going to have to hope he turns his attention to you and away from Mary Bernadette. Lord, that sounded awful. I'm sorry, Megan."

"It's okay," Megan assured him. "I'm here to draw his fire away from the original target. And to find out what he's really up to in dear little Oliver's Well."

CHAPTER 107

"Remember," Pat said, as he and Megan stood in the hall outside Mary Bernadette's private room, "the doctor suggested we keep all stressful topics from her. And that means Wynston Meadows and the OWHA and your—your *crusade* on my mother's behalf."

"Of course." Megan laid a hand on her husband's arm. "Pat? Are you sure you don't want to go in alone for a bit?"

He frowned. "I'm sure."

Those of us who are about to die salute you. Megan didn't know
why those words had come to her just then. Or maybe she did
know. In they went. Pat's manner instantly became stiff and distant.

"Mom," he said. "You're looking well."

Mary Bernadette raised an eyebrow. "Am I? I suppose I should
be grateful for small favors."

Pat nodded. "Right."

Megan resisted a sigh. The emotional distance between Pat
and his mother saddened her. Her husband was not a cold man.
Megan didn't believe that he hated his mother, no matter what
he said about her. Someday soon he would have to face the fact
of her mortality and make peace with the woman who had given
him life.

"How are you feeling, Mary Bernadette?" Megan asked, not-
ing that her mother-in-law wouldn't quite meet her eye. "Are
they keeping you comfortable?"

"As well as can be expected," Mary Bernadette replied.

"That's good."

Megan looked to her husband, who seemed to be out of conversation. He just stood by his mother's bedside—not close
enough so that he could touch her or she him—his arms at his
side, his expression set. Megan repressed a strain of annoyance.
Couldn't he at least make an effort? "All's well at the house," she
told her mother-in-law. "The animals are being looked after.
We're keeping things tidy."

"Thank you."

"We should be going," Pat suddenly blurted.

"It was good of you to come," Mary Bernadette said, her dignity intact as always. "I'm feeling rather tired now, anyway."

Megan went over to Pat and took his arm. "Good-bye, Mary
Bernadette," she said. "Sleep well." And then she led her stone-
faced husband out of the room.

CHAPTER 108

The room was crowded, what with Mary Bernadette's bed and equipment, the three men, and the profusion of cards and flowers that were still pouring in, days after Mary Bernadette's admittance to Oliver's Well Memorial Hospital.

Every surface but the floor was covered with vases; Grace had begun stuffing two or three bouquets into one vase in order to make room for those still coming. There were forty get-well cards—PJ had counted them—and three Mylar balloons. Mary Bernadette had suggested that PJ bring the balloons home for Banshee and Mercy to play with.

PJ had smiled. "You mean, to deflate."

"I won't deny that I don't really care for balloons," his grandmother had acknowledged. "I don't find them appropriate for people over the age of eight."

This afternoon, Father Robert had come by to pray with Mary Bernadette. He informed PJ and his grandfather that he would be reading Psalm 103.

Paddy and PJ each bowed his head and folded his hands before him. Mary Bernadette, sitting up in the bed, did the same.

> "Bless the Lord, O my soul,
> and all that is within me, bless his holy Name.
> Bless the Lord, O my soul,
> And forget not all his benefits.
> He forgives all your sins
> And heals all your infirmities;
> He redeems your life from the grave
> And crowns you with mercy and loving-kindness;
> He satisfies you with good things,
> And your youth is renewed like an eagle's."

"Excuse me. I'm sorry to interrupt." A nurse stood at the door to the room, an apologetic smile on her face. She beckoned to PJ with her forefinger, and he followed her out to the hall. He returned to his grandmother's room a few minutes later. He knew he was scowling, but he couldn't help it.

"What's wrong?" his grandfather asked in a low voice, as the priest read on.

"A massive bouquet of flowers," PJ replied. "That's what's wrong. From Wynston Meadows."

"Where is it?" Paddy asked.

"I threw it in the trash where it belongs."

"You might have offered it to the nurses to give to someone who has no flowers from a loved one."

PJ shook his head. "I didn't even think of that, I was so mad. Can you believe the nerve of that man, sending flowers to the woman he's trying to destroy? The hypocrite *wants* her dead and out of the way."

"Name calling won't help matters."

"But that's what he is, Grandpa, a hypocrite."

"Who is that you're talking about?" Mary Bernadette's voice rose over Father Robert's, causing him to stop midsentence.

Paddy took a step closer to his wife's bed. "Now, don't trouble yourself, Mary."

"It's nothing Grandmother," PJ added. "Sorry, Father Robert."

Father Robert nodded and continued with the prayer.

"For he himself knows whereof we are made;
he remembers that we are but dust.
Our days are like the grass;
We flourish like a flower of the field;
When the wind goes over it, it is gone,
And its place shall know it no more."

PJ leaned in to his grandfather. "Couldn't he have chosen something less grim?"

"The psalm was your grandmother's wish," Paddy explained. *We are but dust.* PJ had never imagined what his life would be like without his grandmother. He knew, of course, that she would die. Everybody died. But it had never occurred to him that most likely *he* would go on living after her. He would *have* to go on living, especially when his wife was pregnant with his child. The thought was daunting and filled him with equal measures of fear and determination.

Father Robert finished reading the psalm and offered a final blessing. "I'll leave you with your family, Mary Bernadette," he said then.

"Wynston Meadows," Mary Bernadette said when he was gone.

"Excuse me, Grandmother?" PJ said.

"That's who you were talking about earlier. Wynston Meadows. What is he up to now?" she demanded. "I have a right to know."

PJ looked helplessly to his grandfather. Paddy cleared his throat, opened his mouth, and closed it again. He went over to the bed and took his grandmother's hand. "It was nothing," he said firmly. "I was just letting off steam."

Mary Bernadette searched his face with her bright, keen eyes and PJ knew she knew that he was lying.

"You're right," she said, withdrawing her hand from his. "The man is a hypocrite."

CHAPTER 109

"Fitzgibbon Landscaping. This is Alexis speaking. How may I help you?"

"Alexis, it's Morgan."

Alexis put her hand to her heart. She was thankful that she was alone in the office.

"Hello."

"I had to call. I heard about Mary Bernadette's stroke. I'm so sorry. If there's anything I can do to help, please let me know."

"Thank you. There's probably nothing. Her daughter's here now and she's pretty much got everything under control. And my mother-in-law is here most times, too."

"Good. Alexis? Are you there alone?"

Alexis nodded and then, realizing the futility of the gesture, said, "Yes."

"Look, Alexis," Morgan went on, his tone urgent. "I really need to apologize for . . . for what almost happened the other day. It was wrong of me, but . . . The thing is, I'm falling in love with you. I know I shouldn't be, but I can't seem to help it."

Alexis was shocked. She had been so concerned with her own troubling emotions she had never stopped to give real consideration to his. He had been falling in love with her, not just playing a game, not just killing time. Not that she had ever really suspected him of trifling with her emotions but . . . She felt herself blush with shame. "I . . ."

"Can you honestly say that you don't have feelings for me?"

"No," she whispered. "But I'm married."

Morgan laughed unhappily. "I'm aware."

Alexis didn't know what she could say to him. She was determined to stick by her decision not to see him again, even as a friend. She didn't entirely trust herself, and she all too clearly recalled Maureen's cautions about the gossip mill in Oliver's Well. And, most important, she loved her husband and was soon to bear his child.

"You deserve better than me, Morgan," she said finally. "I'm a bit of a wreck right now. Aside from being married, I mean." Not exactly the most eloquent way to put things, but it was all she could manage.

"Alexis—"

"No. Morgan, listen to me. Nothing can happen between us. I can't see you again. I mean, not deliberately. If we run into each other in town . . ."

"I should nod politely and walk the other way?"

Alexis swallowed hard. "Yes," she said. "That's the way it has to be."

"I'm not happy about this, Alexis," Morgan said, his tone mournful. "But I'll abide by your decision."

"I'm sorry for hurting you, Morgan. I'm sorry for leading you on. I promise I didn't do it purposely."

"I believe you."

"I should go now. Someone might come in. . . ."

"All right," Morgan said. "Good luck, Alexis. I hope life is good to you."

She couldn't bring herself to reply. She quietly hung up the receiver. She had not told him that PJ refused to see a therapist. She had not told him that she was pregnant. Those things were private. She had no right to share them, and he had no right to know them.

This, she thought, was what life was really about. There were constantly difficult choices to be made and challenging promises to be kept. There were sacrifices to be offered for others. There was unhappiness and sorrow to bear. There were consequences to be paid. How naïve she had been when she married PJ Fitzgibbon, how airy her ideals, how false her notions of marriage. In spite of all evidence to the contrary she had thought, no, she had *expected* it all to be so easy.

With a supreme effort Alexis forced herself to return to the work of helping to run her family's business. And at the end of the workday, she would drive to Oliver's Well Memorial Hospital and pay PJ's grandmother a visit.

Chapter 110

Mary Bernadette was restless. She kicked at the thin sheet covering her legs. It still wasn't settling right. She leaned forward and straightened it with her hands. The sheet felt scratchy. She sat back against the pillows and sighed. She was sure that she would mend more quickly in her own home than in this place of sickness and death. If only she was allowed to *do* something productive instead of lying like an invalid!

There was no use in pretending that she wasn't worried about the health of the OWHA, especially after that disgraceful and utterly false bit of "news" had aired the previous Saturday. She had demanded that the family keep her fully up to date, but so far not one of them had even brought her a newspaper, supposedly on doctor's orders. Her own husband and grandson had lied to her on the day of Father Robert's visit. Something had happened and they were keeping it from her. She was annoyed and insulted. Everyone was being condescending to her, treating her like a child. Just last evening she had called Neal Hyatt in the hopes that he might tell her if Wynston Meadows had made any further incursions on the good reputation of the OWHA. But Neal, as charming as always, had managed to tell her exactly nothing. And just that morning when the doctor had been in to see her, he had reminded Grace that her mother was in a delicate condition and needed complete rest. "*You* try telling her that, Doctor," Grace had replied. They had been talking about her as if she weren't even in the room!

There was a knock at the door, and in came Grace and the twins.

"I was just thinking about you, dear," Mary Bernadette said with a smile.

Grace raised an eyebrow. "What did I do wrong?"

Mary Bernadette ignored her daughter's question.

"How are you feeling, Grandma?" Danica asked. The poor girl looked frightened. She was twisting the end of her braid and her eyes were wide, as if she were trying not to cry. It might be the sight of the ugly machines and the hanging bags full of God knew what sort of fluids that upset her, Mary Bernadette thought. She hoped it was that, rather than her own appearance. She knew she wasn't looking her best, but she *had* applied the powder and lipstick Grace had brought her and her hair was freshly brushed.

"Just fine," she told her granddaughter. "Don't play with your hair."

Danica took her hand away from her braid.

"When will you be getting out of here?" David asked.

Grace chuckled. "You make it sound like she's a prisoner in a jail."

David turned to his aunt. "For someone like my grandmother," he said quite earnestly, "this is a jail."

Mary Bernadette was touched. How acute the boy was! "As soon as the doctors say I may leave," she told him.

"I hate hospitals," Danica said fiercely.

"I don't think anyone really likes them," Grace said, putting her arm around her niece's shoulders.

"The people who get better in them don't mind hospitals so much," David pointed out. "I mean, I know that my surgery isn't going to be fun or anything, but at least when I get back home I'll be able to walk better."

This child must not die, Mary Bernadette thought. *There must be no more loss.* David was smart and self-possessed. He would take the Fitzgibbon name far.

"Well, I'm never going to the hospital," Danica declared. "Ever."

Mary Bernadette smiled. She admired her granddaughter's determination.

"Let's not think about that," Grace said briskly. "Let's focus on making this visit a pleasant one for your grandmother."

"Danica, tell me about school," Mary Bernadette asked. "Are you getting good grades?"

"Yes, but I'd rather tell you about soccer, Grandma, if that's okay."

"Of course." Mary Bernadette had no interest in sports of any sort, but if they were important to her granddaughter, she would do her best to pay attention.

"Once she starts," David warned, "she never stops."

Grace laughed and Danica managed a smile before launching into a story about a game and one of her teammates and a gross injury and an awesome goal. Mary Bernadette listened and nodded and smiled in what she hoped were appropriate moments.

At least, she thought, the children weren't treating her like some sick old lady. She could take a good deal of comfort in that.

CHAPTER 111

Megan was at home in her office, urgent paperwork relating to the CPEE to her right, several e-mails from her colleagues at the law firm waiting to be answered, and a form from the hospital where David would be having his surgery to be filled out and mailed. But first, there was OWHA business to which she had to attend. She still felt a bit anxious about the task she had taken on, but to the other members of the board she would have to be worthy of Mary Bernadette—in other words, she would have to show only strength and determination.

Let the games begin, she thought, as she placed a call to Leonard DeWitt.

"I was half-expecting to hear from you," he admitted, when she had identified herself. "What are you really up to, Megan, joining the board of the OWHA? It's not only to keep Mary Bernadette's voice being heard, is it?"

"In a way, Leonard, it is," she told him. "See, I want to get rid of Wynston Meadows as much as you do. I'm not entirely sure how I'm going to go about doing that, but it seemed to me the first step was to get on the board. The next is to know on whom I might count for help. And that's why I'm calling you."

Leonard laughed. "Are you sure you and Mary Bernadette aren't related by blood?"

"Quite sure."

"All right then, you can forget about Joyce," he said. "She'll slavishly follow Meadows's every command, no matter its unsavory nature. I think she's half in love with the man. And Wallace is too concerned with gaining Meadows's favor to entertain a sensible opinion about him."

"Then what about Norma? Can she be made to see that Meadows is poisonous for Oliver's Well?"

"Possibly," Leonard told her. "She's not an unintelligent woman, but she isn't known for her firm views and strong opinions. Frankly, I've no idea what she thinks about Meadows and his high-handed ways."

"Which leaves you and me and Richard and Neal and Anne and Jeannette. A majority of the board. We're all staunchly pro–Mary Bernadette and just as staunchly pro–Oliver's Well. Can't we just put it to a vote and push Meadows out the door?"

Leonard cleared his throat. "It's not as easy as all that. If it were, Meadows would have been long gone. See, we need a unanimous vote, not just a majority, to dismiss anyone from the board. Well, unanimous expect for the person being voted off."

"What? That's ridiculously restricting! Who came up with that idea?" *And please don't say Mary Bernadette. . . .*

"I don't know," Leonard admitted, "but it's been in the by-laws of the OWHA forever."

"Well, this puts a new spin on things. No wonder you're all feeling so stymied."

"Not all of us. Joyce and Wallace seem content to put up with any sort of bad behavior for the sake of the money. Which so far has been just a phantom."

"Maybe," Megan said, "we can concentrate on the character angle. Convince the others that Meadows's history suggests he can't be trusted." She told Leonard about the shady development deal and the charges of domestic violence.

"But nothing ever came to court, you say?"

"No."

"Then it remains speculation. Suspicion isn't proof."

"But sometimes it can be enough reason for walking away from a deal that seems too good to be true."

"That is a point, but when there's so much money at stake . . . Honestly, Megan, I don't like the man one bit, but if there is a possibility of his coming through with the millions, the last thing I want to do is alienate him. And I'm not alone in that. I think even Mary Bernadette feels the same way."

"I understand. Well, thanks, Leonard, for your honesty."

"What are you going to do now?" he asked.

"I'm not sure," she admitted. "But you'll be the first to know."

Megan remained at her desk when the call was over. It occurred to her again that she might have taken on a losing cause, especially given that insane rule about the need for a unanimous vote to get someone kicked off the board. But there was no way she could walk away from the OWHA now, not without embarrassing herself and bringing further shame on the Fitzgibbon name. There had to be a way to eliminate Wynston Meadows without eliminating the money.

It all came down to the money. But why did the money have to be Wynston Meadows's money? "Of course!" Megan said to her office. It was so simple! If everyone was so afraid of losing Wynston Meadows's promised millions, then she would simply have to find the money elsewhere. And then she would have to convince the board members that the new financial backers were a better bet for the OWHA than the illustrious Mr. Meadows.

Now, Megan thought, her excitement suddenly dampened, *where do I find someone with twenty-five million dollars they're willing to give to little Oliver's Well?*

CHAPTER 112

"None of my family will tell me what's going on with the NOWHA," Mary Bernadette complained. "Jeannette, tell me what you know. What is Wynston Meadows saying about me now?"

Jeannette, who was sitting in the chair beside her friend's bed, sighed. "Honestly, Mary, I don't know anything. And I think everyone would agree that it would be in very bad taste for him to malign a sick woman."

"Everyone but Mr. Meadows would agree," Mary Bernadette retorted. She had dismissed her son and daughter-in-law's warnings about him as ridiculous and insulting. And now . . . Now she was paying for her pride.

"Please, Mary," Jeannette said, "don't drive yourself mad with thinking about the man. Please just concentrate on getting better. We miss you back home, Mary."

Did anyone really miss her? Anyone other than Paddy, of course, and if he did miss her, Mary Bernadette wondered now if it was only because she was a habit for him, someone whose presence punctuated his days and gave them form. It was a terrible thought, but that didn't mean it wasn't the truth.

"I've had a bad shock, Jeannette." The second the words were out of her mouth, she wished she could draw them back in.

Jeannette nodded gravely. "Indeed you have, Mary."

"I never thought that something like this would happen." There, again, were words she had never meant to speak.

Jeannette smiled. "What, that you would grow old like everyone else?"

"Don't mock," Mary Bernadette scolded. "I'm serious. It was foolish of me, terribly foolish to expect I would escape—weakness. Foolish and sinful."

Jeannette reached over and patted her friend's arm. "Now,

don't be too hard on yourself, Mary. We all entertain fantasies of immortality from time to time. Sometimes we do it without even being aware that we're living in a dream."

Fantasies of immortality. "I don't know what to do," she admitted, turning her face from Jeannette.

"There's nothing *to* do Mary, but to rest and get well."

"Poor Paddy."

"We're all looking after him, Mary, don't you worry."

Mary Bernadette turned back to her friend. "Do you think he's been happy?" she asked. The need to speak seemed to be overwhelming. She realized that she desperately wanted to hear the truth, but if anyone knew the truth would they tell it to her?

Jeannette stood abruptly—Mary Bernadette saw her flinch and knew that her back was hurting her—and began to smooth the sheets. "Of course he has! Now, don't go troubling yourself with such silly thoughts."

Mary Bernadette pushed Jeannette's hands away. "Stop fussing over me. I'm not entirely incapable. Not yet."

Carefully, Jeannette sat back down. "The doctors say you're doing much better."

"Then why are they still holding me prisoner?" Mary Bernadette demanded. "When can I get out of this place?"

"Patience, Mary. Patience is a fine virtue."

Mary Bernadette frowned. "Yes, well, that's all very well for you to say when you're not the one eating substandard food. And I haven't had a decent night's sleep since I've been here, what with sick people coughing and buzzers buzzing and machines whirring and beeping. For so long I was—I was terrified of this place! Do you remember when Paddy had the hip replacement, how you sat with him for hours on end because my nerves wouldn't allow me to? Now I'm just sick of it!"

Jeannette sighed. "This too shall pass, Mary. Be thankful that you survived."

Mary Bernadette suddenly reached for her friend's hand. "I *am* thankful, Jeannette," she said fiercely. "More than anyone can ever know."

CHAPTER 113

Pat followed his father through the living room and into the kitchen, Mercy trotting between them. The two men had been at the hospital all morning. Pat had spent only a moment or two with his mother and then had waited for his father in the cafeteria, reading the paper on his iPhone and drinking weak, flavorless coffee. Anything was better than standing tongue-tied by his mother's bed, wrestling with unsettling emotions.

Mercy was now bouncing around the kitchen. In search of a treat, Pat supposed. The mutt never stopped eating, asking to eat, and probably dreaming of eating. Well, that sort of fixation was common in shelter animals. God only knew what sort of awful life Mercy had endured before someone had brought her to safety and then Paddy Fitzgibbon had adopted her.

"Let me make you some lunch, Dad," Pat said, opening a cupboard and scanning the contents.

"Don't go to the trouble, Pat. I'm not hungry."

Pat turned to his father. "You have to eat, Dad. Mom will kill one of us if you lose weight. Look, here's a can of tomato soup. How about soup and a grilled cheese sandwich? And there's beer in the fridge. I brought it in. I won't tell Mom if you won't."

Paddy managed a smile. "No, I won't say a word."

His father took a seat at the table, Mercy ever attentive by his side, while Pat went about preparing lunch. And while he toasted bread and heated soup he thought back to all the times his father had quietly—though sometimes ineffectually—attempted to make up for his mother's frequent punishments and chronic lack of affection. Pat had always been very grateful for his father's love.

Now he brought the soup and sandwiches to the table. "Eat it while it's hot, Dad," he said.

His father picked up his spoon but put it down again. "I

know," he said, "that your mother has been hard on you, Pat. But she's always loved you. I hope you believe that."

Pat choked on his soup. It was the last thing he had expected to hear from his father. The content of their conversations had always strictly remained in the realm of weather, sports, and local politics. Never, ever did they discuss family matters or, God forbid, feelings. Pat fervently wished that Megan would come through the kitchen door right then and rescue them both.

"It's just that something happened to her when William died," his father went on, stirring his soup into a small maelstrom. "And then you coming along so soon after . . . Well, she hadn't finished mourning, I suppose."

"Eat some soup, Dad," Pat repeated, "before it gets cold."

Dutifully, his father took a few spoonfuls of soup and a bite of his sandwich. And then he looked at his son earnestly. "I hope that you can forgive her, Pat. She is, after all, your mother. But I know that's between the two of you."

Pat stared at his plate and considered his father's words. *Could* he forgive his mother her arrogance and her constant criticism? *Could* he forgive her for all the times he had gone to her for comfort and she had turned him away? *Could* he forgive her for the rudeness and disdain with which she had treated his wife? And *could* he forgive her for loving William more than she was ever able to love him?

Automatically, Pat took another bite of his sandwich, but it had no taste for him now. He was half-tempted to give the sandwich to Mercy, but the thought of his mother finding out—no matter that she was in a hospital bed miles away—stopped him. And at that moment he realized that though he might never come to like his mother, he did love her. Though the love wasn't as strong as what he felt for his father or his wife or his children, still, it *was* love. And maybe you owed forgiveness to the ones you loved, even the difficult ones.

Pat cleared his throat. "I promise I'll always do the right thing by her, Dad."

His father smiled at him. "I know you will."

They ate their lunch and drank their beer in silence for a while, each man lost in his own thoughts, while Mercy continued to stare fixedly at Paddy's bowl and plate. "If it weren't wrong to be envious of another person's good fortune," Paddy said suddenly, urgently, "I would be envious of you, Pat. You have all that I lost."

"What do you mean, Dad?" Pat asked, troubled by his father's tone of voice. "What have you lost? What do I have that you don't?"

"You have to understand that I mean no disrespect to your mother."

"Of course not. But I still don't understand."

"I do love your mother, Pat. And I know that she loves me. But things haven't been right in such a long time. . . ." Paddy looked down at his half-empty bowl of soup. "It was different," he said, "when your mother learned she was going to have William. It was—better. We were so very happy. And then when William died, well, it near killed her. My dear wife. She became . . . She grew distant from me, from everyone. She couldn't risk the intimacy, you see. She was so very afraid that she wouldn't survive another great loss so she hardened her heart."

Pat was at a loss for words. His mother, afraid? And his father . . . He had never known how much of his mother's difficult nature had registered with his father; he had never even considered that his father might be unhappy or lonely in his marriage. He felt immensely sorry for the man's suffering. And he felt ashamed of his own lack of sympathy and understanding.

Paddy began to cry quietly. Mercy whimpered and rested her head on his lap. "Good girl," Paddy told her through his tears. "Good girl."

Pat waited patiently for his father to compose himself. Eventually, Paddy looked back up at his son. "I did try to make you feel loved. I did try."

Pat reached across the table and put his hand on his father's. "I know," he said earnestly. "You did the best you could do, Dad. That's all anyone can ask of a person."

"I wish it could have been more."

Pat smiled. "You know what they say, Dad. If wishes were horses, then beggars would ride."

Paddy smiled back. "You sound just like your mother."

"God forbid!"

"Now, there you go again."

Mercy lifted her head from Paddy's lap and barked.

"Eat your lunch, Dad," Pat said. "And try to keep that dog off the table."

Chapter 114

Alexis, Grace, and Megan took the elevator down to the hospital's cafeteria for a cup of coffee. Mary Bernadette had fallen asleep and there was no point in the three of them staring at her. That was what Grace had said.

PJ's aunt was tall and straight shouldered like her mother. Her hair was brown with a few streaks of gray and her eyes were the exact color as her brother's. On the fourth finger of her left hand she wore a simple silver band. There was a silver chain around her neck, and Alexis guessed a cross was suspended from it, but whatever it was rested inside Grace's shirt.

"How are you getting along at Fitzgibbon Landscaping?" Grace asked her when they had found seats at a table by a window. "Yikes, this coffee is awful."

"Fine. It's not a very difficult job."

"Easy for you to say. I don't do numbers. What else are you up to?"

"Not much," Alexis admitted. "Well, nothing, really. I was . . .

I was doing some work for the OWHA but . . ." Alexis felt her cheeks flame. "But that didn't work out."

Grace grinned. "Too strong a dose of the matriarch, eh?"

"You two have such full lives," she blurted. "I mean . . . you have your own lives, apart from . . . apart from Oliver's Well."

"You have to learn to stand up to Mary Bernadette, Alexis," her mother-in-law said. "Unfortunately, nobody else can do it for you. Not even my son, though—God forgive me for saying this— he might be of more help to you than he has been."

Alexis was stunned. Could it be that PJ's mother and aunt had sympathy for her plight?

"Mary Bernadette is not a goddess, Alexis," Grace added, "no matter how formidable she might appear. She's just a flawed human being like the rest of us."

"I guess I know that, but still. When she gives you that look . . ."

Megan laughed. "Ah, the look! She really should have been an actress. I wonder how much of her persona is conscious."

"Good question," Grace said. "I think that my mother is a fascinating example of a person who's highly conscious of the effects she wants to achieve and at the same time largely unknown to her self. Unaware of her real motives. Flailing. In short, desperately staying afloat."

"Maybe that will change," Alexis said. "A crisis can change people for the better. Or so it's said."

Grace looked up at the cafeteria ceiling, as if, Alexis thought, the answer lay in the insulated tiles. "Maybe," she said after a time, looking back at the other two women. "But my mother is one stubborn lady. It might take a miracle to budge her. And I haven't witnessed many of those lately."

"We're Catholic," Alexis pointed out. "We're supposed to believe in miracles."

"Do you?" Grace asked. "Do you really believe in miracles?"

"I don't know," Alexis admitted.

"The problem with my mother," Grace said now, "is that she has no sense of humor. Now, I don't know if she ever did or if it died when William died. Either way, it would do her good to laugh more. To see the ridiculous or absurd side of things once in a while. To learn to make fun of her own foibles. But again, I think we're talking a miracle."

Megan shook her head. "I can't imagine Mary Bernadette giggling. Can you? Think about it. Laughing modestly, sure. But not giggling."

"No snorting milk through her nose, either."

Alexis laughed. "No thigh slapping."

"Everything with her is so—so deadly serious." Grace sighed. "I feel bad for her. I don't think she ever has a moment's peace."

"How much does anyone know about her childhood?" Alexis asked. "Was it a particularly difficult one?"

"I don't think so," Grace said. "But she's never talked much about growing up in Ireland."

Megan nodded. "We do know that she had a brother named William and he died young, in his twenties I think. And both of her parents died before they were sixty. They never saw their grandchildren. No one had the money for travel back then."

"The last of her line?" Grace wondered. "I never heard about cousins, either. There was Aunt Catherine, and I know she didn't have any daughters, but honestly I have no idea if she had any children at all. If she did have sons, they might still be in Ireland."

"So," Alexis said, "apart from us, Mary Bernadette is alone in the world."

The three Fitzgibbon women were silent for a moment.

"You know," Grace said suddenly. "I think my mother is terribly afraid to be happy. I think she believes that being happy only tempts fate. Or, in her case, the punishing wrath of God. *Farewell, thou child of my right hand, and joy; my sin was too much hope of thee, lov'd boy.* That's from a poem Ben Jonson wrote after his son died of the plague. Same notion. Punishment for happiness."

Megan sighed. "I wonder if she was always this way. I wonder if her—let's say, her seriousness—came about only after she lost her child."

"I think it's quite possible. But I'm pretty sure we'll never know. I'm certainly not going to ask Dad a question like that!"

"It would upset him," Alexis said. "He's such a nice man, isn't he?"

"Yes," Megan said. "He is."

"I suppose I'd better get back to Mom," Grace said suddenly, rising from her seat. She smiled at Alexis. "I'm glad we had this time together."

Alexis smiled back. "Me too," she said. "And thanks, the both of you."

CHAPTER 115

"I had a very nice conversation with your mother and your aunt Grace this afternoon. They're such intelligent women. Funny, too," said Alexis.

Alexis and PJ were at the cottage that evening. Alexis was feeling more optimistic than she had felt in a very long time. Grace and Megan had given her hope that someday she might succeed in forging a meaningful and independent life while still being a member of the Fitzgibbon family. Assuming she was still married to PJ.

"Good."

"What do you want for dinner?" Alexis asked, opening the fridge and looking inside. "We've got ground turkey. I could make burgers or meatballs."

"Either one, you pick. Alexis? I need to talk to you about something."

Alexis closed the fridge and turned around. The pained look she saw on her husband's face startled her. "Is it your grandmother?" she asked hurriedly. "Did something happen since I was at the hospital?"

"Grandmother is fine. It's just . . ."

"What, PJ?" Alexis walked over to him and put her hand on his arm. Her heart was beating madly. She was suddenly very, very afraid of losing him.

"It's just that there's a rumor around town that you and Morgan Shelby have been spending time together. People have seen you going into his gallery."

Alexis took her hand away from her husband and willed herself not to blush furiously. *A guilty conscience needs no accuser,* she thought. How true that was! "Yes," she said carefully, "I *was* spending some time with him. I—I was thinking about maybe learning the gallery business. He gave me some advice. But then I decided it wasn't what I wanted to do after all."

"That's all?" PJ asked, his tone pathetically hopeful.

"Yes, PJ," Alexis said. "I swear. That's all."

"Why didn't you tell me you were thinking about working in a gallery?"

"It seemed that you had so much on your mind already."

"You mean you thought I wouldn't listen to you. You thought I'd say you were just complaining about your job with Fitzgibbon Landscaping."

Alexis nodded. "Yes."

PJ shook his head. "You were probably right."

"Who . . . Who are these people who saw me with Morgan Shelby?" she asked.

PJ looked embarrassed. "The wife of one of the guys at work told him she'd heard rumors," he said. "He came to me. He thought I should know."

Alexis felt slightly sick. She could honestly say that nothing had happened, but the thought of people talking as if it had badly frightened her. She remembered something PJ had said, back when Wynston Meadows had started making trouble for the family. The very rumor of wrongdoing could taint even the most innocent of people. And just how innocent *was* she, Alexis wondered. Not as innocent as she should be.

PJ now took her right hand and held it in both of his. "The thought of you falling in love with another man . . . I don't think I could stand it, Ali."

"I'm not in love with another man, PJ."

"I believe you. And I've thought about what you asked, and I *do* want us to see a counselor. As long as we don't tell my grandmother. She's always distrusted therapy of any kind and given her health . . . Well, I don't want to make things worse for her."

And, Alexis thought, *you're still thinking of Mary Bernadette before me. And when I was miserable all by myself you ignored me, but when you thought there might be another man, you listened. Oh, PJ, we both have some serious growing up to do.*

"Thank you," she said. "It might not be easy, you know."

"I know."

"Things will have to change, PJ, or we'll find ourselves right back in the same place a year from now. But with a baby in tow."

PJ's eyes were blurred with tears. "I'm afraid, Ali. I'm afraid of losing you. I'm afraid of what my parents would think of me if I were stupid enough to let you go, if I gave up on our marriage. I'm afraid that no matter how hard I try I'll fail."

"But you still love me?" she asked.

"With all my heart," he said.

"Then we'll be okay," she said, willing herself to believe it. "We *have* to be, for our baby's sake."

"Do you remember our wedding?" PJ asked.

Alexis smiled and gently wiped the tears from her husband's cheek. "Like it was yesterday."

"You for me, and I for thee and for none else."

The words they had spoken before God, family, and friends. "Your face to mine and your head turned away from all others," Alexis responded.

"I vow."

"I vow."

And then PJ took her in his arms and they stood together, quietly, for a long time.

CHAPTER 116

"Megan, good to see you again."

"And you, Sarah," Megan replied, shaking the hand of her colleague. "How's the family?"

"Fantastic. My daughter gave birth to her fourth child last month."

"Fourth? Wow. Girl or boy?"

"Another boy. Mark my words she's going to try one more time to get it right."

Megan laughed and took the seat Sarah indicated. Sarah Simons was a professional fund-raising consultant and one of the best at that. Over the years she had done great work in helping the CPEE find money from a variety of sources, and most recently she had been responsible for raising twenty million dollars to fund a new wing of an esteemed art museum in Chicago. If anyone could help save the Oliver's Well Historical Association from the meddling Wynston Meadows, Sarah Simons was the most likely one to do it.

"So," she said, seated behind her desk, "you said on the phone this isn't about the CPEE."

"It isn't." Megan outlined what had been going on with Meadows and the OWHA, and how she had gotten herself a place on the board—"a miracle, that"—with the admittedly crazy hope of ridding the association of the Great Man. "So far," she went on,

"they—we—haven't seen a penny of the promised first installment of five million dollars. And the CEO tells me that Meadows
has refused to formalize a payment schedule. If you ask me, he
has no intention of forking over the money."

"He's bad news," Sarah said shortly. "Everyone knows that.
People who aren't compelled to do business with him don't. Personally, I think he's mentally unbalanced."

"From what I've seen so far, I think I agree. Look, here's the
thing, Sarah. The OWHA is financially sound. They don't need
Meadows's money to survive, but they do need it—or they think
they need it—to buy a big, important piece of property known as
the Branley Estate. It would be a real coup for them and a benefit for the town as well as for the entire region. The buildings are
in bad shape, but after restoration they hope to open the place as
a museum."

Sarah nodded. "And you want me to do a feasibility study, de-
fine the board's goal, outline how much money it really needs to
raise to buy the property and then to restore it to at least some of
its former glory?"

"Right. And then I want you to work your real magic by finding potentially interested donors and putting me in touch with
them."

"Private donors in this case, since you're not approaching
them through formal procedures. Am I right?"

"Yes. The other members of the board know nothing about
this yet. And I don't want them to know unless—until—I've found
my money."

"So we're not looking at government funding or corporate
sponsorship or even foundations with grants to give."

"Is that going to be a big problem?" Megan asked.

"It shouldn't be a problem at all. Not to be indelicate, but
who's going to pay for my time and efforts if the board doesn't
even know about me?"

"Me," Megan said. "I'm your client."

"I don't come cheap."

Megan smiled. "I'm aware. But I've got the money."

"And what the hell, I'll give you a discount. It'll be fun to try to undermine Wynston Meadows, even in a roundabout way. That is what you're trying to do, yes? Kick him out once you've secured pledges from more reputable donors?"

Megan nodded.

"All right, Megan," Sarah said. "Let's sign the papers."

"Thank you, Sarah. Thank you for believing in my impossible dream."

CHAPTER 117

Alexis and Maureen were at the Pink Rose Café having an afternoon coffee and what Maureen liked to call her "unnecessary constitutional necessity."

"I saw Mary Bernadette this morning," Maureen said, wiping powdered sugar from her chin. "I just decided to show up. Frankly, I can't believe she let me in, but she did."

"Really? How did she seem?"

Maureen grinned. "In fine form. Charming the nurse who delivered her breakfast into giving her extra butter for her toast."

Alexis laughed. "I guess before long she'll be back on Honeysuckle Lane, directing and dominating the Fitzgibbon clan!"

"Looks like it."

Alexis quickly glanced around the café to be sure that no one was in eavesdropping distance. "I have big news," she said. "PJ has agreed to see a couples therapist."

"That *is* big news! Hopefully this therapist can help sort things out."

"Did you try to save your marriage when it started to break down? Did you ask Barry to see a counselor?"

Maureen smiled ruefully. "Oh, yes, I tried all sorts of things to make the marriage work, but Barry wasn't interested in our future together. At least I had the moral satisfaction of knowing that I was willing to forgive him and give the marriage another chance. Cold comfort, but better than nothing."

"His loss," Alexis said, reaching for the last piece of her chocolate croissant.

Maureen shrugged. "I'd argue if I could."

"Are you in touch with him? Do you know where he is and what he's doing?"

"We're not in direct contact, no," Maureen said. "There's no reason to be, not since we didn't have children. But he lives in Smithstown and on occasion I hear a snatch of gossip. He's been married twice since our divorce. Divorced twice, too. I don't know why he bothers getting married in the first place. He's clearly not cut out to be a husband. He can't even *spell* monogamy."

Alexis laughed. "I'm glad you're over him."

"Me too. Although it did take some time. It's amazing how attached we become to people even when all they cause us is misery. Barry treated me shabbily from the first—not that I saw that then!—but I found myself missing him when he'd gone."

"Habit?" Alexis wondered. "A relationship becomes a habit, good or bad."

"And people need habits, don't they? If everything that happened to you and everyone you encountered was always new and changing, life would be unbearable."

Alexis nodded. "I don't mean to equate my husband with something as mundane as breakfast, but if I don't have this particular kind of bread I like every morning, toasted with bitter marmalade, my entire day is somehow—wrong. I want my life with PJ to be that sort of habit. Without him it would just be—wrong."

Maureen laughed. "I'm not sure I'd tell *him* about the toast analogy, but I get your point." She ate the last bite of her donut and wiped the last speckles of powdered sugar from her hands.

"You know, I'm so happy that you're taking steps toward a change for the good. Do you remember when I told you to let PJ know you needed a path of your own, something that belonged only to you and not to the family?"

"Of course I do. It was the day you rescued me."

Maureen smiled. "Be that as it may, I have a confession to make. I'm afraid I haven't followed my own advice."

"What do you mean?"

"What I mean is that I haven't been brave. I haven't been decisive. Sometimes . . . sometimes I think that after what happened to me—the bad marriage and the messy divorce, I mean—sometimes I think that I just . . . stopped. That I just gave up really living for anything other than this vague and far-off notion of 'taking care of the parents.' I think I decided to be safe. Do you know, Alexis, that I don't even have a hobby?"

Alexis flinched. She recalled Morgan Shelby asking her about her life apart from the Fitzgibbons. She recalled having nothing to say. "Well, neither do I," she admitted. "I used to before I . . ."

"And you will again. You'll have a passion all your own. I believe that."

"But if I will—if I can—you can, too," Alexis urged. "You've always seemed so strong. So *sure*."

Maureen laughed. "I guess it's easy to seem strong and sure when your life presents absolutely no challenges and you've organized it that way. Look, I didn't mean to get all depressing. The point is that I'm proud of what you're trying to do for yourself, Alexis. Okay, I'm not your mother, I have no right to be proud, but I am."

"Thank you, Maureen," Alexis said sincerely. "I don't know what I would do without your friendship."

"Without *your* friendship I'd have to eat my donuts all alone!"

Alexis laughed and looked at her watch. "Oops. I should get back to the office. When Mary Bernadette is back on her feet, the last thing I want her to find is a bill unpaid or the candy jar only half full."

"And I should get back to good old Wharton Insurance. Not that anyone will have missed me. . . ."

"Maureen," Alexis scolded, as the two women left the café. "You underestimate your charm."

CHAPTER 118

Back in Annapolis, Megan's campaign to replace Wynston Meadows's promised financing was forging ahead. Sarah's office had completed the feasibility study and had drawn up a detailed schedule for when money for the purchase and restoration of the Branley Estate would be needed over time. The results were heartening.

Ten million dollars would do the entire job—from buying the property to designing the restoration and through to the end of construction. One million up-front would secure the estate and get the restoration team rolling. Finding $1 million was doable. And Megan knew from experience that the hardest part of the fund-raising process was securing money up front. Afterward, especially once work had begun and the project was a reality, donors tended to come on board more readily.

Megan reviewed the list of potentially interested donors Sarah had provided. Some of the names were familiar to her; some were entirely new. Sarah had warned Megan there was a good chance that most if not all of them would make the complete and total absence of Wynston Meadows's involvement a prerequisite for their investing. "In fact," she had said, "you might want to consider making that assurance up-front. The man has made a lot of enemies. But that's your call."

"Hey."

Megan turned around as Pat joined her in the office and sank into the chair by her desk. "You look tired," he said.

"I am tired. I didn't sleep well last night."

Pat frowned. "I'm worried about you, Meg. You're already stretched so thin, what with work and the charity and David's surgery looming."

"It isn't *looming*, Pat. It's coming."

"Meg."

Megan sighed. "Look, Pat, don't worry. I'm fine. Really, I'm on top of it all."

"It's not that I doubt your abilities."

"I know." She did know. Her husband had always been her greatest supporter.

"But I still don't understand why you're doing this," he went on, pointing to the printed list of names still in Megan's hand. "Why have you taken on this Herculean task just for my mother? You don't think you can finally win her friendship, do you?"

Megan laughed. "No! Anyway, I've told you before I'm not really doing this for your mother."

"Well, I certainly hope you're not doing it for me. I don't need you wearing yourself out for my sake."

"Consider the big picture, Pat. I'm doing this because it's the right thing to do."

Pat rolled his eyes. "Meg, there's no need to be noble! Don't sacrifice yourself for the sake of the Fitzgibbon clan! We're not worth it."

"Why shouldn't I do what I can for the family?" Megan argued. "I'm a Fitzgibbon, too, aren't I? And you know as well as I do that Mary Bernadette might be a lot of things, but she isn't a thief or a liar as Meadows has been implying. She's the most aboveboard person I know. And she's PJ's role model, or one of them, anyway. I don't want her tarnished in his eyes."

"PJ is a big boy, Meg. He should be able to handle the fall of heroes and the debunking of cherished myths."

"Still."

Pat leaned closer to his wife. "Meg," he said, "my mother has spent a lifetime hurting the people she claims to love. Whatever her deep, dark motives, and I told you all that Dad told me about what happened after William died, the result was bad. Can't you just forget about this crusade? Most crusaders don't come home alive, you know. And if they do, they're missing a limb or two."

"No," Megan said firmly. "I can't let it go. More to the point, I won't. I'm taking the bull by the horns, Pat."

Pat sighed. "Just promise me that you'll walk away if things become too heated. Wynston Meadows—your bull—can be a brutal opponent. I don't relish the idea of my wife becoming cannon fodder."

"Men and their war imagery. And what do cannons have to do with bulls?"

"I'm right in this case, Meg. Well, I guess I'll let you get back to the crusade."

"Onward Christian soldiers. Now, I've got some calls to make."

CHAPTER 119

Just after seven o'clock Wednesday morning, Mary Bernadette Fitzgibbon suffered a heart attack. The call from the hospital came in on Grace's cell phone; she had asked the hospital staff to notify her or Megan, not Paddy, in the case of an emergency. Now Grace and her father stood in the waiting room at the end of the hall while her mother's condition was being evaluated. Paddy looked utterly drawn and defeated. For the first time since her mother had fallen ill, Grace felt seriously concerned about her father.

The elevator doors slid open and Pat came bursting out into

the hall. "I got here as soon as I could," he said, panting. "How is she?"

"I'm not sure yet," Grace admitted.

Pat put his hand on his father's shoulder. "Dad, how are you holding up?" Paddy just shook his head.

The birth family is together, Grace thought. *Dad and Mom, Pat and me. A unit unto itself. And where does William fit into this unit?*

"What am I going to do if she doesn't make it?" Paddy said, his voice pathetic and thin. "She's my better half and always has been. How will I live without her?"

"Now, Dad," Grace said quietly. "It wasn't a major heart attack, that much we know. Let's not jump to conclusions. Let's just wait until we hear again from the doctor."

"Why don't you have a seat, Dad?" Pat led his father to a row of plastic chairs and helped him into one. Then he came back to where Grace stood, arms folded.

"Mom had better recover," he whispered fiercely. "I realized there's something I've got to do while I still can."

"And that is?"

Pat sighed. "I had a very illuminating conversation the other day with Dad. And then another conversation with Megan. Boy, that woman is smart. And then I got your call this morning. Suffice it to say, I'm finally ready to make some sort of peace with Mom after a lifetime of—of anger. Of bitterness. I want to ease my conscience. It's a selfish motive, I know."

"But that doesn't make it wrong. And maybe Mom will benefit from a reconciliation, too."

"Maybe."

"An offering of peace is never a waste, even when it might seem to be."

Pat frowned. "Putting positive energy into the universe?"

"Something like that." Over her brother's shoulder, Grace saw a man in a white coat coming down the hall toward the waiting room. "Here comes Dr. Wesson."

"Ms. Fitzgibbon," Dr. Wesson said as he joined them. "And—"

"Mary Bernadette's son, Pat." He held out his hand and the doctor shook it. The three walked over to where Paddy was sitting.

"How is she, Doctor," Paddy asked. "How is my wife?"

Dr. Wesson smiled. "She's stable and resting. It wasn't a major episode, as I mentioned earlier, and as she was right here in the hospital we were able to take action immediately. The worst that can be said is that this will delay her release a bit longer. We'll want to keep an eye on her for a few more days."

Pat wiped his hand across his eyes. "What a relief. I mean, that Mom's okay. When can we see her?"

"Now, if you'd like."

Grace offered her hand to her father and helped him to rise. "See, Dad," she said. "There was no point in worrying."

Paddy managed a feeble smile and the family followed Dr. Wesson to Mary Bernadette's room.

CHAPTER 120

Grace stood quietly by her mother's bedside after her father and brother had gone home. Mary Bernadette was asleep. She looked alarmingly disturbed, almost in pain, as if all the struggles and sorrows of her life were alive and torturing her at that very moment.

"I wish you could rest, Mom," Grace whispered. "Truly rest. I don't think you've let go for even one moment of your life. But then again, what do I really know about you? Next to nothing."

It was true, Grace thought. She knew so very little about her mother other than what was readily observable. More precisely, other than what Mary Bernadette allowed her family and friends to witness. She was a wife and a mother and a grandmother. She was a dedicated member of the congregation of the Church of the Immaculate Conception. She was a long-standing and highly respected member of the board of the Oliver's Well Historical Association. Important information, certainly. But Grace suspected that not even her father knew the secrets of Mary Bernadette's heart.

Grace checked her watch. Megan was due soon to relieve her. Amazing woman, Grace thought. Her efforts on behalf of Mary Bernadette's beloved historical society really were admirable. If *she* had been as abused by Mary Bernadette as Megan had been over the years, would she be willing to go to bat for the woman's reputation and peace of mind? Grace sighed. Not likely. She was a nun, not a saint.

A nun who was also a daughter and who, in spite of all, loved her mother. Not long ago Grace had come across an old Irish blessing. The words had stayed with her, and probably for this very occasion, she thought now.

"Oh, aged old woman of the gray locks," she whispered, "may eight hundred blessings twelve times over be on thee! Mayest thou be free from desolation."

Grace paused. There was another line to the blessing, but she was reluctant to give it voice. But then she went on. After all, someday . . . "Oh woman of the aged frame!" she recited. "And may many tears fall on thy grave."

Gently, Grace touched her mother's face. "Megan's on her way," she told her. "And I'm going to pay a visit to William."

There was no indication that her mother had heard anything.

CHAPTER 121

She was late for mass. She was angry with herself. Tardiness indicated laziness of character. She ran out of the house. With long leaps and bounds she sped through the streets of Oliver's Well, deserted in the dusk that had suddenly descended on the town.

The church loomed in front of her. She ran up the stairs and threw open the doors. "I'm here!" she cried. But no one replied to her greeting. The church was empty. She became aware only now that she was wearing a dress she had often worn when she was first married to Paddy. Though she could not see her own image, she knew that her hair was once again brown.

"Father Murphy," she cried. "Where is everyone?" She dashed up the central aisle to the altar and made the sign of the cross. A noise like the beating of a bat's wings made her whirl around. "Hello?" she called. "Paddy?"

She became aware of being frightened and frighteningly alone. Where was Father Murphy? Or was it Father Robert she was meant to meet? Where was her family? Maybe she was in the wrong church. Yes, something wasn't right. Why were the windows covered with black curtains? This was not *her* church at all!

With a small cry of terror, Mary Bernadette dashed back down the aisle and into the preternatural dusk. She found herself in an old cemetery. "This is where William is buried," she said to the crows cawing in the dark. "I must see him." She hurried toward a giant oak tree, under which she knew she would find his grave.

And now she was no longer alone. Jeannette was standing by William's grave, as if protecting it. She was not the aged Jeannette and not the young Jeannette but both, and a middle-aged woman at once, all three ages of woman in one. Mary Bernadette wondered at this.

"Where is everyone?" she cried, reaching out her hands toward her friend. "No one is inside. They were supposed to be here. They promised me!"

Jeannette did not take Mary Bernadette's hands. She replied with a voice filled with infinite sorrow. "Oh, Mary," she said. "You made everyone go away."

"What do you mean I made them go away?" Mary Bernadette demanded. "I love them, all of them, they're my family! I need them here with me!"

Jeannette pointed to the headstone. "Do you see what words are written here?"

Mary Bernadette looked more closely. It was difficult to see in the dim light, but after a moment she made out five words that sent a chill through her heart.

Here lies Mary Bernadette Fitzgibbon.

"But that's William's grave!" she protested. "What's the meaning of this?"

"It's your grave, too, Mary. You've always known that, haven't you?"

"No," Mary Bernadette said defiantly. "No, I know nothing. Oh, I'm so confused. Where *is* everyone!"

Jeannette began to fade into the gloom. "Look for them hard enough and you will find them. God willing."

Mary Bernadette took a step forward and again reached out for her friend. "Where? Where do I look? Help me, Jeannette!"

But Jeannette was gone now. William's grave stood unattended and abandoned. Mary Bernadette ran to it and knelt in the damp earth. It was then she saw that there were other words etched into the stone. Frantically, she wiped the stone with her hand to clear it of dirt and lichen.

"Let my tongue cleave to the roof of my mouth," she read aloud, "if I do not remember you."

She was aware that she was making a sort of whimpering sound. *Where am I? Someone help me!*

"Mrs. Fitzgibbon? Mrs. Fitzgibbon, wake up. You're having a bad dream."

Mary Bernadette opened her eyes to see a nurse leaning over her.

"Yes, yes. I'm awake," she said, her throat dry. "I'm fine. I was . . . A dream . . ."

The nurse smiled sympathetically. "Yes, dreams can be wearying, can't they? Sometimes they just get you in their grip and try as you might you can't escape them."

"Yes."

"Would you like your dinner now?" the nurse asked. "I've kept it aside."

"All right."

When the nurse had left the room Mary Bernadette gathered every bit of her formidable mental energies. It was essential that she not forget the dream; clearly, it was a message from God. And what was He saying to her? What did He want her to know?

Yes. He was telling her that she had been less than what she might have been for her family. She had failed to keep them close, her husband and her son and her daughter. She had in some way abandoned them. *All those Sunday sermons on the importance of love,* she thought. *And did I ever really take heed?*

"Oh," she whispered to the empty room, "what have I done?" Had she indeed permanently alienated her son and his wife, her daughter, even her beloved husband, Paddy? Had she let down her oldest grandchild, of whom she was so fond? Why hadn't she been more lenient with her grandson's wife, less forceful and demanding? At least, she thought, wiping a tear from her cheek, her beloved William was safe; at least he was beyond any harm her failings might cause him.

Despair settled heavily on Mary Bernadette's heart. But despair was a sin. She knew that. Life was the most precious gift God had granted and to throw it away—even to wish it over and gone—was wrong. No matter how difficult the path ahead might be, Mary Bernadette Fitzgibbon was determined to make what amends she could. "Dear God," she whispered. "I ask for your forgiveness and for your strength."

CHAPTER 122

Megan took a sip of tea and sighed. Really, it was amazing how good a cup of tea could make her feel. *I'm an addict,* she thought. *I am addicted to tea.* Which was a lot better than being addicted to power and control. She thought back to the last meeting of the board of the OWHA. They had been discussing a problem with the Kennington House. Just the year before, a reputable company had been hired to repaint the exterior. As far as anyone knew, proper procedures had been followed. But for some reason the paint was not adhering to the clapboard.

"It might be a moisture issue," Richard had pointed out. "I've seen it before."

"So," Neal had asked, "how do we ascertain if that is the problem?"

"Call in an expert. If moisture *is* at fault, then we might need a vapor barrier. And that involves removing the plaster or Sheetrock, installing plastic sheeting, and then adding a new wall finish. It's a big job, and it doesn't always solve the problem."

Leonard had frowned. "And by big job you mean expensive job."

"Well, we certainly can't ignore it."

Megan had been reading up on the problem of peeling paint and had another idea of what might be the culprit. She had gotten as far as saying, "It might also be—" when Meadows had cut her off.

"With all due respect," he had said, tapping away on his iPhone, "given the fact that you are a temporary member of this board, I think that you should be seen and not heard." At this point he had finally looked at her. "Unless, of course, you have something truly profound to add to this discussion."

Megan had simply smiled; she would share her information with Leonard at another time. She had almost been amused by

Meadows's rude behavior. Having heard from so many people during the course of her campaign that he was so disliked took a good deal of the sting out of his words. She was nothing special to him, just another person to torture and bully.

"What he doesn't know is that I'm a pit bull in sheep's clothing," she had told her husband that morning over coffee, after having related the Great Man's latest little abuse of power.

"I think I'm becoming a bit afraid of you," he had replied. "It's kind of appealing."

"Don't be weird, Pat."

"Sorry."

Well, Megan thought now, glancing up at the words of her beloved Saint Francis, let Meadows have his pathetic amusements. What mattered was that she had made good progress with her campaign to save the integrity of the OWHA. It had been easier than she had imagined, convincing people to rally to her cause, and she couldn't help but wonder how many of them had agreed to help fund the OWHA to the initial tune of one million dollars only to see Wynston Meadows derailed. "I wouldn't touch that man with a ten-foot pole," one of them had said. "What were these people thinking when they invited him on the board?" To which Megan had carefully replied, "Unfortunately, they weren't well informed." That $1 million up-front wasn't $5 million up-front should not be an issue. Sarah Simon's expertise had determined the OWHA didn't *need* $5 million to get the ball rolling. And Megan would make the others heed that fact.

Now she was ready to approach her fellow board members—excluding Joyce, Wallace, and, for the moment, Norma—with the good news.

Megan picked up her cell phone and punched in the first number. "Leonard," she said. "I've got it. I've got us the money."

CHAPTER 123

Megan and Grace and Jeannette and Maureen were at the Fitzgibbon house. They had come to water the plants, do the laundry (Mary Bernadette was concerned that Paddy had a clean shirt to wear every day), dust and polish the furniture ("Mom's going to give every surface the white glove test as soon as she gets home," Grace had warned), and vacuum the carpets ("That mutt of Paddy's sheds like a demon."). Paddy had taken the offending Mercy for a walk, and Banshee had removed herself from the scene of activity.

"Probably hiding in Mary Bernadette's closet," Megan said. "The poor thing's been spending a lot of time in there since her mommy's been in the hospital."

The women had been working for more than an hour when Megan suggested they gather in the kitchen for a break. She and Grace and Maureen could work on without rest, but Jeannette suffered from a bad back. Some respect had to be paid to the condition she never mentioned.

"There will have to be some big changes around here," Grace said when they were seated around the table with cups of tea and a plate of cookies. "For one, Dad and Mom are getting cell phones whether they like it or not."

Jeannette frowned. "You know Mary. She doesn't trust technology."

"Tough. She's going to have to change her mind. I'll get them something elder friendly."

"And one of those Life Alert systems," Megan said. "It wouldn't hurt to have one of those for when either Mary Bernadette or Paddy is alone in the house."

Grace laughed. "Assuming we can make them use it. Or remember to use it."

"And at least one more landline extension," Maureen said. "It's ridiculous in a house this size to have only two."

"She's going to fight us all the way, you know," Megan said.

Grace shrugged. "I don't care. It's for her own good, and Dad's. If we can't convince her to take care of herself, we'll appeal to her belief in duty to others."

"And she shouldn't be driving for a while, I would think. I can certainly help in that regard, take her shopping or to church."

"Thanks, Maureen. That will take some of the burden off Paddy."

"And I'll keep an eye on her, of course," Jeannette said. "For what good it will do."

"She values your friendship, Mom," Maureen said earnestly. "She needs your companionship."

"As I need and value hers."

Maureen sighed and fiddled with her teaspoon. "I never thought I'd be polishing Mary Bernadette's furniture and talking about—about all that's going to change. It feels like the end of an era. God, how dramatic of me. Sorry."

"The end of an era maybe," Megan said, "but not the end of the entire story."

Grace reached for a cookie. "Jeannette," she said, "tell us about my mother in the early days. Tell us about William."

"It's a difficult thing for me to talk about," Jeannette said, smoothing her dress unnecessarily. "I promised Mary Bernadette I would never mention William to anyone."

"I'm sorry," Grace said, putting her hand on the older woman's arm. "I shouldn't have asked."

Jeannette sighed. "No. Things have changed and you have every right to know about your brother. He was a lovely little boy. Your mother doted on him as if he were a prince, and indeed he charmed everyone. I sometimes think about what he would have become had he lived. . . . Something great. Something good."

Megan wondered how much of Jeannette's memory of the child had been colored by Mary Bernadette's idealized vision of her son. But did it matter?

"After he died, the poor soul, I despaired of Mary's ever regaining her spirits," Jeannette went on. "She was in a terrible way. I'd never seen a human being so shattered. But I should have known that someone with her strength of character would revive."

"But not actually recover?" Grace wondered.

"Was she . . . was she at all happy when she learned she was pregnant with Pat?" Megan asked.

Jeannette's eyes filled with tears. "She couldn't be. It was too soon. It seemed somehow—cruel."

Megan nodded. "I see."

"And when she was pregnant with me?" Grace asked.

"Eight more years had passed. She was better able to take some pleasure in the thought of another child. And, well, your being a girl somehow made it easier for her."

"She couldn't compare me to her version of William the way she could compare Pat. Sorry. Probably shouldn't have said that."

"Well, that's all in the past," Maureen said hurriedly. "What's done is done."

No, Megan thought. *The past is never truly past. What once happened is always happening.* But it was no good in arguing that point now.

"More tea, Jeannette?" she asked.

"No, thank you," Jeannette replied, rising from the table with some difficulty. "I think it's time I got back to my cleaning."

Chapter 124

Pat stood in the hallway outside of his mother's hospital room, hands in the pockets of his pants, a frown on his face. He was working up his courage to finally make peace with Mary Bernadette Fitzgibbon.

The conversation he had shared with his father over soup and sandwiches had changed him. Well, as he had told Grace, the conversation, the unsettling knowledge of his father's loneliness, the fact of his mother's heart attack, and the good example of his wife. He had told his father that all you could ask of anyone was that she do her best. Well, maybe his mother *had* done her best by her son, and God knew she wasn't the sort to do anything by halves. Mary Bernadette made the effort, you could say that much about her.

Still, Pat hesitated to enter his mother's room. He just wasn't sure that he had the stomach to talk to her honestly about their relationship. He also wasn't sure that it would be the right thing to do at this late date. The woman was old. She was sick. He had no desire to hasten the death of his children's grandmother. Well, he could only hope that he would know what to do when the moment for speaking arrived. Pat took a fortifying breath and knocked on his mother's door before going inside.

"Mom. How are you this morning?" he asked. He noted that she had applied her usual lipstick and powder and took that as a good sign.

"As well as can be expected," she replied. "I can't complain."

"Good. I mean, it's good you're not in pain or anything. Are you?"

"No."

Pat lowered himself into the chair by her bedside. "I need to tell you something, Mom," he said, before he could lose his nerve. "It's not easy for me to say. I know we . . . I know we don't get along, but I do love you. I just wanted you to know that."

Mary Bernadette nodded. "Thank you, Pat."

Now, he took his courage in both hands. "But I felt abandoned by you, Mom. Unwanted. As a kid, I mean. I always felt . . . I always felt that I was a disappointment to you. I always felt that I could never live up to the image of my older brother. Of William."

His mother said nothing in reply but looked down at her hands, folded in her lap.

"I'm sorry, Mom," Pat went on, "but I had to say something. There have been too many years of silence. I won't bring it up again. I promise."

Pat felt close to tears. He hoped he hadn't made things worse between them. His mother looked up at him now. He thought he saw a glimmer of a tear in her eye, too, but he couldn't be sure.

"I'm sorry you felt that way," she said quietly. "Abandoned. Unwanted. A disappointment. It must have been very hard for you."

All he could do was nod.

"I did care, Pat," Mary Bernadette went on. "I do care, more than you know. You're my son. My only son."

She reached for his hand. Pat hesitated for a moment before giving it to her. He couldn't recall the last time his mother had touched him. Her hand felt bony. The skin felt dry. His mother was old and time was passing. He was her only son.

To expect more from his mother simply wasn't fair. If she wasn't the mother he might have chosen, so be it. He had had it better than a lot of people. There were worse wounds than the ones that had been inflicted by Mary Bernadette Fitzgibbon.

An aide came into the room then, bearing a tray of food. "Lunchtime," he announced brightly as he placed the tray on the moveable table at Mary Bernadette's bedside. When the aide had gone, Pat let go of his mother's hand and removed the plastic lid from the tray. He grimaced.

"How about I get you some real food, Mom," he said.

Mary Bernadette sighed as if, Pat thought, a very large and cumbersome burden had been lifted from her shoulders. "That would be an act of great kindness. A ham and cheese sandwich and a real cup of tea would be heaven."

"You got it."

Pat replaced the lid on the tray and turned to leave.

"And make sure they use real mayonnaise on the sandwich," his mother called out in her famously imperious voice. "Not that dreadful substitute some people find acceptable. And no artificial sweetener for the tea."

Pat looked back. For half a moment he wondered if his mother should be eating something as fatty as mayonnaise after having suffered a heart attack. And then he laughed. What Mary Bernadette wanted, Mary Bernadette would have. "Real mayonnaise it is," he said.

CHAPTER 125

PJ and Alexis sat in their car in the parking lot outside the office of Roz Clinton, Certified Marriage Counselor. Her stomach was in knots. PJ was drumming his fingers on the steering wheel. They both sighed at the same time.

"Ready?" PJ asked, turning to her.

Alexis thought she had never seen him look more serious and determined. It gave her hope. She nodded. So much was at stake. Alexis said a silent prayer for her marriage and for the child she and her husband were bringing into the world.

They got out of the car, and hand in hand they went inside the small building in Waterville that also housed the offices of an acupuncturist and a homeopathic healer. Roz Clinton's office was on the second floor. She opened the door on the first knock.

"Welcome," she said. "PJ and Alexis? Call me Roz."

According to the biography on her website, Roz Clinton was seventy-three. One of the reasons Alexis had chosen her was because of PJ's close relationship with his grandmother. She thought he might feel more comfortable opening up to an older person. If he would open up at all, and that was still to be seen.

Roz Clinton led them inside and asked them each to take a seat on the couch. She sat in a big, squishy-pillowed chair facing them. Alexis noted that her clothing—a flowing top in a paisley pattern and a many-tiered skirt that came to her ankles—was unlike anything Mary Bernadette would ever wear. In her ears she wore large hoops. Her necklace was a string of irregularly shaped turquoise beads. There was a ring on every finger of both hands. *A benevolent Being on her throne*, Alexis thought.

"Is this your first time meeting with a counselor?" Roz asked. Her voice was warm and pleasant. Her smile was reassuring.

PJ cleared his throat and nodded. Alexis burst out crying, and PJ put his arm around her.

Roz handed her a box of tissues.

"Have a good cry, my dear," she said kindly. "I find that it always helps me."

CHAPTER 126

Megan was sitting at the table in the Wilson House along with her fellow board members, waiting for the Great Man to arrive. She did not join in any of the desultory conversations going on around her. Her thoughts were enough to keep her occupied.

The truth was that Megan was disappointed that the fact of potential new donors to the OWHA hadn't met with more enthusiasm. Leonard, at least, was excited. Richard, however, was hesitant to commit his support. For some reason the idea of several private people funding the future growth of the OWHA disconcerted him. "Not that I think what you're proposing is all that unusual," he had told Megan. "Just that it sounds—risky." To which Megan had replied, "Any riskier than being beholden to one domineering man with a vision completely at odds with ours?" Still, Richard hesitated.

Neal was less wary than Richard but not 100 percent sure it was the way to go. He seemed almost physically repulsed by Wynston Meadows, but that extreme antipathy wasn't enough to override his need for further assurance that Megan's proposal had a good chance of succeeding. He wanted, he said, to know more about the donors and what other projects they had funded.

Megan speculated that Jeannette's suspicious reaction to her proposed scheme was a result of her lack of experience in the wider world. Apart from her work for the church and the OWHA, Jeannette's life had been solely dedicated to the care of her family. "What if they all turn out to be like Mr. Meadows?" she had asked Megan. "Then we'll really be in trouble." The fact that every potential donor had made it a requirement of their support that Meadows be gone from the OWHA didn't seem to count with her.

As for Anne, well, Megan didn't really understand Anne's reluctance to accept her proposal as viable. Perhaps she was simply under too much strain with running the store, caring for her husband, and putting up with the disruptions to the usually smooth workings of the OWHA to invest energy in what she saw as a long shot.

But what did it matter if in the end Joyce, Wallace, and perhaps Norma refused to abandon their adherence to Wynston

Meadows, in spite of the promise of money unencumbered by ridiculous demands and bad behavior?

Richard shook his head. "I've sent Meadows three texts in the last twenty minutes and no reply to any of them."

"The man is busy."

"We're all busy, Wallace," Leonard countered. "But not too busy to send a text or an e-mail explaining our absence at a meeting."

"This is ridiculous," Neal said. "I'm calling this meeting to order."

After Leonard had presented his report, a difficult bit of old business was addressed. Wynston Meadows's latest suggestion was that the tiny gift shop housed in one of the eighteenth-century additions to the Wilson House carry baseball caps with the name of the town across the front. The idea had met with protest from all but Joyce and Wallace. Even Norma had found the gumption to point out that the kinds of items the gift shop carried were of an entirely more sophisticated nature—biographies of past American worthies, small notebooks made with good hand-crafted paper, exact replicas of period jewelry, reproductions of recipe books kept by colonial housewives.

"And how does any of that precious stuff get the name of our town out there?" Meadows had argued. "How does any of that market Oliver's Well? I think we should do T-shirts as well as baseball caps. Commission a cartoon of a guy in seventeenth-century clothes tumbling into a well, something to really catch people's attention."

Megan had said a silent prayer of thanks that Mary Bernadette wasn't in the room to hear this blasphemy.

"Can anyone at this table really be in favor of selling this sort of tourist nonsense in our shop?" Leonard demanded now.

Joyce, without the Great Man's presence to prevent her from speaking her mind, admitted that the idea of T-shirts depicting an early settler falling into a well was a bit over the top.

"It's ludicrous," Neal said forcefully.

"But almost everyone wears baseball caps and T-shirts," Wallace argued. "They would make us a lot of money."

"At what cost?" Leonard demanded. "The cost of our dignity? We'd be the laughingstock among our colleagues nationwide."

Wallace then suggested that the issue be tabled once again until all members were present for a vote. "After all," he said, "it was Mr. Meadows's idea. It wouldn't be right to take a vote without him." The others agreed. Megan could barely hide her annoyance. Not even the threat of gimmicky merchandise could instill the courage to resist the whims of the Great Man.

After the meeting, Megan found herself walking out to the parking lot with Neal.

"Why do you think Meadows didn't let us know he wouldn't be at the meeting today?" he asked her.

"He enjoys playing with people, Neal. It's a power thing."

"Yes. And he probably feels he's beyond accountability at this point in his life."

"Mary Bernadette would say that he'll be held accountable on the Day of Judgment."

"Do you think she really believes that?"

"Yes, Neal," Megan said. "I think that she does. And I sincerely hope that she's right."

CHAPTER 127

Mary Bernadette was sitting in the chair by the bed. She had already taken two turns around the hall, and though she felt a bit tired, she felt stronger than she had in days. It was only her thoughts that were troubling her. The things that Pat had said to her. . . . She had badly wanted to press the call button to bring a nurse along, anything to stop having to listen to the words coming out of her son's mouth. But she had resisted the temptation to turn away from him. Pat was only repeating one of the truths her dream had revealed to her. She had failed her family.

Dear, sweet William! Mary Bernadette had long assumed that Pat and Grace had found out about her firstborn at some point. People could be dreadful gossips, and there *was* the fact of the headstone in Oliver's Well Memorial Cemetery. But until the conversation with Pat she had never considered the possibility that her husband might have shared the story with his children. But indeed, he might have done so.

Poor Pat, she thought now. He had flinched when he had taken her hand. She was sorry for that. She had held her grief for her lost son closer to her heart than she had held the son who had survived. It was true, wasn't it, that in some ways she, too, had died when William died.

"Knock knock."

It was Grace. Mary Bernadette cleared her throat. "Good afternoon," she said.

"Hi, Mom. How about another walk around the floor?"

"Yes. I have to regain my strength. There's so much I have to do. . . ." She took her daughter's arm and they began their parade up and down the hallway.

"Is Banshee well fed?" she asked, for what she knew was the hundredth time since she had been brought to the hospital. "You know she likes her food in her special bowls, one for the wet and one for the dry. And her water changed twice a day."

"Yes," Grace said. "She's being treated like the Queen of Sheba. Though she does miss you, Mom. That's clear."

"And that Mercy hasn't torn apart the couch, has she?"

Grace laughed. "Since when does she chew on the furniture?"

"There's a first for everything."

"I assure you the couch is intact. Though sometimes I wish that it wasn't. Really, Mom, it's like sitting on a concrete bench, and the armchairs aren't much better."

Mary Bernadette widened her eyes. "I never noticed such a thing."

"You wouldn't! Anyway, I've just talked to the doctor and he says you should be out of here in a day or two."

Mary Bernadette crossed herself. "Thanks be to God!"

"And thanks be to your doctors and nurses, too."

"And," Mary Bernadette added, "thanks be to my family."

CHAPTER 128

PJ and Alexis had just returned home from their second therapy session with Roz Clinton. Alexis had immediately made two cups of tea, and now she and her husband sat shoulder to shoulder on the couch.

"I'm exhausted," PJ said.

"Me too."

"She's very smart."

"She is."

"And she's very kind. She's not judgmental."

"Yes." *Well*, Alexis thought, *if she is judging us, she's very good at hiding it.*

"Do you think Roz always dressed like that? So Bohemian?"

Alexis shrugged. "I have no idea. It suits her, though, doesn't it?"

"Yeah. Alexis?" PJ shifted so that he could look directly at her. "How does anyone ever make a marriage work over a lifetime? How have my grandparents pulled it off? How have my parents or your parents done it? More and more it seems to me that it takes a sort of miracle—maybe a whole bunch of them—to get it right for the long haul."

"Maybe you're right," Alexis said thoughtfully. "Maybe you do all that you can possibly do and then you pray to God or whatever spiritual power you believe in to send along a miracle of—of kindness and patience and understanding and sympathy."

"Are you sure you don't regret becoming a Catholic for me?" PJ asked. It was one of the topics that had come up in this second session with Roz Clinton. "It was an awfully generous thing of you to do."

"No," Alexis replied promptly. "I don't regret it. But honestly, I'm not sure how long it's going to take to really feel like I *belong.* It's so different from your experience, always *being* a Catholic. Like always having black hair and blue eyes, no big deal, just what's always been *there.* But I have to make a conscious choice to believe. It's hard."

"I'm honored you made the choice for my sake. You gave me a great gift, Alexis. I just hope I can make it worth your while. I hope I can give you what *you* want in return for what you give me."

Alexis smiled. "It's takes two to tango. Sorry, silly cliché. But it's true, PJ. For our marriage to be a success, I have to create a meaningful life of my own. I guess I'm learning that a husband is not meant to be a knight in shining armor."

"But I really want to be," PJ said earnestly.

Alexis took his hand. "But don't you see, that's not fair. No one should have to be the solution to another person's life. I have to make me happy. It's *my* responsibility."

"As long as your being happy includes me as your husband, shining armor or not."

"It does, PJ! Even in sweatpants you're the man I want."

PJ laughed. "Really? I've been dying for you to say that."

"No!" Alexis shrieked. "Please, no sweatpants."

"Darn. One other thing. I was thinking that maybe we should tell my parents that we're going to therapy. I want them to know that we take this marriage seriously and we're not going to let the strain of these past months destroy something beautiful. Are you okay with that?"

Alexis smiled. "Yes, that's a very good idea!"

"But I still think we should keep Grandmother in the dark."

"Also a very good idea!" The last thing any of the Fitzgibbons needed, Alexis thought, was for Mary Bernadette to have another heart attack.

"Chinese takeout for dinner," PJ said suddenly. "What do you think? We haven't done takeout in . . . I can't remember how long it's been."

Alexis kissed her husband's cheek. "I think it sounds like fun," she said. "And I want spicy sesame noodles."

CHAPTER 129

Megan was en route to the grocery store. She felt exhausted. She felt anxious. There was CPEE business she had been neglecting. Danica had reminded her that she had promised to make three dozen brownies for her class bake sale the next day. The night before Pat had wanted to talk at length about the conversation with his mother in which for the first time ever William had been mentioned. Megan was afraid she hadn't paid as much attention as she should have and she felt bad about it. A few days earlier David had admitted that he was in fact scared about having surgery, and Megan's own fears and sense of helplessness had roared into life, momentarily rendering her at a loss on how to answer his concerns. She felt bad about that, too.

And on top of it all, she was afraid she had come to a dead end in her plan to rid the OWHA of Wynston Meadows. Leonard, and now Richard and Neal, were willing to lose Meadows's promised twenty-five million dollars in favor of the one million dollars Megan had already secured and her assurance of more money to come, but Jeannette and Anne were still hesitant to accept the fact that the new potential sources of money were indeed real and not phantoms born of desperation. And to get a unanimous vote against Meadows, she would have to convince Joyce, Wallace, and Norma as well, and there's where she saw real trouble. Jeannette and Anne would probably come around, but the two or possibly three who were in thrall to the Great Man would never vote against him for anything less than—than what? A truly nefarious deed.

Okay, she thought, *so what's the worst that could happen?* She might fail to get Wynston Meadows ousted from the board. The financial pledges she had secured would then fall through; the private donors she had lined up had made it very clear they wanted nothing to do with the man. The OWHA might buckle under Meadows's bullying tactics. He might then buy historical properties from the now-bankrupt OWHA, tear them down, and put up hideous concrete office parks. He might effectively break Mary Bernadette Fitzgibbon's spirit, if he hadn't done that already.

No, Megan thought, tightening her grip on the wheel, *I cannot fail. I simply cannot.*

CHAPTER 130

Mary Bernadette Fitzgibbon was back home on Honeysuckle Lane. As she crossed the threshold, she said a silent and fervent prayer of thanks. She was installed in one of the armchairs in the living room and asked if she would like a proper cup of tea. She said that she would, and Megan went to the kitchen to prepare it. Banshee screamed her welcome and jumped onto Mary Bernadette's lap. Mercy stood by the chair, tongue lolling and tail wagging. Mary Bernadette was glad to see them all.

David and Danica had made a huge WELCOME HOME sign and

hung it over the door to the kitchen. Jeannette, Danny, and Maureen came by to deliver the cards and flowers gathered from her hospital room. (The balloons had been disposed of long before.) Katie and Bonnie stopped by bearing a plate of Mary Bernadette's favorite raspberry scones, warm from the oven.

As soon as the excitement of her arrival had settled down, and the twins had gone outside to play, Mary Bernadette expressed her intention of surveying the house to be sure that nothing had been broken or put back in a wrong place and that everything was as spic-and-span as she had left it. She was eager to reestablish herself over her domain. But her family wouldn't allow her to climb the stairs to the second floor, so she had to be content to inspect the rooms on the first floor. She found that everything was in order. She felt a bit disappointed that things had carried on so well without her. But she thanked her daughter and daughter-in-law for their efforts.

"I'm so happy to have you home in time for my birthday," Paddy said when Mary Bernadette had taken her seat again. "Grace said that she'll make the cake, to spare you the effort."

"I'm perfectly capable of making my husband a birthday cake," Mary Bernadette replied briskly. And then she said, "But if Grace wants to do it, then of course she may."

"And you don't have to worry about the everyday running of the household," Grace said. "We all know how hopeless Dad is with the domestic arts—sorry, Dad—so Katie and Bonnie and Megan and I have made a housekeeping and cooking schedule. We'll rotate duties among us."

Mary Bernadette opened her mouth to protest.

"Now, Mom," Grace went on in that annoyingly mock severe tone she seemed to have adopted in the past weeks. "We're not intending to usurp your kingdom, just to help out while you regain your full strength. I'm sure you see the wisdom in that."

In fact, Mary Bernadette did see the wisdom in her daughter's argument. "And now," she said, "I must admit to feeling a bit tired."

Megan and Pat wished her a pleasant rest and went off to fetch the twins. Grace and Paddy escorted her into the small first-floor bedroom that David sometimes used; it would be hers until she grew stronger. Banshee immediately settled herself on the bed and began to purr.

Paddy kissed her cheek and Grace closed the door behind them. Mary Bernadette was alone. *How*, she thought, *did I suddenly become so old that I can permit myself a nap?* She *was* tired, but sleep didn't come right away. Instead, she stared up at the ceiling, Banshee tucked under her arm, thinking of the difficult changes she would have to accept. She knew that she should wholeheartedly accept the assistance so generously offered her. But it was hard not to chafe under what she felt to be restraints on her will and her independence.

She remembered then an old bit of wisdom her father claimed to have heard from his own father. "Have sense, patience, and self-restraint, and no mischief will come." All these years later and Mary Bernadette could still clearly remember sitting at her father's feet before the peat fire in their home. She had loved him dearly. But how well had she adhered to his words of wisdom?

Banshee roused herself and stepped onto Mary Bernadette's stomach, where she curled into a ball. Before long the two ladies had fallen asleep. Mary Bernadette did not dream.

CHAPTER 131

"I'm on pins and needles, Neal. What made you call this meeting?"

Megan was at her desk in Annapolis, addressing her fellow board member via her computer screen. Around Neal, in the main room of his gallery, were arranged Richard, Anne, Leonard, and Jeannette.

"I think," he said, "that I might just have the information we need to finally put an end to the disaster that is Wynston Meadows."

"Well, come out with it then," Leonard urged.

"You all know my friend Harry Duran? He's an agent with Hollytree Real Estate."

There were murmurs and nods in the affirmative. "He's got a good reputation," Megan noted. "And he donates to the OWHA."

"Well," Neal went on, "as in any given industry, word gets around, even things that are supposed to be top secret, deals and promises and the like. And just this morning Harry had it on good authority from a friend of his at Toth Realty that since he's been resident in Oliver's Well, Wynston Meadows has been in secret negotiation—through his lawyers, of course—with the Baker family."

"The owners of the Branley Estate," Richard said.

Megan could not restrain a grin. *Patience,* she told herself. *We haven't won yet.*

"One and the same. It seems that he's intending to buy the estate for himself. And, though it's unclear if the Bakers know this bit of the story, he's planning to tear down what survives of the old buildings, clear all that lovely land, and put up a housing development."

Jeannette put a hand to her heart.

"I can't say that I'm surprised," Megan said. *Surprised and cautiously elated,* she added silently.

"Are you sure of this, Neal?" Leonard asked.

"As sure as I can be. Harry wouldn't have passed along the information if he didn't take it seriously. Now the question is, what do we do with it?"

"I can't believe Mr. Meadows has been going against the OWHA all along. Pretending to be our benefactor." Anne sighed.

"While still holding on to his money," Jeannette said angrily. "And treating the rest of us like doormats."

"I say we confront him at the next meeting."

"You know as well as I do, Leonard, that he'll deny any wrong-doing," Richard said. "He'll say it's only a nasty small-town rumor."

"But that might be enough," Megan argued. "What I mean is, even the rumor of a board member acting for personal gain could very well turn away other potential donors, or even our long-standing ones. We tell him we can't afford the possible fallout."

Richard shook his head. "I hate to be the naysayer here, but to that Meadows will say he's got more money than all other donors put together, so who cares if the rest go scurrying off."

"And Joyce and Wallace and Norma might still think it's worth the risk to keep him around," Jeannette said gloomily. "I don't understand what they hope to gain from the man."

"Who was it who came up with that silly rule about needing a unanimous vote to dismiss someone from the board?" Anne asked.

"Some oddball in the board's storied past," Leonard said. "The point is, the time's come to act. I suggest that at our next meeting we reveal that we've got new financial backers lined up, and then we present the information that Meadows has been acting against the interests of Oliver's Well, and not only regarding the Branley Estate. What about his wanting to cancel the Independence Day Parade and cut the education program? We just might get that unanimous vote."

"We have to try," Neal said. "That's for sure."

Megan nodded. "Just be sure we make no mention—not even a hint—of what new business we'll be addressing. Maybe the element of surprise will work to our advantage, not so much with Meadows but with Joyce, Wallace, and Norma. The last thing we need is for one of them to get wind of our intentions."

"Mum's the word," Neal agreed. "Shall I call this clandestine meeting adjourned?"

"See you all on the battlefield," Megan said. "Good night." And she went downstairs to pour herself a cautiously celebratory whiskey.

CHAPTER 132

It was six o'clock in the evening. Grace was out at the grocery store. Paddy was in the kitchen, heating one of the casseroles Bonnie had provided. Mary Bernadette was propped against a pile of pillows in the bed in the little first-floor bedroom, several unopened novels by her side. She had been home for two days and still the house seemed almost frighteningly quiet after all that time in the hospital where one never had a moment's peace. Machines beeping and whirring and voices, always the voices, of nurses and doctors and visitors and the patients themselves, complaining or crying out, whispering or weeping. Mary Bernadette had longed for the blessed peace of her home on Honeysuckle Lane.

But now, the quiet seemed oppressive. There was too much time to think, and she didn't want to think. For one, she had realized that in the past few days she had lost almost all interest in knowing the latest news about the OWHA. Not once had she asked for a copy of the *Oliver's Well Gazette*; not once had she even thought to call Leonard or to question Jeannette when she stopped by. She suspected that her sudden disinterest was a result of her spiritual despair, and she had prayed for God to lift her from the depths. But in the pit she remained.

She thought about other things, too. She had come to see that it wasn't only her family who had suffered because of choices she had been making for the past fifty some-odd years. By erecting such a strong guardrail around her heart she had deprived *herself* of so much happiness as well. Over the past weeks she had watched how her son and his wife behaved when they were together, how simply and truly affectionate they were, how warm and comfortable they seemed. It was a sad thing to admit, but she and Paddy hadn't experienced that sort of easy intimacy since before William's death. So many years! She was so very sorry now for having deprived her husband of her whole self. She was ashamed of it, but she felt envious of the relationship her son and daughter-in-law shared. She realized now that she longed for a sort of love with her husband it might be too late to cultivate. Paddy had stuck by her through all of life's vicissitudes. He had never once complained. He was a quiet hero of a man. And oh, how she loved him!

Paddy came into the room with her dinner on a tray. He stopped short when he saw the tears streaming down his wife's face. He put the tray carefully on the bedside table and took her hand in his.

"Now, Mary, what's wrong?" he asked gently.

"Will you forgive me, Paddy?" Mary Bernadette pleaded. "Will you forgive me?"

Her husband leaned down and gently kissed her forehead. "There's nothing to forgive, Mary," he said. "Absolutely nothing."

There was nothing more for either of them to say.

CHAPTER 133

"I've been given a reassignment to Virginia," Grace was telling the other Fitzgibbon women, gathered in Mary Bernadette's kitchen. "The order has granted me a year, and we'll see after that."

"Paddy will be so relieved," Megan said.

"I'm glad, too. Where will you be working?" Alexis asked.

"At the hospital, in the pastoral care department. I'll be visiting with patients in their homes once they're released. I'll try to help them deal with the emotional fallout of their illnesses. I'll pray with them if they want me to."

Alexis shook her head. "I could never do what you do."

"My daughter has a gift," Mary Bernadette said. "A true calling."

Grace turned to her mother. "And Mom, now that you're confined to the house for a bit, I'm going to introduce you to the wonders of the Internet."

"I have no interest in the computer."

"Too bad. You're a captive audience. I'll get you set up on Skype so you can be in touch with your grandchildren. And we bought you and Dad each a cell phone."

"Oh Lord."

"Don't take the name of the Lord thy God in vain, Mom."

"Yes, dear. But those things are supposed to give you cancer."

"And frogs give you warts. You'll learn to take the phone with you when you go out. And to be sure that it's turned on."

"Since when have you become so bossy?" her mother asked.

Grace grinned. "I've always been bossy," she said. "Just not with you."

Mary Bernadette laughed. The sound was so unexpected that Grace, Megan, and Alexis exchanged looks of surprise.

"Well," Mary Bernadette said then, "I'm afraid that I need a nap." She got up from her chair and walked slowly out of the kitchen, Banshee dashing ahead.

Grace spoke softly, though they had heard the bedroom door close. "Did you notice that since Mom's been home from the hospital she hasn't once asked about the OWHA? At least, not in my hearing."

"Nor in mine," Megan said. "It's as if she's lost all interest."

"Or she's pretending," Alexis suggested. "Maybe she's secretly talking to one of her friends on the board."

Megan shook her head. "Her friends would never break their promise of silence. And Mary Bernadette wouldn't give any credence to the likes of Wallace or Joyce or Norma. No, I think for some reason we can't fathom she's lost interest."

"I hope it's only temporary," Grace said. "The OWHA is her

life. It would be a shame if it were lost to her. And after all your hard work, Meg."

"Well, I had help finding other sources of money to replace Meadows's cash. And now with what Neal's uncovered . . ."

"What's that?" Grace asked.

Megan explained. "And so we're going to confront Meadows at the next meeting and see where that gets us. Hopefully it will convince the holdouts that he's downright bad for Oliver's Well."

"I have to admit that PJ and I are only vaguely aware of what's been going on. We've been so self-focused. . . ."

"I haven't been advertising my efforts," Megan told her daughter-in-law. "And your priority should be your marriage."

"Wait," Grace said. "Do you actually have to *prove* wrongdoing to vote Meadows off the board?"

"No," Megan said. "It's not a court of law. But concrete proof might help convince the holdouts."

"Maybe he'll be so angry that someone finally had the nerve to confront him that he'll leave the board without your needing to put it to a vote."

"I doubt it, Alexis. He's perverse enough to stick around and torture us, at least until he can make off with the Branley Estate."

If only there was something else I might do to help our case, Megan thought now. And then, like the proverbial lightbulb suddenly turning on in her mind, it came to her. There *was* one more thing she might do! Why hadn't it occurred to her before?

"I've been praying for your success," Grace said now. "Your cause is righteous."

Alexis frowned. "I thought you weren't supposed to pray for something specific to happen, like one person to win and the other person to lose. I don't mean to criticize," she added hurriedly. "I'm just trying to figure it all out."

"You pray for God's will to be done," Grace explained. "You pray for the courage to accept whatever form that will takes. And sometimes you give the man upstairs a little nudge. But in this case, I'm pretty sure God knows that Wynston Meadows and his money are not what's best for Oliver's Well."

"But Wynston Meadows might still get his way," Alexis argued. "Unfair things happen all the time. Good things happen to bad people. Bad things happen to good people. So does that mean that God ignored your prayer?"

"No," Grace said. "It means that He sees the bigger picture, what we can't see. He's got a reason for all that happens. A reason beyond all human understanding."

Alexis shook her head. "It's all so complicated."

"That's where faith comes in," Megan said. "No matter what religion you belong to. Without faith, life is hardly bearable."

"I think this discussion has gone on long enough," Grace announced. "How about I make a run to Cookies 'n Crumpets? I've found that a good cookie can solve even the most convoluted theological debate."

Alexis sighed. "Yes, please! And could you get me a corn muffin, too?"

"Count me out," Megan said. "I've got some pressing business to attend to." *Like emptying out my bank account.*

CHAPTER 134

This is it, Megan thought as she took her seat at the table in the former dining room of the Wilson House. *God, if you care a whit about the OWHA, now's the time to prove it.*

When everyone was gathered, Neal called the meeting to order. Leonard, as CEO, gave his report and then Neal read the minutes of the previous meeting—at which Wynston Meadows had been absent. "We did delay getting started," he said now, "but as we had no word from you and couldn't be sure you would join us. . . ."

Wynston Meadows said nothing, but showed his teeth.

After dealing with the old business, Neal turned the meeting back over to Leonard.

"We have no new business to discuss?" Meadows asked, raising an eyebrow. "As far as I'm concerned there's a great deal that needs attention."

"Yes," Leonard said, in his most commanding voice. "There certainly is a great deal that needs attention, most urgently the question of your continued tenure on the board of the OWHA."

Meadows laughed. "Excuse me?"

Leonard went on. "To begin with, the board of the OWHA has always chosen to conduct our business in a democratic, even a friendly, fashion. You seem to favor an autocratic approach, which quite frankly doesn't sit well with the majority of the board's current members."

"Not me!" Wallace protested. "I mean, I have no problem with your—with your style, Mr. Meadows."

"Nor do I," Joyce intoned.

Norma looked toward the windows. Meadows showed his teeth again.

"More to the point," Leonard went on, "you have made it abundantly clear that you do not share many of the board's priorities. I cite your arguments against the continuation of the educational program as only one instance of this conflict."

"Because the program loses money," Norma said. "Doesn't it?"

Leonard shook his head. "It does not lose money, Norma. You can look at the books for proof if you'd like."

"But Mr. Meadows said—"

Leonard looked to Meadows as if to allow him a reply, but he merely glared. Leonard now cleared his throat. *Here we go,* Megan thought. *The final stretch.*

"In short, Mr. Meadows, we have found another source of funding to help see us into the future."

"What?" Joyce cried.

"This is preposterous!" Wallace crowed. "Why are we only hearing about this now?"

Leonard nodded at Megan. "I think the younger Mrs. Fitzgibbon should explain."

Megan looked around the table at each member of the board in turn. "Let me begin," she said, "by stressing the fact that the OWHA is in a healthy financial position. It has been for some time now. We do not need Mr. Meadows's money for survival. We need only additional sums for new projects. The notion of a $25 million gift excited us, understandably. But it excited us too greatly. At the same time we grasped at the money, we abandoned reason and good sense. We almost abandoned the true purpose of this association. All too aware of this, I recently took it upon myself to bring in someone with professional expertise to do a feasibility study of a purchase and restoration of the Branley Estate and then to point me in the direction of potential interested donors. As a result, I've discovered a new path ahead for the OWHA, one that doesn't involve our selling ourselves to one person."

"This is preposterous!" Wallace cried. "Who gave you the authority to spend the OWHA's money?"

"No one," Megan replied. "With my own money I hired a fund-raising consultant with whom I've worked over the years in the interests of the Cerebral Palsy Education Effort. She and her staff have defined our real financial needs as follows. To purchase the Branley Estate in the immediate future, we need one million dollars in hand, with a stream of ten million over the next three years. I have copies here of the study in all its detail."

From the tote by her side, Megan took a stack of folders and handed them to Richard, seated on her right. "If you'll each take one and pass the rest on . . ."

"I don't understand," Norma said.

"I do." Joyce leaned forward in her seat and pointed a boney finger at Megan. "It's just like Mr. Meadows has been saying. Another Fitzgibbon trying to take control of everything! Manipulators!"

"Joyce." Leonard's tone was warning enough to quiet the woman.

"Of course," Megan went on, "to most of us here at this table, one million dollars seems like an enormous amount of money—albeit not as enormous as five million. But it *is* a viable financial needs goal. And so I approached the private donors suggested by Ms. Simons and have secured this initial amount with one proviso—that Mr. Meadows have no attachment to the OWHA."

"Who are these private donors?" Wallace demanded.

"I'm afraid that I'm not at liberty to divulge their names until the OWHA has cut all ties to Mr. Meadows."

Meadows grinned and shook his head. But he said nothing.

"You could be making this up!" Joyce cried. "Maybe the donors don't even exist!"

"Now, why would she do that?" Anne snapped. "She used her own money to hire that firm, she did all the legwork."

Joyce spluttered but had no answering argument.

"Understandably," Megan went on, "this is a lot to take in, so let me help set your minds at ease. Securing the start-up money is always the most difficult part of the fund-raising process. But I've done that now. Once the design and construction begins, once the project is seen to be a reality, the money invariably flows more readily. I've never seen it happen otherwise."

"I've read about Sarah Simon," Neal said. "Her credentials are outstanding. I remember a few years back she was responsible for identifying funding for the new children's oncology wing at State University Hospital."

"There's a full bio of her firm in your folders," Megan pointed out. "It should reassure you all."

Still, Wynston Meadows remained silent.

"But why are these so-called donors interested in us?" Wallace asked. "Who are we to them? At least Mr. Meadows has a personal interest in—" Wallace reddened.

"In what?" Leonard said. "I very much doubt our newest board member spent his childhood poring over history books and artifacts as he claimed to."

Wynston Meadows said nothing. His silence, Megan thought, was becoming deafening.

"Wallace's question is a good one, though," she said. "You might have heard the term *venture philanthropists*. These are people who have a tremendous amount of money and an interest in funding relatively small but worthy ventures or organizations that haven't had the time to prove themselves. Sarah Simons selected a group of such people she knew to be interested in organizations like the OWHA and, well, I approached them with our hopes for the Branley Estate."

"And they said yes. They really said they would help us?"

"Yes, Norma. This particular group of people did."

There was a long moment of silence as Joyce, Wallace, and Norma absorbed this unexpected turn of events. And as Wynston Meadows . . . as he what? Megan shot a glance in his direction. He was staring at the wall over Richard's head. His expression was almost detached, unconcerned. *God*, Megan wondered. *Had he even been listening to me?*

Leonard cleared his throat. "Given the fact that we have an alternative source of funding in place," he said, "and given a circumstance that has recently come to our attention, the board of the OWHA would prefer not to accept your money and the ties that come with it."

This caused Meadows to finally break his silence. "What circumstance?" he asked, his tone icy.

Megan glanced quickly at Neal. He nodded ever so slightly.

"It has come to our attention," Leonard went on, "from a very reliable source that you have been in secret negotiations to purchase the Branley Estate for your own purposes. In short, it has come to our attention that you propose to tear down the surviving buildings and put up a housing development."

Wynston Meadows grinned. "You people really do like to hear yourself talk, don't you?"

Joyce giggled.

"Frankly," Leonard continued, undeterred, "even the whiff of a scandal on the part of a board member could cause lasting damage to the reputation of the OWHA. And we can't have that, now, can we?"

Megan watched as Meadows's expression hardened. *What's he up to*, she wondered.

"Are you going to let me explain my actions, Mr. DeWitt, or are you going to continue blustering?"

Leonard inclined his head.

"You people," Meadows began, "have no experience of how things happen at this level of business. Yes, you've purchased properties before, but never on this scale. I've been working behind the scenes to gather information about the Branley Estate. I've been working to understand the financial motives behind the Baker family's need to sell. I've been working to accurately assess the real value of the property. This, at times, has involved what you people in your innocence might call subterfuge. Let me explain, as I see from several faces around the table, that my meaning escapes you. In the past weeks I've conducted several casual discussions with a developer to more fully understand the value and the challenges of such a property. This is in no way proof that I've been trying to make a back-door deal. But I suppose an unsophisticated observer might construe my actions as against the interests of the OWHA. But I assure you, that perception only goes to prove the naïveté of said observer."

Meadows, with a self-satisfied smile on his face, waited for a reaction to his words. Megan was almost tempted to applaud his performance. She had never heard a speech so filled with presumption and condescension. *He truly believes we're a bunch of idiots*, she thought. *And maybe, to some extent, we have been.*

"A fine bit of self-justification," Neal said. "And I'm not buying any of it."

"You spoke to a developer?" Wallace said. His face was ashen. "There would be no need for us to consult a developer."

"Not unless we planned to tear down the estate," Norma said, her eyes wide. "And we would never . . ."

"Research," Meadows snapped. "All to gather information."

"Information that has nothing to do with the matter at hand," Leonard thundered. "Do you think we're complete idiots, man?"

Meadows shrugged.

"And the educational program." Wallace, emboldened, looked at Meadows. "I had been planning an entirely new set of workshops for the summer camp. But they wouldn't have happened, would they, not if you had your way."

"Still a schoolmarm at heart, Wallace?"

Megan thought that Wallace looked sick.

"And let's not forget Mr. Meadows wants to cancel the Independence Day parade," Richard pointed out.

"What does it matter?" Joyce spat. "He's still the one with the money. And it's a lot more than what Megan Fitzgibbon managed to scrape up!"

"Loyal little Joyce!" Meadows chuckled. "I know your type well, my dear. I've seen you making eyes at me."

Joyce gasped.

Cruel man, Megan thought. She didn't like Joyce Miller very much, but the woman didn't deserve to be publicly mocked.

Leonard frowned. "I think we've heard enough to put this matter to a vote. Neal, would you distribute the ballots?"

Always expect the unexpected, Megan thought now, picking up her pen. It was something Mary Bernadette often said. At the last minute the vote could go either way.

A moment later, Neal collected the ballots and counted them into one pile. He looked to Leonard and nodded, a ghost of a smile playing around his lips. Megan felt lightheaded with relief.

Leonard straightened his shoulders. "The board of the Oliver's Well Historical Society unanimously votes to dismiss you, Wynston Meadows, effective immediately."

Wynston Meadows laughed incredulously. "Do you people have any idea what you're doing? If I'm not on the board you don't get my money, end of story. You're throwing away an enormous sum you badly need just because some part-time lawyer has convinced you that she knows more about business than one of the richest, most successful men in the country."

One more moment, Megan told herself. *Let him taunt us for just a bit longer.* . . .

"We know exactly what we're doing, Mr. Meadows," Neal said, his expression grim. "There is no more to be said."

"Yes, there is. You've screwed yourselves completely. I still have more money than you'll ever have, and I'll still get the Branley Estate—and I'll tear it to the ground. Meadows High-Rise Housing Complex. It has a certain ring to it, doesn't it?"

And there it is.

"You wouldn't!" Norma cried.

Joyce put her hand over her mouth. Richard began to sputter. Megan rose from the table. "If I may?" she said. "I don't think that you *will* get the Branley Estate, Mr. Meadows. You see, only yesterday I took an option on the property." *And it was the best ten thousand dollars I ever spent,* she thought, fighting back a grin.

"What are you saying?" he demanded.

"Is this true, Megan?" Leonard asked. The others looked too shocked to speak.

"Quite true. The option," Megan went on, "allows me to hold the estate for four months, during which time a sale to the OWHA will be completed, thanks to our financial angels. The owners were more than happy to work with me, especially once they'd heard the, the *rumor* of Mr. Meadows's intended use of the land. The Baker family might need the money, but their dedication to the history of Oliver's Well is staunch. So you see, Mr. Meadows, even if we hadn't been able to vote you off the board, the property would still be safely in the hands of the OWHA, during which time I guarantee you I would have been able to find another group of donors to help us complete the purchase." *At least*, Megan added silently, *I hope I would have.*

"Hear, hear!" Neal cried.

"You're worse than the old one!" Meadows spat.

Richard made to stand, but Megan shook her head to stop him. She opened the leather portfolio on the table before her. "I would now like to present a document that assigns rights under the option to the Oliver's Well Historical Association. Neal, I believe you are a notary?"

Neal grinned. "And I happen to have my seal with me." A moment later, the transfer was made official. Richard began to clap, and the others joined in. All, of course, but Wynston Meadows, who got to his feet, roughly pushing his chair away from him.

"You provincial idiots can go to Hell."

"There are ladies present, Mr. Meadows," Leonard said in his voice of peacekeeping authority. "I suggest you watch your language."

Without another word—really, Megan thought, what could he say now?—Wynston Meadows stalked from the room. A moment later the front door of the Wilson House slammed shut.

"What bad manners that man has," Jeannette said with a laugh.

Joyce sniffed. "I never liked him from the start. I was just pretending to go along with his ideas so that . . ." She cast her eyes down at her bony hands on her bony lap.

"Well," Wallace huffed. "Well, well, well."

Anne shook her head. "Frankly, he frightened me. He had so little respect for any of us."

Neal nodded. "A bully. And most certainly not a gentleman."

"To think I invited that man into my home," Norma said, her hand to her heart. "What made him do it? Why did he even bother with us in the first place if he didn't care about the OWHA?"

"I don't think we'll ever know the entire truth behind his motives," Megan said. "Greed, a need for power and control, a desire for notoriety?"

"Well, whatever his motives, good riddance," Richard said. "A huge burden has been lifted from the OWHA."

"And from Mary Bernadette," Leonard added. "And it's all thanks to Megan."

"No," Megan said firmly. "In the end we all pulled together." She looked purposefully at Joyce and Wallace. "In the end it was our dedication to the ideals of the OWHA that won us the day."

And a good bit of luck, she thought. "Let's never again forget our true purpose."

"Amen to that," Richard said. "And I think Megan should be the one to share the good news with Mary Bernadette. And the one to tell PJ that he still has the Stoker job."

Leonard nodded. "I'll have our lawyers expedite the contract. And I'll inform the other contenders that the job is no longer open."

Megan gathered her leather portfolio and her tote. "Then I'll be off," she said. There was another round of applause.

CHAPTER 135

"I have some good news to share with you all," Megan announced. The family was gathered in the living room of the Fitzgibbon House on Honeysuckle Lane.

"You're having the twins baptized," Mary Bernadette said.

Pat groaned. "Mom!"

"What is it, Megan?" Paddy asked, putting a hand on his wife's shoulder.

"Yeah, Mom," PJ said. "Don't keep us in suspense."

Megan took a deep breath. "Wynston Meadows," she said, "was voted off the board of the Oliver's Well Historical Association."

Mary Bernadette put a hand to her heart. "But his pledge . . . the Branley Estate . . . What will happen to it now?"

"All taken care of," Megan said. "I'll tell you the details later. All you need to know for now is that the threat is gone. The OWHA will go on as always. And there *will* be enough money for the purchase of the Branley Estate." Megan turned to her older son. "And PJ, the board would be honored if you would accept the contract for the Joseph J. Stoker House. Again."

"You bet I will!" PJ drew Alexis into his arms.

Grace clapped, and Danica joined in.

Pat beamed. "And my genius wife did it all singlehandedly!"

"Now, Pat, I—"

"How?" Mary Bernadette asked, her voice agitated. "How did you do it?"

"I was voted onto the board as a temporary member," Megan explained carefully. "I was accepted as a voice for the Fitzgibbons. I hoped to be able to set things right again. Frankly, I wasn't at all sure I would succeed. I'm still having trouble believing things turned out as well as they did."

"Here, Mom," David said, looking up from his iPhone. "Listen to these headlines. Some are from papers in D.C."

"Headlines already?" *Well*, Megan thought, *anything to do with the Not So Great Man probably makes the papers. Even an ignominious defeat.*

"Washington Area Big Wig Brought to Heel by Mom of Three."

Danica peered over her brother's shoulder. "Local Family Takes Down Corporate Giant. That's pretty good. And listen to this: He Thought He Could Pull the Wool Over Our Eyes: The Takedown of a Hedge Fund Billionaire by a Local Historical Society."

"That's a bit dramatic," Grace said. "But I like it."

"Here's another," David said. "Part-Time Lawyer Stops Bigwig in Tracks."

Megan raised her eyebrows. "I'm a bit more than just a part-time lawyer!"

PJ laughed. "Oh no, the fame is going to her head!"

"God forbid!" Megan laughed. "I'm not cut out for the limelight. I do very well working behind the scenes." *But I did enjoy my little performance. . . .*

Mary Bernadette still seemed stunned. "I don't understand," she said. "You did all this for . . ."

"For us," Megan said firmly. "For the Fitzgibbon family and for Oliver's Well."

"This calls for a celebration," Paddy announced. "Dinner at The Angry Squire!"

"Great idea, Dad," Grace said. "Mom, I'm going to have to borrow something decent to wear."

Alexis smiled. "I do love their steak. But I think that tonight I'll try the lamb."

Mary Bernadette cleared her throat. "The lamb," she said, "is also excellent."

CHAPTER 136

M ary Bernadette was in her temporary bedroom on the first floor. She had asked to talk to Megan alone before they left for dinner at The Angry Squire. And while she waited for her daughter-in-law, the words of the proverb came to her. "Who shall find a valiant woman? . . . Strength and dignity are her clothing. . . . She opens her mouth with wisdom, and the teaching of kindness is on her tongue."

Perhaps, Mary Bernadette thought, Megan was the truly valiant woman of the Fitzgibbon clan, and in her blindness and arrogance she had failed to see the truth. Maybe it was now time to become a promoter of happiness, rather than the person who inhibited the individual members of the Fitzgibbon family from claiming their rights.

There was a knock on the door and Mary Bernadette called, "Come in."

"You wanted to see me," Megan said.

"Yes." Mary Bernadette gathered her native courage and generosity. "You've saved the good name of the Fitzgibbons," she said. "I'm grateful. More grateful than you can know."

Megan nodded. "Thank you. It was my pleasure, Mary Bernadette. This family means a lot to me, as does Oliver's Well."

"You're sure the finances of the OWHA . . ."

"I'll explain it all to you tomorrow if you'd like, but there's nothing to worry about. Wynston Meadows isn't the only one with deep pockets. And as I'm sure you suspected, his concerns were entirely selfish. He didn't care at all about Oliver's Well, its past, present, or future."

"I must say it all seems a bit of a miracle."

Megan laughed. "Honestly, it seems the same way to me. There were too many moments when I thought I'd never be able to convince the board members to trust me. It was almost as if Wynston Meadows was holding them under a spell."

"He was," Mary Bernadette said. "The spell of money."

"Yes."

"Well, I'm forever grateful to you, Megan. I'm sure we all are." Mary Bernadette straightened her shoulders. "And I do hope that you will forgive my earlier—my earlier unhappy words."

"Yes," Megan said. "I do forgive you. But I must also request that from now on there will be no more unhappy words. No more criticism of my parenting choices, or of Pat's, either. Harsh words linger far longer than physical wounds."

Mary Bernadette agreed with a firm nod. "Now," she said, "I think we should meet the others for our celebration."

CHAPTER 137

It was the day after the celebratory dinner at The Angry Squire, and Alexis and her husband were having tea with the family. It really had been an amazing evening. People had never stopped coming to the table to shake Mary Bernadette's hand and tell her that she looked well, to congratulate Megan on having ousted Wynston Meadows (word, of course, had gotten around), and to wish PJ the best of success on the Joseph J. Stoker House project. The Fitzgibbon family was indeed local royalty.

"Did you enjoy the lamb?" Alexis asked Mary Bernadette now.

She nodded. "I defy any big-city chef at one of those overpriced fancy restaurants to best Richard's kitchen."

"And those mashed potatoes!" Paddy turned to his wife. "Not as good as yours, of course," he added.

"Grandmother, Grandpa. Everyone." PJ put down his cup and got up from his perch on the arm of the couch. "Alexis and I have some good news to share." He smiled and nodded at his wife.

"I'm pregnant," Alexis announced, her voice breaking with emotion. "We're having a baby!"

"A great-grandchild," Mary Bernadette said, tears glistening in her eyes. "That I would live to see the day. . . ." Paddy took her hand, tears in his own eyes.

Pat shook his son's hand and kissed his daughter-in-law's cheek. Megan hugged them both.

"I'm going to be an uncle," David said. "Cool!"

"And I'm going to be an aunt. Awesome! Wait." Danica made a face. "I won't have to change diapers, will I? 'Cause, ew."

"I'll change diapers," Grace assured Danica. "I just love babies!"

"And if I'm going to be a grandmother," Megan said, "I should probably learn to knit."

Alexis laughed. "Not unless you want to."

"Thank God. I tried to learn once and I hated it."

"We brought some champagne for a toast," PJ told them. "It's in the fridge."

"I'll get it." Alexis turned to her mother-in-law. "Megan, would you help me?"

"I know what you're thinking," Alexis said as she brought the bottle of cold champagne from the fridge and her mother-in-law took glasses from a standing cabinet reserved for Mary Berna-dette's good Waterford crystal. "Getting pregnant now probably wasn't the smartest thing to do. But PJ told you that we're seeing a therapist. We're totally committed to making our family work. I promise."

Megan smiled. "I have faith in you and PJ. You have my full support. Pat's, too."

"Thank you. I love your son very much. I have since the moment I first saw him."

"I'm sure of it. Now, shall we?" Megan carried the tray of glasses back into the living room while Alexis followed with the champagne.

"Can I have a taste?" David and Danica asked in unison.

To which Megan, Pat, Mary Bernadette, Paddy, and Grace replied, "No!"

CHAPTER 138

Alexis stood outside the tiny used bookstore on Main Street. Maureen had just sent her a text to say that she was running a few minutes late. *No matter*, Alexis thought. The sun was warm and after too many months of resenting Oliver's Well, she was happy to once again appreciate its charms.

Alexis waved to a woman she recognized from church. The man who supervised the produce section at the grocery store passed by and smiled. And there, across the street, was Morgan Shelby, coming out of the post office. Alexis's heart contracted for a moment, but she knew without a doubt that she had made the right decision in walking away. She wished him well and she hoped that he soon forgot—and forgave—her.

"Alexis! Sorry I'm late." It was Maureen, hurrying toward her, hair flying.

Alexis smiled. "No worries. It's a beautiful day. I'm enjoying the sunshine."

"Some idiot—sorry, some annoying—customer forgot his appointment and came running in at quarter to five. When I told him he'd have to reschedule, as I had an appointment of my own to keep, he had the nerve to throw a fit."

"Yikes. What did you do?"

Maureen shrugged. "I told him I was sorry he was upset and that I would be glad to see him tomorrow, and I left. For all I know he's still there, making a fool of himself."

"I'm glad I don't have your job! Do you want to walk down to Oliver's Grove?"

"Sure. I could use some fresh air. The person who sits next to me at the office—and I name no names—wears the most dreadful cologne I have ever smelled in my life. It's like a combination of frog sweat and bear urine."

"Maureen!" Alexis laughed.

"Well, it's pretty bad."

"Another reason I'm glad I don't have your job!"

"So, enough about me," Maureen said. "What's going on with you? You look great, by the way. Pregnancy agrees with you."

"So far, so good. I want to share something with you. Top secret, of course."

"Mum's the word."

"PJ has made some real personal progress in therapy," Alexis told her friend. "It's been tough for him, but the other day he finally was able to admit to Roz—well, and to me—that he realizes he'd grown too attached to his grandmother. He talked about how abandoned and confused he had felt when the twins were born and his parents were so concerned about David. He said that his grandmother saved him—his exact words—and made him feel like he mattered again."

Maureen let out a whistle. "For a Fitzgibbon that's an amazing bit of self-awareness."

"I thought so. Look, Maureen, I really want to thank you again for helping me when I thought I was losing my mind."

"No big deal. We all threaten to lose our mind at some point in our lives."

"Do you think that's really true?" Alexis said. "I mean, I wonder if there are some people who have it all figured out from the start. Life, I mean."

Maureen laughed. "I don't believe that for a second."

"Yeah, I guess I don't, either. But I really did think for a while that Mary Bernadette was perfect. That she never had a doubt or a worry."

"We do that sort of person—the sort who appears to be in complete control of her life—we do that sort of person a big disservice when we forget that she's only human. Who knows how many times over the years Mary Bernadette wanted to ask for help and just couldn't because she felt trapped in the character she'd created for herself—or that others had foisted on her."

"Do you know something I don't know?" Alexis asked.

Maureen shrugged. "My mother is Mary Bernadette's dearest friend. Over the years she's let enough information trickle through to allow me to know that Mary Bernadette was never quite as tough as people thought she was. Things were hard for her. She took on so much responsibility. She didn't make life easy for herself."

"Or for other people! Sorry. I guess I shouldn't say that after all she's been through."

"Well, all that's in the past now," Maureen said. "At least, I hope that it is. I hope that Mary Bernadette can find real peace in the years she has left."

"Yes. I do, too," Alexis said. "And there's something else, Maureen. PJ and I were wondering if you would be godmother to our baby."

Maureen gave Alexis an enthusiastic one-armed hug. "Of course! Wow, thank you both! That's the second piece of good news I got today."

"Oh? What's the first?"

"Remember when I was going on that day at the café about how my life just stopped after the divorce? How I *let* it stop?"

"Yes?"

"Well, since then I've been doing a lot of thinking. And while I'm not saying I'm ready to make huge changes in my life—or lots of small changes, at that—I am ready to start doing something other than just going to and from work every day."

Alexis laughed. "The suspense is killing me."

"And so I signed up for swimming lessons at the Y in Somerstown! The deadline for registration had already passed, but someone dropped out and I got her place."

"Good for you, Maureen."

"And it's really thanks to you. You're my inspiration."

"Me? But I'm just stumbling around."

"Stumbling forward, more like. And that's a lot better than standing still."

It was something she had never expected to be, Alexis realized. Someone's inspiration. It felt pretty good.

"Well, here's the park," she announced as they came in sight of the lacebark pines and magnolia trees the Grove was famous for. "What now?"

Maureen made a face. "I know you can't drink, but we each have things to celebrate. . . ."

Alexis laughed. "The Angry Squire it is!"

CHAPTER 139

It was six-thirty in the evening. Mary Bernadette had cooked dinner for her family, though she had accepted Grace's offer to set the table and Megan's assistance in peeling the potatoes and she had allowed PJ and Alexis to load the dishwasher after the meal. *There's always a first time for everything,* she told herself.

Pat, Megan, Grace, and the twins had gone for an after-dinner stroll, leaving Mary Bernadette and Paddy alone with PJ and Alexis. The four were sitting in the living room—Mary Bernadette and Paddy in the two armchairs and PJ and Alexis on the couch.

"We'd like to talk to you both," PJ said, clearing his throat as if he were nervous.

Paddy nodded, and Mary Bernadette experienced a sharp twinge of anxiety—*Is there something wrong with the baby?*—and said, "Of course."

"Well, now that we're starting our family, we've decided to leave the cottage just as soon as we find a place of our own."

"But—"

Paddy gave her a look of warning. Mary Bernadette protested no more.

"We're not abandoning the family," Alexis assured them. "Or Oliver's Well. And we'll always be grateful for your having let us live in the cottage."

"It's a fine idea," Paddy said. "Isn't it, Mary?"

"Yes," she said, her voice even. "We wish you well."

Alexis smiled at her husband. "Also, I've joined the Oliver's Well Players, as an assistant set designer," she said excitedly. "And I'm going to pursue a master's degree in photography." Alexis turned to Mary Bernadette. "And if it's okay with you, Mary Bernadette, I'd like to start the Day in the Life project again. I was thinking that maybe I could work it up into a thesis project!"

Mary Bernadette nodded. *It would be foolish not to accept the girl's offer*, she thought. Besides, hadn't she always wanted the OWHA to be a true family affair?

"You'll be the busiest woman in town," Paddy said with a smile.

"About that, Grandpa. What with a baby on the way, and grad school, and the Players, and the OWHA, I was wondering—*we* were wondering—if Fitzgibbon Landscaping might not hire someone part time to help Alexis run the office."

Paddy frowned. "We've never had anyone other than family behind the desk. What do you think, Mary?"

All eyes turned to her. Mary Bernadette schooled her expression to reveal none of the discomfort she felt with this latest suggestion of change. *I cannot continue to control it all*, she told herself. *I must allow for the happiness of my family.*

"I think, Paddy," she said finally, "that we can find someone suitable."

"Thank you, Mary Bernadette," Alexis said. "Thank you."

PJ got up from the couch, came over to Mary Bernadette, and hugged her. "You're the best," he said. "You, too, Grandpa."

"I hear the others on the front path," Mary Bernadette replied, releasing herself from her grandson's grasp. "Alexis, would you put the kettle on?"

CHAPTER 140

Pat, Megan, Grace, and the twins joined the others in the living room for tea and a delicious peach pie that Bonnie had dropped off earlier that day. *That woman is going to make me fat*, Grace thought, helping herself to a second slice. *And I don't care.*

PJ and Alexis filled the others in on their latest news. Megan said she had heard of a charming little house on Vine Street that had just gone on the market. Pat admitted that he had had no idea Alexis was interested in theatre. Grace offered to help interview candidates for part-time office work at Fitzgibbon Landscaping. The twins fought over the last piece of pie.

"And if it's all right with you, Mom and Dad," Grace said, "once Alexis and PJ move out, I think I'll stay at the cottage rather than in my old bedroom here. Unless you decide you want to rent it out."

"There'll be no strangers living in my backyard," Mary Bernadette said.

Grace smiled. "And I guess I'm not allowed to throw any wild parties?"

"Our rebel," Paddy said fondly.

The others continued to discuss the impending changes to the lives of the Fitzgibbons. Grace, half-listening, reflected on her decision to move back to Virginia. There was some truth to that old adage: Absence makes the heart grow fonder. Living several thousands of miles away from her mother had helped Grace to exorcise unpleasant memories and to focus on the positive aspects of their relationship. Still, there was something to be said for living in the presence of a difficult loved one, for the challenges it presented and for the joys it might unexpectedly bring.

Anyway, now she and Megan could be friends in the flesh. And Grace felt that she owed her sister-in-law. Megan had been on the front lines for too many years. It was all well and good to go off and save the world, but it was also important to help the ones at home. In other words, as Voltaire had opined, it was important to cultivate one's own garden. Of course, Voltaire probably hadn't been considering the likes of Mary Bernadette Fitzgibbon. . . .

"Grace?"

"Yes, Mom?"

"I was thinking that you might want to refresh your wardrobe now that you'll be living in Oliver's Well. I hear California is ter-

ribly casual, but things are different here. My dear friend Anne
owns a wonderful dress shop on Main Street. I'll let her know
you'll be coming by."

Alexis hid her face in her napkin. Megan bit her lip. Grace
forced a smile and said a silent prayer for patience. "Thanks,
Mom," she said. "That's very nice of you."

CHAPTER 141

"**I**'m perfectly capable of making the tea," Mary Bernadette
protested. "I've already made dinner for my family."

Jeannette and Mary Bernadette were in the Fitzgibbon kitchen. Jeannette was boiling the water and putting out the plate
of cookies.

"I know, Mary. You told me several times. But the doctors said
to take things slowly. There's no good in taxing your energy."
Jeannette brought the tea things to the table and sat. "Now," she
said, "a nice hot cup of tea will do you wonders."

"I'm not sick, Jeannette. Just—"

"Impatient."

"Yes." Mary Bernadette took a small sip of her tea and sighed.
"We were so young once, Jeannette. When we first met."

"Mere girls."

"And now . . ."

"Everyone grows old, Mary. If she's lucky."

Unlike William, Mary Bernadette thought. *My poor unlucky child.*
"I'm not who I used to be," she said. "All those years ago . . . I
made the wrong decisions."

"Now, Mary. You did what you had to do."

"But I was wrong, Jeannette. Why deny it now?"

"Have a cookie, Mary. They're the shortbread ones you like."

"I still can't help but wonder . . ."

Jeannette sighed softly. "Wonder about what?"

"If I'm somehow to blame." Mary Bernadette looked directly into her friend's eyes.

Jeannette reached over and put her hand on Mary Bernadette's. "Mary, after all these years you can't still be worrying over that."

"Can't I?"

Jeannette sighed and sat back. "Of course. If I were the one who had lost a child I would be mourning until the day I, too, died. And wondering. No, Mary, I can't blame you. But that doesn't mean I'm not sorry it has to be this way for you."

"Don't listen to me," Mary Bernadette said briskly, waving her hand in dismissal. "I'm being morbid. And I do still have Pat. And Grace. And my dear Paddy."

"And the grandchildren. And Megan and Alexis. And a great-grandchild before long. You're blessed, Mary. Don't ever forget that."

"No. I won't forget it. Do you know, Jeannette, I was thinking that maybe Wynston Meadows was right."

Jeannette looked horrified. "Lord, Mary, what can you mean?"

"Right about it being time for a change. Maybe it is time for younger people to lead the way."

"And what will you do, sit back quietly and watch? I don't think that's likely, Mary. Besides, you have more to give, I know you do. And the OWHA has never gone wrong since you've been our guiding spirit."

"Well, that *is* true," Mary Bernadette admitted. There was never any point in false modesty. "But I'm tired, Jeannette. It might be nice to share the burden of responsibility."

"With Megan? She's done such a fine job of putting things right."

"Yes. She has. But once I'm fully recovered she'll be relinquishing her position on the board. And there are others who are also worthy of a larger role. Neal makes a fine appearance. He might do very well giving interviews to the press."

"Yes. But let's not think about that now. More changes. Let's just enjoy our tea."

Banshee appeared at Mary Bernadette's feet and let out a horrible wail. "Would you like a wee bit of milk?" Mary Bernadette asked the cat.

Jeannette shook her head. "You spoil the creature, Mary."

"I know that I do."

CHAPTER 142

"Heads up!"

Megan ducked as a Frisbee sailed by her left ear.

"Sorry, Mom!" Danica called.

"Play with that thing behind the cottage," she called back. Her daughter dashed by and retrieved the Frisbee. Megan shook her head. Danica was fantastic with her feet—she was the best all-around player on her soccer team—but lousy with her hands.

The Fitzgibbon family had gathered on the lawn before Mary Bernadette and Paddy's house for a Fourth of July barbeque. Pat and PJ manned the grill while David and Danica (when they weren't chasing a wayward Frisbee) carried plates of burgers and hot dogs to the three picnic tables that had been set end to end. Jeannette, Danny, and Maureen were there too, as were Katie and Bonnie. Even Mike and Lucy Burrows were in attendance, at the invitation of the elder Fitzgibbons. Mike brought two six-packs of beer and his wife brought a vat of potato salad. Megan had noted that Mary Bernadette had eyed it with suspicion, no doubt wondering since when potato salad was made with red potatoes and green olives. Still, she had graciously accepted a helping and then, Megan noted, another. Alexis had made a pasta salad full of vegetables and herbs. Bonnie had brought a corn and avocado salad, and Jeannette and Maureen had made three trays of red velvet cupcakes, decorated with white frosting and red, white, and blue sprinkles. Megan had contributed the new red-and-white-checked tablecloths, as well as the paper plates and napkins and the plastic utensils and cups. Grace had stocked and set up the drinks table. *A real group effort*, Megan thought, surveying the feast. *A gift from us all, to us all.*

Now that the OWHA was no longer in thrall to the bullying Wynston Meadows, it was free to play its traditional role in the town's Independence Day celebrations and the parade was most definitely on. For the first time in her long tenure, Mary Bernadette had declined to march; she simply didn't feel up to the strain as yet. So the other board members had arranged for the parade to be rerouted onto Honeysuckle Lane on its way to the finale celebrations at Oliver's Grove. In that way, Mary Bernadette Fitzgibbon could still be involved.

"How are you feeling, Mary?" Jeannette asked.

"Just fine," Mary Bernadette replied. "Why wouldn't I be?"

Megan bit back a smile. "Would anyone like more corn and avocado salad?"

"Yes, please," Katie replied. "I can never get enough of that dish."

Bonnie laughed. "It's how I've kept her happy all these years."

"I keep Mike happy by scratching his back every night."

Lucy's remark was met with silence until Grace cleared her throat and asked for someone to pass her another hot dog.

"I can't wait to see the library's new float," Maureen said to Alexis. "I hear the staff has been working on it since last summer."

"You know, I've never marched in a parade."

Grace raised her eyebrows. "Really? Not even as a kid?"

Alexis shook her head. "Nope."

"You can march with the OWHA, now that you're once again the Contemporary Archivist," Mary Bernadette told her.

"Thanks, Mary Bernadette," Alexis said. "I'll definitely participate next year."

"I hear the marching band!" David called out. Mercy began to bark and chase her tail.

Mary Bernadette sighed. "Someone put a leash on that mutt before she gets herself run over by a float!"

"Here they come!" PJ called.

Three of Oliver's Well's best high school athletes—one girl, flanked by two boys—came into view carrying a horizontal banner across which was printed the town's name and the date of its incorporation. They were followed by a group of Oliver's Well's more civic-minded residents waving small American flags. The town's two surviving WWII veterans saluted as they drove slowly by in the backseat of a convertible driven by Sheila Rogers, the mayor's wife. The library's new float met Maureen's expectations, boasting a huge papier-mâché replica of an early printing press.

Next was the high school's marching band. As they came abreast of the Fitzgibbon house, they broke into a rendition of "It's a Grand Old Flag," a song everyone knew to be one of Mary Bernadette's favorites. A troop of Boy Scouts followed the band; a troop of Girl Scouts followed them. The members of the board of the Oliver's Well Historical Association who were not seated in the Fitzgibbon front yard rode by on a float depicting a replica of the Kelleher House, the town's oldest surviving structure. They nodded and waved to Mary Bernadette as the float rolled by.

When the last of the parade had vanished in the distance, Mary Bernadette, in her well-known commanding tone and with her famously dazzling smile, called for a toast. "To the Fitzgibbons," she said, when everyone at the tables had raised a plastic cup. "And to our dear friends gathered here today. Long life and may God bless us all!"

The applause—even from Pat—was thunderous.

EPILOGUE

On a Saturday in the middle of the following January, the Fitzgibbon family was gathered at PJ and Alexis's new house on Vine Street. The house was small—the living room doubled as a dining room when guests came for meals, and there was only one bathroom—but it suited them perfectly. The furniture was an eclectic mix of new pieces and things Alexis and PJ had found at secondhand shops. They had bought their dishes, flatware, mugs, and glassware at Goodwill.

At the moment the men of the Fitzgibbon family were in the backyard and the women were in the kitchen with Alexis as she put the final touches on the dinner. Baby Maeve Olivia, barely a month old, was asleep in her car seat in the corner of the kitchen.

Alexis turned from the oven. "Danica, would you mind setting the table? The plates and silverware are stacked on it already."

"Sure," Danica replied, dashing into the living room.

Mary Bernadette followed her. "The knives go on the right, Danica," she said.

Danica frowned at the place she had just set. "Oh."

"No harm done," her grandmother assured her. "Everyone makes mistakes. Just the other day I forgot to replace the hand towels in the powder room."

Mary Bernadette went back to the kitchen and took a seat at the tiny table. Eight months had passed since the stroke that had temporarily felled her, and she was feeling almost her old self again. In spite of an initial reservation, she had decided to retain her role as the chairman and official spokesperson of the Oliver's Well Historical Association. Really, she had told her family, there was no good reason to abdicate the position she had held for so long, and indeed Leonard, on behalf of the entire board, had pressed her to continue in her duties. Some things had changed, however. She was now using e-mail—though not regularly—and had managed to receive a few calls on her cell phone. She had Skyped once with David and Danica and had decided that it was *not* for her. Grace had acceded this point. Unwelcome but accepted was the presence of the Life Alert system. "It's an ugly thing," Mary Bernadette had said when she had first laid eyes on it. "It doesn't go with any of my clothing." Grace had sighed. "Vanity, Mom."

A much more welcome change was that Mary Bernadette and Paddy were closer than they had been in many years, and in spite of the traumatic way this had come about, she was deeply pleased by it. And she was very happy about the fact that Paddy had fallen into the habit of taking her hand as they sat on the couch of an evening to watch a bit of television before bed. It was like the old days—the very old days—but somehow more poignant, being tinged with old sorrows. As for her relationship to William, her private grief would never entirely lose its power over her, but now, as she had promised God that she would, she made it a point to focus on the care of those still living.

"Should I drizzle some olive oil on the hummus?" Megan asked.

Alexis nodded. "Sure. Use that bottle by the toaster. It's the good stuff."

"Hummus?" Mary Bernadette asked her daughter in a low voice.

Grace patted her mother's hand. "You'll like it, I promise."

Megan had overheard her mother-in-law's question and allowed herself a smile. Sometimes on her own and sometimes accompanied by Pat and the twins, she continued to visit Oliver's Well regularly, and though she was no longer officially involved with the OWHA, she was available to offer advice regarding the funding for the acquisition (just completed) and the restoration (soon to begin) of the Branley Estate. Wynston Meadows was now just an unhappy memory. He had sold his house in Oliver's Well and gone back to D.C. where he belonged. As for life within the bounds of the family Fitzgibbon, it seemed to have settled into a new pattern, one in which Mary Bernadette asked her daughter-in-law's opinion on matters ranging from the best way to get red wine stains out of a tablecloth to the fastest way to bake a potato. Of course, Mary Bernadette already knew the answers to these questions, but Megan saw the act of asking as an offering of peace, if not exactly one of friendship. And there had been no more comments about the pagan lifestyle of the Annapolis branch of the family.

"The meat is done," Alexis announced. "Dinner in about fifteen minutes."

Alexis Fitzgibbon was happier than she had ever been in her life. She adored being a mother, and she was thrilled to be living in her own home with her husband. She was enrolled in a graduate program at the local campus of the state university (her classes were in the evening, allowing PJ to be home with the baby), and what with her membership in Oliver's Well Players, her photography work for the OWHA, her part-time day job at Fitzgibbon Landscaping, and her weekly drinks date with Maureen (who was dating someone she had met through her swim class), Alexis was always on the move. And, as if she wasn't already busy enough, she had undertaken an informal study of the history of the Catholic Church. There was so much to learn, much of it inspiring, some of it horrifying, all of it fascinating. PJ had joked that before long she would "out–Mary Bernadette Mary Bernadette." Alexis wasn't sure that was possible.

Now that they had a granddaughter to spoil, Olivia and Lester Trenouth had promised to visit Oliver's Well once a month. And Alexis no longer accepted checks from her parents. She had told them that if they wanted to help her new family they might instead contribute to Maeve's education fund, and they were happy to oblige.

"Everything smells wonderful," Grace said.

Alexis, face flushed from the heat of the oven, smiled. "Thanks. I hope it tastes as good as it smells."

Grace, who had eaten many a meal at Alexis and PJ's home, knew that it would. She was enjoying her job at the hospital and found that living in her parents' backyard had its benefits. One was that it allowed her to see her brother's family more often, and of course to keep an eye on her ageing parents. Another was that she had access to her mother's cooking, too, and as she tended to eat pretzels and peanut butter for dinner when left to her own devices, this was a real treat.

"So, what's the deal with boys?" Grace asked Danica, when she had come back to the kitchen and dropped into a chair. "I mean, do you like them?"

Danica made a comically horrible face. "The deal with boys is that they're dumb! Well, not all of them. David's okay and Dad's all right. And PJ and Grandpa, too. But most of them are stupid and boring. Besides, I have soccer and debate team and school-work. I don't have time for boys. I mean, if I wanted to hang out with them. Which I don't."

Grace nodded. "You know, you're pretty smart. Maybe some-day you'll think about becoming a nun. We work to empower women. We fight for peace and social justice."

"And you pray, of course," Mary Bernadette added.

"That, too."

Danica considered this for a moment. "That's all great," she said finally, "especially the fighting part, but I do really like shopping."

"Shopping," Alexis said, "is definitely a good thing."

"Well," Megan told her daughter, "you've got plenty of time to think about your future."

"Look, Maeve is waking up! Can I hold her?" Danica asked, jumping up from her seat and going over to her niece, who was making little mewling sounds.

"Of course," Alexis said. "Do you remember how I taught you to pick her up?"

Danica rolled her eyes. "Seriously?"

Paddy, Pat, and David were in the backyard, watching PJ's progress on a garden shed. Paddy, good with his hands, offered suggestions. Pat, not good with his hands, had no suggestions to make. David watched with a critical eye.

"Did Marty give you a professional discount on the lumber?" Paddy asked his grandson.

"Yup. And I'll give him one when he finally decides to deal with that overgrown, weedy lawn of his."

Paddy shook his head. "Don't count on that happening any time soon. His lawn has been a disgrace since I've known the man, and that's over thirty years. If I was still what I used to be I'd take a mower to it myself, whether he liked it or not."

It was true that his wife's illness had taken a toll on Paddy, but good things had also come from the time of crisis. Mary Bernadette had mellowed in the aftermath of her distress, and Paddy felt a comfort in his marriage that had long been missing. That indeed was a blessing.

"So, what's this girlfriend of yours like?" Paddy asked his younger grandson.

David shrugged. "I don't know. She's nice."

"Does she have a name?" PJ asked.

"Duh! Her name is Emma."

"Is she a good student?" Paddy wanted to know.

David laughed. "Yeah! She's, like, the top of our class."

"And she's pretty."

"Dad!"

Pat shrugged. "What? She is."

"Yeah," David admitted. "She's pretty. Not that it matters or anything."

David's surgery the previous July had been a success; he felt strong and in far less pain than he had been before the operation. He was now fascinated by golf. This pleased his father, as he, too, was fascinated by the game, though he wasn't very good at it. David and Pat now routinely spent Saturday mornings at the golf course, sending balls wildly into the air and narrowly avoiding getting hit by their own clubs.

"You know," Pat said to his older son, who had just muttered in frustration, "you could have just bought a prefab shed."

"Where's the challenge in that? David, hand me that box of nails, will you?"

David did so.

"Maybe someday you'll join Fitzgibbon Landscaping," PJ suggested. "We could rename the company The Fitzgibbon Brothers Landscaping."

"No thanks," David said. "I'm going to law school."

"Well, maybe when you're in high school you can work summers for me."

"You just want cheap labor, don't you?"

Pat clapped David on the back. "You'll make a fine lawyer, my boy!"

"Just like his father," Paddy added.

Pat smiled. These days he felt closer to his father, as well as to his mother, than he ever remembered feeling. Though Mary Bernadette was still the domineering woman she had always been, it was not as consistently. And his parents seemed happier together. Pat hoped they had rediscovered some of the emotional intimacy his father had told him was lacking in their marriage. His own marriage to Megan was as good as it had ever been, which was excellent. Pat was happy, too, to see Grace more often. He had great fondness as well as great admiration for his sister. And he was thoroughly besotted with his granddaughter. No doubt by the time she was old enough to talk, Maeve would have him wrapped completely around her little finger. Pat couldn't wait.

"Do you remember the time you tried to build that fort in the backyard, Pat?"

Pat turned to his father. "What do you mean tried to build? I *built* a fort."

Paddy chuckled. "It lasted about three minutes before the entire thing collapsed on itself."

David hooted and PJ grinned. "I guess talent skips a generation," PJ said to his father.

PJ felt very grateful at that moment. Well, pretty much at all moments since the awful few months the year before. Life was not perfect, but it was good. He was still learning how to pay attention to his wife in a way that mattered to her, but this process was helped by the fact that Alexis had developed her own interests and was establishing her own identity apart from—but in relation to—his. He knew that he had acted unfairly, expecting her to ease in to his own life without any real support. He had failed to understand that she was a complete person of her own. There had been no malice in his thinking, just ignorance, which he had come to realize was often just as bad.

With the help of Roz Clinton—he and Alexis saw her once every six weeks—he was also learning how to fully separate from his grandmother while still expressing his love and respect for her. It wasn't always easy to say no to Mary Bernadette—saying yes had been a habit for a very long time—but she, too, had made an effort to let him live life on his own terms. It wasn't a huge effort, but it was enough that both he and Alexis had noted. And then, of course, there was his gorgeous, angelic, and absolutely perfect infant daughter.

Megan appeared at the back door then and called the men in for dinner.

"Finally," David said, and hurried ahead of his elders.

Alexis had made a Middle Eastern feast, complete with hummus, baba ghanoush, tabouli, pita, and lamb kabobs.

"It's not at all hot," she assured Mary Bernadette, whose expression was wary. "And it's all good for you."

"It smells awesome," David announced.

The Fitzgibbon family took their seats at the table in the living room. Even with the table's two extra leaves, it was still a tight fit. Alexis thought it was cozy. Paddy said grace and they began their meal.

"So," Grace said, spooning tabouli onto her plate, "I've done some research on places to stay in Dublin and Cork. There are a few options that look good for all of us, considering our varying budgets."

"I can't believe we're finally going to Ireland," Danica said. "I am so psyched."

"A family pilgrimage," PJ said. "Four generations all together."

"As long as my Mary continues in good health," Paddy said, taking his wife's hand.

"I swear by the Almighty Father, His Loving Son, and the Holy Ghost—and the Virgin Mary, of course—that I will! Now, would someone pass me that—what did you call it, Alexis? Baba-something? It's very tasty."

Alexis smiled. "Baba ghanoush," she said. "And gladly."